CAMPUS GOD

JENNIFER SUCEVIC

Campus God

Copyright© 2022 by Jennifer Sucevic

All rights reserved. No part of this book may be reproduced in any form or by any electronic or mechanical means, including information storage and retrieval systems, without written permission from the author, except for the use of brief quotations in a book review.

This is a work of fiction. Names, characters, businesses, palaces, events, locales, and incidents are either the products of the author's imagination or used in a fictitious manner. Any resemblance to actual persons, living or dead, or actual events is purely coincidental.

Cover Design by Mary Ruth Baloy at MR Creations

Editing by Evelyn Summers

Home | Jennifer Sucevic or www.jennifersucevic.com

Subscribe to my newsletter -) https://www.subscribepage.com/l5v9e4

ALSO BY JENNIFER SUCEVIC

Campus Flirt (novella)

Campus Heartthrob

Campus Hottie

Campus Player

Claiming What's Mine

Confessions of a Heartbreaker

Crazy for You (80s short story)

Don't Leave

Friend Zoned

Hate to Love You

Heartless

If You Were Mine

Just Friends

King of Campus

King of Hawthorne Prep

Love to Hate You

One Night Stand

Protecting What's Mine

Queen of Hawthorne Prep

Stay

The Boy Next Door

The Breakup Plan

The Girl Next Door

1

BROOKE

"Girl, I'm in desperate need of a break," my bestie says as we hustle our way through the crowd of students traveling across campus like a herd of slow-moving cattle.

"Easton wearing you out already with all that sex?"

Sasha's eyes widen as she knocks her shoulder into mine. "What? Of course not!"

I grin as her face turns beet red.

Uh-huh, sure...

I know *exactly* what's going on in the room across from mine. Those two are so loud it would be impossible *not* to know. Although, I can't begrudge Sasha for finding her happily ever after and enjoying every moment of it.

That girl deserves it.

She's been crushing on her best guy friend since they were kids and didn't think there'd come a time when Easton saw her as anything more than his soccer-playing gal pal. But dreams really do come true, because here we are. They've been going strong for about a month now.

And it's all thanks to yours truly. I'm the one who pushed her into going out with my hockey-playing cousin, Ryder. That was all the prompting Easton needed to see her for the gorgeous woman Sasha has grown into. And the rest is relationship history.

They fit so perfectly that it's almost like they've been together for years. Two pieces of the same puzzle.

Am I a wee bit jealous of what they have?

Of course not.

All right, maybe a little. Who wouldn't want to be with a guy who looks at you like you hung the moon in the sky especially for him? That's exactly the way it is with Easton.

My last relationship ended in spectacular disaster. We're talking flames, plumes of black smoke, and no survivors.

Andrew Hickenlooper.

Football player.

More like all-around player.

We were together for almost a year when I'd learned that he'd been cheating.

A nasty chlamydia diagnosis was the ultimate tip-off. Imagine sitting on a table in a doctor's office, only to be told you had an STI. And since I wasn't screwing around on the side, I knew exactly where it had come from.

The only thing worse than that was when he tried to deny it. When that didn't work, he'd attempted to tell me that I caught it from a toilet seat.

Ummm…no.

It's not called a sexually transmitted infection for nothing.

The situation jackhammered to an all-new low when I found out that almost everyone at Western knew he was screwing around behind my back, and that it had been going on throughout most of our relationship. I won't lie, for a few minutes, I'd considered transferring colleges.

But here's the thing—I didn't do anything wrong.

Even though it wasn't easy, I held my head up high and ignored all the ugly gossip until it eventually died down. Now, if Andrew would take a hint and leave me alone, I could finally put the whole nasty mess behind me, where it belongs.

"You might not have noticed, but the walls in our apartment are paper thin."

"Oh, god," she groans, cheeks growing more flushed with every step we take.

I can't resist the chuckle that slips free.

"If we could go to his place, I would. But you know what it's like over at the football house. Constant parties and cleat sniffers looking to get laid. I'd prefer to keep them away from my man."

"Like you have anything to worry about. That guy only has eyes for one girl and that's you, my friend."

It's sweet.

The smile that blooms across her face tells me that she knows it as well. Just as she opens her mouth to respond, strong arms wrap around her from behind and sweep her off her feet.

Literally.

Speak of the devil...

Sasha beams as Easton presses her against his muscular body. By the besotted look in my bestie's eyes, the world around her has completely fallen away. People jostle past, shooting irritated looks in their direction, but neither cares. It wouldn't surprise me to see little red and pink hearts dancing above their heads.

Ugh.

They're seriously too cute for words. It's enough to induce vomiting.

Just as I'm about to sigh, movement catches the corner of my eye. A shiver of awareness slices through me and the delicate hair at the nape of my neck prickles as my gaze lands on the figure loitering a few feet away.

Crosby Rhodes.

Left tackle for the Western Wildcats.

My initial reaction is to step away and put more distance between us, but I refuse to give him the satisfaction. Instead, I steel myself for a confrontation. I've spent too much time around him not to know exactly how this interaction will play out.

And that's badly.

The funny part—if there's anything amusing about this situation—is that he has a reputation on campus as a real player. The guy doesn't *do* girlfriends. To my knowledge, he's never entertained the idea of one. Even with his surly disposition, he can still charm the panties off any female within a ten-mile radius.

Except me.

To me, he's a total dickhead.

As soon as I make eye contact, his gaze drops, slowly crawling down the length of my body. Even though he's not physically touching me, that's exactly what his perusal feels like. It takes every ounce of self-control to remain motionless, so he doesn't see how much his scrutiny bothers me. Instead, I straighten my shoulders and grit my teeth before jutting out my chin in defiance. If he thinks he can burrow under my skin that easily, he's seriously mistaken.

By the time his onyx-colored depths return to mine, there's a slight curl to his upper lip and a dark look filling his eyes.

"Nice tits, McAdams. New push-up bra? They look bigger than usual. I like it."

"Fuck off, Rhodes." It takes effort to resist the urge to hunch over so that my breasts aren't as noticeable. Although, let's face it, when you wear a D cup, that's difficult to do. I've always been sensitive about the size of my boobs, and somehow, Crosby has figured it out.

He smirks as if pleased by my reaction. I have no idea what I did to provoke his ire, but it's been directed at me since Andrew first introduced us. If it had been possible to avoid the surly boy with the messy dark hair and lip ring, I would have done so after just one meeting. Unfortunately, that was impossible given that Andrew and Crosby are teammates, friends, and roommates. They share an apartment together off campus.

In the beginning, I went out of my way to be nice, figuring that with enough time and kindness, his attitude would thaw and he'd soften his stance. That never happened. If anything, his temperament grew nastier. Once it dawned on me that we were never going to sit around a campfire and sing Kumbaya, I avoided and ignored him.

Even though Andrew and I broke up six months ago, I still run into Crosby on campus and at parties. Sure, I could avoid the football players all together, but I refuse to give either of them that much power over my life. That being said, am I going to miss any of them, with the exception of Easton, when I graduate from Western in the spring?

Nope. Not even a little.

That's not to say they're all bad dudes. A couple of Sasha's soccer teammates are dating football players and they seem like nice guys. But after Andrew's total mindfuck, I have zero interest in getting wrapped up with another self-absorbed jock. There are too many girls at Western throwing themselves at their feet. Most of the ones who hooked up with Andrew knew he had a girlfriend and didn't give a crap.

So much for girl code.

After I dumped his ass, a good number of them came out of the woodwork to share all the gory details. Then they were all about pussy power and solidarity. Not so much when they were hoing around with my man behind my back.

"What?" He grins. "It was a compliment. You should take it that way."

"Please," I snort, "nothing that comes out of your mouth could be misconstrued as complimentary."

His smile widens, and the tiny silver hoop pierced through the corner of his lip glints in the sun. Without realizing it, my gaze drops to the metal. His tongue darts out to play with it, and a punch of arousal explodes in my core.

His voice dips as he looms closer. "Is that what you want, McAdams? My sweet words?" He practically purrs the question.

My heart kicks into overdrive as my attention snaps to his eyes. An unwanted sizzle of electricity snakes down my spine. One would think from our contentious past, the only thing he would do is piss me off.

Turns out that's not the case.

For whatever reason, Crosby is the only guy on this campus capable of making my hormones sit up and take notice. If there were away to stomp out the unwelcome attraction rushing through me like liquid fire, I'd do it in a heartbeat.

But there's not. Trust me, I've tried. Which is precisely why I go to such great lengths to avoid him. I would say like a clap diagnosis, but…

That hits a little too close to home.

I clear my throat. "Hardly."

He eats up more distance between us until it becomes necessary to tip my chin upward to hold his flinty gaze. It takes every ounce of self-control to stand my ground instead of scrambling backward in retreat.

The buzz of attraction zipping through my veins is not only disconcerting but refuses to be extinguished. His bright white teeth flash in the sunlight, and my attention is reluctantly snagged by the small metal hoop. I've never been attracted to guys with piercings. Or who are dark and moody.

Crosby is—and has always been—the exception to the rule.

When he reaches out to trail a finger down the front of my sweater, I jerk out of the strange stupor that has fallen over me and knock his hand away.

"Don't touch me," I growl, baring my teeth like a rabid dog. He's lucky I don't take a chunk out of him. At the very least, he'd think twice about messing with me in the future. Then again, nothing seems to deter him. He enjoys taunting me.

A slow grin spreads across his face as dark humor dances in his inky-colored irises.

Unwilling to get drawn into any more of a verbal skirmish, I spin on my heels and stalk through the crowd. Now that Easton has captured Sasha's attention, it's doubtful she'll notice my abrupt departure.

There's only so much of Crosby Rhodes I can take.

2

CROSBY

I stare after Brooke as she shoves through the crowd in order to get away from me. Her long, caramel-colored hair floats around her shoulders and down her back in bouncy waves. The urge to reach out and twirl a thick lock around my fingers had thrummed through me like a heavy drumbeat. My hands are still clenched at my sides so I wouldn't do just that.

Have I fantasized about wrapping the wavy length around my fist while thrusting deep inside her body?

You bet your damn ass I have.

Even now, I have to tamp down the boner rising in my boxer briefs.

Would she have bitten off my hand if I'd even attempted to touch her?

Yup. I risked both life and limb just stroking my fingers over the front of her sweater. That girl hates me with the passion of a thousand burning suns. Most of the females on this campus fall at my feet, begging for my attention, wanting to get fucked by yours truly.

She's the exception.

By design.

I've spent the last year doing everything in my power to piss her off, so she'll keep a healthy distance between us. Especially when she was dating my roommate, Andrew.

Call it a defense mechanism of sorts. I'm not saying it's right, but it was, in fact, necessary.

The only girl at Western I'm interested in is the very same one I can't have. Andrew still has a hard-on for his ex. If he has his way, he'll convince her to give him another chance. We've been friends for too long to let some good-looking chick with a nice rack wedge her way between us.

So…if that means I need to drop a few nasty comments to make certain she steers clear, then that's exactly what I'll do. From the disdainful way she glares at me to how she snaps and bares her teeth, it doesn't take a genius to realize my plan has worked like a charm. If there happens to be a flicker of guilt attempting to flare its way to life inside me, I stomp it out before it can take root and do permanent damage.

Just as Brooke disappears through the sea of students, Easton throws an arm around my shoulders. When I glance at him, he nods toward the last place I saw Brooke before she vanished from sight.

"I've never met a chick who hates you more. It's kind of comical. Although, let's be honest, you're a real dick to her."

He's not wrong. He just doesn't understand the rationale behind my actions. And I'm not about to fill him in, either.

I shrug, pretending I couldn't give a shit about her or her feelings. "And?"

"Just saying that she wouldn't spit in your mouth if you were dying of thirst."

Again, I have to stomp out the remorse attempting to take root inside me. I'd prefer to avoid Brooke until graduation, but that's not possible. Plus, as much as I hate to admit it, there's a tiny part of me that enjoys trading insults with her. That enjoys having her ire directed my way. Because let's face it, if she's focused on me then I don't have to worry about her with someone else.

Don't think I'm not aware of how sick and twisted my behavior is.

I totally get it. There's just nothing I can do about it. Or maybe it's more accurate to say there's nothing I'm *willing* to do about it.

Before I can shoot back with a comment, he continues. "What's the deal between you two anyway, huh?"

I plow a hand through my hair.

Yeah...there's no way I can admit the truth.

When I remain silent, he says, "Brooke is actually a super sweet girl. You know what Andrew did to her was fucked up, right?"

Of course I do. It's not even a question in my mind.

"Who's to say she didn't know what was going on and was cool with it?" Believe it or not, there are girls who enjoy the status of dating a Western Wildcat. Especially when the guy has a chance of being drafted and making millions a couple of years down the line. You can't believe some of the shit these chicks are willing to put up with. As long as they're the ones walking around with them on campus, they don't give a damn. Or they're willing to let it slide.

Do I really believe Brooke fits into that kind of merciless category?

No. She was totally clueless about Andrew's side pieces. The hurt that had radiated off her when she'd discovered the truth was palpable.

He rolls his eyes. "No way, dude. She had no idea what was going on. Andrew's an asshole for what he did."

Agreed.

Here's the problem—Andrew and I have known each other since third grade. Say what you want about him, but he's always had my back. I might not agree with the decisions he makes, but I'm not about to end our friendship over it. When I broke my leg freshman year of high school, he's the one who helped me rehab it and pushed me to get back on the field when all I wanted to do was sit around and feel sorry for myself. Without him, who knows what would have happened. Maybe I wouldn't be at Western playing football or have a chance of getting drafted to the pros this spring.

I owe Andrew a lot, and he deserves my loyalty. I'm unwilling to throw our friendship away because he's been known to make dubious decisions.

Before Easton can comment further on the situation, I say, "Let's get moving."

His brows rocket skyward. "Since when do you care about getting to class on time?"

I don't. What I care about is shutting down this conversation.

"Since now."

3

BROOKE

"Are you sure you're good with being here?" Sasha asks as we shove our way through the thick crowd at the football house.

Is she kidding?

This is the last place I want to be. More than likely, I'll run into the two guys I have zero interest in seeing. But I refuse to allow them to stop me from hanging out with my friends and enjoying myself. Even if I have to grit my teeth and fake it the entire time.

I paste a smile on my face and hope she buys it. "Yeah, of course."

She scrutinizes my expression before looping her arm through mine. "I know you do. I promise, we won't stay long. There are plenty of other parties going on."

My spine loses some of its rigidity as my muscles loosen. "There's a ton of people here. Maybe I'll get lucky and won't run into…" My voice trails off as my gaze collides with bright blue eyes.

Damn.

Naturally, my ex is knee-deep in fangirls, all who are vying for his attention.

When I first caught sight of Andrew on campus freshman year, I was instantly besotted. He's blond, handsome, and tall with a muscular body honed from years of lifting weights and playing football.

It wasn't until the end of sophomore year that he finally noticed me. We started talking and he asked me out. I felt like the luckiest girl in the world. This guy could have any girl he wanted, and he chose to spend time with me.

Me.

Even more dizzying than that, Andrew wasn't a guy known to get serious with one girl. I was the first. I'm not going to lie—it made me feel special and blinded me to the telltale signs in front of my face. After all, if you're more interested in sleeping around, you're not going to be in a committed relationship…right?

Wrong.

Instead of acknowledging him, I swing away. The last thing I want to do is get sucked into a conversation.

"Uh-oh," Sasha mutters, gaze pinned over my shoulder, "incoming."

Great. And we haven't even been here for five minutes.

Just as I attempt to shove my way through the sea of partiers, a heavy hand lands on my shoulder, halting my movements. A second later, I'm spun around.

"Hey, babe," Andrew says, flashing me a charming smile that gives him a boyishly innocent look.

I huff out an exasperated breath. "I'm not your babe."

"Aw, come on. Don't be like that." He pulls me forward until his brawny arms can wrap around me and I'm inundated with his fresh, citrusy scent. Once upon a time, I would have melted in his arms and clung to all that chiseled strength, never wanting to let go.

Those days are long gone.

When he brushes his lips against the crown of my head, I fight my way free. If I'm not careful, he'll glom onto me for the rest of the night, and I won't be able to shake him loose. It's happened before, and I'm unwilling to spend the next couple of hours trying to escape from him.

I push against his chest until he releases me. As soon as he does, I take two quick steps back. When I've put enough distance between us, his gaze meanders down my body. "You look gorgeous as usual."

"Thanks."

"No problem, babe."

I draw in a steady breath, hoping it'll calm everything that rages inside me. "Andrew, we've been through this. I'm not your babe. You need to move on."

He reaches out and snags my fingers before toying with them. His blue gaze flickers from them to mine. "What if I don't want to move on? What if I want to give us another shot? Come on, you can't deny that we weren't good together."

Is he crazy?

Of course I can. But that would only lead to more discussions, and that's what I'm trying to avoid.

Instead, I shake my head. "We aren't getting back together," I repeat. "Not after what happened."

With a shift of his weight, he cocks his head. "I've already apologized a thousand times. Why can't you just forgive me so we can move past this?"

It's on the tip of my tongue to say I'm sorry, but I stop myself before the words can tumble free. I'm not the one whose behavior was reprehensible. And he's right, he's apologized over and over again, but it doesn't change the fact that he cheated on me. Multiple times.

Instead of getting drawn into an argument, I point toward the kitchen at the back of the house. "I need a drink." Probably more than one. "Have a good night."

Before he can respond, I push through the press of bodies, needing to get as far from him as I can.

"Wait," he calls after me. "I'll come with you."

"No thanks," I yell over my shoulder, hoping he'll take the hint and finally move on.

What?

A girl can hope.

I glance around for Sasha and realize that she's stepped in front of Andrew to block him from following me. And that, my friends, is exactly why she'll always be my ride or die. If she weren't already my bestie, her sacrifice would seal the deal. Who knows…maybe she'll be able to talk some sense into him.

Although that's doubtful.

I'll kill a little time by grabbing a drink and then circle back. With any luck, Andrew will have disappeared, and I'll be able to avoid him for the rest of the night. It takes a few minutes to make my way to the kitchen before finding the keg and stepping in line.

When the guy standing in front of me swings around, I blink, realizing it's my cousin, Ryder.

"Hey," I greet, pulling him in for a quick hug. "I'm surprised to find you here." More like shocked.

The football and hockey players don't necessarily get along. Even though we're supposed to be one big, happy Western family, the two teams are always competing to be top dog on campus.

"Trust me, I'm not happy about it either," he grumbles, glancing around the crowded party. "Hopefully, we won't stay long. I got dragged here because someone's girlfriend's brother is on the team."

Looks like we're both stuck in the same miserable boat.

Instead of telling him that, I slip my arm through his. Even though Ryder is my cousin, he's more like a brother to me. "Well, it's always good to see you. How are Aunt Sadie and Uncle Cal?"

His expression softens. "They're good. You should stop by for a visit. They miss seeing your face. Actually, she made a batch of cookies for you a couple of weeks ago."

My brows pinch together. "Really? I never received them."

His lips curve into a grin as he pats his flat belly. "I know. But I told her you thought they were delicious."

I snort and swat at his arm. "You're a big jerk."

This only makes him grin more. "I'll let you know the next time we're getting together for dinner."

"That sounds good." While I avoid getting together with my own mother, it's the opposite with Ryder's parents.

We chat for a few more minutes before he grabs a beer and drains the glass in one thirsty gulp. "There's nowhere near enough alcohol to dull the pain of this party." Before I can respond, his eyes darken. "You're not here by yourself, are you?"

I shake my head. Of course not.

Does he think I'm a complete idiot?

"Nope, Sasha's around here somewhere." I don't mention that she's holding off my ex. Andrew has never been a fan favorite with Ryder.

"Just make sure you stick with her tonight, all right?"

"I will." I give him a peck on the cheek before shooing him away. The last thing I need is a keeper.

And then he's gone, plowing through the sea of students. Although, honestly, most scatter out of his way. Ryder is well over six feet and broad in the shoulders. Whether he's walking around campus or skating on the ice, no one wants to get run over by him.

Once my beer is in hand, I swing around to retrace my steps. Hopefully, I'll be able to find Sasha without running into my ex again.

I don't get more than a step before slamming into a hard body. The drink gets splashed across the front of my loosely knit cotton sweater, making the thin material cling to my breasts as I lose my balance and stumble a couple of steps. Strong fingers wrap around my upper arms to stop me from tumbling backward.

A gasp slips free as beer drips down the material and puddles at my feet. I glance up, gaze slamming into familiar dark eyes.

Crosby.

Of course it would have to be him.

Had I known that tonight would turn out to be such a clusterfuck, I would have stayed home, ordered pizza, and curled up with a good movie. Maybe read a book. Instead, I'm here. Dealing with the two guys who top my shit list. It's like a cosmic joke.

When his attention drops to my breasts, my nipples tighten under the intensity of his scrutiny. Heat fills my cheeks as embarrassment slams into me full force. I could try to convince myself it's from the cold liquid that has soaked the front, but deep down I know it's a lie. It's the heat of his stare that has my body reacting this way.

I steel myself for a nasty comment. Instead, his jaw tightens as the muscles tic in his cheek. When he releases his hold on my shoulders, a little sigh of relief escapes from me. It's short lived as his fingers lock around my wrist before he drags me through the congested kitchen and into the dining room. The music continues to thump around us as the lights remain low.

"Hey! Let go of me!" My feet stumble to keep pace with him as I try to jerk my arm free. "What are you doing?"

"Taking you upstairs."

Ummm...excuse me?

Hell, no.

I don't want to go anywhere with this guy.

When I yank my arm for a second time, attempting to break his hold, his grip turns punishing and I wince. The press of people part for him like the Red Sea as they try to scurry out of his way. I can't say I blame them. Given half a chance, I'd scramble out of Crosby's way as well. Thirty seconds later, I'm dragged up the staircase. Each step has my heart rioting more painfully against my ribcage until the organ feels like it'll explode from my chest.

"Crosby," I grunt, continuing to struggle as we reach the second-floor landing and move steadily down the hallway. He stalks past two closed doors before grabbing the handle of the third and throwing it open. I've been here enough times with Sasha to know this is Easton's room. He drags me across the threshold before slamming the door shut behind us. Only then am I released. I stumble backward, trying to put enough distance between us. But how much is enough?

I have no idea.

This is the first time we've been alone together.

Warily, I rub my wrist and glare, just to make sure he understands I'm not a willing participant in whatever he thinks is going to happen here. I take my gaze off him long enough to glance at my wrist. It feels like the flesh has been scalded by his touch. It's almost a surprise when I don't find burn marks.

Crosby and I might exchange barbs whenever we're around one another, but he's never laid his hands on me.

Not like this.

The thought sends a fresh wave of shock flooding through me as goosebumps spring up, skittering across my skin.

Eyebrows lowered, my upper lip curls. "What's your problem?"

"I don't have one," he says calmly as his fingers settle at the hem of his navy T-shirt before slowly dragging it up his body and over his head.

Even with the dim lighting in the room, my eyes widen as a bare chest rippling with well-honed muscles comes into view.

Holy cow.

I might have spent a lot of time hanging out at Andrew's apartment when we were together, but I never caught a glimpse of Crosby without his shirt on. A mental fog descends as my mouth turns cottony at the sight of it. For a long stretch of silent moments, the only sounds that can be heard are the muted music from the party raging downstairs and my heartbeat as it pounds viciously in my ears.

"See something you like?" His voice sounds as if it's been scraped from the bottom of the ocean. It slips beneath my skin and does strange things to my insides before twisting them up into a painful knot.

I don't have to glance at his face to realize there will be a mocking smirk curving his lips. That notion is enough to puncture the sexual haze clouding my better judgment. Heat floods my face as I drop my gaze to my hands.

Ugh.

The last thing I need is for this guy to suspect just how much he's able to affect me. That would be a mistake. One he would never let me live down.

I clear my throat. "I'm leaving." I take a tentative step toward the door, knowing that I'll have to sidle around him since he's blocking it.

What's he going to do?

Keep me trapped inside?

A burst of fear-spiked excitement explodes inside me.

His lips twitch as he shifts his stance, shadowing my movement and blocking any avenue for escape. "You're not going anywhere until you take off that shirt."

My eyes widen. There's no way in hell I heard him correctly. "Excuse me?" The question is barely a squeak that leaves my lips.

He jerks his head toward my chest as his gaze once again settles there. Awareness sizzles through me before I ruthlessly tamp it down.

Why him?

Why does my body always react to him like this?

It doesn't make the least bit of sense. I can't stand Crosby Rhodes. And yet…

My libido has a mind of its own where he's concerned. It's frustrating. Especially since he's such a dick.

I blink to awareness as he stalks toward me. With every step he takes, the intensity filling the room ratchets up until it feels as if all the oxygen has been sucked from it and it becomes impossible to breathe.

A glint sparks to life in his eyes. "I said you're not going anywhere until the sweater comes off."

Even though I'm a full head shorter than him, I straighten to my full height.

Who the hell does this guy think he is?

As I open my mouth to blast him into next week, he says, "Look down."

Thrown off by the snapped-out command, I blink before narrowing my eyes. I'm afraid of what he'll do if I look away for even a moment. He continues to stare as my breathing turns labored and my teeth nibble at my lower lip.

"For fuck's sake," he growls, "stop staring at me and just look at your damn sweater."

The gravel filling his voice has me dropping my gaze, only to find the thin, cream-colored material plastered across my breasts. Now that it's soaked, it's practically translucent. Not only is the outline of my bra perfectly clear, but so are the dusky-tipped nipples poking through the sheer material. Eyes flaring wide, I gasp and quickly cross my arms over my chest. If warmth had been filling my face a few minutes ago, it now feels like I'm burning up inside with embarrassment.

Oh god.

How many people caught sight of me like this?

A tortured groan escapes from my lips.

"That's exactly why you need to take it off and put something else on," he grounds out.

When I remain frozen in place, lost in the turmoil of my own thoughts, he eats up the distance between us with two long-legged strides before pressing his shirt into my palm. My gaze lifts to his bare chest, and an unwanted shot of electricity sizzles through my veins before settling in my core.

Say what you want about the guy, but he has an amazing body. He's all rippling muscle and sinewy strength. If he were anyone else, I'd reach out and run my hands over his pecs to see if they're as hard and chiseled as they appear. Instead, my fingers bite into the cottony material to keep from doing exactly that. I can't imagine what his response would be if I were to touch him. He'd probably sneer and make a barbed comment meant to inflict as much damage as possible.

Already I can feel the burn of his gaze boring into the top of my head as I force myself to take a step in retreat. I need a few inches of separation before this situation can spiral any further out of control. Anything that will help clear the fog from my brain so I can think straight.

"You might not realize it, but the only way this will work is if you take off your sweater first."

I draw in an unsteady breath and attempt to regain my bearings. It's not easy with him standing inches away. Instead of Andrew's citrusy aroma, his is woodsier and more masculine in nature. Something smoky that slyly wraps its way around me and assaults my senses. I'm almost tempted to inhale a big breath of him and hold it captive in my lungs.

It takes effort to clear both my throat and head. "Turn around."

"Why?" As he shifts closer, his muscles flex and bunch. "I don't get to ogle your chest the way you did mine?"

A smirk simmers in his deep voice.

"Just turn around," I snap, losing my patience. The way he can so easily befuddle me is irritating.

"It's not like you have anything I haven't seen before."

Air becomes trapped in my lungs as he invades my personal space. I feel the heat radiating off his body in heavy waves as he whispers in my ear, "Or touched. Or sucked into my mouth."

The deep scrape of his voice has arousal exploding in the pit of my belly. Actually, it detonates much lower. My panties are dampening as we speak. There's so much attraction zipping through my veins, searching for an escape route.

I sway toward him before catching myself. "That might be so, but you've never seen me, and I'd prefer to keep it that way."

His gaze drops to my stiffened buds as his tongue peeks out to play with the lip ring. Stare intensifying, he flips the metal back and forth until it feels like the moment could shatter. Just when I can't take another second, he retreats and turns away.

Air escapes from my lungs in a relieved rush.

When he folds his arms across his chest, the grooved and corded muscles that make up the wide expanse of his back constrict. He's all solid and carefully constructed strength. A wall of impenetrable steel, from the broad set of his shoulders to his traps, deltoids, and lats.

Why does he have to be such a good-looking jerk?

So tall and powerful.

And the lip ring…

A reluctant shiver works its way through me before settling like a dull ache in my core.

I yank the shirt over my head before forcing my arms through the holes and pulling it down my body. It's a few sizes too big, but it's better than the cold, wet sweater I'd been wearing. As the material settles around my body, I'm once again inundated with the masculine scent of him. Unable to resist, I bring the soft cotton to my nose and inhale another lungful.

Not wanting him to catch me, I release the fabric and smooth it down just as he swings around. Everything in me stills as his gaze rakes over my length. I'm like a rabbit frozen in place as a predator decides whether to make a tasty meal out of me. And there's not a damn thing I can do about it.

Self-preservation and past run-ins leave me bracing for the unexpected. Instead, he swings toward the dresser before yanking open a drawer, grabbing a maroon T-shirt, and covering his chest.

Only then does he glance over his shoulder and meet my gaze. "Ready to go?"

More than ready.

I nod and fly past him to the door before practically ripping it off its hinges. It's so much easier to breathe in the hallway. The air isn't nearly as thick or oppressive as inside the room. My heart pounds a painful beat as I race down the staircase.

No matter how swiftly I move, I'm uncomfortably aware of Crosby's intimidating presence silently stalking me.

As I rejoin the crowd, my feet stutter with the realization that he could have easily given me a shirt from the dresser. Instead, I'm wearing the one off his back.

4

CROSBY

My attention stays riveted to the girl with the long, caramel-colored hair standing on the other side of the living room. The very same female who is now wearing my shirt. In a weird way, it feels like I've marked her as my own and she now belongs to me.

Brooke would, no doubt, have something to say about that.

And none of it would be good.

The thought is enough to make my lips twitch. I probably shouldn't take such perverse pleasure in pissing her off, but I can't seem to help myself. It's just too easy. A few carefully placed comments and she goes off like a shot.

I like the way she looks when she's all riled up. Her eyes light with fury as the edges of her mouth sink. There are times when I wonder if I've pushed her too far and she'll rip me to shreds, times when a strange, combustible energy fills the atmosphere and my cock stiffens as all the blood drains from my brain.

"Hi, Crosby."

I blink back to the present and realize that Shandi Miller has sidled up next to me while I wasn't paying attention. With a knowing smile, she flattens both palms against my chest before stroking them down to the waistband of my jeans.

"Hey. How are you?" Gaze focused on her, I bring the bottle of beer to my lips and take a long swig.

Her heavily made up eyes lower to half-mast as a sly smile tugs at her lips. "Better now that I've found you." Her voice is nothing more than a purr that holds the promise of enough pleasure to make my eyes cross.

She presses closer until I can feel the tight points of her nipples against me. Shandi doesn't have a shy bone in her trim little body. She's a girl who knows what she wants and goes after it with single-minded determination. You have to respect a woman like that. My guess is that she's trolling for a hookup. Since she's one of the girls I fuck on a regular basis, I would normally be up for a couple hours of no-strings-attached sex.

But not tonight.

Tonight, my thoughts are filled with the curvaceous girl who is pointedly ignoring me from the other side of the room. Even though I know nothing can happen, that doesn't stop me from wanting her.

From craving what will never be mine.

My thoughts tumble back to earlier this evening when she'd knocked into me, spilling the drink down the front of her shirt. The golden liquid had turned the delicate material practically sheer before becoming plastered across her breasts like a second skin.

I've spent years fantasizing about what her tits would look like beneath her clothing. Now I have a visual to tuck away for later use. Unfortunately, I wasn't the only one taking mental snapshots. From the corner of my eye, I watched a few guys do double takes, ogling her with hungry gazes. Unable to stand the idea of a bunch of jerkoffs drooling over her, I grabbed her hand and towed her up the staircase to Easton's bedroom. Could I have given her one of his shirts to wear for the remainder of the night?

Sure.

Instead, I'd yanked off my own T-shirt before forcing her to pull it on. Even though it's a couple sizes too big and swallows her up, I like the way she looks in it. The thought that a piece of my clothing is wrapped around her body does things to me.

"Oh?" I say, half distracted as my attention wanders back to Brooke. And the guy who is now talking to her.

What the fuck?

Shandi slinks closer, attempting to regain my distracted attention. "I was thinking we could get out of here. Maybe head back to your place for a while."

My brows snap together as the guy inches closer before picking up a thick lock of her hair and twirling it around his finger.

I know exactly what kind of dirty thoughts are running amok in this asshole's head, and it's not going to happen. I'll make damned sure of it.

"Crosby?"

My gaze snaps back to the blonde who is staring up at me. If my main objective is to get naked and enjoy myself for a couple of mindless hours of pleasure, this girl is here for it.

"What?"

Irritation flickers across her pretty features. "Do want to get out of here?"

"Nah. Not right now."

She blinks before frowning. "Really?" Disbelief weaves its way through her voice.

I shake my head as my attention slides back to Brooke and the douchebag attempting to make moves on her. Even in an oversized T-shirt, she still attracts male interest.

For a handful of seconds, we both remain quiet. Shandi seems knocked off kilter by the sudden turn of events. This is the first time I've turned her down. As far as fucks go, this girl is perfect. She understands that an hour or so of fooling around between the sheets doesn't equate to a relationship. She also realizes that I'm going to screw other girls and she's free to do the same. What I've discovered is that Shandi enjoys a little girl on girl action and is no stranger to threesomes.

So yeah…

No red-blooded guy in his right mind would turn her down.

There are a lot of chicks who swear up and down that they're cool with one-night stands, but very few actually feel that way. I've been burned a couple times. So, I'm careful about who I jump into bed with, which is exactly why the groupies who hang out at the football houses are my first choice. It's kind of hard to claim you thought it was the start of something beautiful when you've spread your legs for half the team and counting.

If I were smart, I'd take the nubile blonde up on her offer. A hard come just might help clear Brooke from my head. She's the last person I need to be focused on. But…there's no point in screwing one girl when I can't stop thinking about a different one. I've attempted that feat before, and it doesn't work. I'm usually left with a vague sense of dissatisfaction and regret. I'm better off going home and jerking off to thoughts of her.

How fucking pathetic is that?

I clear my throat and shift my weight. "Sorry. I'm not in the mood." Which is also a first for me.

She rears back as if I've bitch-slapped her into next week. "Are you being serious?"

"Yeah." Unfortunately.

"All right." Her hands fall away as she retreats a step. "If you change your mind, come find me."

"Will do."

As soon as she spins on her heel, I take off toward Brooke and the jackass who seems to think he'll be getting into her pants tonight. Like a man on a mission, I plow my way across the room until someone steps in front of me, blocking my path. My irritated gaze snaps to his.

Andrew.

Fuck. How the hell did I forget about him?

"Hey," he says, looking a little bleary-eyed.

When I give him a chin lift, he frowns before glancing over his shoulder toward his ex-girlfriend.

"Why is Brooke wearing your shirt?" His words are all slurred together, which is par for the course on a Saturday night. He works hard on the field and likes to play even harder off it. He's certainly not the only one of my teammates with that mentality.

"She spilled a drink down the front of her sweater, so I gave her mine to wear. It's not a big deal," I tack on, hoping we can drop the conversation.

He searches my eyes, holding my gaze for an uncomfortable amount of time before saying, "You know that she'll always be my girl, right?"

My shoulders slump.

"Yup." Mostly because he never allows me to forget it.

He stumbles a few paces before bringing the glass to his lips and sucking down half of it. Belching, he drags the back of his hand across his mouth. "You think I should talk to her again?"

In this condition?

"That's probably not a good idea."

With a groan, he swings around to stare at her. "Why won't she forgive me?"

I huff out an exasperated breath. "Because you fucked around behind her back."

He waves a hand. "So what? Plenty of guys do. Is it really that big of a deal?"

I glance at the girl in question as she tucks a stray lock of hair behind her ear. "Yeah, I guess to her it was."

Tipping the cup to his mouth, he taps the bottom when he finds it empty. With a grumble, he staggers off toward the kitchen without another word. I glance at Brooke and find a smile curving her lips as she flirts with the guy. After a few moments, her eyes flicker to mine. As our gazes collide, any happiness filling her face drains as she quickly dismisses me. Her attention resettles on the jerkoff she's talking with. Only this time, her smile looks more forced than before.

Even though I had every intention of stomping over and breaking up the little love fest going on, I reconsider my decision.

What would be the point?

When it comes to Brooke McAdams, I'm not going to do a damn thing.

I can't.

She's not mine.

And she never will be.

5

CROSBY

"Come on, dumbass," I grumble, half dragging Andrew through the door of our apartment. What I should have done is left his ass at the party to sleep it off.

He mutters something indecipherable before staggering through the small entryway, past the dark kitchen, and into the living room where he faceplants on the couch, landing with a heavy thud.

I can only shake my head in disgust.

This drunken behavior was all fine and dandy when we were eighteen-year-old freshmen living on our own for the first time. But that's no longer the case. We're seniors, one semester away from graduating, and he's still pulling the same crap. The guy gets hammered and makes an ass of himself every Saturday night like clockwork. I never thought I'd say this, but it's getting old.

I slam the apartment door shut and reluctantly trail after him into the living room before dropping onto the armchair. It's after two in the morning. I'm tired and just want to hit the sack. The problem is that I don't need him choking on his own vomit.

I pull my phone from my back pocket and scroll through a couple of notifications before tossing it on the coffee table to contemplate the situation. Well, at least he's passed out on his stomach. If I remember correctly, he can't asphyxiate in his own puke unless he's on his back. Or is it the other way around?

I probably should have paid more attention during the mandatory seminars we were forced to sit through freshman year.

I glare at Andrew as he snores softly with his mouth hanging open before huffing out a breath and rising to my feet, ready to hit the sheets. There's not much else I can do for him. I don't take more than two steps before his eyelids fly open and he flips over onto his back before digging his phone out of his pocket and staring at it.

He taps the screen before pressing it to his ear. A moment of silence passes before he mutters, "Can you believe she blocked me?"

The *she* in question is obvious.

"Yeah, I can."

"But I love her," he whines, stabbing the end call button.

I scrub a hand tiredly over my face. My eyes feel like they're burning.

"Then maybe you shouldn't have cheated on her," I mutter for the second time tonight. Or given her an STI.

Curable, but still...

It's doubtful that matters in the grand scheme of things.

"I didn't realize what I had until it was gone."

Yeah, well...tough shit. There's no way to go back and fix the situation.

Even though I've never voiced those thoughts out loud, I don't understand how he could have cheated on Brooke. The girl is a perfect ten. She has it all going on—looks, brains, and amazing personality. It's a lethal combination capable of bringing a grown man to his knees.

At first, I wondered if she knew what was going on and simply chose to turn a blind eye. It was easy to lose all respect and drop her neatly into the same category as all the other jersey chasers.

After a few months, little comments here and there made me realize that she was totally clueless. Then I disliked her for being stupid and refusing to see what was going on right in front of her face. It's only in hindsight that I realized I needed a reason to dislike her and clung blindly to any excuse.

"Do you think she'll come around at some point?" he asks, voice slurring.

"Probably not."

When he groans, I swing around and head to the kitchen for a couple of bottles of water. He's going to need it. Plus, I'm not interested in fielding more questions regarding his ex. Andrew needs to move on. It's like he's stuck on her for dropping him like a hot potato.

When I return to the living room, he's sitting up with my phone in his hand.

My brows jerk together. "What the hell are you doing?"

He glances at me before staring at the cell. "She hasn't blocked your ass, so I'll call from your phone."

"What? No way."

Jesus Christ…this guy. He just won't give up. The girl is going to take out a restraining order if he doesn't knock this shit off. And I wouldn't blame her for it.

Tossing the bottles on the chair, I dive across the coffee table and swipe the slim device from his hand. There's a small tussle as Brooke's sleepy voice comes over the line.

"Hello?"

Fuck.

"Hello?" There's a pause as her husky voice grows more alert. "Who is this?"

I swing away before stabbing the disconnect button and falling onto the couch next to him.

"What the hell, dude?" He's one stupid motherfucker.

Andrew gives me sad, puppy dog eyes in response. That might work with the chicks on campus, but not me. "I just wanted to hear the sound of her voice." His head lolls back against the top of the cushion as his eyelids fall closed. "She has the softest pussy I've ever fucked." There's a pause. "I miss it."

A painful knot twists in the pit of my belly. The last thing I want to dwell on is the two of them having sex. Or all the nights she crashed at our place. The grunting and noises that would emanate from across the hall. I'd lay awake, staring up at the ceiling, trying not to think about what they were doing. Anytime Brooke was around, I'd belt back a few drinks and text a random girl to come over, hoping it would be enough to take the edge off.

Did it ever work?

Nope.

I was all too aware of what was going on. Hell, it was impossible not to think about. Impossible not to admit how much I wanted to be the one fucking her and then falling asleep with her curled up next to me.

"I'm going to bed," I grumble, pushing away from the couch.

As soon as I rise to my feet, Andrew slumps over. A snore escapes from him before his head even hits the cushion.

So fucking annoying.

Just as I step over the threshold into my bedroom, a message pops up on the screen.

Did you call me?

I stare at the question and contemplate my choices. Ignore it or...

Sorry. Wrong number.

There. That should take care of it.

Are there really any wrong numbers?

A slight smile tugs at the corners of my lips as I shake my head. Brooke sure as shit wouldn't feel that way if she knew who she was texting with.

That's quite a philosophical question for three in the morning, don't you think?

Instead of answering, she responds with...

Is this what now constitutes philosophical discussions? If so, that's really sad.

That's all it takes for the tentative smile hovering around the corners of my lips to turn into a full-blown grin. It never crosses my mind not to respond.

The world as we know it is in serious trouble.

A second wind hits me as I sink to the mattress and stare at the phone, eager for another text to pop up.

Agreed.

There are three laughing emojis tacked on before the dreaded question is asked.

What's your name? Do I know you?

I shove a hand through my hair and consider setting the phone on my nightstand and ignoring the questions. There's no way I can tell Brooke the truth. All it will do is give her more ammunition to hate me with. Plus, she'll know her ex was once again attempting to get ahold of her.

Before I can think better of it, my fingers fly across the miniature keyboard.

Don't know. Who are you?

Part of me wonders if she'll bother to be honest. As far as she's concerned, this was nothing more than a random call, and we don't know each other.

Brooke. I'm a senior at Western.

Well, hell. That was unexpected. But still, there's no point in admitting the truth. The girl would flip her lid. And she hates me enough as it is. I don't need to add kerosene to that particular fire.

That's a coincidence. So am I.

I evade the main question, hoping she won't notice.

But you didn't tell me your name.

Fuck.

What to do...

What to do...

I glance around the room until my gaze falls on an official university letter lying half-opened on the nightstand.

It's addressed to Crosby C. Rhodes.

Crosby Christopher Rhodes.

Chris.

Air gets wedged in my throat as I hit the green send arrow. There's a lengthy hesitation before three little bubbles appear on the screen.

Hmmm. I don't know anyone named Chris.

I give her a tiny nugget of truth, so I don't feel like such a damn liar. Then again, what does it really matter? We'll text for a couple of minutes before this convo loses steam and we say our goodbyes. In the morning, this exchange will be forgotten and we'll both move on with our lives.

I don't get out much. I'm a mechanical engineering major and usually buried under a ton of homework.

Interesting. I'm majoring in fashion merchandising. Pretty much opposite ends of the spectrum and yet we're both housed in the same building.

That's true.

You can always tell the difference between the fashion students and the engineering ones who wear pocket protectors and look socially out of place with the crowds of people.

All right...

This little back and forth has gone on long enough. All I'm doing is prolonging the inevitable and digging my grave deeper. Instead of responding, I toss the phone on the nightstand and yank off the T-shirt and jeans before sliding beneath the covers. For good measure, I turn on my side and face the wall, so I won't be tempted to pick up the cell.

I squeeze my eyelids closed as the slim device pings.

Nope. I'm not going to do it. I'm not—

Less than ten seconds later, I roll over and snatch it from the nightstand.

Fuck me.

6

BROOKE

My eyelids crack open when there's a knock on my bedroom door. The garbled-out words must be loud enough for Sasha to hear, because she pushes the thick wood open and takes a peek inside my room.

"Hey, are you up?"

"No. Go away. Still sleeping."

Instead, she pads into the room, and I catch a whiff of maple syrup and warm butter. I open my eyes more fully to see a fresh stack of pancakes.

With a groan, I push myself up into a seated position and shove my hair out of my face. "Oh my god, that smells amazing."

She waves her hand in front of it until the tantalizing scent penetrates my senses and my belly grumbles.

"I made them just for you," she sing-songs.

As soon as she hands over the plate, I dig in. Without question, breakfast is one of my favorite meals of the day. Especially when I'm not the one cooking it. Sasha has always been an early riser and loves to putter around the tiny kitchen. Although, with soccer and classes, she doesn't have a lot of spare time to do it. But it's fully appreciated when she does.

As I shove a forkful of fluffy goodness into my mouth, she settles on the edge of my bed.

"You know it's ten o'clock, right?"

My eyes widen as my fork stalls midway to my mouth. "Seriously?"

She nods. "I checked on you a few times to make sure you were still breathing."

I smirk and devour another bite. "You're a good friend," I say around a mouthful of pancake.

With a shake of her head, she squints. "I'm sorry, I couldn't understand that." She makes a few tsking noises. "What would Elaine say if she heard you talking with your mouth full?"

It's tempting to stick out my tongue, but that would probably be gross. The girl did, after all, make me breakfast. So, I'll let the comment slide.

Once I've swallowed down the mouthful, I say, "We both know my mother would be aghast at my lack of manners." Ugh. Elaine is the last person I want to discuss first thing in the morning. In fact, I try not to think of her unless absolutely necessary.

"She'd probably make you take a refresher course on etiquette."

She's not lying about that.

"Why are you such a sleepyhead this morning? We both got home at the same time last night, but I'm pretty sure I was up later than you," she waggles her brows, "if you know what I mean."

I roll my eyes. "Yup, I heard."

My bestie is usually mortified when I mention the decibel level of their little love sessions. This time, she grins, looking as pleased as a cat that just ate the canary.

Rather than delve into her sexcapades, which will only depress me since there haven't been any shenanigans for me since Andrew, I say, "Actually, I was up texting until five this morning."

"Ohhhh." Her eyes widen as she rubs her hands together. A giddy expression settles on her face. "Wait…don't tell me. Let me guess." A moment of silence ticks by as she stares at the ceiling with narrowed eyes. "Was it that cute Sig Delt I saw you talking with? FYI—he couldn't take his eyes off you."

Her hand snakes out to slap my arm.

"Ouch!" I wince. Sasha works out and can do some major damage if she wants. I've been on the receiving end of her playful punches for years. They're not always so playful. "You almost made me drop the plate."

"Why didn't you tell me on the way home?"

I raise my brows. "For one, it's not that guy. And two, you were so busy sucking face in the backseat, you wouldn't have heard anything I said."

A dull flush stains her cheeks. "We were *not* sucking face."

"Yeah, you were." I distinctly remember thinking there was an excellent possibility that he was going to hoover her tonsils right out of her body.

She waves away my observation before turning the conversation back to the topic at hand. "If it wasn't the frat guy, then who did you spend all night texting with?"

Now that I've plowed my way through half the stack and my belly is full, I set the plate on the nightstand and resettle against the pillows.

"His name is Chris," I hedge, unsure how much to divulge. The entire thing is crazy.

"Chris?" Her brows pinch as she purses her lips and racks her brain. "From the swim team?"

"No, I don't think he's a swimmer."

She shifts. "Did you meet him last night at the party or somewhere else?"

My teeth sink into my lower lip before worrying it.

When I remain silent, she makes an impatient hand gesture. "Come on, tell me. I'm dying here."

"I haven't exactly met him...yet."

"I don't understand." Before I can respond, she groans. "Please tell me this isn't someone you met on a dating app. I thought you deactivated your profile after the last guy sent you a bunch of dick pics." She scrunches her face. "They weren't even that impressive."

Yeah...we're not going to talk about that dumpster fire of a situation.

"No dating app was involved."

"Then explain how you're talking to someone who you haven't actually met. Was it a random number?" she asks with a laugh.

One glance at my face has the mirth fading from her lips as her eyes widen until it looks like they might fall out of her head. "OMG, you're talking with a random number?"

I huff out a breath and shrug. "Yeah. One thing led to another, and we ended up texting for two and a half hours."

When she remains silent, a concerned expression settling over her pretty features, I clear my throat and say hastily, "I doubt anything more will happen."

"You don't think so?"

I shake my head, no longer wanting to discuss the situation. I'd fallen asleep last night with a smile on my face. Out of everyone I spoke with at the party, this is the conversation I enjoyed most. And it had all taken place through text. We'd clicked instantly.

"Okay." She rises from my bed before grabbing my plate from the nightstand and heading into the hallway. "Let me know when you want to do a little shopping, the cupboards are bare," she calls on her way out.

I snuggle into the covers before grabbing my phone and scrolling through our messages. There are so many. It's funny, I have no idea what this guy even looks like, but we discussed a lot of different things and in a strange way, I feel like I got to know him. What I've discovered only makes me curious to learn more. The realization that this was just a one-time deal has a kernel of sadness blooming to life inside me. Before it can take root, I shake it off.

It was a wrong number, nothing more. Honestly, there's no reason for us to text ever again.

Just as I toss off the covers, ready to head to the bathroom, my phone dings with a message.

Hey. Sleep well?

A smile springs to my lips as my fingers fly over the keyboard.

7

BROOKE

*E*ven though there's an entire wing dedicated to the engineering sciences, I glance around the open space, wondering if Chris might be here hunkered down as well. He mentioned spending a lot of time studying at the library. My gaze slides over a couple of guys.

There's a dark-haired one over there. Could that be him?

Or maybe the lanky blond studying by the stacks?

Or what about the muscular Prince Harry lookalike across from us?

My brows draw together as I contemplate the situation. The problem is that I could literally run into him on campus and not realize it. We've spent the last couple of nights texting for hours, but I still don't have any idea what he looks like.

Instead of keeping our banter light and easy, we've delved deep and really gotten to know each other. It's to the point that I look forward to sliding between the sheets at the end of the day. I can't deny that the more I discover, the more I like.

When it comes down to it, I have no idea who this guy is. He could literally be anyone. Maybe that's the attraction and why it's so easy to open up and be real with him. In a short amount of time, we've managed to strip away all the pretenses. Or maybe there weren't any to begin with. Neither of us is worried about images or pretending to be something we're not.

It's refreshing.

And kind of addicting.

All right...more than kind of.

When I should be focused on my homework, I'm daydreaming about Chris.

It's only when Sasha waves a hand in front of my face that I'm force back to the present. "What's going on with you?"

"Hmmm?" I blink, attempting to refocus my attention. "What do you mean?"

She narrows her eyes as if I'm not fooling her at all. "You're thinking about that guy. What's his name?" Before I can respond, she supplies the answer. "Chris."

Heat floods into my cheeks.

"I can't believe you two are still texting."

Embarrassed, I huff out a breath before jerking my shoulders. "I like talking to him," I mumble. "Why is it such a big deal?"

She jerks a brow and gives me a hard stare. "Because you're not actually talking. You're texting."

"So?" I shift on my chair, wishing there were a way to shut down this conversation.

"So?" She leans forward, closing some of the distance between us. "What if he's not who you think he is? What if you're being," her hand flutters in the air between us, "catfished or something like that?"

Catfished?

Oh, come on.

The look in her eyes tells me she's as serious as a heart attack. The gurgle of laughter dies a slow death on my lips.

"What do you really know about him?"

"His name is Chris, and he's an engineering student at Western." I could rattle off a bunch of things, but I don't want to share them with her.

"Are you the one who brought up going to school here or did he?

Don't you think it's awfully coincidental that some random guy calls you and ends up attending the same university?"

A small pit settles at the bottom of my belly.

I don't know...

Maybe?

Silently I dig through my memories, trying to recall who mentioned Western first. I think it might have been me.

"How do you even know that he's a *he*?"

I...

Because he said his name was Chris and I just assumed.

When I press my lips together, her face scrunches and she spears me with a skeptical look.

"I don't know, Brooke. I think it would be a good idea to pull back a bit and be more cautious where this person is concerned." She drops her voice. "What if this guy is some creepy Russian dude halfway across the country who's like seventy years old and wants to snatch you up for the sex trade? Have you even considered the possibility that you're being played?"

The small pit in my belly grows until it's roughly the size of Rhode Island. It takes effort to force out a weak chuckle. "I think you've been watching too many Lifetime movies."

"Sometimes I watch *Dateline*, and everything I just said actually happens." She raises a brow. "Especially to naïve college girls."

"I'm not naïve," I mumble, feeling like an idiot. I've seen the same news reports, and what she's saying is true.

"How long was Andrew cheating on you before you finally figured it out?"

I wince, both surprised and hurt she would throw that in my face. "That's a low blow."

She releases a steady breath before reaching across the table and laying a hand over mine. "You're right, it was. But it doesn't make it any less true."

As much as I hate to admit it, maybe Sasha *is* right. Maybe I've been way too trusting where Chris is concerned. It's all together possible that he's not who he claims to be. Just because I wouldn't lie to a stranger, it doesn't mean other people have the same standard of honesty. As painful as it is to admit, she's right about Andrew. He lied to me for most of our relationship and I never questioned him.

"I'm not trying to be a downer here. Just get a little more information before this goes any further, okay? And for god's sake, if you actually decide to meet up with him, do it on campus in a busy place during the daytime."

I roll my eyes. "I'm not a complete idiot."

Her expression softens. "I never said you were. I just want you to be careful, that's all."

"I know you're thinking the worst, but I highly doubt he's been lying to me."

Sasha gives me a noncommittal grunt. "Time will tell, won't it?"

I straighten, wishing I felt as confident as I'm trying to appear. "Yes, it will."

"Hey. What are you two talking about?"

Startled by the deep voice, we glance up at Ryder, who has sidled up to the table we're camped out at. When Sasha's gaze flickers to me, I give my head a little shake. Even though I'm close with my cousin, he doesn't need to know about this situation.

"Brooke has a little something-something going on—"

Argh!

"I do not," I cut in. Sasha's more than aware of how overprotective Ryder can be. Especially after the whole Andrew debacle. I'm really going to kill her for bringing this up in front of him.

He straightens to his full height before cracking his knuckles. "Oh, yeah? Who's the guy?"

"It's no one," I say before Sasha can divulge any more state secrets. The last thing I need is Ryder getting all up in my business.

His expression darkens. "I want a name."

With a groan, I slump in my chair. "That's not necessary, all right? We're just talking." If Ryder has his way, it'll never progress to anything beyond that.

"Why are you so afraid to tell me who it is?" His expression turns thunderous. "You'd better not be back with that cheating asshole."

I roll my eyes. "Do you really think I'd do that?"

"I hope not."

"It's not Andrew, okay? Can we just drop this?"

"Better not be a football player. They're all a bunch of—"

"Watch it, my boyfriend is one of those guys," Sasha says, jumping into the conversation.

Ryder smirks. He knows exactly who she's with. It wasn't so long ago that I set them up on a date. Only now am I glad it didn't work out. Like I need to be tag teamed by these two?

No, thanks.

"As far as we know, this guy isn't an athlete," Sasha supplies.

Ryder shifts, gaze darting between us. "What do you mean?"

"She hasn't exactly met him," Sasha explains. "It was a wrong number and they got to texting."

"Please tell me you're joking," he mutters.

I huff out a breath and glare. First at him and then at my traitorous roommate. I am so over this conversation.

"Don't worry, I told her that she needs to investigate the situation before it goes any further, or they decide to meet up."

Ryder shakes his head before crossing his brawny arms over his chest. "You realize this person could be messing with you, right?"

"So I've been informed." The pit has gradually grown throughout this conversation to the size of Texas.

"Yup, catfished," Sasha adds. "It happens. I've watched a few shows on it."

Ugh.

These two…

Unwilling to listen to either of them for another moment, I rise to my feet. "Now seems like a good time for a break." I stare pointedly at my cousin. "Hopefully, when I return, you won't be here."

"That's not very nice," he grumbles. "I'm just concerned about you, that's all."

"I'm not a moron." Again, my gaze slides between the pair of them. "I won't put myself in a bad situation, and I'm not going to meet up with someone unless I know exactly who it is. Okay?"

They both grumble out responses.

With nothing more to say, I spin around and stalk toward the bathroom. As much as I want to dismiss the thoughts circling around my head, that's now impossible. I really hope Sasha is wrong about Chris being anything other than an engineering student at Western.

Although, as much as I hate to admit it, she's right about one thing—I need to do a little more recon and make sure this guy is who he says he is before this relationship progresses any further.

Because at this point, that's exactly what it feels like.

A relationship.

8

CROSBY

After a grueling two-hour practice, I strip off my pads and jump into the shower, washing off sweat and bits of turf that are stuck to my damp skin in record speed. Instead of standing around and shooting the shit with the other guys the way I normally would, I throw on my clothes and hitch my duffel bag over my shoulder before heading toward the exit.

"Dude." Andrew slides in front of me before holding up his hands. "What the hell? Aren't you going to wait for me?"

I shift the bag on my shoulder, antsy to take off. "I will if you get your ass in gear. I've got a lot of work to do." That's not necessarily the truth. All right, fine. It's a flat-out lie, but what am I supposed to say?

That I'm impatient to lock myself in my room and text his ex?

No way.

I can just imagine how that would go over.

And that's like a lead balloon.

Irritation flickers in his blue eyes as he waves me away. "You know what? Forget it. I'll catch a ride with Asher. I was gonna hang out at their place for a while anyway."

The tension gathering in my shoulders gradually evaporates as relief rushes in to fill the void.

Fuck.

What I'm doing is so wrong.

Each day, I tell myself that I'm going to back off and let this thing die out. And yet, I can't. I have no idea how a few innocent messages spun so far out of control. I hate how much I enjoy texting with her, getting to know her on a deeper level, exchanging funny little stories or reminiscing about our childhoods. I've discovered more about Brooke in the past week than I have in the three and a half years we've attended the same school.

I might not know where all this is leading, but I realize at some point, it's going to explode in my face.

How can it not?

I've spent almost eighteen months tamping down all my feelings. I've tried to convince myself that she's not as cool, smart, or funny as I imagined she might be.

You know what?

Turns out that she's all those things and more.

Now that I know this, the last thing I want to do is keep my distance. The more I get to know her, the more I like her.

It's a fucked-up situation.

"Rhodes, you coming over or what?" Asher asks, standing around totally buck naked with his junk flapping in the breeze.

Er...not that I'm looking.

But it's kind of hard to miss.

"Nah, don't think so." Sitting around with these assholes, drinking beer, and playing video games is the last thing on my mind.

He shifts and grabs a towel from the bench before drying his hair. "Did you forget about the rematch in NHL that you owe me?"

"Sorry, it's not happening tonight. I've got some homework to finish up. Not all of us are BS communications majors."

He flashes a grin before grabbing his boxers from his locker and hauling them up his thighs. "You're just jealous that it'll be my pretty mug on TV after I'm done playing ball."

I snort. "You've got more of a face for radio." Actually, nothing could be further from the truth. Asher Stevens gets all the chicks he could want. Most of the time, he has a girl tucked under each arm. Hell, they show up at the house he shares with Rowan, Brayden, Easton, and Carson on a regular basis to do his laundry.

It's just as ridiculous as the degree he's working on.

"Come on, dude," he whines like a big, six-foot baby, "I've got Allison and Beth coming over tonight. I'm sure they've got a few friends who would be more than happy to tag along and keep you company."

I shake my head. "Nope, still not interested."

"Hey," Andrew pipes up, "what about me? I could use a little company."

The words shoot out of my mouth before I can rein them in again. "Thought you were working on getting back together with Brooke."

Not even a flicker of guilt flashes across his face as he shrugs, grabbing a T-shirt from his locker and dragging it over his head. "I am. So what?"

"You think banging other girls is gonna help with that objective?"

He frowns as if seriously contemplating the question. "No, but what am I supposed to do? Sit around and twiddle my thumbs while I wait for her to change her mind?"

Un-fucking-believable.

Just as I open my mouth to blast him, I slam it shut again.

What the hell am I doing?

The best possible outcome would be for Andrew to move on and leave Brooke alone. I need to get out of here before I get sucked into any more conversations or inadvertently convince Andrew that he should remain focused on his ex.

Without another word, I slink out of the locker room before exiting the athletic center. I pull the gray hoodie over my damp hair and make my way to my black Mustang and slide behind the wheel. I rev the engine a few times, enjoying the rough purr before gunning it out of the parking lot. It takes less than five minutes before I'm pulling into the parking garage beneath the apartment building.

Like I'd park my baby on the street.

Even though the surrounding area near Western's campus is fairly safe, crime still happens. It only took my vehicle getting broken into one time freshman year before I installed a state-of-the-art alarm system. When I moved off campus junior year, underground parking was non-negotiable.

A couple guys say hello and tell me that they're looking forward to the game this weekend as I push my way through the door and into the lobby. As I head toward the elevator, I spot a group of girls. Like hell am I trapping myself inside with them. All the giggling and sly looks directed my way drive me batshit crazy. Before they can catch sight of me, I yank open the metal door that leads to the stairwell and take the steps two at a time. Once I reach the fourth floor, I'm breathing heavy.

After the drills Coach put us through, I'm beat. If I weren't looking forward to texting with Brooke, I'd finish up my homework and hit the sheets.

With Andrew heading over to Asher's place, the apartment is dark and quiet. I grab a protein bar from the kitchen cabinet and head into my room to hit the books. These engineering classes are no joke, but it's important to my parents that I earn a degree that's practical. Something I can use if my plans for the NFL fall through. Mom has a doctorate in anthropology and teaches at Columbia. My father is an orthopedic surgeon with his own practice, and my older brother is following in his illustrious footsteps. For years, my parents attempted to push me the med school route, but that was never going to happen. My brother might be cut out for that kind of life, but I'm not.

It's not difficult to feel like the black sheep of our family. Even from a young age, I realized their life wasn't the one I wanted. They might not have liked it, but I've managed to carve my own path. Hopefully, the NFL will be part of that future. Even if it's just for a handful of years. It's more than some guys get.

After devouring the bar, I take out my books and get to work. Every twenty minutes or so, I find myself glancing at my phone and checking the time. I'm antsy to text with Brooke. It's all I can do to force myself to concentrate and finish up the reading and homework that's due tomorrow. It's crazy how much I've come to look forward to our convos in a short period of time.

Just as I wrap up my studies, my phone dings with a message. I can't stop a grin from spreading across my face. If that's not perfect timing, I don't know what is. I practically pounce on the slim device in my haste to read the text.

Hey...I have a few questions for you.

Hmmm. That's not the greeting I was expecting. Concern flares to life inside me as air gets wedged in my throat.

Has she somehow figured me out?

I can't imagine she would be this calm if that were the case. Or even bother to contact me again. It takes effort to get my fingers to move.

Ok...shoot.

Three little bubbles appear before the questions pop up.

We've spent a lot of time texting, but how do I know you're really who you say you are? Or that we even attend the same school?

My muscles loosen as I force the pent-up breath from my lungs. All right...she hasn't figured me out, but it looks like her Spidey senses are tingling.

For all intents and purposes, this charade has run its course. I should do the right thing and ghost her. Maybe block her number so she can't contact me again. Walking away before this blows up in my face would be the best thing for both of us. Whether Brooke understands it or not. If she discovers I'm the one behind the messages, she'll probably freak out before stringing me up by my balls. She'd hate me even more than she already does.

That's one of the things I've enjoyed about our conversations. She might not realize it, but we were able to hit the reset button. With her, I'm not Crosby, the guy she hates with the passion of a thousand burning suns. I'm Chris. She's gotten to know me on a deeper, more intimate level. And she obviously likes what she's found, because she keeps coming back for more.

Fuck.

It feels like I've reached a fork in the road. Unsure what to do, I plow my hand through my hair. Needing a few moments to clear my head, I gravitate to the window, crank open the blinds, and stare. All I know is that I'm not ready to end this. Before I realize what I'm doing, I snap a photo of the university bell tower that can be seen in the distance before hitting send.

There's the view from my bedroom.

Okay. So you live near the university. But do you really attend Western? Or are you some seventy-year-old dude?

A reluctant smile tugs at the corners of my lips before I yank up my sweatshirt and take a pic of my abs. The joggers I threw on after practice graze my hipbones. If they were any lower, I'd be in danger of sending her an entirely different kind of photo.

And just to be clear—I don't send pics of the goods.

Like I need that shit surfacing later in life.

Or for my grandma to catch sight of it.

She'd probably keel over from a heart attack.

My parents would fucking kill me. I've already made enough dubious choices during high school. I don't need to do anything more to solidify the black sheep title.

There's a long stretch of silence that jacks up my nerves before she finally texts back.

For an engineering guy, you've got a nice six pack.

A chuckle escapes from me as I walk back to the bed and settle in for our conversation. Now that I've offered up proof, it feels like we're back on track.

Exactly what are you implying about engineers?

She replies with a laughing emoji.

All right...I showed off some skin. Any chance you'll return the favor?

As much as I'd love for Brooke to send me a titty shot, I know that's not going to happen. But a guy can hope, right?

Hands down, Brooke McAdams has the best breasts I've ever seen. They're spectacular. Way more than a handful. Which is precisely why I dragged her ass upstairs at the party as soon as I noticed how sheer her sweater had turned. She'd looked like a contestant in a wet T-shirt contest. No fucking way was I going to have every asshole in the place ogling her.

I've never been a jealous guy. I get all the pussy I could possibly want. But there were times when she was with Andrew and I'd run into her in the hallway at night. She'd be wearing nothing more than a tank top and panties. The thin material would be stretched across the rounded curves of her breasts, and it would take every ounce of self-control not to yank her to me. It was times like that, when I was eaten up with jealousy, that I actually hated my friend.

My phone chimes with a photo, and the smile I'd been wearing somehow grows wider.

It's a pic of her bare belly. I drag my thumb over the photo as if it's possible to touch her. It's more than enough to have my cock stiffening up.

That's all you get.

I hunker over my phone and shoot off a response.

I'll take it.

We go back and forth about our day. I tell her everything, omitting details about football practice. And then she does the same, telling me about her classes and friends.

Even though I'm pretty sure I know the answer to this question, I ask it anyway.

Do you have a boyfriend?

Bubbles appear as every muscle becomes whipcord tight. I mean... it's possible that she's been seeing someone. Even though I try to keep tabs on her, I don't know everything. If she is, I'll be forced to rip the guy limb from limb.

Nope.

Relief has my muscles turning lax.

How long has it been since you were involved in a relationship?

I don't know why I'm asking. Maybe, on some level, I want her to verify that she no longer has feelings for Andrew. Because if she does...

Wow. We're really getting into it, aren't we?

I smirk. She has no fucking idea just how into it we're about to get.

Yup. Now spill.

I haven't dated in six months. I got burned pretty badly by the last guy I was with.

What happened?

Cheated on. Lots of times.

Ouch. That must have hurt.

It did. I felt like an idiot because I was totally oblivious. Kind of hard to trust anyone after that kind of mindfuck.

I drag a hand across my face. There were too many times to count when I was tempted to pull Brooke aside and clue her in as to what was going on behind her back. Or send her an anonymous note.

Something.

Anything.

But Andrew is one of my oldest friends. How could I really turn around and betray him like that? Even if he was in the wrong. It was a shit place to be.

I'm sorry that happened to you.

That, at least, is the truth.

Me, too.

So...you're done with dating? You've resigned yourself to spinsterhood and a couple of cats?

At least a dozen. Lol!

Another chuckle escapes from me. This is exactly the way it is with this girl. Talking to her—even through text—makes me happy. I've never felt like that before. Then again, when have I ever spent time just talking with a chick? Actually drilling beneath the surface and getting to know someone?

The answer to that would be never.

Brooke is a first. And I don't want it to end.

Before I can fire off another text, a second one rolls in.

When I finally decide to get back out there again, it's going to take the right guy. Or maybe I should say that I won't be dating any more athletes. Please tell me you're not one of those.

I wince.

Fuck.

The lies just keep piling up.

But what can I do? Tell her the truth? I'm already in too deep to do that.

Nope.

Are you sure? You've certainly got the abs of one.

Umm...thank you?

She responds with a laughing emoji.

I like to work out. There's no shame in my game.

Clearly.

I'm sensing you might want more pics.

I certainly wouldn't say no...

Christ...my cheeks are beginning to hurt from all the smiling. Honestly, this isn't me. It's never been me. Brooke would be shocked if she discovered that I was the guy behind the texting. She knows me as a moody bastard. Surly. Always ready with a shitty comment to keep her at arm's length. And now look at me. I'm like a giddy schoolgirl.

This is bad. Really bad. It's like quicksand. The more I flail about, the deeper I get sucked in.

With abs like that, I imagine you have a girlfriend.

Is that your way of lowkey asking if I'm available?

Maybe.

I blow out a steady breath.

Nope. No girlfriend.

When was the last time you were involved in a relationship?

Do I tell her the truth?

I fucking hate all these lies. There's already enough I'm keeping from her. I should be honest whenever possible.

Never.

That response is met with a long silence.

Like, ever?

Nope.

Hmmm.

Hmmm?

And you're NOT an athlete?

Fuck

Nope.
Because I refuse to date another one.
Interesting. So does this mean we're going to date?
The words are flying across the keyboard before I can stop them.
What the hell am I doing?
She sends back a laughing emoji.
A second message rolls in before I can fire off another.
You're really easy to talk to.
I feel the same.

This is the first time I've had a genuine conversation or connection with a girl who wasn't interested in me because of my status on the team. They talk about dudes bagging as many girls as they can. But you know what? Chicks can be just as mercenary, and don't try to tell me different. It's like some of these jersey chasers have a team roster they're carefully working their way through.

Brooke doesn't give a shit if I play for the Wildcats or that I'll be entering the draft in the spring. Hell, if she knew the truth, she wouldn't give me the time of day.

The irony of this situation isn't lost on me.

I should go. Talk tomorrow?
Same time. Same place.

I set the phone down and plow both hands through my hair before grabbing the back of my head.

What the hell am I going to do?

Even though I know I should put an end to this madness before it goes any further, I also realize that isn't going to happen.

Best case scenario—it blows up in my face.

Worst case…

I don't even want to think about what that would look like.

9

BROOKE

I blow dry my hair until it floats in artful waves around my shoulders and down my back before returning to my room to get dressed for the day. Since it's supposed to be unseasonably warm this afternoon, I grab a short, plaid tweed skirt that hits midthigh with a frayed trim and pair it with a lightweight black sweater that has a high neck and hugs all my curves. A wide black belt with a silver buckle gets added to the ensemble, along with a pair of sleek black boots that lace up the backs of my calves.

Voilà.

And now we're ready to face the day.

I add a bit of eye shadow, mascara, and lip gloss before swiping my phone from the nightstand and heading into the hallway. Just as I cross over the threshold, a text pops up across the screen. My feet stutter to a halt as I scan the message.

Morning, beautiful.

That's all it takes to have my heart slamming into my ribcage as a grin spreads across my face. Normally, we text in the evening before we go to bed. Even though I'm trying to put the brakes on whatever this is, that feels impossible. Our relationship is growing, seeping into more of our lives.

Morning. You're up early.

Yup. Had to get a quick lift in. I was just about to head out the door for class.

Is it totally crazy how much I like this guy?

I mean...I don't even know what he looks like. Only his abs, which, I'll admit, were spectacular. Trust me, I spent a good amount of time drooling over the photo after we said our goodbyes last night.

I'm just about to head out the door, too.

Oh yeah?

Dressed and everything.

Send me a pic.

Air gets trapped in my lungs as I consider the request. It doesn't take more than a handful of seconds before I'm spinning around and walking back inside my bedroom. I step in front of the full-length mirror propped up against the wall and stare at the reflection that greets me. My teeth sink into my lower lip before worrying the flesh.

I'll admit part of me is terrified to send him a photo.

What if he doesn't like what he sees?

What if I'm not his normal type and he decides to ghost me?

I'm not one of those rail-thin girls who subsides on salads and Diet Coke. I like to eat. And I have the curves to show it.

Most of my high school years were spent trying to live up to my mother's rigorous standards of beauty. Not only did I spend a great deal of time hangry, but it made me feel bad about myself. Inadequate. And ultimately, it didn't work. All I have to do is look sideways at a piece of chocolate cake and I gain five pounds.

Before I have a chance to overthink the request, I hold up my phone and snap a shot, making sure the camera covers my face. Maybe I'm willing to take a chance and send him a pic of my body, but I'm not ready to put it all out there just yet.

One hesitant step at a time.

For a long moment, I scrutinize the photo. It would be all too easy to pick apart every flaw, but I've made a concerted effort to stop doing that since I realized it only fed the monsters in my head and made me even more self-conscious than I already am about my weight.

I stab the green send button so that I don't chicken out or spend the next fifteen minutes trying to get the perfect lighting and angle to make it more flattering. If Chris doesn't like what he sees or I'm not his type, then it's better to realize it now and move on before I invest any more time in this fledgling relationship.

That thought leaves me faltering.

It hasn't even been a week. And yet, we've spent so much time texting. We've had more in-depth conversations than Andrew and I ever did.

And we were together for almost a year.

How sad is that?

Nerves dance down my spine as I wait for his response.

Any response.

When one minute slowly ticks by without a reaction, disappointment bubbles up inside me as I realize that maybe this little texting flirtation has come to an abrupt end.

And that's fine. It's not like this was actually—

Three flame emojis pop up on the screen.

Damn. You're smoking hot.

Relief rushes through me as every ounce of tension gathered in my muscles dissipates and my knees weaken.

You're way out of my league.

Before I can text back, a third one rolls in.

Have a good day, beautiful. Talk tonight.

A smile stretches across my face as I practically tap dance through the living room on my way into the kitchen, where Sasha sits on the counter, wolfing down a bowl of cereal as she swings her legs back and forth.

With narrowed eyes, she points the spoon in my direction. "You look way too happy for eight o'clock in the morning. Take that shit down a couple of notches before I have to do something about it."

I snort and flutter my lashes. There's way too much giddiness careening through my veins. "Sorry, can't do that."

Her face scrunches. "Let me guess…this has something to do with Chris, your mystery man."

Unable to help myself, I grin like a lunatic before grabbing a granola bar and a banana to eat on the way to class. "Maybe," I sing-song obnoxiously.

"Please girl, there's no maybe about it. I haven't seen you this excited about someone since…" Her brows furrow as she tilts her head and stares off into space. "Well, never."

Hmmm. She might be right about that. I don't even think I was into Andrew this much. I mean, I was…but there was something different about it. Like I just felt lucky to be with him. As if he'd plucked me from obscurity like a rockstar at a concert. In hindsight, I treated him like he was something special and didn't hold him accountable for his behavior.

I don't know what it is about this guy, but I'm eager to see where it could lead. We have a lot in common and he's so easy to talk to. And those abs…

"I know." There's a pause as I reluctantly admit my deepest fear. "He almost seems too good to be true."

There. I said it. Out loud.

"Maybe he is." She shoves another spoonful of Apple Jacks into her mouth before chewing them thoughtfully. "Has he sent you a photo of his face?"

"No." Although…it's not like I'm dying to send him a pic that's up close and personal either. We're taking everything slow and getting to know each other without worrying about the physical.

"What if he turns out to be hideous?"

I turn the question over in my head. It's not like I haven't pondered it before.

"I don't know," I answer truthfully. "The thing is, I really like his personality. You know how you meet someone and maybe at first, you're not attracted to them physically, but the more you get to know them, the more appealing they become?" When she nods, I continue. "I think it would be like that."

"*Cyrano de Bergerac.*"

I tilt my head. "Huh?"

She waves her spoon in the air before swallowing down her breakfast. "You know, like that old movie *Cyrano de Bergerac*."

"I think the movie was actually based on a play."

Sasha rolls her eyes. "Yeah, that is so not the point."

"This is more like that reality show *Love is Blind*. It's kind of like I'm blind dating this guy. Except, we're not actually dating."

Yet.

"Who knows," she adds, "maybe this one will turn out to be your dream man."

I rein in the snort and try not to get my hopes up. Have I secretly thought the same thing?

Maybe.

"I won't hold my breath, but I like what I've discovered so far."

Setting the empty bowl on the side, she leaps down from the counter. "Anyone would be better than that asshat."

Asshat is Sasha's pet name for Andrew. I have to admit that it's a fitting description.

Not wanting to get dragged into another conversation about my ex, I grab my jacket from the back of a dining room chair along with my messenger bag and head for the door. "Are we still on for lunch?"

"Yup. I'll be there."

"Okay, see you later."

With that, I step into the narrow hallway before taking the stairwell to the first floor and exiting the building. Campus is about a twenty-minute walk from the apartment. On a gorgeous autumn day when the sun is shining brightly overhead, it doesn't feel so bad. During the winter, when the temperatures plummet or the sidewalk is full of snow, I usually take my Volkswagen Jetta. It was a gift from my stepfather for my sixteenth birthday after he and Mom tied the knot. As far as stepparents go, Garret is a good one. He's never been anything but kind.

The morning passes by in a blur of classes before I hit the library to sneak in a little studying, and then it's time to meet up with Sasha at the union. Am I guilty of being distracted for most of the morning and peeking at my phone to see if Chris has texted again?

Yup.

Does my heart beat out of control every time my phone dings with an incoming message?

Guilty.

As I walk through the large space which is crowded with students who have the same idea, I glance at the different restaurants. There's pizza, sandwiches, bowls, and salads.

I can almost hear my mother's voice chirping in my ear that I should pick something low calorie. It's for that reason that I beeline for the chicken sandwiches. Elaine spent years clucking her tongue and making passive aggressive comments about the foods I needed to stay away from. It wasn't until I moved away and started seeing a counselor freshman year of college that I realized how dysfunctional our relationship was.

Once I reach the counter, I grab a sandwich along with a fruit bowl instead of French fries, and a bottle of water. Those are my concessions. What I learned in counseling is that it's all about moderation. I can have something I'm craving if I balance it with other healthy options. After my tray has been loaded, I look around for Sasha. As soon as I do, she pops up like a meerkat and waves wildly from a booth.

"Hey, girl," she says as I slide onto the opposite side of the table before pointing to my tray. "This is exactly why we're such good friends. Great minds think alike."

That's when I notice her lunch mirrors mine, down to the water and fruit cup. I grin as we both dig in.

"I'm famished," she says around her chicken sandwich.

"Me, too."

Sasha is the goaltender for the Western Wildcats women's soccer team. She could probably eat several sandwiches in one sitting and still burn off all the extra calories running around the field for a two-hour practice. The girl can pack it away and never gain a pound.

Bitch.

I'm halfway through my meal when my phone dings. I glance down and find a photo of myself eating lunch.

You're even hotter in person.

Eyes widening, I nearly choke on my chicken before swinging around to scan the vicinity. Exactly who I'm searching for remains a mystery. Maybe I thought he'd be standing a few feet away with a smile on his face and somehow, I'd instantly know it was him. Instead, people are strolling by with their lunches in hand, talking with friends and finding a place to settle.

My heart jackhammers beneath my breast as I tap out a message with shaking fingers.

You're here?

Was. Had to grab something and run.

Disappointment wells up inside before nearly drowning me. I can't believe we were so close. Why didn't he say something? More than anything, I want to put a face to the guy I've been spending so much time thinking about. At this point, I don't care what he looks like. Short or tall. Thick or thin. Handsome or not...

All right, so maybe I know he has a jacked body.

Before I can fire off another message, Easton drops down beside Sasha and presses a kiss against her lips. These two...

They're so stinking perfect for one another. I have no idea how they couldn't see it before a month or so ago. Especially since they can't seem to keep their hands off one another.

They also make me realize how wrong Andrew and I were for each other and how I tried to fool myself into believing that we weren't. Instead of acknowledging my concerns and doing something about it, I swept them under the rug and pretended they didn't exist. I will never allow that to happen again.

I'm slammed from those thoughts when a hard body slides in next to me. When a hip brushes against mine, I quickly scoot over so there's a bit of space between us. I glance at the person next to me, only to find Crosby's dark eyes staring back.

Everything inside me freezes. I'm like a deer trapped in the headlights of oncoming traffic. This is exactly what he does to me.

Why is he here?

Invading my personal space.

Not to mention, my peace of mind.

I automatically steel myself, waiting for a snarky greeting. I'm sure he'll have something ugly to say. He always does.

When I raise my brows, only wanting to get it over with, he gives me a chin lift in greeting. "Hey."

I glance around the table, confused at what's unfolding. Under normal circumstances, we go to great lengths to avoid each other, and yet here he is, sitting next to me as if it's the most natural thing in the world. Weirder than that, a full minute has ticked by without him attempting to cut me to pieces with his sharp tongue. Even his ever-present smirk is strangely absent.

I'd love to brush aside the greeting and ignore him, but the manners Elaine drilled into my head win out, making it impossible.

"Hi," I mumble, unsure where we go from here. We've never actually engaged in a civil conversation.

Feeling as if I'm adrift in the middle of a raging sea, I glance at Sasha and Easton for help, only to see that they're busy playing kissy face. I gulp down the nerves that are rising in my throat and shift uncomfortably, wishing escape was an option. An awkward silence descends as I stare at my phone. If I can't physically get away, maybe mental escape is a possibility. Hopefully, if I ignore him long enough, he'll get the hint and take off.

Even though I'd been starving a handful of moments ago, my appetite has vanished. I have no idea if it's because of the guy parked next to me or the one who just texted. As much as I wish it weren't the case, Crosby makes me nervous and twitchy. As if I'll come right out of my skin. I hate it.

Even though my attention is focused on my phone, I'm hyper-aware of him sitting six inches away from me. Every shift of his body. Every inhale of breath. Every rise and fall of his chest.

I feel it deep in my bones.

The heat that wafts off him in heavy, suffocating waves. Crosby Rhodes is way too good looking.

And that lip ring...

A reluctant shiver dances down my spine as goose flesh breaks out across my arms. It's as if someone has thrown a heavy stone deep inside me and it ripples outward until it can reverberate in my fingers and toes. On more than one occasion, I've wondered what it would feel like to kiss him. I tell myself that it has nothing to do with him and more to do with the fact that I've never made out with a guy who has a piercing.

Deep down, I know I'm lying to myself. As much as I wish it didn't, it has everything to do with Crosby. Once I realize what I'm doing, I silently chastise myself before refocusing on my phone.

"What are you looking at that's so interesting?"

His voice breaks into the chaotic whirl of my thoughts. Unable to help myself, I glance at him, only to find his gaze pinned to mine as he shifts his body. Our knees brush as an unwanted bolt of lightning shoots through me, electrifying my insides.

My mouth turns cottony as I force out a response. "Nothing."

Sasha breaks away from Easton long enough to ask, "Did you get another text from that guy?"

A rush of heat floods my cheeks as Crosby's gaze flickers to my friend before slicing back to mine. If it's possible, there's even more intensity filling his dark depths. "What guy?"

I grit my teeth and glare at Sasha.

What the hell is she doing?

First she blabs to Ryder, and now Crosby?

If she's looking to lose her best friend, she's doing an excellent job. She must realize that the last person on the face of this Earth I'd want knowing any of my personal business is the guy sitting beside me, invading my space, and sending my senses into a tailspin.

I don't think he's ever been anything but an asshole. All right, so maybe he was sort of nice at the party when he gave me the shirt off his own back, but that's certainly never been his MO. If his past behavior is anything to go by, this nicer, kinder Crosby won't last long. At some point, he'll turn, and I don't want to be taken by surprise when he does. It's much easier to keep him at a firm distance than to let my guard down.

"None of your business," I grumble, shooting him a frown. If he thinks I'm going to set aside everything that's happened between us just because he's decided to act like a human being for once, he's sadly mistaken.

A few seconds of silence tick by before he clears his throat, once again drawing my attention back to him.

"You look nice."

My eyes widen. It's like the real Crosby Rhodes has been taken by body snatchers and replaced with this imposter. I'm not saying the one sitting next to me isn't a better version, but it's still freaky.

He shifts as I continue to stare. "What?"

It's tempting to lay my hand across his forehead and check for a fever. I need something that will make sense of this abrupt change in behavior.

When I remain silent, unsure what to say, he follows that up with another question. "Do you have a problem with me complimenting you?"

"No," I say cautiously, choosing my words with the utmost care. It's as if I'm navigating a minefield. One wrong step and I'll be blown to smithereens. "I'm just waiting for the punchline."

He cocks his head. Not once do his penetrating eyes deviate from me. It makes me feel as if he can see beneath the surface to my deepest thoughts. Ones that consist of him. It's unnerving, and I can't resist squirming beneath their intensity.

"Punchline?"

His tongue peeks out to swipe over the silver ring, flipping it leisurely back and forth. My gaze drops to the movement as a burst of unwanted arousal blooms in the pit of my belly. Actually, the sensation has taken up residence much lower. I clench my thighs to stifle it.

"I don't understand what you mean," he adds, continuing to play with the metal.

Focus, Brooke!

I clear my throat and drag my gaze up to his. "I'm waiting for you to say something nasty and cut me down. You like to be a dick. Especially to me." I pop a shoulder with far more casualness than I'm feeling. "It's kind of your thing."

There's a pause as something flickers in his eyes. It can't possibly be guilt. Or regret. That's not in his repertoire. Crosby Rhodes doesn't feel remorse. Certainly not where I'm concerned. The only thing this strange behavior is doing is filling me with confusion and putting me on edge.

I don't need it.

Nor do I want it.

Tension ratchets up between us until it reaches a frenzy, and I can barely stand it. My chest constricts with the need to escape his impenetrable gaze. Even though I haven't finished my lunch, I grab my messenger bag.

"Would you mind moving? I need to go."

That's not necessarily the truth, but I can't be in his enigmatic presence for another moment, or I'll come undone. Maybe burst at the seams. And I refuse to allow that to happen.

Especially in front of him.

10

CROSBY

*F*uck.

This isn't going the way I imagined it in my head. In fact, it's the exact opposite.

With her bag hoisted over her shoulder, Brooke stares at me like I'm the devil incarnate come to drag her to hell.

And to her, I probably am.

It's not like I have anyone else to blame for how she feels other than myself. Somehow, I need to right this relationship. Whether that's possible after everything I've said and done over the last eighteen months remains to be seen. But I have to try, right?

Instead of rising from the bench and allowing her to flee—because she'll take off like a bat out of hell if I do—I remain seated. There's no way for her to get past me unless I do. The expression on her face tells me that she realizes it as well. It's a cross between wanting to rip my head off and wanting to shrink away.

The temptation to drag her into my arms and soothe away her anxiety pounds through my blood like a steady drumbeat. It's tempting to give in. She's like a frightened animal that needs coaxing and a gentle touch. Instead, I keep my hands to myself. She's liable to scream bloody murder if I do. I can see it in her eyes.

Had we never started texting, perhaps I could continue to treat her with disdain and keep her at a firm distance, but that's no longer possible. Brooke has unwittingly shared personal details that she keeps hidden deep inside. I know about her hopes and dreams. Past demons that continue to haunt her. Fears and insecurities that keep her up at night. I've peeled back the layers and shared the same. There's no way to erase it all from my brain and pretend we're no more than acquaintances. Whether she realizes it or not, everything has shifted between us.

"Can we talk outside?" The question pops out of my mouth before I can fully think it through.

For the second time in a matter of minutes, she stares at me with a strange mixture of surprise and uncertainty. It's like she has no idea who the hell I am.

When she remains silent, my brows rise. "Brooke?"

"There's nothing for us to discuss," she says through stiff lips.

I should have realized it wouldn't be that easy. She's nothing like the other girls on campus. She's not going to simply roll over and spread her legs because I've decided to be nice. I've hurt her dozens of times, and now she wants nothing to do with me. Honestly, there might not be anything I can do to salvage this relationship.

I search her eyes carefully, looking for any hint of softening.

There's none whatsoever.

As we continue to stare, she straightens her shoulders and presses her lips together until they're nothing more than a thin, bloodless line. I glance at the couple across from us, only to see that they're still wrapped up in each other. Good. The last thing I need is an audience.

"It'll take less than five minutes, and then, if you want to tell me to get fucked, you can do it."

"I don't need to waste two seconds before telling you that," she shoots back, heat gathering in her pale cheeks.

True enough.

I drop my voice. "Please?"

She sucks in a sharp breath before forcing it steadily out. "You've got three minutes."

"I'll take it." I have no idea if that's nearly enough time to convince her that I'm not the guy she thinks I am. The one I've been so intent on proving that I was.

"You don't have much choice in the matter," she snaps as I rise from the bench and hold out my hand to assist her.

She stares at it briefly like it's a snake before sliding out on her own. With the strap of her bag settled on her shoulder, she grabs her tray of half-eaten food. Sasha and Easton break apart as if only now remembering there are other people they were dining with.

Her roommate's brows slide together. "You're leaving already?" She glances at the tray. "You didn't even finish your lunch."

When the expression on Brooke's face becomes strained, it hits me that I'm probably the reason for her lack of appetite. I mentally comb through the last ten minutes and realize she didn't touch her food while I'd been sitting next to her. I hate that I make her feel that way. Although, she does the same to me. But for different reasons.

"Yeah. I need to get moving."

Sasha's curious gaze bounces between us. "Wait a minute, you two are leaving together?"

I shift my weight before nodding. "There are a few things we need to discuss."

Concern flickers in Sasha's eyes. I certainly can't blame her for being leery of my intentions. I've gone out of my way to treat Brooke like shit, and everyone knows it. Including her best friend.

And mine.

A frown tugs at the corners of her lips. "Are you sure that's a good idea?"

Easton's dubious expression mirrors his girlfriend's. "Yeah, I mean…" His voice trails off awkwardly.

The fact that he's actually concerned for Brooke's wellbeing chafes my ass. And yet, when it comes down to it, I can't blame them for being skeptical. I deserve the concerned expressions being aimed in my direction. I have, unfortunately, earned them.

I shift my weight and grumble, "It'll be fine. Rest assured; I don't plan to chop her up into tiny pieces."

"Are you sure about that?" Sasha shoots back, voice growing harder.

I roll my eyes and shackle my fingers around Brooke's wrist. Her pulse beats erratically against my thumb, like the wings of a hummingbird. Already, I know there's nothing I can do or say that will settle it. A small gasp escapes as I drag her from the table and through the packed union before either of them can convince her to rethink her decision.

Instead of swearing under my breath, I smash my lips together before shoving through the glass doors. Brooke's boots click a steady staccato against the tile floor as she hastens her steps to keep pace with me, all the while trying to break free of my grip.

She has no idea how much I want to lay my hands on her. It's taking all of my self-control not to hoist her into my arms and take her someplace where we can be alone. I get the feeling I'd be able to quiet all the rioting voices in her head if my lips were to crash on top of hers.

Would she turn all soft and pliant in my arms?

Or continue to fight me tooth and nail?

"You can let go of me now," she growls, words escaping in short bursts.

Yeah, that's not happening. There is no damn way I'm relinquishing my hold. She'll take off in the blink of an eye.

Once outside, a fresh breeze wafts over us, slapping at our cheeks. As I tow her along the path, people scurry out of our way. The glower on my face says it all.

I glance around, searching for a quiet place where we can talk that's away from student traffic before heading for a grassy knoll as she continues to twist in my grip.

"Where are we going?"

As soon as our feet grind to a halt, a grunt leaves her lips as she yanks her arm from me. Now that we've come to a stop, I don't have any other choice but to set her free. If she flees, there won't be much I can do about it.

Surprisingly, she stays put. She scowls at me before rubbing small circles across the delicate flesh of her wrist. It's tempting to take it in my hands and check for damage. The last thing I want to do is hurt or bruise her.

"Make it quick," she snaps. "I need to go." She crosses her arms against her chest and hunches her shoulders as if preparing for an attack.

Now that I have her to myself, my brain empties, and I have no idea what to say. An uncomfortable silence stretches between us as I shove my hands into the pockets of my jeans before shifting my weight.

Her expression darkens as she impatiently taps her foot. "Well? I'm waiting. What was so important?" Her voice rises with each bitten-out word.

Instead of easing into the conversation the way I imagined, I blurt, "Is it possible for us to wipe the slate clean and start over?"

The tapping instantly stills as her frown intensifies. "Are you joking?"

It's slowly that I shake my head.

She blinks as questions flicker through her eyes before she gives voice to them. "Why would you want to do that? You've always been such a dick. The entire time I was with Andrew, you never had one kind word to say to me. *Not one*. In fact," she adds, "you could barely act civil."

I flinch as the accusation whips from her mouth.

She's not wrong. There's nothing I can say to justify my actions. Every jab and poisonous dart were purposeful, carefully aimed to illicit the most damage, and there's no way to come back from that.

I glance away before plowing a hand roughly through my hair.

Instead of revealing the truth—that I pushed her away because she was dating my best friend and I had feelings for her—I give her an inadequate platitude. "I'm sorry."

Her jaw turns slack before she whispers, "Seriously?"

It takes effort to swallow past the thick lump of wet sawdust now lodged in the middle of my throat. "Yeah. I shouldn't have treated you the way I did."

She blinks away the shock as laughter slides from her lips. "Sure. Right. Whatever you say." She slips her phone from her pocket before glancing at the screen. "If we're done here, I have some place to be."

Anxiety spirals through me, flooding every cell in my body. "No."

Her humor transforms into a scowl. "Your three minutes are almost up."

Afraid that she'll walk away, I spring forward.

Her eyes widen as she scrambles back a few steps in retreat before throwing up her hand to ward me off. "Don't! You're the last person I want touching me."

Her words feel like an icy dagger through the heart. I draw in a sharp breath and force myself to keep a few feet of distance between us.

"Why now, huh? Why bother to make amends when we're a little more than a semester away from graduation?"

Air escapes from my lungs like a tire with a slow leak. It would be all too easy to come clean. To tell her that I'm the one she's been texting with late at night. But then she'd hate me even more than she already does. I can see it in her eyes. Anything she feels for Chris would be immediately snuffed out. She'd assume I was fucking with her for shits and giggles. There wouldn't be a way to convince her otherwise.

So, no…the truth isn't an option.

"Because there's no reason for us to be at odds with one another."

Gaze boring into mine, she cocks her head and tightens her arms against her chest. The self-protective stance doesn't escape me.

"That's the funny thing. We never *were* at odds. You were just an asshole for no reason. There's a difference, and I really hope you understand that. For some strange reason, you took an instant dislike to me, and no matter how pleasant or forgiving I was, it didn't make a difference. In fact, it only spurred you on. And now, after all the shitty comments and embarrassment you've caused me, you want forgiveness?" There's a pause. "You want me to forget because *you've* suddenly decided that we should make nice?" Her features resemble carved granite as she shakes her head. "I feel like this is just another game you're playing, and guess what? I refuse to engage."

When I take a desperate step in her direction, she flinches.

"I promise you it's not."

She huffs out a mirthless laugh. "And I'm just supposed to put it all behind me and trust that you're being honest?"

My tongue darts out to moisten my lips. This is going so much worse than I expected. "Of course not. I realize it'll take time to prove my sincerity. All I'm asking is that you give me a chance to do it."

Instead of shooting down the request like it's a plane flying over enemy territory, which is what I fully expect, she mutters with a shake of her head, "I don't know."

A tiny spark of hope ignites inside me. "I know I've been a giant dick. I'm just asking for a chance to show you that I can be different. That's all."

She presses her lips together as her shoulders stay hunched. I can almost see the thoughts churning through her head and the temptation burning within her to tell me to go to hell. The last thing I want is for her to walk away without making at least a small bit of progress in the right direction.

Unsure what else to do, I thrust out my arm. "Truce?"

Her gaze drops to my outstretched hand as a heavy silence falls over us. The noise of our surroundings fades to the background until it's only the two of us. Just when I think she'll leave me hanging, she cautiously places her fingers in mine. As soon as they touch, my grasp tightens, holding on for dear life.

Little does Brooke realize that she's just sealed her fate with that one innocuous gesture.

Her eyes flare as she quickly tugs her fingers free and scrambles away. Now that she's agreed to a truce, there's only so long I'll allow her to hold me at a distance. The electricity that snaps and sizzles between us makes me want her even more. I've spent years denying myself the one girl I've always wanted, and I refuse to do it any longer.

"I need to go," she mumbles before spinning away and taking off through the sea of students.

Just as she's about to disappear through the throng, she sends a glance over the curve of her shoulder. Her confused gaze fastens onto mine as a slight smile tips the corners of my lips and I raise a tentative hand. She doesn't return the gesture. Instead, a frown settles on her features before she turns away and vanishes from sight.

Once she's gone, I release the air trapped in my lungs as my muscles loosen. Sure, I'll admit it was a little touch and go there, but, in the end, the conversation went better than expected. Whether she realizes it or not, her agreement to wipe the slate clean is just the beginning.

When my phone chimes with an incoming message, I dig through my pocket before peering at the screen.

It's unfair that you know who I am. I want a pic of you.

I snort out a mirthless laugh.

Yeah…that's not going to happen.

At least not yet.

One thing's for certain, I have my work cut out for me. Most girls on campus think I'm a charming bastard. I guess it's time to prove just how charming I can be.

11

BROOKE

I hasten my pace as another shiver of unease slides through me. All right...so maybe it's not one hundred percent apprehension. It might be something more along the lines of—

Nope.

I refuse to go there.

It takes effort to shake away the feelings Crosby rouses so effortlessly within me. How is he able to twist me up into a series of complicated little knots?

Even if I'm physically attracted to the guy, I can't stand him.

So yeah...that conversation makes no sense. All he's managed to do is confuse me.

Of all the things I expected him to say, an apology for past transgressions wasn't one of them. Honestly, I would have expected hell to freeze over before that occurred.

Even though I agreed to wipe the slate clean, does that mean I'm going to forget everything he said and did to me?

Hell no.

The guy has a shit ton to prove before I could ever consider trusting him.

My brows pinch together as I carefully turn the conversation over in my head. The question I'd posed had been legitimate. We'll both graduate in the spring and move on with our lives. Why bother now of all times?

There's no point in being friends or getting to know one another on a deeper level. The only upside I can see is that I'll no longer have to worry about him embarrassing or insulting me. Tension won't fill every muscle, making me jittery and on edge at the thought of running into him.

Instead of pretending to be friends, I'd rather we ignore each other. Then we could coexist peacefully. There's no reason for us to interact. Maybe the irrepressible energy that snaps and sizzles when we're in the same vicinity would finally dissipate.

Just as I'm about to turn onto the path that leads to McKinney Hall where my next class is located, Sasha catches up to me.

She huffs out a breath, looking winded as her gaze does a quick scan of my person. "What was that all about?"

I shake my head and scrunch my face. "Your guess is as good as mine. Maybe he's done the impossible and grown a conscience. If so, that would prove that miracles really do come true."

When her expression fills with confusion, I reluctantly admit, "He actually apologized for his shitty behavior and claimed we should," I make air quotes with my fingers, "wipe the slate clean and start fresh."

Sasha's eyes widen. "Get out of here."

"Nope." I pop the 'P' for added emphasis.

"Holy crap. Now that's a plot twist I didn't see coming."

"Maybe." I jerk my shoulders and continue walking. "Then again, maybe not."

There's a moment of hesitation before she asks, "You don't believe him?"

That's the million-dollar question.

"I don't know. He has a lot to prove before I trust anything that comes out of his mouth." The conversation continues to play on a loop in my brain as I lower my voice. "It wouldn't surprise me if this were all some kind of twisted game to lull me into a false sense of security before doing something awful."

Her eyes widen before she whispers, "No way. Do you really think Crosby is that diabolical?"

Honestly?

I have no idea. When it comes down to it, I don't know him very well. How could I? All he's done is shut down every attempt I made to get to know him, all the while treating me like shit.

So, yeah…in my opinion, he's capable of almost anything.

A rush of air escapes from my lungs. "I don't know." But I refuse to give him the benefit of the doubt or take a chance and get hurt again.

"I hope you're wrong," she murmurs before nibbling on her lower lip. "I will literally kick his ass if he attempts to pull something like that."

Her grumbled out words bring a genuine smile to my face. Sasha and I met during freshman orientation and hit it off right away. We ended up rooming together in the dorms sophomore year and then moved off campus to an apartment junior year. This will be our last year living together before we go our separate ways after college. Out of all the friends I've made throughout my life, Sasha is probably the one I feel closest to. I hope we'll always be in each other's lives. It'll be weird not to see her face on a daily basis next year.

There's a moment of silence before she asks, "But you're going to give him a chance?"

My lips flatten. "I guess."

Do I really want to?

No, but we have the same friend group. When I show up at a party, not only do I worry about seeing Andrew, but Crosby as well. If I'm being truthful, the thought of running into him gives me more anxiety than coming face to face with Andrew. I can deal with my ex and easily shut down his persistent advances. For whatever reason, it's not as easy with the dark-haired guy.

So…maybe this is for the best.

It's one less person to worry about.

"All right, girl. I gotta get to class. I just wanted to make sure you were okay."

I paste a smile on my face. "I'm fine. No worries."

With a wave, Sasha takes off. "See you later."

"Bye," I call after her retreating form, watching as she catches up to one of her teammates.

I don't get more than a handful of steps before my name is shouted above the low babble of conversation. Instantly recognizing the voice, I wince and hasten my pace.

First Crosby and now Andrew.

Can this day get any worse?

Don't answer that. It was more of a rhetorical question. Everyone knows it can.

And probably will.

When he calls my name for a second time, only louder, I realize I won't be able to lose him in the crowd. He's much closer than he was just a handful of seconds ago.

Damn.

Not a minute later, a large palm lands on my shoulder, making escape impossible. Sometimes, I get the feeling that he's trying to wear me down.

I mean, is that really what he wants?

For me to give in and agree to be his girlfriend because I'm too tired to continue fighting him?

That thought is disturbing on so many levels.

"Hey," he says, pulling up alongside me with a smile. It's the same one he'd shoot my way before we got together. It's all boyish charm and aren't-I-adorable.

The worst part is that I fell for it. Hook, line, and sinker.

"I've been calling you, trying to get your attention. Didn't you hear me?"

That's the funny thing. It would never cross Andrew's mind that I was deliberately ignoring him. His ego is way too big for that.

I huff out an exasperated breath. I'm still rattled from the strange conversation with Crosby to focus on my ex. Before I can pull any excuses from my ass, he tosses a brawny arm around my shoulders and hauls me against his muscular body. It takes a bit of finesse for me to duck from beneath his arm and put some much-needed space between us.

He shoots me a wounded look. "There used to be a time when you couldn't get close enough. I miss those days."

"That was before I realized you enjoyed being close to a lot of girls and weren't owner specific."

"Babe," he sighs, "we've been through this before."

Yes, we have.

"And I've apologized a hundred times for what happened."

"That's because you cheated on me roughly that many times," I remind, refusing to allow him to guilt trip me into forgiving him.

"You're exaggerating," he mutters.

I open my mouth, ready to fire back with a scathing retort before slamming it shut and grinding my teeth. Relief pumps through me as the engineering building looms in the distance. I speed up, only wanting to reach it as quickly as possible.

Instead of responding to the comment, I brush it aside. "Look, I've really got to go. I need to speak with one of my professors before class begins," I lie.

I brace, expecting him to dig in. Instead, he says, "What were you talking with Crosby about?"

I blink, surprised by the abrupt change in conversation. "What?"

Suspicion flashes in his blue eyes before disappearing, making me question whether it was there in the first place.

"I saw you with Crosby and wanted to make sure everything was all right." There's a pause as emotion seeps into his voice. "You know I'd kick his ass if he was ever mean to you."

A snort of disbelief escapes from me before I can rein it back in. "He was always mean, and you never did a damn thing about it."

"Babe," he tilts his head as his expression softens, "I tried to give the two of you space to hash out your issues. That's all. I was always ready to jump in if I was needed."

I roll my eyes.

That is such a lie. He'd sit his ass on the couch with a beer and watch us as if we were that night's entertainment. After Crosby cut me to pieces and I was on the verge of tears, Andrew would wrap his arms around my body before steering me toward the bedroom as if sex would fix everything. That was it. He never said a damn word to his friend.

How did I ever believe I was in love with him?

All I can say is never again. I will *never* get tangled up with another lying, cheating athlete again. I'd rather be alone than be in a shitty relationship.

"How about I take you to that little Mexican place you love so much, and we can talk everything out?"

I stop so abruptly that the girl walking behind me slams into my back.

"Sorry," I call out as she flips me off and stalks away before turning my attention to Andrew. "We don't have a relationship. We are *never* going to have one again. Period. End of story. Full stop." I search his eyes. "Do you understand?"

He blinks and shifts his weight before dropping his voice to a low rumble. "Are you riding the cotton pony? Because you're being awfully bitchy."

My mouth drops open.

It would be all too easy to reach out and throttle him. It takes every bit of willpower not to do exactly that.

Am I riding the cotton pony?

Is this guy serious?

"Actually," I say with more calm than I'm feeling, "I'm not. I'm just annoyed at having the same conversation every time I run into you. It's like that movie *Groundhog Day*. It's exhausting, and it needs to stop."

"So," he says slowly as if wrapping his brain around a difficult concept, "what you're telling me is that I should give you a little more time?"

I open my mouth to blast him into next week before slamming it shut and stalking away.

No.

Just…no.

12

CROSBY

*A*s soon as Coach blows his whistle, I jog off the field to grab a bottle of water. Now that we're deep in the season, every second spent on the field counts. Every snap. Every play. Every hard-fought yard. We all realize that the small things can be the difference between winning and losing.

Lifting the squeeze bottle to my lips, icy cold water fills my mouth before hitting the back of my throat. It's only when I get jostled from behind that liquid gets dumped down my chin and the front of my practice jersey. Fist clenched around the bottle, I swing around, ready to knock the stupid fucker on his ass.

Instead of a clueless underclassman, I find Andrew, narrowed gaze pinned to mine. His jaw is tight and his arms hang tensely at his sides. From all outward appearances, he looks ready to throw down.

When I raise a brow, he gives me a chin lift.

I shift my stance under the intense scrutiny. "What's up?"

Clearly something is. I've known him way too long to be fooled by his silence. He's simmering inside, ready to blow. He's always had a quick temper. It's just not usually directed at me.

"What's up with you and Brooke?"

Every muscle goes whipcord tight. Has he somehow found out I've been texting her?

I rack my brain. There's no way. I've been so careful. I don't even have her listed by name in my phone. She's only identified as Perfect Ten.

So, I have no idea how he could have figured it out. I drag a hand through my hair as my mind continues to spin, searching for an explanation.

"Yeah, I saw you talking with her at lunch." His gaze turns frosty. "Thought you couldn't stand her?"

The air trapped in my lungs escapes in a slow leak as I jerk my shoulders. All right...he doesn't know anything. Not really. I overreacted and jumped to conclusions. This is what happens when you keep secrets from your best friend and roommate. You become paranoid.

It takes effort to keep my voice nonchalant. "Easton wanted to stop over and say hi to his girl. It wasn't anything more than that." Even though I should keep the questions locked up deep inside where they can't see the light of day, they burst free. "What's the big deal? I'm not allowed to have a convo with her?"

He tilts his head as if reassessing me and my comment with new interest. "Just seems weird that you were always an asshole to her when she was my girlfriend, and now that we're broken up, you're all chummy."

"I wouldn't go that far," I mutter, knowing there's no way in hell Brooke would consider me a friend. She could barely tolerate my presence for the five minutes or so that we were together before hightailing it away as fast as she could.

"Just do me a favor and stay the hell away from her."

I straighten to my full height as my muscles stiffen. "Excuse me?"

He steps closer as a dull red flush seeps into his cheeks. "You heard me. Don't mess with her. Just stay the fuck away."

I narrow my eyes. "That's funny. You certainly didn't have a problem when I messed with her before."

Even though his lips crook at the corners, his blue eyes remain glacial. "Honestly? I liked that the two of you couldn't fucking stand each other. I didn't have to worry about her falling for your bullshit broody charm the way all the other chicks do."

I can only stare as his words roll around like marbles in my head. When I think back, I realize that Andrew never bothered to defend her. Sure, he'd comfort her, but he never told me to knock that shit off. At the time, I figured he didn't want to get in the middle of our verbal skirmishes. Only now do I realize how wrong I was.

I shake my head, losing even more respect for him. Pretty soon, there won't be anything left.

"You're a real fucking dick," I snap.

When a slow smile spreads across his face, I realize he's aware of it but doesn't give a damn.

"You gotta know that Brooke actually loved you, right?" Before he can fire off a response, I step closer and growl, "She would have done anything for you. She was the perfect girlfriend, and you threw her away without so much as a second thought."

Fuck.

Why the hell did I allow all of that to escape?

The smile disappears as his lips twist into an ugly scowl. "Seriously, Rhodes? It almost sounds like you have a hard-on for my ex."

There's a beat of uncomfortable stillness.

Instead of firing off a firm denial that will get us back onto solid ground, I remain silent. I'm so damn tired of lying to him and myself about what I feel. I've been doing it since I first saw her on campus.

"And I know that can't be true. *Right?*"

The words sit perched on the tip of my tongue. It wouldn't take much to push them out and tell him the truth.

Tell *someone* the truth.

Then I can let the chips fall before picking up the pieces. Part of me feels like it would be easier than constantly guarding myself and keeping everything shoved deep down inside where it can't see the light of day. Because that's exactly what I've been doing, and it's killing me inside.

He advances another step before shoving a hand against my chest and forcing me back. The barely-contained aggression is enough to knock me off balance.

"You never answered the question. You're not trying to get with my girl, are you?"

A couple guys turn and stare as Andrew's voice escalates. As much as I want to come clean, this isn't the time or place for this conversation.

My shoulders collapse as the lie escapes. "No."

Even though he nods, he continues to stare suspiciously. I don't think he's ever looked at me like he doesn't know who the fuck I am.

Is this really what I'm intent on doing?

Blowing apart our friendship?

Fuck.

Fuck.

Fuck.

Because this is a foolproof way to do it. He's not going to move on until he gets her back again.

"Good. I don't want you even looking sideways at my girl."

"She's not your girl," I remind him. "She dumped you six months ago."

"No matter what happens between us, Brooke will always be mine. She's angry and needs more time to cool off. You watch, she'll come to her senses and crawl back to me."

It takes everything I have inside not to snort. Hell will freeze over before that happens. But there's no way I'm going to tell him that. By the intensity written across his face, he believes it wholeheartedly. And, more than likely, he'll spend the rest of senior year trying to make it happen.

"Stay out of my way, or I'll fucking take you out."

My eyes widen at the pent-up rage vibrating off him in thick, suffocating waves.

"You need to settle the fuck down." If he thinks he can intimidate me, he's out of his mind.

"Do I?" His hands bunch and release at his sides. It wouldn't surprise me if he tried to throw a punch. There's a red haze clouding his vision. He isn't seeing clearly. If he were, he'd walk away.

"Yeah. You're acting like a fucking nut."

It takes a moment for his shoulders to loosen and him to twist his head from side to side, cracking his neck as if working out the tension. "I just can't stand the thought of her with someone else."

"I know."

And if I didn't before this conversation, I do now. Andrew will never be all right with me having anything to do with his ex. For the first time since Brooke and I have gotten closer, I seriously consider backing off.

The smartest thing to do would be to end things. It's not like we have an actual relationship. We've just been texting back and forth.

Would I like it to be more?

Yeah.

But it'll be at the expense of my friendship, and I'm not ready to go there.

Not yet.

13

BROOKE

*E*xcitement stirs in the pit of my belly as I grab my phone and settle into bed.

Is it sad how much I look forward to texting Chris at the end of each day?

Probably.

After my bizarre conversation with Crosby this afternoon and then the run-in with Andrew, it's exactly the balm I need to smooth out all the rough edges.

Instead of waiting for him to make first contact, I let my fingers fly across the keyboard.

Hey. How are you?

I hit send before staring at my phone, willing him to respond. Even though he seemed to find my photo attractive, there's a part of me that worries I'm not really his type and he'll end up ghosting me. I don't think I could take that today of all days.

Hey, beautiful.

A relieved smile spreads across my face as all the doubts circling viciously through my head dissipate. My fingers hover over the screen as I work up the courage to hit the send button.

Want to FaceTime? It's only fair since you already know what I look like.

As soon as I press send, my heart lodges itself in the middle of my throat before pounding into overdrive. The seconds that slowly creep by drag like hours. A mixture of anticipation and fear spiral through me, ratcheting up my nerves to unprecedented levels.

Sorry, I'm not ready for that just yet.

A tidal wave of disappointment crashes over me, threatening to drag me under. I'm so desperate to put a face to the person I've gotten to know over the past week.

What about a call?

I blow out a steady breath, fully expecting him to nix that idea as well. Only now does it occur to me that I might have made too much out of this little texting thing we have going on. Maybe this doesn't mean anything to him, and I need to pull back. If the guy doesn't even want to FaceTime or—

When the screen lights up with an incoming call, I jerk upright as my heart nearly explodes.

I stab the green button and answer it. "Hello?"

"Hey."

His voice is unexpectedly deep and tickles something in the far recesses of my brain. Before I can think too much about it, a swarm of butterflies erupts in the pit of my belly before searching frantically for an escape route. I lower myself down before curling onto my side and hugging the phone to my face.

I blurt out the first thing that comes to mind. "I can't believe we're actually talking."

He chuckles. "It's nice to hear your voice."

As crazy as it sounds, I already feel like we know each other. This is more a formality than anything else.

"Yours, too." So good. "I can't believe you were able to recognize me on campus."

There's a brief pause, and all I hear is the light intake of breath before he clears his throat. "I was at the Union grabbing lunch and I noticed you. Then I realized it was the same outfit you sent a picture of earlier. I took a chance and snapped the photo. I'm glad I was right."

I cling to the first part of his explanation, not allowing too much hope to take root. "So, I'm your normal type?"

"You're *definitely* my type."

Another explosion detonates in my abdomen as a silly grin spreads across my face. Reining it in would be impossible. There's no point even trying.

"And you won't send me a photo in return?"

There's another long pause. "Not yet."

"You know that I don't care, right?" My voice dips, turning serious. "I just want to put a face to the person I've been spending so much time texting."

"I...just need a little time, okay? Is that cool?"

"Yeah, of course."

If he's not ready to take that next step, then I'll wait until he is. I'm just happy to hear his voice. It feels like we've reached a new level.

I pull the covers over my body and snuggle into them as he says, "Tell me about your family. You're an only child, right?"

"Yup. My parents divorced when I was seven, and then it was just my mom and me for a long time. When I was fifteen, she married my stepfather, Garret."

"And you like him?"

"Yeah, I do. He's super easy going and treats me well." There's a pause before I admit, "My mother, on the other hand? She's kind of the opposite. Our relationship is more strained."

"Why is that?"

It takes a moment to formulate a response. "Our values don't necessarily align, and she's always been critical."

"I'm sorry to hear that. I bet it was tough to deal with growing up. Do you mind me asking what she's so judgy about? You seem pretty damn perfect to me."

The compliment has my belly doing a little flip.

It feels a little surreal to talk about this with someone I don't actually know in real life. But that's the strange thing...because it does feel like I know him. Maybe I couldn't pick him out of a lineup, but I feel like we have a connection. Sadly, it's more than I've found with the other guys I've dated.

When I don't immediately respond, his voice softens. "Hey, you know what? Forget I asked. We don't know each other that well, and the question was probably way too personal."

I release a pent-up breath and realize that I want to be honest and share private experiences with him that I normally wouldn't with people I have nothing more than a superficial relationship with. Sasha is aware of the issues with my mom, but she's one of the few. In the beginning with Andrew, I tried to open up, but he didn't have any interest in jackhammering below the surface. When we were together, he wanted to have sex. The few times I mentioned my mom, he told me that she was great, and I didn't have anything to bitch about. So, I didn't bring it up again.

"No, it's all right. I want to tell you. My mother's name is Elaine. She's more into materialistic things and enjoys all the perks that go along with being married to a wealthy man with social standing. It's the life she always wanted for herself, and it's something my dad couldn't give her, which is why they divorced when I was a kid. Honestly, I think they're both much happier with the partners they're now married to."

"Okay," he says softly, "but that doesn't explain why your relationship with her is difficult."

No, it doesn't.

His comment makes me realize just how intently he's paying attention to the conversation, and warmth blooms in my chest.

"She's always been super critical of my appearance." I pause before forcing myself to admit the truth and bare wounds that run deep. "And my weight." Heat suffuses my cheeks as shame tries to take hold. It's always been a sensitive topic for me, and it's doubtful that will ever change. No matter how much counseling I have.

"Your weight?" Confusion weaves its way through his voice.

"Yeah." I suck in a deep breath before releasing it. "While I was growing up, she was hyper focused on my weight. She always made a point of commenting on the kind of foods I was eating or if I was having too much or not fitting into my clothes properly. I became obsessed with how many calories I was consuming and working out to burn it off. It was really unhealthy, and I try not to get sucked back into those old thought patterns."

A long silence stretches between us as my heartbeat picks up tempo. My teeth scrape against my lower lip, and I wonder if I've inadvertently revealed too much of myself. This isn't an issue I ever considered sharing with Andrew. In fact, when he saw photographs of me in high school, he commented on how amazing I looked and then squeezed my side as if to silently show me that he could see the difference. I can only wince at the memory.

"Fuck. That's really messed up. I'm sorry, I didn't realize."

I force out a laugh to cover my embarrassment for the overshare. "Why would you? We barely know each other."

He clears his throat. "Right. For what it's worth, I think you're perfect. No one should ever make you feel like you're not enough. No matter what size you are."

The pit at the bottom of my gut gradually dissolves. "I spent most of high school on a low-calorie diet and then tried to burn off everything I'd consumed. There were times when I would stuff myself with food. All the sugary sweets my mother frowned upon and banned from the kitchen. I'd feel so guilty afterward that I'd force myself to throw it up. For a long time, that cycle seemed unbreakable. Like I would be trapped in it for the rest of my life. Each time I gave in, I'd feel such shame for losing control and being weak. I'd tell myself that it wouldn't happen again. But it did. For a while, I'd be able to control the urges and I'd feel invincible. Strong. Even though my body was weak. And then I'd break down, binge, and feel like shit. Worthless. I spent so much energy trying to live up to her unrealistic expectations. I wanted to be the perfect daughter, but it was never enough."

Even though I've talked about this in therapy and worked through it in my head, there's something oddly cathartic about sharing my past with him. About giving him a glimpse into the person buried beneath the façade. I don't want to pretend to be anyone other than who I truly am. If he's unable to accept that—accept *me*—then he's not worth my time.

"I really wish I could hold you right now."

Everything inside me melts. "Me, too."

"Close your eyes and imagine that I am."

I do as he instructs, picturing him there with me, and somehow, it makes everything better.

"Is this an issue you still struggle with?" he asks hesitantly.

"No. Once I left for college, I was able to take a step back and realize how unhealthy my relationship was with not only food, but also my mother. I started seeing a counselor on campus and that really helped me to understand what I was doing. It took a long time to recognize that these were her issues and not mine. I've also come to accept that I will never be a twig, but I can still be happy and healthy." It's Sasha that I have to thank for that. She was instrumental in helping me to understand that I wasn't seeing myself clearly when I looked in the mirror.

"I really hate you went through all that."

"Me, too." I've spent a lot of time grieving my childhood, wishing things could have been different. But the past can't be changed. I can only make my peace with it and move forward.

"I give you a lot of credit for being able to do that. You're really strong."

"It wasn't easy, but I'm much happier now." Another burst of warmth rushes through my veins as I clear my throat and steer the conversation in a different direction. I've talked enough about myself. "What about you? Are you close to your family?"

"Like your parents, mine are also divorced. It happened around the same age, so I guess we have that in common." There's a trace of humor in his tone. "Dad's currently on wife number four."

My eyes widen. "Oh. Wow. That's…"

"A lot?" he asks with an easy chuckle. "Yeah, it is. He's a surgeon and spends more time at the hospital than he does at home. Wife number two used to joke that he was married to medicine rather than her. Sadly, it's the truth. When she finally came to grips that it wouldn't be changing, she left. It was pretty much the same with wife number three. Wife number four doesn't seem to mind that he's not really present."

I search my brain for any other information I've gleaned about his family from our previous texting. "You have an older brother, right?"

"Yup. He's in his second year of med school."

"But you weren't interested in doing that?"

There's a long stretch of silent moments that leaves me wondering if I've unintentionally stepped on a landmine. What I've come to realize from my own past is that we all have them. Whether we realize it or not.

Just as I open my mouth to tell him that we don't have to talk about it, he says, "No. Engineering is more up my alley. My father probably works eighty hours a week. He's always on call for his patients. Both he and my brother feel like it's a higher calling and are passionate about the profession. You need that kind of dedication and willingness to sacrifice other parts of your life. I'm unwilling to do that."

It sounds like he's given this a lot of thought. It's not something I would have necessarily considered when thinking about a medical career, but it makes sense.

"I can understand that. Is your family disappointed by your decision?"

"Maybe a little, but they also realize that my interests lie elsewhere."

"And that's with mechanical engineering?"

There's a slight hesitation before he says, "Yeah, engineering."

"What are you going to do with that?"

"I don't know. Probably something in the auto industry."

"It's hard to believe that we'll graduate next semester. Were you able to do an internship? Do you have any prospects lined up yet?"

"There are a few options, but nothing concrete. I'll know more in the spring." He quickly turns the question back on me. "What are your plans after graduation?"

"I was lucky enough to land an internship last summer at a department store, and they've offered me a full-time position working with their buyer. It's not exactly what I want to do, but it's definitely a jumping off point."

"That's really cool. Congrats."

"Thanks."

A smile blooms across my face as we spend the next couple of hours talking about what feels like everything under the sun. Interspersed throughout it all is a ton of laughter and joking. I don't think I've ever connected on this kind of level with anyone. It feels like I could tell Chris anything and he would understand. It's a shock when I glance at the clock on the nightstand and realize that it's after one in the morning. Where did the time go?

"I'm sure you've heard this before, but you're really easy to talk to," I admit, reluctant to end our conversation. "I dated someone for almost a year, and I don't think we ever spoke this much or got this deep the entire time." I force out a small laugh. "How sad is that?"

"It just proves that he wasn't the right guy for you."

"No, he wasn't."

We both lapse into silence.

"I should probably let you go. You'll be a zombie tomorrow morning."

A mixture of sadness and longing fill me as I reluctantly agree. "Yeah, okay." My teeth sink into my lower lip. I don't want this to be a one-time thing, but I'm afraid to ask for more or come off as needy.

"Talk tomorrow?" he asks.

Relief washes over me. "Definitely."

"Night, beautiful."

"Goodnight, Chris."

With that, I reluctantly hang up.

14

BROOKE

I flip the page of the book I'm reading and jot down a few notes before glancing at my phone. I've got about an hour of studying to get through before I head home and call Chris. Even the thought of settling between my sheets and talking with him is enough to bring a ridiculously giddy smile to my face.

It's crazy just how much I like this guy.

We've been texting all the time, not just at night. It's become a problem. Which is exactly why my ass is here at the library. The last thing I can afford to do is slack off in my classes when I'm this close to graduating.

Plus, Easton and Sasha were holed up in her room. Once the bedframe started to hit the wall, I packed up my bag and hightailed it out of there. Sitting there and listening to them go at it made me feel like a huge perv.

"Hey."

Knocked out of my thoughts, I glance up and find Crosby staring at me. A shiver of awareness skitters down my spine as an unwanted burst of nerves explodes in my belly.

Why?

Why is it always like this with him?

If I'd thought his apology would help smooth everything over between us, that hasn't turned out to be the case. The sexual tension has ratcheted up to unprecedented levels when all I want is for it to go away.

"Hi."

"You're working late."

I shift on my chair before making a concerted effort to rip my gaze away from his onyx-colored eyes. Sometimes, if I'm not careful, it feels like I could get sucked into them.

"Yeah, I have some reading to finish up." I shrug. "It's easier to concentrate here than at the apartment."

"I take it Easton's there?" he asks with a smirk.

My lips lift as a chuckle slips free. "Unfortunately, noise canceling headphones aren't always enough."

"Yeah, that's not an image I want in my head." He shifts the backpack on his shoulder before pointing to the chair parked across from me. "You mind if I work here, too?"

Any humor that had been filling me drains away.

"Umm—"

Tell him no. Tell him that you're waiting for someone.

"Ah...I guess."

If he notices the hesitation in my voice, he ignores it and drags out the chair before settling on it. As he pulls out his computer and a few books, I refocus my attention. I promised myself that I'd get through one more chapter before heading home and calling Chris. That's my little reward for staying on task, and I'm not about to allow Crosby to derail it.

Except...my gaze repeatedly settles on him.

Thank god he doesn't notice. Every time I find myself studying him, or even worse, staring at his lip ring, wondering what it would feel like—

I have to mentally shake myself out of those thoughts.

Shifting on the chair, I glance at my phone again and realize that thirty minutes have slipped by, and I've barely plowed my way through four pages. At the rate I'm going, I'll never be able to leave and call Chris.

I glance at the reason for my distraction, only to find him already watching me. Goosebumps break out across my arms when he continues to hold my gaze and doesn't look away.

My mouth turns cottony.

He's not the person I want to feel this way about.

"Are you almost done?" he asks.

Is it my imagination, or does his voice sound strangely gravelly?

Maybe it would be best if I am. With enough time and distance, these feelings will eventually fade. Although, it's been this way for a while and that has yet to happen.

"Umm, yeah. I've gotten through most of what I needed to." That's a lie. "I should probably head home." Relief pumps through me at the idea of getting away from him and the unsettling emotions he rouses inside me.

With a nod, he shuts down his computer and closes the cover before shoving it in his backpack.

I blink. "What are you doing?"

"Leaving with you."

A fresh burst of nerves explodes in my belly as I shake my head. "No, you just got here. Don't leave on my account. You should stay and study." My voice continues to rise. "I'm sure you'll get more accomplished by yourself." Although, my presence didn't seem nearly as distracting to him as his was to me.

"It's fine. I wasn't planning on staying long, but I needed to get this assignment wrapped up for tomorrow. I can complete the rest at the apartment."

Damn.

"Oh. All right."

Once his bag is packed, he rises to his feet. "Did you take your car or walk here?"

I glance toward the staircase and wonder how rude it would be if I just took off. "I walked."

His brows lower as a frown settles across his face. It only makes him even more handsome.

"You shouldn't be walking home alone when it's dark. It's not safe."

I shift my bag on my shoulder, itching to get away from him. "I know, but it isn't that far."

"Come on, I've got my car. I'll give you a lift."

When I open my mouth to argue, he shakes his head and everything inside me deflates.

Great.

Instead of getting away from him, I'll be trapped inside the confines of his car.

I can't help but drag my feet as we head to the first floor before beelining for the exit. Standing much too close for comfort, Crosby stretches his arm around me and grabs hold of the door before opening it. When I stare, his lips tremble around the corners as if he knows exactly what's going through my brain.

Since when does this guy have manners?

As soon as I step outside, the chilled night air hits my cheeks. It makes me wish I'd grabbed a jacket before heading out the door earlier this afternoon. I rub my hands up and down my arms to ward off the cold.

Not a second later, Crosby steps closer before throwing an arm around my shoulders and tugging me against his body. The woodsy scent of his cologne inundates my senses. Just as I'm about to inhale another breath, I stop.

What the hell am I doing?

It's so tempting to fight my way free, but his warmth feels much too good.

"Is that better?" His husky voice has a shot of need exploding deep within me before settling uncomfortably in my core.

I clear my throat along with those unruly thoughts. "Yeah, thanks."

When we're about halfway to the parking lot, I notice a group of three girls walking toward us. There aren't many people still on campus at this hour, just a few either heading to the library or the dorms. Their gazes stay fastened on the guy next to me. When they're about ten feet away, one waves as a big smile lights up her face.

"Hi, Crosby. I was just at the football house looking for you."

"Oh yeah?"

"A ton of people are over there partying. I was kind of hoping you'd be one of them."

"Sorry, not tonight," he says easily. "I've still got a lot of homework to plow through."

The blonde's curious gaze settles on me before she hikes a brow. I've seen her on campus and at the football parties. She's gorgeous, with the kind of trim body I can't help but envy.

Since I can imagine what she's thinking from our proximity and it couldn't be further from the truth, I decide it would probably be a good idea to separate myself from him. Except, when I try to step away, Crosby's arm tightens around me, anchoring me to his side.

He clears his throat. "Maybe another time, all right?"

Her attention returns to him before she closes some of the distance between them.

"I'm free if you need any help studying." Heat flares to life in her eyes. "It's all about the proper incentives."

Umm, okay.

When one of her hands settles on his chest, I glance up to get a read on his thoughts. This conversation has definitely taken a turn for the uncomfortable.

Just as Crosby's mouth opens, she turns to me and cuts him off. "I'm not sure if we've met before. I'm Shandi. Any friend of Crosby's is definitely a friend of mine."

Ummm.

"Hi. Brooke."

My eyes widen when she reaches out and slips my hand into hers before giving it a gentle squeeze.

"Maybe we could help Crosby study," she winks, *"together."*

It takes a moment to snap out of the mental stupor that has fallen over me and tug my fingers free. "I think you've got the wrong idea."

Before I can say anything more, Crosby brushes her other hand from his chest and pulls us back a step. "Sorry, Shandi. You'll have to find someone else to party with."

Her gaze bounces between us before she pops her shoulders. "No worries. Maybe another time. You two have fun."

And then the trio takes off, giggling as they go.

Wait a minute…did she just imply what I think she did?

Crosby propels me forward as I shake my head, trying to make sense of the strange conversation. After a couple of steps, my feet grind to a halt as I swing toward him.

He glances down at me with raised brows. "What's the problem?"

"I don't know who that was, but if you'd rather hang out with her, feel free. I'm more than capable of getting home on my own."

Not once does his gaze deviate from mine. "I have no interest in hooking up with Shandi."

"Are you sure? Because it's none of my business what you do."

"Yup, I am."

When I remain frozen in place, uncertain how to proceed, his arm tightens around me. "Come on, it's cold. Let's get you home."

Reluctantly, I nod and follow him.

Silence settles around us as we make our way to the parking lot and the lone car a couple of rows away. Normally, during the day, the lot is jampacked and spots are at a premium. That's not the case now.

Once we reach the vehicle, his arm disappears from around me and the cold immediately rushes in. He opens the door and ushers me inside before closing me in the small cabin. With a quick jog around the hood, he slides onto the leather seat and starts up the engine. Allowing it to idle for a couple of minutes, he pulls out of the lot and onto the tree-lined street. I rack my brain for something to say but can't stop thinking about Shandi.

If I had to describe the kind of girl Crosby spends time with, she would fit the description perfectly. She's a carbon copy of the ones I've seen hanging all over Andrew. What's apparent is that she didn't care if Crosby was spending time with another female. In fact, she was more than willing to join in on the action. It's yet another unnecessary reminder as to why getting tangled up with an athlete at Western is a terrible idea.

Not that I'm in any danger of getting involved with another jock.

I give Crosby a bit of side-eye.

And it certainly wouldn't be the jock sitting next to me.

Can you even imagine?

Laughter bubbles up in my throat before I choke it down so it doesn't have a chance to break loose.

"Penny for your thoughts," he says.

There's no way I'm telling him the truth.

"I'm just thinking about what I still need to get done tonight."

"Oh?" He flicks a glance at me. "I thought you finished everything at the library."

"It's just a little reading," I mutter, hating that he's caught me in a lie.

It's a relief when he pulls up in front of the building. After he shifts into park, his dark gaze spears mine and it feels as if I'm being pinned to the seat. Even though my fingers are curled around the handle and I'm all but ready to jump out, I find myself unable to move.

"We could have stayed at the library if you needed to work. I wasn't in a hurry to leave."

I gulp as my mouth turns cottony. "It's fine," I whisper. "No big deal."

With a nod, he turns more fully toward me. "Any plans later tonight?"

Chris forces his way into my brain, and for some reason, I'm loath to bring him up to Crosby. My relationships are none of his business. Just like his are none of mine.

"No. I'll probably go to bed early. It's been a long day." I force myself to stop rambling before I admit the truth.

Why does this guy make me so nervous?

As I force myself to break eye contact, I glance down and a lock of hair falls over my eyes, shielding him from my view and making it so much easier to breathe. Just as I exhale, ready to leap from the car and make a quick getaway, he reaches out and sweeps the thick strands out of the way, carefully tucking them behind my ear.

The intimate gesture has the air clogging in my lungs. My wide gaze rises to his. The look of intensity filling his eyes makes my heart pound into overdrive as the oxygen gets sucked from the small space. His fingers slide slowly across my cheek before falling away.

It's the sharp ringing of my phone that releases me from the strange paralysis. I blink and fumble for it before hitting the green button and holding it to my ear.

"Hello?" When I finally find my voice, it's nothing more than a painful rasp. As if I haven't had a drop of water in days.

"Brooke?" There's a pause. "Where are you?"

Sasha.

I couldn't be more thankful for the timely interruption. I'm afraid to think about what could have happened otherwise. And that's a difficult admittance to make.

"I'm right outside the apartment building." I reluctantly glance at Crosby. "I'm just about to walk in."

"Good." Her voice becomes chastising. "I was worried when I found the apartment empty."

"I'm fine. I'll see you in a few minutes."

"Okay."

My fingers shake as I disconnect the call and slip my phone back inside my bag.

"Guess you need to go."

"Yes." I definitely need to go. My fingers curl around the handle before popping it open. Even though cold air rushes in, it does nothing to clear my brain. "Thanks for the ride."

"Anytime."

I jerk my head into a nod before slipping unsteadily from the car. It's only when I slam the door closed that I'm able to draw in a breath and rush toward the building. It takes everything I have inside not to throw a glance over my shoulder. Even though I resist the urge, I know he's there, watching me. I can practically feel the heat of his stare burning holes into my flesh.

It's only when the elevator doors close that my knees weaken, and I almost collapse against the wall. For just a sliver of a moment, it had felt as if Crosby might kiss me.

And even more damning than that?

I'd wanted it.

A gurgle of disbelief bubbles up in my throat as I squeeze my eyes tightly closed. What I need is to make more of an effort to stay as far from the dark-haired football player as I can get.

Otherwise…

I'm afraid to think about what could happen.

15

BROOKE

I slam the bedroom door closed before slipping my phone from the bag and setting it on my desk. I've been looking forward to calling Chris and talking with him all day. After what almost happened with Crosby, it now feels more important than ever. I drop to the bed before hitting his contact info. A moment later, his phone rings. On the third one, he picks up, his deep voice coming over the line.

"Hey, beautiful."

Everything inside me loosens as I push Crosby from my brain and focus on Chris. It's not like I'm messed up or am confused about them. Chris is the guy I'm interested in. So what if I'm physically attracted to someone else?

It doesn't mean anything.

"Hi. I missed talking with you."

"Yeah, me too," he says as a car door slams. "Today's been busy."

A huff of breath escapes as I fall onto my back and stare at the ceiling. "Is this a bad time?"

"Nope. I'm just getting home."

Relief floods through me. This is exactly what I've looked forward to all day. Just hearing his deep voice is enough to settle me.

For the next hour or so, we delve more into our pasts and what we hope will happen in the future. We debate our favorite movies—he's all about Marvel and I prefer Harry Potter— along with our favorite alt rock music—he's into Royal Blood and I like Billie Eilish.

"You're so easy to talk to," I finally sigh. Other than Sasha, there's no one else I've ever shared so much of myself with. "I feel like we could hang on the phone for hours."

"I think we have," he says with a chuckle.

A smile curves my lips. He's right. Our longest marathon session lasted four hours.

It's kind of surprising that we never run out of stuff to say. At least, we haven't yet.

I squeeze my eyes tight and force the question from my lips. "Do you ever think about me during the day?" It feels like I obsess about him all the time. It's only been a few weeks and already I'm in deep. It's like quicksand. If he doesn't feel the same, then I need to find a way to pump the brakes.

"All the damn time," he says, voice dipping and turning rough.

Relief rushes through me. "I think about you a lot, too."

"Oh, yeah? What exactly goes through your brain when I pop into it?"

My teeth sink into my lower lip before I admit, "Just that I want to see you. Reach out and touch you." I should stop now before revealing too much, but the words escape before I can stop them. "Kiss you."

My eyes widen at the beat of silence that follows. I'm sure my neediness will have him running for the hills.

"I'd like to do more than that," he says gruffly.

"What do you wish we could do?" I ask, curling onto my side and holding the phone firmly against my ear so I don't miss a single syllable.

He releases a slow breath, and it's as if I can feel the warmth of it ghosting across the delicate flesh of my face.

"If I were there with you now, I'd pull you into my arms until I could feel every inch of you pressed against me. You're so gorgeous, and I love your curves. I'd take my sweet damn time worshipping every single one of them."

A shaky exhalation leaves my lips as my belly hollows out. The low timbre of his voice along with what he's saying are like the strike of a match. That's all it takes to ignite a firestorm of need deep inside me. I shift against the sheets and clench my thighs. We're not even in the same room, and I'm more turned on than I've ever been before.

"Tell me what you like," he encourages.

My heartbeat thunders almost painfully against my breast. I've never talked about my desires with anyone. Andrew never asked or cared about what I liked. Everything in our relationship revolved around him. Especially sex. It's like he knew that he could get it anywhere from any number of girls. He'd drop little comments that made me feel like I needed to perform to keep him satisfied.

In the end, it wasn't enough.

Maybe *I* wasn't enough.

For a while, I allowed his unfaithfulness to mess with my head along with my confidence. It took some time to realize that he was the problem, not me. And he certainly wasn't the only athlete cheating behind his girlfriend's back. It's like an epidemic on this campus.

The interaction with Shandi pops into my brain, and thoughts of Crosby swiftly follow. For all I know, he decided to head over to the football house and meet up with her. Or one of the other girls clamoring for his attention. Then again, it doesn't matter what Crosby Rhodes does with his time. I shake away thoughts of him and focus on the conversation at hand.

"Hey? Are you there?"

"Yes. Sorry."

"Is this too much for you?" Instead of a growl filling his voice, hesitation does. It's the last thing I want.

"Not at all." It takes effort to push out the words. I've thought them plenty of times but never said them out loud, let alone to another person. "What I like most is having my breasts played with."

"Mmm. Are they sensitive?"

"Very." They always have been.

"Are you touching them right now?"

"What?" My eyes fly open. I glance at the door, hoping that Sasha or Easton didn't hear the near shout, before lowering my voice to a whisper. "No, of course not!"

"I want you to do it while I'm on the phone."

Oh god.

"You want me to..." My words trail off into nothingness as my throat turns bone dry.

"Touch yourself?" he says matter-of-factly like it's no big deal. "Yeah. I want to imagine you playing with your breasts while pretending I'm the one doing it."

A groan escapes from me as I roll onto my back and consider the request.

Before I can give him an answer, he continues, "I want you to strip off all of your clothes and slide naked between the sheets."

For a moment, I remain still, deciding if I can actually go through with this. I'm no stranger to masturbation. There were too many times to count when I didn't get off with Andrew. He never made sure I was there with him before he came. Arousing me wasn't exactly a high priority for him. Within five minutes of rolling onto his back, he'd be snoring soundly, and I'd have to finish myself off. He was never the wiser. Maybe that's part of the problem and I should have told him. Maybe then he wouldn't have thought he was so amazing in bed.

"Have you taken off all your clothes?"

"No," I say tentatively, "not yet."

"What are you waiting for?" he growls.

Instead of overthinking the situation, I let my inhibitions go and do as he asks.

Setting down the phone, my fingers rise to the hem of my sweater before I yank it up my body and toss it to the floor. Then I unfasten the bra and pull it from my arms, allowing it to drop. I unsnap the button and lower the zipper of my jeans before quickly working them down my hips and kicking them free. Left in my panties, the cool air of the room wafts over my warm flesh. My nipples tighten as my heart riots. Once I've shimmied out of my underwear, I slip beneath the sheets and pull the covers over my body. There's something delicious about the feeling of cool cotton against my naked flesh.

"Okay, I'm done."

"Good girl," he says softly.

Good girl.

Those two little words are all it takes for a burst of arousal to explode in my core.

"Now close your eyes and run your fingers along the valley between your breasts. Back and forth. Nice and slow." There's a moment of silence. "Are you doing it?"

"Yes," I whisper, following his instruction to the T. No longer do I wonder if I can do this.

I *want* to do it.

"Good. Now run the tips of your fingers to the top of your pussy before dragging them upward again. "How does that feel?"

Mmmm. It's so good. Especially when I imagine that he's the one caressing me. That thought has me shifting on the mattress as need unfurls deep within my core.

"It's really nice."

"Now bring the same hand to your breast and trace little circles around your nipple without actually touching it."

My teeth sink into my lower lip as I do exactly as he commands. There's something so strong and compelling about the way his deep voice washes over me.

"I want you to give the same attention to the other one. Lazy circles that make you crave more."

Oh god…they're so stiff. Already my breasts feel heavy and achy.

"Now tweak the first one with your fingers. Give it a good pinch. I want you to feel it straight down to your pussy."

A whimper escapes from me as I follow his directives. It only takes one tweak for my core to flood with liquid heat.

"Do you like that?"

"Yes," I whisper in surprise, "a lot."

The world shrinks down until it's only able to encompass the two of us. "I wish I could watch you touch yourself while getting off to the sound of my voice. I bet you look so fucking beautiful, spread out on the bed."

The throbbing between my legs grows in intensity, becoming almost too much to bear.

"I just want to get my hands on you. Stroke those perfect titties before sucking them into my mouth. I bet you'd love that, wouldn't you?"

"Yes," I moan, imagining him doing exactly that. My eyes are squeezed tightly shut, and it takes a moment to realize the guy filling my thoughts is…Crosby. It's his dark eyes staring back at me. His large hands coasting over my flesh. Even though I know it's wrong, that mental image only stokes the flames of my desire. I tell myself that it's only because I don't know what Chris looks like.

That has to be the reason. It can't be anything else.

"Now pinch the other nipple, just like you did to the first one," he says, voice cutting sharply into my thoughts.

A gasp slips free from me as my back bows off the mattress.

"Put me on speaker," he growls, "so you can use both hands."

What?

My eyelids fly open as my movements still. "No, I can't do that. I don't want my roommate to hear you."

Or me.

Especially me.

"Don't worry, I'll keep my voice low. No one else will hear you come. The cries that fall from your lips are only for me." There's a pause. "You want to get off, don't you?"

I chew my lower lip for a handful of seconds before finally caving in. There's too much arousal crashing through my body for me to turn back now. And it's been so long since I've had a good orgasm. Touching myself has never felt like this. In the past, I've always used my vibrator to take care of business, and it never lasts more than five or ten minutes. There's always an end goal in mind, and that's what I'm focused on reaching.

I've never taken the time to touch or play with my breasts,

tweaking the little buds until they stiffen. I don't slowly stroke my hands over my body, arousing myself to the point of no return. There's no teasing whatsoever. The act is straightforward.

It's not a conscious decision to hit the speaker button before setting the phone next to me on the pillow. More like a deep-seated need to see this experience through.

"Okay," I whisper, "I'm ready."

A low growl vibrates in my ear. "Your ex had no idea what he threw away, did he? What an idiot."

I can't argue with that. What makes no sense is that this guy—the one I have yet to meet—seems to understand my needs better than the person I was with for a year.

"You really are fucking perfect, you know that?"

"Hardly."

"You're so perfect I can barely stand it."

My heart flips over beneath my breast, wishing that were true.

"Are you ready for more?"

"Yes." So much more.

"I know you are, and I'm going to give it to you." He clears his throat. "I want you to cup your breasts with both hands and feel the fullness of them. Now imagine that I'm beside you, admiring every gorgeous inch while I play with your body."

The image he sears into my brain is so hot.

"Are you squeezing all that softness?"

"Yes." I arch off the mattress as I massage my breasts. "Mmm, it feels so good to touch myself."

"I bet it does," he groans.

"I want you to roll your nipples with your forefingers and thumbs."

My breath escapes in a shaky rush before I gasp, sucking it back inside.

"Give them a little pinch before tugging them."

A shot of pleasure-infused pain spirals through me as a moan escapes from my parted lips.

"Fuck," he grunts. "Do you have any idea how much I want to get my hands on you?"

"I want that, too." It's the only thing that would make this experience better.

"I want you to cup your titties and press them together. Are they big enough to do that?"

"Yes." It used to embarrass me that my breasts were so full. But at the moment, listening to the rasp of his heavy breathing float across the line and knowing he's imagining the very same thing, I'm glad they are. And I like that it turns him on.

"I'd love to slide my cock right between them."

The thought of him straddling me, pinning me to the mattress as he thrusts his dick against my flesh has a burst of pure heat exploding in my core.

"I'd drive it slowly back and forth. With each pass, I'd bring the tip to your lips for you to kiss and lick."

The erotic image he paints is such a turn-on that it's impossible to keep the whimper locked inside where it belongs.

"I want you to keep one hand on your breast and let the other trail down your belly to that sweet little pussy." I can almost hear every intake of breath over the line as he pauses. "Are your fingers there?"

I jerk my head into a nod before forcing myself to give voice to the response. "Yes."

"Kick off the covers so you can feel the cool air against your bare skin."

It's on the tip of my tongue to tell him no. Instead, I swallow it down and do as he instructs. My body is on fire, and I'm burning up inside. Once the comforter and sheet are removed, the air of the apartment wafts over my skin, raising goosebumps in its wake. I shift against the cotton and realize that I didn't lock the bedroom door. Not that Sasha is in the habit of barging in without at least a courtesy knock, but it could happen. The danger of being caught only heightens the desire thrumming wildly through my veins.

"Now, I want you to spread your legs. Let them fall all the way open."

I widen my thighs until my knees practically touch the mattress. Years of gymnastics has made my body pliant and flexible. As the cool air caresses my damp flesh, I know I've never felt so wanton in all my life.

"I bet you're a fucking picture, all spread out with your hair tangled like a halo around you."

Air gets wedged in my throat at the guttural sound of his voice as it washes over me. It occurs to me that I haven't even touched myself —not really—and already it feels like I could splinter apart into a million jagged pieces.

"I want you to trail your fingers gently over your parted lips and tell me how it feels."

I caress one plush side before carefully circling the entrance. As I touch myself, sharp shafts of need shoot through me and my back arches off the bed. Even though I'm alone, I feel strangely open and vulnerable.

Totally at his mercy.

"Tell me what your pussy feels like, baby."

My heart stutters at the endearment. "My lips are silky smooth and so soft."

"Mmm. I bet they are. Keep going. I want to know more. I want to know everything."

"They're wet because I'm so turned on." My fingers continue to circle, not daring to dip inside. But I want to so badly. "And hot. The more I stroke them, the fuller they feel. It's as if they're swelling with need."

"Fuck," he hisses. "Do you like touching yourself?"

"Yes," I groan, enjoying this more than I ever thought possible.

"What about having your pussy licked and eaten? I bet you like that, too."

"I do, but my last boyfriend," I pause, searching for the nerve to force out the rest, "didn't like to do it that often."

"How could he not?"

Even though he can't see me, I shrug. "I don't know. He liked it more when I did things to him."

He snorts.

"I'd lick that sweet little pussy all the damn time. There's no way

I'd ever be able to get enough. Do you know that? All. The. Damn. Time."

His words send a straight shot of need to my core, leaving me to twist restlessly on the bed.

"What do you want now?"

"I want to play with my clit," I whisper. It feels like it's pulsing with a life all its own, and I'm dying to touch it.

"Don't you dare. Not yet. Keep touching yourself with nice, slow circles that make you feel like you're going to go insane."

It won't take long for that to happen. I'm precariously close to splintering apart. I have no idea what this guy is doing to me, but I love it.

I moan, needing more. Instead of arguing, I do exactly as he commands, knowing he'll force me higher and higher until I explode. And when I do, it'll be the best damn orgasm I've ever experienced.

Just when I don't think I can stand another moment, he says, "All right, dip your finger inside, but don't go all the way. Only a knuckle or two. It's all about teasing. Never giving yourself too much."

Another moan slips free as I follow the instruction.

"Do you need more?"

"Please."

"Mmmm, I love hearing you beg. You can pump your finger in and out a few times, but keep the movements shallow."

I groan as my muscles stiffen, becoming impossibly tight.

"Now touch your clit and imagine that it's my fingers stroking over the little nub." His voice grows increasingly rough.

That first touch has me gasping as sensation continues to ratchet up. My back arches as everything inside me constricts, coiling tight as a scream builds deep inside. My eyes screw shut as I stroke my flesh.

"My fingers are wrapped around my cock, strangling the fucking life out of it as I imagine you spread out, touching yourself for me." His voice is nothing more than a harsh rasp as his breathing turns labored, echoing in my ears until it's all I'm aware of.

It's the mental image of him stroking his dick that sends me careening right over the edge into oblivion. My body convulses as I moan out my orgasm. I don't stop rubbing until every drop of pleasure has been wrung from my pussy. His groans, and the slap of his own skin mingles with mine as we both find our pleasure.

Without question, it's one of the most intense orgasms I've ever given myself. And it's certainly better that anything I've experienced with Andrew.

It takes a few moments for the sexual haze to clear so I can catch my breath. "Chris? Are you still there?"

"Yeah," he says, sounding winded, like he just ran a marathon. "I'm here."

I grab a Kleenex and swipe it over my fingers before picking up my phone and clicking off the speaker. "Thank you."

He chuckles. "I'm pretty sure I'm the one who should be thanking you."

"That was," I pause, trying to find adequate words to describe what just happened, "kind of amazing."

"You're damn right it was."

"Promise me we'll do it in person some time?" The question is out of my mouth before I can stop it.

There's a beat of silence as his voice turns serious. "Yeah, I promise."

My teeth sink into my lower lip before I force out the next question. Considering the intimacy we just shared, it seems strange I would even have to ask. "Do you think we could meet up tomorrow? Maybe for coffee or something."

A burst of nerves explodes inside me when an answer isn't immediately forthcoming.

My tongue darts out to moisten my lips. "Please?" I don't know why it feels so imperative he agree to this meeting, but it does. If he puts me off after what we just did...

I'll be crushed. There's just no other way around it.

"Okay," he says hesitantly before adding, as if trying to resign himself to the idea, "sure, we can do that."

"Really?" Air rushes from my lungs as cautious anticipation takes root inside me. I'm almost afraid to get my hopes up that I'll finally be able to put a face to the guy I've gotten to know so well.

"Yeah."

"Good." A smile tips the corners of my lips. "Eleven o'clock at the Roasted Bean?"

"That works."

It's so tempting to squeal, but I keep the sound trapped inside.

For now.

"I'll see you tomorrow," I whisper, feeling almost giddy with the excitement rushing through me.

"Tomorrow."

16

CROSBY

What the hell had I been thinking? Oh...that's right, I hadn't been. I'd been much too wrapped up in what we'd been doing and all the strange feelings of need prickling beneath the surface of my skin, attempting to claw its way free. Afterward, when Brooke had asked to meet up, I'd caved like a cheap house of cards.

I'm regretting that impulsive decision now. She's not ready to discover the truth. She can barely tolerate being in my company. At the library yesterday, she couldn't get away from me fast enough.

I plow a hand through my hair and continue pacing outside the Roasted Bean. It's ten fifty-five. There's a massive boulder sitting at the bottom of my gut. And nothing I do banishes it.

Of course I realize that at some point, I need to come clean. It's not like I can keep this charade up indefinitely. Especially after what happened last night. Even thinking about how we masturbated over the phone has me popping wood. I've fucked a lot of girls, and that's probably the sexiest thing I've ever experienced.

Screw it. I straighten my shoulders and draw in a deep breath.

All right, here's the plan...I waltz in there, make a little bit of small talk, and then lay it on her that I'm Chris. She'll be pissed off at first—

that's to be expected—but hopefully I'll be able to sweettalk her out of it. Believe it or not, I can turn on the charm when the occasion calls for it. And this one definitely does. I'll apologize again—profusely, if need be—and beg her forgiveness.

Who knows...maybe she'll even see the humor in it. The entire situation is kind of funny when you think about it.

Yeah. That's exactly what I'll do, and, in the end, it'll be fine. Just last week, we buried the hatchet. This can be part of that fresh start.

I stop and swing around to stare at her through the oversized picture window in front of the coffee shop. She showed up ten minutes ago and is already camped out at a small table, waiting for me to make an appearance. Her caramel-colored hair tumbles around her shoulders and down her back in soft waves. A lot of girls like to throw their hair up into a ponytail or messy bun, but not Brooke. She usually wears it long and loose.

I fucking love it.

There have been too many times when I've been tempted to reach out and stroke my fingers through the silky strands. Since I'm not a guy who normally enjoys taking my own life into my hands, I've always kept them to myself.

She's wearing another short skirt that shows off a tantalizing amount of long leg and a pale pink sweater that hugs her curves. Curves that she willingly stroked her hands over at my command last night.

That's not a thought I need in my head right now. I came when she did over the phone, but then I had to rub another one out before I was finally able to fall asleep last night.

I blink back to awareness when she shifts on her chair, alternately glancing around the crowded shop before staring down at her phone. Even from this distance, I can see a mixture of anxiety and excitement swimming around in her green eyes. No matter how much I try to convince myself she'll be all right with the truth, deep down I know that's a lie. There's an excellent chance she'll wring my neck when she realizes I was the one on the phone with her last night.

Unsure what to do, I suck my lip ring into my mouth before flipping it back and forth with my tongue. The way I see it, there are only two options. One, I walk away and never talk to her again. Or two, I man up and tell her the truth. Those are the only ways this can play out. My head spins with indecision as I stare through the window and weigh my choices.

The urge to bolt is what finally prods me into movement. I have to at least try and explain how an innocent text snowballed out of control before I could put a stop to it.

It's not like I deliberately set out to deceive her.

All right, so maybe I did keep texting her, knowing that she thought I was someone else, but it hadn't been with malicious intent. She has to understand that, right?

Ever since I first laid eyes on Brooke, she's made me feel things I wanted to ignore, and for a long time, I was able to put my friendship first and do that. This past couple of weeks have only intensified those feelings, forcing me to realize that I couldn't ignore them anymore. I don't want to lose what I've only just found.

We've spent so much time talking and texting, getting to know each other on a deeper level. When it comes down to it, *I'm* the guy she's gotten to know. And like. Even if she doesn't realize it yet.

What I have to do is plead my case and hope she understands.

Before I can chicken out, I spin around and grab the handle of the door, forcing my feet over the threshold before cutting a direct path to her. It's only when I reach the tiny table that I stutter to a hesitant halt. When my shadow falls over her, she lifts her head and meets my gaze. The hopeful light in her wide eyes dims when she discovers me standing next to her.

If I were in need of further proof that I'm the last person on the face of this Earth she'd hoped to see, this confirms it. "Oh. Hi, Crosby."

All of the carefully compiled explanations arranged in my brain evaporate as she shifts, attempting to look past me as if I'm blocking her view.

Instead of taking off, the way every instinct inside is screaming for me to do, I force the words through stiff lips. "Hey. What are you up to?"

Her distracted attention flits to me briefly before sliding away.

"Umm," she cranes her neck as the chime over the glass door trills and someone steps inside the shop, "meeting up with a friend."

"Oh, yeah?" *Tell her. Tell her right now before this goes any further.* "Anyone I know?"

Fuck.

What the hell am I doing?

No, seriously.

That would have been the perfect segue way to say—yeah, I'm Chris, I'm that friend.

Instead, I keep the words buried deep inside. How can I tell her the truth when it's obvious from the barely concealed disinterest on her face that I'm the last person she wants to have a conversation with? I think if she could shoo me away from the table without being overtly rude, she'd do it in a heartbeat.

"I'm not sure," she finally admits as a hint of color touches her cheeks. "It's kind of a blind date."

Say the words.

Do it.

Stop being such a pussy.

"Huh." My hand rises to stroke my jaw. "Interesting."

It's official—I'm a pussy.

She jerks her shoulders. When the door opens for a second time, she perks up and peeks around me.

All right, I can still change the trajectory of this conversation.

It's now or never.

I clear my throat, fully prepared to blurt out the truth. "Listen, I—"

"I think my date just walked in." She swiftly rises to her feet. "Can we talk another time?"

"Huh?" My brows slam together as I swing around and scan the nearby area until my gaze lands on a tall blond dude who is now staring at Brooke with a smile on his face.

Oh, hell no.

"Wait—"

Before I can stop her, she pushes past me. Excitement dances across her face. The expression is night and day from the one she'd been wearing while staring at me. Unsure what to do, I watch as the guy plows a hand through his hair, shoving the strands away from his eyes before grinning.

Instead of stalking over and grabbing her the way every instinct is clamoring, I hightail it out of the Roasted Bean. As I push through the door, a chilly breeze wafts over me, cooling all of the emotion that riots beneath the surface of my skin. After a couple of steps, I pull out my phone and fire off a quick text, apologizing for being a no-show.

Do you really think for one damn minute I'm going to let her think that the asshole inside is the one she's been texting with?

No fucking way.

17

BROOKE

As soon as I park my car in the half-filled lot, I flip down the visor and take one last look in the mirror, making sure that my hair and makeup are on point. There's no need to give Elaine any further ammunition to use against me. I blow out a steady breath, knowing that no matter how much I straighten and smooth, my mother will find something to comment on. It's taken a couple of years and a shit ton of therapy sessions to come to that realization.

Most of the time we meet up, my armor is firmly intact and I'm able to use the counseling tools in my toolbox to get through the visits relatively unscathed. That's not the case today. After Chris bailed on me, I'm feeling a little vulnerable. My high hopes had ended in crushing disappointment.

Maybe I shouldn't be so surprised that he flaked. Although, after last night, I guess I am. Masturbating while on the phone with a guy is certainly a first for me. I'm not going to lie—it was super-hot, but still…

The only consolation I have is that he texted right away to let me know he couldn't make it. Unfortunately, the damage had already been done. I'd assumed the cute guy I'd caught the eye of across the shop was him and went over to introduce myself. When I'd asked if his name was Chris, he'd said, and I quote, that he could be any guy I wanted him to be. I'd thought he was trying to be cute until the real Chris's message rolled in, letting me know that he'd been held up by one of his professors. Extricating myself from the coffee shop situation had been embarrassing.

The rest of the day had been downhill from there. And now, I'm going to cap it off by having dinner with my mother. I'm sure by the end of the meal, I'll want to hurtle myself off the nearest bridge.

With a resigned huff, I steel myself for two hours of unpleasantness, all the while tiptoeing through a minefield of topics. The evening will be exhausting, which is why I can only deal with seeing her every couple of weeks. Lord knows it'll take that long to undo all the damaging subliminal—and not so subliminal—messages she'll bombard me with. If it's a real shitshow, I'll make an appointment with my counselor on campus to discuss my unresolved issues.

Exiting the vehicle, I smooth down my skirt and head inside the restaurant. The quicker I get in there, the sooner it'll be over with, and I can head home to lick my wounds in private.

"Hi," I say with a forced smile when I reach the hostess stand, "I'm here to meet Elaine Bollinger."

The younger woman nods before stepping from behind the sleek desk. "She's already been seated. If you'll please follow me, I'll show you to your table."

It takes everything I have inside to keep the pleasant expression pasted across my face as I catch sight of Mom strategically positioned in the middle of the elegant dining room where she can see everyone who comes and goes. Once she catches sight of me, she rises to her feet and throws open her arms.

"Darling," she coos, "it's so good to see you. It feels like it's been forever."

I'm immediately enveloped in a sultry cloud of Chanel as she air kisses both cheeks, behaving as if she's from a sophisticated European country instead of a holler in Eastern Kentucky, where she was born and raised before hightailing it from there when she was seventeen years old. The only times she's returned to her roots are when her parents died, and she sold the tiny hovel she'd grown up in. Mom always had big dreams and, say what you want about her, she made damn sure to attain them.

I stare longingly after the hostess as she silently retreats to the front of the restaurant, wishing there were a way for me to escape with her.

"You too, Mom."

She pulls back just enough to search my face before the smile fades and a look of concern fills her bright blue eyes. A cool hand drifts to my cheek.

"Brooke, you look tired. Haven't you been sleeping well?"

And so it begins...

"I've been sleeping just fine." Especially after that cataclysmic orgasm last night. I was dead to the world until my alarm went off this morning. Although, it's highly doubtful Mom would want to hear all the juicy details.

The thought of sharing my little self-love sesh with her brings a tiny smile to my lips. The shock and horror that would settle over her expression might be worth the price of admission, but then I would never hear the end of it. And that, I'm unwilling to deal with. She'd probably faint, and I'd have to call Garret to come retrieve her.

She presses her injection-filled lips together, making her look more like a duck than usual. Lisa Rinna has nothing on Elaine Bollinger.

"I don't know," she studies me carefully, "you have the appearance of someone stressed. Is school not going well?"

I untangle myself from her embrace before putting a few steps of distance between us. The cloying scent of her perfume is already fast at work, giving me a headache. When I take a seat opposite of where her bag is set, she does the same. Although, she lowers herself with far more poise and grace.

"School is great. It couldn't be better."

She nods, discretely checking her makeup in a small, gold compact before snapping it shut with a click and sliding it into her latest Birkin.

"I'm delighted to hear that. Garret will be so pleased."

I clear my throat, relieved for a change in conversation. "How's he doing?"

"So busy." She waves a perfectly manicured hand through the air. "You know the kind of hours he puts in."

Yes, I do. It's those very hours that leave Mom free to fill up her days with spa treatments, salon appointments, and charity functions. Despite her rocky start in life, it's what she was born to do. It's the kind of wife she always wanted to be. Dad didn't make nearly enough money for her liking. When they were married, she constantly nagged him to climb the corporate ladder and look for a better job that paid more money. One that could afford all the luxuries she felt she was owed. When it became apparent that Joe McAdams wasn't interested in doing her bidding, she cut him loose and found a way to marry the kind of man she deemed worthy.

Garret is in his late fifties and has two older sons I met for the first time at the wedding and at a couple of holiday parties afterward. I get the feeling Brett and Derek don't care for Elaine. Luckily, they've always been kind to me.

Mom is forty-four, but with all the work she's had done, she looks more like a woman in her early thirties. There have been too many times to count when she tried to pass herself off as my older sister.

What else can I do but roll my eyes and play along?

A waiter stops by and takes our order. I would dearly love an alcoholic beverage to take the edge off, but then I would have to sit through a sermon on the evils of alcohol. And when I say evils, I mean how it prematurely ages you. Even though she's told me repeatedly that I have excellent genes passed down by her, there's no reason to tempt fate. So we both order two glasses of sparkling water with a wedge of lemon.

For a few moments, she pretends to study the menu. I'm not sure why she bothers with the ruse. We both know she'll end up with a spinach salad. Dressing on the side. No croutons.

She gives the waiter a flirtatious smile before ordering exactly what I suspected. I consider ordering a carb-heavy pasta dish, but then I'd have to listen to her talk about how terrible carbohydrates are.

For me.

It would be the perfect segue to discuss my weight, and I don't have the energy for that conversation this evening. Instead, I order the grilled salmon on a bed of greens.

Yum.

Not really.

I hate salmon. Too fishy. But I know she'll wholeheartedly approve of the selection. And she'll be even more impressed when I barely touch it. Maybe I'll hit a drive thru on the way home and eat a burger in her honor.

This is exactly why it took years of counseling to undo all of her twisted teachings and reprogram my brain to a normal setting. Every time I'm in her presence, it's a fight to not slide back into old habits.

We're halfway through dinner when she brings up another subject I have zero interest in discussing.

"Have you spoken to Andrew lately?" she asks, carefully picking at her salad and only daring to spear dark, leafy greens before popping them into her mouth one at a time and chewing methodically.

I push the salmon around on my plate to give the illusion that I've taken a few bites. "Yup. Saw him yesterday."

Unfortunately.

She angles her head and pouts. "I do miss him. He was such a sweet young man. And so handsome." She gives me a knowing look. "Perfect marriage material, if you ask me. He's a man who is going places."

I clench my jaw, refusing to take the bait. Although it's tempting. Since when is being a self-centered, cheating asshole considered perfect marriage material?

When I remain stoically silent, she continues blithely, "I seriously hope you'll reconsider getting back together and giving your relationship another chance. It would be such a shame to let him slip through your fingers." She waves her fork. "In no time at all, another woman will snap him up and you'll be kicking yourself for not thinking long term. Trust me, bitter regret is *not* a good look on a woman."

Perhaps. But from what I've learned, Botox, laser treatments, and plastic surgery are a dream at erasing it.

I wince at the uncharitable thought, hating how snide I've become in her company.

It takes all of my self-control to carefully set down my fork on the fine bone china plate instead of hurtling it across the spacious room.

"You know he cheated on me, right?" A small part of me keeps hoping she'll acknowledge the pain he inflicted, but that has yet to occur.

Her demeanor turns serious as she nods. "So you've mentioned."

It's impossible to keep the sharpness out of my voice. "Not just once but many times."

There's no hint of softening around her eyes or mouth, but that could be the Botox. "I'm not saying his actions weren't distasteful, but doesn't he deserve a second chance to prove he's changed?"

Distasteful.

I think what his cheating ass deserves is a much stronger adjective.

"No, he doesn't." A steady drumbeat begins to throb behind my temples.

"Brooke." She actually has the nerve to cluck her tongue as if I'm a recalcitrant child.

"What, Mom?" I snap. "Should I have turned a blind eye to what he was doing and allowed it to continue? Or maybe I shouldn't value myself as a woman who deserves better? Is that really the motherly advice you're giving me?"

This dinner needs to end before I totally lose it.

"Of course not, darling." She gives her head a little shake as if I'm the crazy one. "But he loves you so much, and you shouldn't forget that his father owns a Fortune Five Hundred company. I just don't want you to regret an impulsive decision because your pride is wounded. You need to consider the kind of life he'll be able to provide for you." She gives a tiny shrug. "Sometimes it's necessary to overlook lapses in judgment in order to stay focused on the prize. I don't want you to make the same mistakes I did because I was young and stupid. There was no one to help guide me. That's not the case for you."

This isn't the first time I've been told how her marriage to my father was a mistake, and it's doubtful it'll be the last.

"I don't want a man who can't keep his—"

"They all cheat," she cuts in sharply before giving me a pitying look. "Please don't delude yourself into believing they don't. They're men. Unfortunately, it's in their nature."

I straighten on my chair and say through clenched teeth, "That's not true. And I have no problem with providing for myself. It's the reason I'm attending college and working toward a degree that will eventually pay the bills. I don't need or want a man to take care of me."

Elaine would vehemently disagree and tell you the reason she sent me off to school was to land a wealthy husband who I could sink my claws into, just like she would have if given the opportunity. But her parents couldn't afford to send her to college. So, she took off for a big city, waitressed in an upscale establishment where she could meet a man who wore a suit and expensive silver watch for a living. There were a few bumps in making the dream come true, but the rest is history.

Thankfully, the waiter stops by and asks if we need anything else.

"Just the check," I mutter, fed up with the conversation.

"Would either of you care to hear about our dessert selections for the evening?"

Mom waves a hand. "Gracious no, I'm stuffed."

The younger man glances at her barely-touched salad before turning to me. His expression never falters.

"And you, miss?"

"Nope." I make a big production of patting my belly. "Also stuffed."

He gives a slight bow and whisks both plates away.

I open my mouth to say goodbye when she beats me to the punch. "I almost forgot to mention the fundraiser we'll be hosting at the estate this weekend."

Everything in me wilts as my tongue darts out to moisten parched lips. "Oh, ah, I wish I—"

Her mouth thins as her eyes harden with disapproval. "It is not a request, Brooke. Garret would be extremely disappointed if you didn't make an appearance at such an important event. Do you need to be reminded that he pays your tuition along with all of your living expenses every month without fail?"

"No," I grumble, "that's not necessary." Mostly because she trots this out anytime I need to be manipulated and forced back into line. I can only stew silently and remind myself that next year will be different. I'll have an income and will be able to pay my own way. I won't need Garret's money for anything. At times like these, it's the only thing I have to cling to.

Her expression smooths at my easy capitulation, and she bestows a smile upon me. "Good. I'll text you all the details tomorrow."

"Fine."

When the waiter arrives with the padded folio, Mom takes out her pink Chanel wallet and tucks a hundred-dollar bill into the pocket before rising from her chair.

"Well, this has been quite lovely."

And then I'm once again enveloped in another perfumed hug before being released back into the wild. As we head to the front of the restaurant, she runs into a woman she co-chairs numerous charities with, and I quickly duck out the door before I can be drawn into a conversation that will make me want to slit my own throat.

The throbbing in my temples has turned more into a full-blown headache as I slip behind the wheel of my Jetta and pull out of the parking lot like the hounds of hell are snapping at my heels. Although, that's to be expected, which is why I popped a few Tylenol before leaving the apartment earlier this evening.

Even though I'm famished, and it feels like my stomach is consuming its own lining, I don't bother to stop. I just want to get home, curl up in bed, and call Chris. I need to hear his voice. Somehow, he's able to make everything better. He apologized about this afternoon, and I'm not going to hold it against him.

At least, not this time.

I mentioned that I would be having dinner with my mother, and after everything I told him over the course of the last couple of weeks, he seemed to understand that I'll need to be talked down from the ledge afterward. I like that about him. He's intuitive and hears more than the words that come out of my mouth.

Fifteen minutes later, I pull into a parking space outside my building and cut the engine. Instead of exiting the vehicle, I suck in a deep breath and allow my forehead to fall against the padded steering wheel. I don't understand why it has to be like this. As far back as I can search my memory, I don't remember a time when we were together and I didn't walk away feeling like shit.

I just wish we could have a normal mother-daughter relationship like some of my friends do. They might envy the money my family has, but I'm jealous of the real connections they have with their moms.

What would that feel like?

It's not something I can imagine, because I've never come close to experiencing true maternal love. It's times like these that leave me feeling even more bereft, because I realize deep down that Elaine isn't capable of being the kind of mother I long for. If I've learned anything from years of therapy, it's to make peace with the things outside your control. Otherwise, it would be all too easy to waste a lifetime twisted up with bitterness.

Giving myself a couple of minutes to wallow in self-pity and acknowledge the hurt that has been inflicted makes it easier to pack it back up and put it to rest. A nice hot bath won't hurt, either.

Just as I lift my head, ready to exit the vehicle, there's a tap against the window. A scream wells in my throat before bursting free as my gaze settles on the face peering at me from the other side in the darkness.

18

CROSBY

So maybe rapping my knuckles against the glass when she wasn't paying attention wasn't the smartest way to announce my presence. Brooke's eyes widen to the point of comicalness as she opens her mouth and lets out a bloodcurdling scream. With the luck I'm having, someone will call the police and I'll cap off this day by getting hauled away.

It takes a second or two before recognition sets in. She blinks as the sound of her fright dies a slow death on her lips. For a long moment, we just stare. When her brows jerk together, I retreat a few steps so she can pop open the door. Her cheeks remain devoid of color as her mouth settles into a tight slash.

"What the hell are you doing sneaking up on me like that?" Her voice wobbles as she flattens a palm against her chest as if to keep everything rioting dangerously beneath it inside. "I almost had a heart attack!"

I clear my throat and force out the lie. "Sorry. I was jogging by and saw you sitting in your car. I thought something might be wrong." Actually, I've been loitering outside her building like a creeper for the past thirty minutes. Trust me, it's not a proud moment, but after what happened at the coffee shop today, I decided I needed to step up my game where she's concerned.

My response throws her for a loop, and her brows pinch together in confusion.

"Oh."

When we fall into another uncomfortable silence, I shift my stance and clear my throat. "Are you all right? Is something wrong?" I'm hoping she doesn't brush off the question, because there won't be much more I can do but walk away.

"No." There's a pause before she tacks on, "Not really."

It doesn't escape me that if she knew she was talking to Chris, there'd be zero hesitation on her part. She'd already be spilling all the grisly details. But the guy standing in front of her isn't Chris.

It's Crosby.

And she doesn't trust him as far as she can throw him. And just to be clear, that's not far. At this point, I'm not sure if there's anything I can do to alter her perception. In no way does that knowledge deter the crazy need coursing through me that demands I get as close to her as possible. What's hilarious—not really—is that it's completely one sided. In fact, Brooke would probably be delighted if I said a quick goodnight and took off, never to be seen or heard from again.

Somehow, I need to change that.

Or die trying.

I shift my stance and lighten my tone. "So…is that a firm no? Or a yes, but I don't really want to tell you about it because you've always been an asshole?"

She blinks, and it takes a few moments before her mouth twitches. It just might be the first hint of a smile I've received from her. As miniscule as it is, I'll consider it to be progress made in the right direction.

"It would be a yes, but I don't want to tell you about it because you've always been an asshole."

I press my lips together and nod. "That's fair."

She searches my eyes before the tension in her shoulders gradually drains and a reluctant puff of air escapes from her. "I just got back from dinner with my mother, and it was as delightful as ever."

It's on the tip of my tongue to tell her I know all about it, but I can't do that unless I plan on outing myself right here and now. After the Roasted Bean fiasco, I now realize it'll take more time to earn her trust and friendship.

"You two don't get along?" I ask, hoping to carefully draw her out of her protective shell.

Her expression becomes strained as she turns the question over in her head. "Unfortunately, it's more complicated than that." She gives a tiny shrug, attempting to play down the situation. "It's not really that big of a deal."

Except I know from our previous conversations that it is.

"That can't be true if it tanked your evening."

She examines me for a long moment before begrudgingly admitting, "Maybe." There's a pause. "I usually need some time to decompress after our visits. I love my mother," she adds quickly, "but we're two very different people and don't always see eye to eye. Her values don't necessarily align with mine."

I stuff my hands into the pockets of my sweats. "I get that. The parentals try to mold us into their likeness, but it doesn't always work. At the end of the day, we're our own people with our own thoughts and beliefs. It can cause friction."

She blinks before studying me. "You're right about that."

With a small shake of her head, she clicks the locks on her Volkswagen until the alarm beeps and hitches the strap of her bag over her shoulder. When she walks toward the entrance of her building, I fall into line beside her. I'm nowhere near ready to abandon this sinking ship.

She gives me a bit of side-eye but remains silent.

My lips lift as I take the bull by the horns. "I'm just walking you to the door to make sure nothing happens."

"Like someone coming out of nowhere and scaring the crap out of me?"

"Exactly like that."

She nods, her expression turning thoughtful. "Hmmm, interesting. I never pegged you for a gentleman."

Probably because I've never tried to be one. "Are you forgetting that I opened both the library and car doors for you yesterday?"

A snort leaves her lips. "I think it was more of a deviation from normal behavior than anything else."

"Isn't it possible that I've reformed my ways?"

Looking unconvinced, she shakes her head. "I think you're blowing smoke up the wrong person's ass."

I flash a grin. "Or, maybe, you don't know me as well as you think you do."

"I wonder why that could be?" Eyes narrowed, she taps her pointer finger against her chin. "Is it because you were too busy acting like an ass for me to get to know you?"

Ouch. Unfortunately, she's spot on. I did everything in my power *not* to get to know her. And vice versa.

"Touché."

Once we reach the glass door, she stops and pulls out a key ring from her pocket before sliding the thin metal into the lock and opening it. Her questioning gaze flickers to mine. I still, unsure what she's looking for. All I know is that I want to stay and continue our previous conversation.

Just as the moment turns awkward, she blurts, "Do you want to come in for a bit?"

19

BROOKE

Someone please tell me that I didn't just invite Crosby Rhodes up to my apartment.

From the surprised expression that has morphed across his face, it's much too late to snatch the words from the air and pretend they never escaped. All I can do at this point is cling to the miniscule hope that he has better things to do and declines the offer. If not, it'll blow apart the rest of my evening and there will be no salvaging it.

This is precisely what spending time with Elaine does to me. It makes me lose my mind.

"Sure."

Damn.

My shoulders collapse under the weight of his agreement. There's nothing else to do other than reluctantly nod as he reaches around me and grabs hold of the door before stretching his arm toward the lobby.

Fate sealed, I step inside the building as Crosby allows the door to swing closed before following me to the elevator. I stab the button and silently berate myself.

What the hell had I been thinking?

Now I'm stuck spending time alone with the one guy I try to avoid at all costs.

Ugh.

Once the doors of the elevator slide open, he waits for me to step inside before following. He's so close that I can feel the heat of his body and smell his cologne. It's so tempting to inhale a big breath of him. Instead, I punch the floor button. Seconds later, the doors close, trapping us inside together.

Air stalls in my lungs as a strange, combustible energy snaps and crackles around us. The more time that slowly ticks by, the more explosive the atmosphere feels. It's as if all of the oxygen has been sucked from the small space. I've never understood why my body reacts to him like this. The fact that I find him so attractive considering our tenuous past is disconcerting on so many levels. I want to be indifferent where he's concerned. The energy that wafts off him is almost suffocating in its intensity. It's almost like a magnet. One that continually pulls at me, never allowing me to get too far.

When I can't stand another moment, I shift before giving him a bit of side-eye. "I hope you don't think I've invited you up to have sex," I blurt.

He blinks before his nearly black gaze pierces mine. "The thought never crossed my mind."

Heat stings my cheeks as I jerk my head into a tight nod. Could I sound any more like an idiot? "Good," I mutter. "I just want to be clear so there aren't any misunderstandings."

His lips tremble as he presses them together in an effort not to smile. "Trust me, there aren't. I'm not under any illusion that you want to sleep with me."

If only that were true.

I almost wince at that thought.

Thankfully, the elevator doors open, saving me from drowning in further conversation. Crosby keeps pace easily with me down the long stretch of brightly lit hallway until I grind to a halt in front of my door. My fingers shake as I open it.

"If you're not cool with me being here, I'll leave. It sounds like you've had a rough night. Maybe you just want to hit the sack and put it all behind you."

Thrown off by the comment, I glance at him in surprise.

Everything inside me loosens and I hear myself say, "No, it's fine. Are you good with watching a movie?"

"Sure. Whatever you want to do."

The apartment is swathed in darkness as I step inside. My guess is that Sasha is out with Easton. Those two have always been close, but now they're more like cojoined twins. They've known each other for so long and are such great friends. I can't imagine finding someone who knows me inside and out like that.

Is it strange that Chris immediately pops into my brain?

We haven't known each other for very long—just a couple of weeks—and yet, I've shared so much with him. Both my past and present. We've even talked about what we want our futures to look like. I'd planned to call him when I arrived home, but that will have to wait.

Shoving him from my thoughts, I flick on the lights as Crosby strolls further inside the apartment. There's a narrow entryway with a credenza shoved up against the wall. A beveled mirror hangs above it, and there's a ceramic bowl for keys sitting on top of the shiny surface. I set my purse on the table before trailing after him.

Like most of the student housing near campus, this place is compact. There's a small kitchen to the right that has barely enough space for two people to maneuver, and a breakfast bar with a couple of stools tucked neatly beneath the counter. A small couch, over-stuffed chair, glass coffee table, and television are arranged in the room. At the far end of the area is a small balcony with views of the university in the distance. It's a two-bedroom apartment, so Sasha and I each have our own space. Although, she's the one who ended up with a private bathroom. After the rental agreement was signed, we flipped for it.

I lost.

Crosby drops down onto the couch, and I consider taking a seat on the chair before nixing the idea and settling on the opposite end, making sure to leave plenty of room.

"What kind of movie are you interested in watching?" He stretches his arm across the back of the cushion, making him feel closer than he actually is.

After the night I've had?

"Definitely something funny."

He nods as I pick up the remote and cue up Netflix before flipping through some comedies and settling on a new one with Ryan Reynolds.

"Let me guess," he says with a snort, "you're one of those girls who think this guy is sexy." The disdain filling his voice would be hard to miss.

My eyes widen. "Are you telling me that you don't find him good looking?"

"Objectively speaking, he's all right." There's a pause. "You know, if you're into his brand of handsome."

I raise my brows. "Just to be clear, I am *totally* into his brand of handsome. In fact, you might have to wipe the drool from my chin."

He turns more fully toward me. "Is that so?"

"Yup. If you're not careful, I'll make you watch another flick as punishment for even suggesting that his status as sexiest man alive isn't well deserved."

A grin breaks out across his face as he hoots. "Sexiest man alive? Give me a break."

"I stand by the comment, and nothing you say will change my mind. He's sexy as hell, and the fact that he's funny makes him even more so. End of story."

His broad shoulders shake with barely concealed mirth. "Just start the movie and let's get this over with."

I narrow my eyes and do exactly that. "Keep it up and we'll marathon it."

It only takes ten minutes before the tension filling me drains away and my muscles finally loosen. A large dose of comedic relief is exactly what I needed after that dumpster fire of a dinner with Elaine.

Another half an hour slides by, and we're both cracking up.

"See." I point toward the television. "Not only is he sexy, but he's funny. Even you have to admit that the guy is the total package."

He rolls his eyes for what feels like the umpteenth time before begrudgingly admitting, "Yeah, fine. He's funny. Okay? Are you happy? Can we just watch the movie?"

Delighted that he's finally admitted the truth, I flash him a grin as our gazes lock and hold. Electricity dances down my spine as a burst of arousal explodes inside me. When the tips of his fingers strum the top of my shoulder, I startle to awareness.

Up until this moment, I hadn't realized he'd been touching me.

Almost as if in slow motion, he scoots closer, eating up the distance between us. "Brooke—"

Before he can say anything more and ruin the lighthearted mood we've managed to find, I leap from the couch and carefully back out of the living room on unsteady legs. My heart gallops against my ribcage as I jerk a thumb over my shoulder. "I'm going to grab a couple bottles of water and make a bowl of popcorn."

I don't give him a chance to respond before bolting to the safety of the kitchen. Once there, my knees buckle, and I practically collapse against the counter. It takes a minute or so to settle everything rioting dangerously inside me.

What was that?

Just like last night, it almost felt like he was going to—

I shake my head to clear it of those thoughts.

No.

No.

No.

Absolutely not.

I don't even like Crosby.

Sure, I find him sexy as hell, but I'm certainly not alone in that assessment. Most of the girls at Western find the guy irresistible. All that messy black hair practically begs female fingers to plow their way through it. Not to mention, those dark eyes that have a way of appearing almost fathomless. And his muscles. My god, the muscles. He's perfectly honed solid strength. Then there's the lip ring...

Yup, the guy could be the definition of catnip for the female species. Once my heart is no longer racing, I carefully sneak a peek into the other room, only to realize he's paused the movie.

I release a steady breath and try to clear the mental fog that has descended before grabbing a bag of popcorn from the cabinet, unwrapping the cellophane, and setting it in the microwave.

You know the easiest way to evict Crosby from my brain?

By focusing on the guy I'm actually interested in. The one I wish were here instead.

Inviting him up was a mistake. When he gave me an out, I should have grabbed hold of it with both hands and agreed that I was tired. Instead, here I am, hiding out in the kitchen of my own apartment.

I nip the phone from my back pocket before firing off a text.

Hey. I'll call in a little bit. Watching a movie with a friend. Would much rather be talking with you.

20

CROSBY

I slide my phone from my pocket when it chimes with an incoming message and glance at the screen.

What the hell?

I'm a little surprised to find a text from Brooke. With a quick glance at the kitchen, I silence the cell. The last thing I want is for her to put two and two together and figure out that I'm Chris. She needs a little more time to get to know me better. Maybe then she won't feel like I deliberately deceived her.

Even though that's precisely what I'm doing.

How the hell did my life become so complicated?

It's beyond ridiculous that I've allowed this situation to spiral so far out of control.

And yet...how can I rein it back in again?

We're way past the point of me ghosting her. I could have walked away from the coffee shop this morning but wasn't able to do it.

I scan the text for a second time.

So she's watching a movie with a friend, huh?

I suppose there are worse things she could have referred to me as. With another quick glance toward the kitchen, I tap out a response and hit send before I can stop myself.

Oh, yeah? What kind of friend? Someone I should be concerned about?

My heart kicks up a few notches as I shift on the couch and wait for a reply.

Not at all.

Then she tacks on a few laughing emojis to twist the knife deeper.

My lips sink into a frown as I drag a hand over my face. I can't believe I'm seriously jealous of a persona I created. How messed up is that?

The faint ding from the microwave knocks me out of my thoughts as I shove the phone back into my pocket. A handful of seconds later, she returns with two bottles of water and a big bowl of popcorn for us to share.

The sexual tension that had been simmering in the atmosphere just minutes ago is now long gone, only to be replaced with the same strain as when I startled her in the parking lot. For a moment or two, I consider bringing up the elephant in the room before quickly discarding the idea. The last thing I want to do is make Brooke more uncomfortable than she already is. If I'm lucky, she'll loosen up again and I can make a little headway before she sends me home. The text she just sent pops into my brain before I promptly shove it away.

It's just going to take a little time for me to change her opinion.

Without a word, I pick up the remote to restart the movie as we dig into the popcorn. Even though we aren't doing anything more than hanging out, there's nowhere else I'd rather be.

The movie is almost halfway through when a plot twist happens, and I can't resist rolling my eyes and telling her how lame it was. She smirks before throwing a piece of popcorn at me. Since it's the last thing I'm expecting, the kernel hits me square in the chest before dropping to my lap. She laughs as I pick it up and toss it back at her. But she's way ahead of me and bats it away before dissolving into a fit of giggles. The movie continues to unfold on the screen as her gaze drops to my mouth. Unconsciously, my tongue darts out to play with the small silver hoop.

Her laughter falls away as she tilts her head and studies it. "What does it feel like to kiss someone with that?"

"Are you interested in finding out?" The question shoots out of my mouth before I can think better of it.

When she doesn't immediately nix the idea, every muscle tightens, going on high alert as my voice turns raspy. "Are you thinking about it?"

"Maybe."

Her honesty is like an electric shot straight to my dick. I don't consider the ramifications of my actions as I close the distance between us before wrapping my hand around the back of her neck and slowly pulling her toward me.

It's almost a surprise when she doesn't slap her palms against my chest to halt my movements. Once the warmth of her breath feathers over my flesh, I brush my lips across hers until she's able to feel the metal. A delicate shiver works its way through her body.

It's not an uncommon reaction. Chicks love the lip ring. Crazy as it sounds, it somehow brands me as a bad boy. I had no idea what a magnet it would become when I pierced it senior year of high school. What I was looking for was a way to piss my father off. Girls tripping over themselves to make out with me ended up being a bonus.

With Brooke, it means so much more.

Her breath catches as I angle my head and sweep my mouth across her upper lip before doing the same to her lower one. There's no need to nudge her into opening for me. She does it without hesitation. When her lips part, my tongue slips easily inside her mouth to mingle with her own. Need explodes in the pit of my gut, and I have to make a concerted effort to keep everything locked down tight when all I want to do is crawl on top of her and devour every sweet inch.

Maybe it's a little underhanded to use the information I've acquired over the past couple of weeks, but I don't give a crap. I understand exactly how Brooke secretly longs to be kissed and touched.

It's only when she twines her arms around my neck and presses her body to mine that I realize she's as into this as I am. It's all the green light I need to deepen the kiss and devour more of her.

Unable to resist, I drag her onto my lap until she can straddle my legs. When the short skirt she's wearing rides up her thighs, a groan escapes from me. It's so tempting to shove the material away so I can catch sight of her panty-covered pussy.

How fucking long have I dreamed about that?

Instead of giving in to the desire, I pull her closer until my erection is nestled against the vee between her thighs. She whimpers as I grind myself against her.

Fuck.

With all her soft curves, she feels even more amazing than I imagined. The thought of sinking into her heat turns me on like nothing else.

"You feel so damn good," I whisper between greedy kisses, running my hands up and down her ribcage, allowing my fingers to brush the sides of her rounded breasts. I keep everything light and gentle, never pushing it too much or too far. I want to take the time to heat her up and drive her just as crazy as she makes me.

Is that even possible?

I have no idea, but I'm going to damn well find out.

As much as I want to slip my hands beneath her skirt or sweater, I don't make a move. It's all but killing me to hold back. When she rolls her hips against me, I know that taking a softer approach with her is key. Has anyone ever taken their time to touch her?

Just when I consider taking this a little further, her phone chirps, shattering the silence of the apartment. Her eyelids flutter open as she breaks the kiss and stares at me with a dazed expression.

The urge to wrap my hand around the nape of her neck and pull her back for more pounds through me. When I lean forward to capture her lips for a second time, she presses her palms against my chest to hold me at bay. Each second that ticks by has the reality of this situation crashing over her features. If I didn't know better, I'd think she just had an out of body experience.

Before she can tell me it was a mistake, I growl, "Do you have any idea how long I've wanted to do that?"

Her eyes widen as she slowly shakes her head.

When she remains silent, I say, "Too fucking long."

Confusion flickers in her eyes as her teeth sink into her lower lip. Her gaze darts away before she clears her throat. "You should go."

Fuck.

It was too much, too soon.

"Is that what you really want?" The urge to brand this girl as my own so everyone knows who she belongs to—including her—pounds through me until it's all I can focus on.

When her gaze falls to my lips, it takes every ounce of self-control not to release the groan trapped within my chest as I suck the small metal hoop into my mouth.

Her pupils dilate as she shakes herself out of the mental stupor she's fallen into. "It would probably be for the best."

When she doesn't scramble off my lap, my hands settle around her waist before carefully hoisting her off me.

Slow, I remind myself.

I need to take this nice and easy.

Once I've set her on the cushion next to me, she rises to her feet before staggering toward the kitchen like a drunk. I'm tempted to reach out and steady her, but I know she'll shy away from my touch. Already, the recriminations are setting in. I can see the play of emotion on her face. I mentally will down the boner in my athletic shorts and drag a hand through my hair before following her out of the living room and into the entryway where she waits.

With the door held open.

If I'm not careful, she'll boot my ass out before I can even say goodnight.

Just as I pass her, I stop. "So, what did you think?"

She blinks in confusion. "Of what?"

"The lip ring."

When a blush blooms in her cheeks, I whisper, "Now imagine it against your clit."

Her eyes grow impossibly wide as her jaw turns slack. A smirk curves my lips as I close the door and head for the stairwell.

And that, my friends, is exactly how you make an exit.

21

BROOKE

Seconds tick by as I stare at the closed door in shock. My fingers tremble as they rise to my lips before gently sweeping across the plump flesh. Without looking in the beveled mirror hanging over the credenza, I already know they're swollen. I have no idea how long we kissed. It could have been minutes or hours. It's all a blur. What I do know is that when I finally pulled away, the movie had ended.

Crosby Rhodes.

I just made out with Crosby Rhodes.

The bad boy of the Western Wildcats football team.

No matter how many times I silently repeat his name in my head, it still sounds just as farfetched. Did he actually admit that he's wanted to kiss me for a while, or was I in some kind of fugue state?

No way. It can't be true. He's always been such a jerk. There have even been a few times when I wanted to punch him in the face. And just to be clear, I'm not the kind of girl who loses her shit and gets violent. That's never been my style. But over the last year and a half, Crosby has managed to find a way to push every single button.

Almost like it was purposeful.

I shake my head to clear it of all the warring thoughts in my brain.

I have no idea if this changes anything between us. It's not like we were friends to begin with.

So…what does that make us now?

As I walk into the living area, another guy pops into my brain and I stumble to a halt.

Oh my god…how could I make out with Crosby when I'm interested in someone else?

A mixture of disgust and disbelief bubbles up in my throat. The only rational explanation is that I was out of sorts from my visit with Elaine. I can't imagine something like this happening under any other circumstance.

At least…I don't think it would.

As I step across the threshold of my bedroom, my gaze gravitates to Crosby's neatly folded T-shirt on my desk. Had I been thinking clearly, I would have given it back to him. Although, I think we can all agree that if my brain had been functioning properly, I wouldn't have made out with him in the first place.

I peel off the skirt and sweater before unsnapping my bra. A groan of relief slides from my lips as the tight fabric falls from my shoulders. I don't have cute little bras that are delicate and decorative in nature. Nope, the ones I buy are purely utilitarian. And if I can find something that minimizes the girls a cup size or two, the happier I am.

Normally, I'd grab a tank top from my dresser drawer and pull it on. Instead, I gravitate to the navy T-shirt. I'd meant to wash and return it but haven't gotten around to doing it. For a moment, I stare at the fabric before raising it.

Don't do it.

Ignoring the voice in my head, I hold the soft cottony material to my nose and inhale deeply. The scent of Crosby's woodsy cologne inundates my senses, just like it did when I was settled on his lap only a handful of minutes ago.

Ugh.

Why does he have to smell so damn delicious?

My eyelids drift shut as my belly flutters with newfound awareness. Being wrapped up in his scent is all it takes to remind me of what it felt like to have his mouth coasting over mine and his lip ring dragging across my flesh. Arousal flares to life deep in the pit of my belly as my core floods with heat. If I'm being completely honest, the feel of the metal was just as sexy as I thought it would be.

Now imagine it against your clit.

I have to clench my thighs together in an attempt to stifle the need coursing through me. The problem is that I can totally picture it. I can imagine exactly what it would feel like.

Before I realize what I'm doing, I tug the material over my head and smooth it down my body. From the corner of my eye, I catch a glimpse of myself in the full-length mirror. Another spiral of electricity sizzles through my veins before being followed by a rush of guilt.

Allowing him to kiss me had been a mistake.

One that can never be repeated.

When my phone rings, cutting through the silence of the room, I startle, forcing the dark-haired guy from my head before swiping the slim device off the dresser. I've been waiting all day to talk with Chris.

As soon as I hit the green answer button, his voice floats over the line.

"Hey, beautiful."

"Hi." I settle on the bed, rolling onto my stomach so I can swing my legs back and forth. Chris is exactly the kind of guy I need in my life.

Not Crosby.

My breath falters as my eyes flare.

Holy crap.

Why would that thought even enter my head?

There's no way I'd date Crosby Rhodes. He's just another player like my ex. How stupid would it be to trust someone like him? Someone who blows through girls like Kleenex?

No, thank you.

We kissed. It wasn't a big deal, and it certainly doesn't mean anything.

"Sorry about being a no-show today," he says, interrupting the whirl of my thoughts.

"It's fine. No worries."

"Thanks for being so understanding." There's a pause. "I've been thinking about you all afternoon. How did dinner go?"

The way he's so easily able to tell me that I've been on his mind sends a burst of warmth rushing through my veins. That feeling is immediately chased by thoughts of my mother. I groan, attempting to steer the conversation in a different direction. She's ruined enough today. I don't want her tarnishing this, too.

"I'm sure that's the last thing you want to hear about."

"I know you were dreading it, and I want to make sure you're okay. You can talk to me about anything. I'm here for you."

My heart spasms in my chest. Could I like this guy any more than I already do?

He almost seems too good to be true.

As soon as that thought niggles its way into my brain, I shove it away. There's no reason for me not to trust Chris. He's been nothing but upfront and honest. How many guys can you say that about?

"Come on, beautiful. Tell me what happened."

That's all the prompting it takes to give him a blow-by-blow of dinner.

When I finally run out of steam, he says, "I'm sorry. That really sucks. Are you all right?"

"Yeah, I'm fine. Honestly, I feel better after talking to you about it." Which is strange but true. Somehow, I feel lighter. Buoyant. More like myself again.

"Good. I'm glad." His voice softens. "There was no way I could go to bed without checking on you."

His genuine concern only makes me fall harder for him. Have I ever dated a guy who took time to make sure I was all right?

It doesn't take much mental searching to discover the answer.

A groan slips free when I remember the party I've been strongarmed into attending.

"What? Did something else happen?"

"It's not a big deal," I mutter. "Just a fundraising event this weekend at their estate. The only positive is that Mom will be busy playing the part of gracious hostess, so our interactions will be limited." And that's always for the best.

"Hmmm. Sounds painful."

He has no idea.

"Oh, it will be."

"Sorry, babe. I wish I could be there for moral support, but I've got a family thing this weekend."

My heart constricts that he would even throw the offer out there. After our failed attempt to meet for coffee today, I was afraid to mention us getting together again.

"I appreciate that."

"I know it's not much, but just remember that I'm only one phone call away. I'll support you however I can, all right?"

How is this guy so sweet?

And how hasn't he been snatched up already?

"That really means a lot to me. Thank you."

We talk for a few more minutes before he asks what movie I watched with my friend. I cringe as Crosby forces his way back into my brain for the umpteenth time. Unwanted memories flicker through my head like a slow-motion picture show of me straddling his muscular thighs and what it felt like to kiss him. Or rub myself against his thick erection. And it had, in case you were wondering, been thick. Guess the rumors I've heard swirling through campus all these years are true.

Heat rushes in to flood my face. The only saving grace is that Chris isn't here to see it.

"Oh, just something with Ryan Reynolds," I mumble, hoping he doesn't ask any more questions. "It was pretty funny." From the little I remember. How it ended is anybody's guess.

"Sounds chill. Exactly what you needed after that dinner."

I wince. "Yeah, it was."

Until it wasn't...

"I wish I could have been there with you."

"Me, too." I press my lips together as remorse eats away at my insides. I'm not a liar. I've never been particularly good at it. As much as I want to keep everything contained inside, I can't. "Do you know who Crosby Rhodes is?"

The phone goes quiet as the atmosphere between us changes, becoming more tense. Is it just me, or does he feel it as well?

As I open my mouth to ask if he's still there, he says, "Sure, I've seen him around."

I release a steady breath and silently berate myself for bringing him up. I should have kept my big mouth shut. "He's my ex's roommate, so I've known him for a while. The entire time I was with Andrew, he was a raging asshole. The comments he would make were just plain mean and hurtful. It got to the point where I hated being in the same room with him and tried to avoid him as much as possible. The crazy part is that I have no idea what I did to make him dislike me so much."

Another silence follows before he bites out, "The guy sounds like a real shithead."

"Yeah." I nibble on my lower lip and admit, "I ran into him on campus last week. He apologized for being such a jerk and asked if we could start over."

"Interesting."

"Yeah," I agree. "It totally threw me for a loop."

"Do you believe him?" he asks carefully. "Do you think he was being sincere?"

I turn the questions over in my head. I've thought about them a lot. "I guess so." It takes effort to push out the rest. "I ran into him after dinner, and we started talking. One thing led to another, and I invited him up to watch a movie."

Even though I haven't come clean about everything that happened this evening, it's enough to assuage some of the guilt eating at me.

"It went all right? He didn't do anything to upset you?"

I blink, surprised he isn't pissed off that I spent part of the night alone with another guy.

"Yeah, it was fine."

"Good. I'm sure that helped you relax and get into a better headspace."

Again, I'm pleasantly surprised by his nonchalant attitude. All the anxiety filling me drains away.

"Yeah, it did."

"I'm glad he was able to do that for you."

It's tempting to pull the phone from my ear and stare at it in stunned amazement. How is this guy so understanding and emotionally mature?

If I thought I liked him before this conversation, it's nothing compared to how I feel now. I'm chalking up what happened with Crosby as a lapse in judgment. We kissed. It wasn't a big deal. It was probably just a regular Wednesday night for him, anyway.

Except he didn't get laid.

"You have an early class tomorrow, right?" he asks, drawing my attention back to the conversation.

"Yup. Bright and early at eight." I glance at the clock on my nightstand and realize just how late it is.

"Then I should probably let you go so you can hit the sack."

"Okay. Night, Chris."

"Night, beautiful. Talk to you tomorrow."

After hanging up, I set my phone on the nightstand before sliding beneath the sheets. Even though I don't want to mentally rehash dinner with Mom, that's exactly what I do. It takes twenty minutes of tossing and turning before I'm finally able to find sleep. When I do, my dreams are a strange tangle of two boys. One who is dark-haired and the other who's murky. Sometime during the night, they end up melding into the same person.

22

CROSBY

With two cups of steaming coffee in my hands, I stroll up the walkway to Brooke's apartment building. Just as I reach the door, a couple of junior football players walk out.

"Hey, Rhodes. What are you doing here?" one of them asks.

I shrug. "Visiting a friend."

The mouthy one jabs his sidekick in the arm. "Doesn't the walk of shame work the other way around? Shouldn't you be going, not coming?"

I hike a brow and glare.

I don't know who these two jokers think they are, but they better remember who they're talking to. And that's a fucking senior on the team. I'll pummel their asses on the field without so much as a second thought.

When they finally realize that I'm not amused, the smiles fade as they mumble a quick goodbye before scurrying away. It's the smartest move they could have made. Actually, the shrewdest decision would have been to keep their pie holes closed in the first place.

I shake my head before strolling inside the lobby and hitting the elevator button with my elbow. Once inside, I wait for the doors to slide open and walk down the hallway. I have to rearrange the cups, holding one against my chest and forearm before rapping on the thick wood with my knuckles.

Is it totally ridiculous that my heartbeat picks up its tempo at the thought of seeing her again?

I search my brain, unable to come up with a time when a girl has made me this nervous. I've never liked anyone enough for that to happen. But that's exactly how it is with Brooke. The fact that I might not be able to turn this around and change the way she feels about me is like an anchor around my neck, dragging me down.

The door swings open, and Sasha fills the space. The greeting perched on the tip of her tongue dies a quick death as her eyes widen before narrowing to slits.

"Crosby?" The way she says my name sounds more like a question than anything else. "What are you doing here?"

I clear my throat and hold up the coffees. "I came to see Brooke."

"Brooke?" she echoes, brows snapping together as her face scrunches. "Why would you do that?" Before I have a chance to respond, she straightens to her full height and folds her arms across her chest. "If you're here to cause trouble, you're in for a world of hurt." She uncrosses her arms and takes a step toward me before drilling a finger into the middle of my chest. "I know you and Easton are friends, but he loves Brooke like a sister, and he'll beat your ass if you even think about fucking with her." She rams her finger none too gently into my chest again. "Have I made myself perfectly clear?"

"Crystal."

My solemn answer seems to knock her off balance. She studies me silently before shaking her head and mumbling something under her breath. It's probably for the best that I can't decipher the grumbled-out words.

"Wait here."

As I open my mouth, the door is slammed in my face. Two seconds later, it snaps back open, and she points to the cups I'm still holding. "Is one of those for me?"

Even though that hadn't been my original intention, coffee seems like a small price to pay to smooth over this disastrous interaction.

"Absolutely."

With a grunt, she nips one of the steaming cups from my hand. "Thanks."

Then the door is slammed in my face for a second time. I shift from one foot to the other, wondering if she plans on returning or if I've been conveniently forgotten about.

I should have realized that a tentative friendship with Brooke would be a tough sell for her roommate. It only makes me wish I could go back in time and alter the course of our relationship. Or, more accurately, that I hadn't been such a raging asshole, as Brooke put it so eloquently on the phone last night.

Just as I consider knocking again, the door opens, and I find Brooke standing on the other side of the threshold. She looks as surprised as her roommate was to find me here.

"Um, hi." Unvoiced questions swirl through her green eyes.

"Hey."

The atmosphere turns tense as she shifts her weight before tucking an errant lock of hair behind her ear. A slight blush blooms in her cheeks, and I can't help but wonder if she's thinking about my parting shot last night. Trust me, I'd be more than happy to give her a first-hand demonstration. That thought alone has my cock swelling with interest.

Her tongue darts out to moisten her lips. "What are you doing here?"

Having almost forgotten about the drink, I thrust the large cup of coffee toward her. "I thought you might appreciate something to jumpstart your day."

Her gaze drops to the container of java. She blinks, looking adorably confused by the gesture. If anything, it only reinforces what a jerk I've been.

"You brought me a coffee?" Surprise laces her voice.

"Yup." When she doesn't make a move to grab it from my outstretched hand, I give it a little jiggle. "Here, take it."

The command snaps her out of her strange paralysis, and she tentatively reaches out, wrapping her fingers around the container.

Our hands brush and her eyes widen before darting to mine. She takes a quick step in retreat as if to put a safe amount of distance between us before lifting the cup to her nose and inhaling the pungent aroma.

A sigh escapes from her lips as her eyelids flutter shut. "I do love the smell of coffee."

Yup, I'm aware of it.

When she'd stay the night with Andrew, she'd make coffee in the morning without fail. When it was ready, she'd pour a steaming cup and lift it to her nose to enjoy the scent before blowing on it and taking that first sip.

Did I happen to pop wood while listening to her sounds of pleasure as she puckered her lips?

Every damn time.

Did I also bite her head off before stomping away?

Almost nearly as often.

But still…as much as it pissed me off to get turned on, I always made sure my ass was in the kitchen, waiting for her to make an appearance. It was a fucked-up situation. One I wish I could take back. Since that isn't possible, I can only attempt to make amends and hope she eventually forgives me.

Her brow furrows as she sniffs again. "Is this freshly ground Arabica?"

"Yeah."

When more questions dance in her eyes, I force myself to admit, "I remembered that you used to drink it." Since I don't necessarily want to bring Andrew into the conversation, I finish with a lame, "Before."

"It's my favorite," she acknowledges with a nod. "Thank you."

"You're welcome."

Another silence falls over us as we stand with the apartment door open and stare. As it turns awkward, I say, "I have my car. Do you want a ride to school?"

"Oh."

My attention drops to her mouth as she chews her bottom lip with indecision. It takes every ounce of self-control not to close the distance between us, pull her into my arms, and kiss her the way I did last night. I couldn't stop thinking about it after we got off the phone. There were so many times when I wanted to blurt out the truth. In the end, I pussied out. I'm afraid that it'll push her away when all I want to do is hold her close.

When she makes no move to accept the offer, I cajole, "Come on. You can enjoy your coffee on the way to class instead of walking six blocks to campus."

Another handful of seconds slowly trickle by before she finally gives in with a reluctant nod. "Okay. Let me grab my bag and we can go."

Instead of slamming the door in my face, she leaves it open before swinging around and beelining to her room. As I glance inside, Sasha steps out from the kitchen with the coffee meant for me. Her eyes narrow as she uses two fingers to point at her face before aiming one of them at me like a weapon. She repeats the gesture a few times just to make sure I understand that she'll be there every step of the way, watching me like a hawk.

I wouldn't expect anything less. The two girls have been friends since freshman year and have always had each other's backs.

It's almost a relief when Brooke returns with her bag. "Ready to go?"

"More than ready," I mutter, shooting one last glance at Sasha's now smirking face before swinging away.

Brooke closes the door behind us and falls in line beside me. Instead of waiting for the elevator, we take the stairwell to the lobby before pushing our way out into the chilly sunshine. She tugs the black leather jacket she's wearing over a short white sweater more firmly around herself.

"It's cold this morning."

"Guess it's a good thing you've got a ride," I shoot back easily.

Her lips lift into a slight smile. "I'll let you know once we reach campus if that turns out to be the case."

I snort. "Touché."

Once we arrive at my Mustang, I click the locks and open the passenger side door. She hesitates, angling her head to give me a considering look. It only proves how much my previous behavior hurt her.

"Thank you," she murmurs before slipping inside the vehicle.

The engine purrs to life before I shift the gear and reverse out of the parking space, taking off down the tree-lined road that leads to campus. We only have a handful of minutes to ourselves, and I don't want to waste any of them.

Between sips of coffee, her attention flickers to me. Even though I stay focused on the ribbon of road beyond the windshield, I can feel the burn of her gaze. The questions and confusion that continue to simmer at my sudden shift in attitude. I search my brain for something that will lighten the atmosphere, but my mind remains frustratingly blank. I've always been smooth with the ladies.

Brooke is the exception to that rule.

It's almost a relief when she clears her throat. "About last night…"

Even though traffic has picked up, becoming heavier the closer we get to the university, I can't stop myself from stealing a glance at her. "I enjoyed it a lot."

When she leaves me hanging, twisting in the wind, I chance another look in her direction, only to find her staring at the cup in her hands as a rush of color pinkens her cheeks.

"And I want it to happen again," I add, just so we're clear and there are no misunderstandings as to what's going on here.

Even though I should slow my roll, I find myself unable to do that. After that kiss last night, all I can think about is how good it felt to have her in my arms and on my lap, grinding against my erection.

By the time I swing into the parking lot near the athletic center, the tension filling the small space is almost suffocating in its intensity. I kill the engine and turn toward her so we can face each other. My hand slips into her hair before wrapping around the nape of her neck.

"Are you interested in that, too?"

When her teeth scrape against her plush lower lip, a groan escapes from me and I drag her closer until my mouth can settle on hers. It only takes one sweep of my tongue across the seam of her lips before she's opening. The kiss itself is fleeting. There and gone before I can fully sink into it.

It's a struggle not to take more and consume every drop of her.

To demand everything.

"I don't know." Her eyes cloud as she searches my gaze. "It wasn't all that long ago you could barely tolerate my presence. Suddenly that's changed, and I still don't understand the reason for it."

It's so tempting to come clean, but I know if I told her the truth, she'd hate me even more for pretending to be someone I'm not. She'd realize that I encouraged her to share personal pieces of herself that she never would have revealed otherwise.

"Brooke—"

She cuts me off. "Last night you claimed to have wanted to kiss me for a while. Is that true?" Again, her gaze searches mine. "Or was it just a line you fed me in an attempt to get into my pants?"

I wince as her tone turns steely and can't blame her for being skeptical of my motives.

"It wasn't a lie. I meant every word."

When I lapse into silence, she raises her brows, urging me to continue.

Even though it's a risk, I give her a small piece of the truth. "I wanted to kiss you the entire time you were with Andrew."

She stills before slowly shaking her head. "You're lying."

"I'm not. It's the truth."

"But you've always been such an asshole." She swallows thickly, and the delicate muscles in her throat constrict. "Right from the beginning, before you ever had a chance to get to know me. I never understood what I did to warrant such hatred."

"You didn't do a damn thing," I say gruffly. Revealing the truth is so much harder than I thought it would be. The pain that flickers across her face is like a dagger through my heart. Maybe I don't deserve her forgiveness. "It was just easier to keep my distance if you hated me."

Air hisses from her lungs. "Are you being serious?"

Unfortunately, I am.

23

BROOKE

No...that's just not possible.

There's no way I heard him correctly.

I shake my head to clear the growing buzzing sound before squeezing my eyes tightly closed to find my bearings.

It takes a few moments before I'm finally able to wrap my lips around the words. "So let me get this straight," I whisper, "you treated me like shit because you actually...*liked* me?" Disbelief threads its way through my voice.

When he doesn't immediately answer my forced-out question, I open my eyes, only to find him staring with a stricken expression. The silver metal of his lip ring glints in the early morning sunlight, momentarily distracting me from our conversation.

"Yeah," he finally mutters, "that would be the gist of it."

Heat burns the backs of my eyelids as my mind tumbles over the last eighteen months and all the nasty swipes he took. There were so many times when I was left reeling, feeling like shit, or humiliated in front of our friends and his teammates.

I've wracked my brain, trying to figure out what I'd done to deserve his treatment. And now I find out that it's because he had *feelings*?

Not in a million years would I have suspected that reason.

I blink out of those thoughts when he gently sweeps his thumb across the fragile skin beneath my eye. I don't realize tears are leaking until the blunt pad comes away with wetness.

"I know there's nothing I can say or do to take away the pain I've caused," he whispers before pulling me closer and kissing away the moisture that continues to trek down my cheeks. "I was a prick, and my behavior was immature. I tried to protect myself at your expense, and it was wrong."

"I just..." I shake my head, unsure how to respond.

Sorrow fills his eyes as he nods. "I get it and don't blame you for wanting to be cautious. I haven't given you any reason to trust me." His gaze burns brightly into mine. "But I will."

What I hate more than anything is the tiny kernel deep inside that desperately wants to believe his motives are sincere.

And I hate that. I wish I could stomp it out.

Life would be so much easier if his apology had no effect on me. If I could tell him to take his stupid explanation and shove it right up his ass before slamming out of the car and stalking away. But the words refuse to be summoned. My body remains frozen in place. I can only stare, searching his dark eyes for the truth as morning sunlight pours over us.

My mind tumbles over all our previous interactions. Even when Crosby was being an asshole, there was always something brewing beneath the surface. A combustible energy that threatened to explode.

One look.

One touch.

It always felt as if I were on the cusp of splintering apart and coming undone. I'd assumed it was all one sided.

Turns out I was wrong.

He felt it, too.

I shake my head to clear the thoughts. "Why now? Why bother saying anything when we're so close to graduating and going our separate ways?"

The silence that stretches between us becomes almost unbearable.

It makes my skin prickle with awareness as the air in the vehicle turns oppressive.

"Because it's exhausting to keep everything buried deep inside and continue acting like I don't like you when nothing could be further from the truth. Not only couldn't I do it anymore, but I didn't want to. I have no idea if it's too late, but you needed to know that my behavior didn't have anything to do with you."

It takes effort to blink away the wetness filling my eyes. "You really hurt me, Crosby." There is so much emotion inside me, fighting to break free. "All those nasty comments and the looks…"

"I know." His voice turns raspy. "I fucking hate myself for putting you through that. If I could go back and do it all differently, I would."

He pulls my face closer until his minty breath can ghost over my parted lips. After everything he's done, it doesn't make sense that all I want to do is close my eyes and inhale a giant lungful of him.

A fine tremble wracks my body. His closeness has always had the power to make me feel weak. After everything he's divulged, that hasn't changed. In this moment, as our breath continues to mingle, becoming one, all I can think about is his mouth coasting over mine, forcing me to forget the ugliness of our past.

"I realize that I'm asking for a lot, but give me a chance to prove I'm not the guy you think I am. One chance is all I need."

Unable to hold his gaze any longer, I squeeze my eyes closed as his words circle viciously through my brain. "I don't know. I need some time." Time away from him to clear my head. That's not possible when he's invading my space.

"Whatever you want, I'll give you."

Another thought pops into my head. "And what about Andrew? What would he say if he knew?"

Even if I were to forgive him, there's his best friend to consider.

"We both know he'd be pissed off," he reluctantly admits.

That's an understatement.

"Yes," I agree, "he would. Maybe you need to think about that before this goes any further."

Guilt flickers across his face as he shakes his head. "Don't you understand that it's all I've been able to focus on? I've done everything in my power to stay away from you, and I can't do it any longer."

When he drags me to him for a second time, I flatten my palms against his chest to keep him at a firm distance. It takes effort to pull away, but I'm afraid of what will happen if I don't. I'm precariously close to shattering into a million jagged pieces.

Without a word, my fingers fumble for the door handle before popping it open. Cool air fills the car as I drag in a cleansing breath, hoping it will settle everything rampaging dangerously inside me. As I step from the vehicle and onto the pavement, I slam the door closed, only to find Crosby waiting for me near the hood of his Mustang. I release the pent-up breath held captive in my lungs.

I have no idea if it's possible for us to move forward. What I realize as our gazes cling is that he doesn't just want to wipe the slate clean and be my friend.

He wants more.

24

BROOKE

*A*fter forty-five minutes on the road, I pull into the winding, tree-lined driveway of the stone mansion Garret moved us into after he and Mom got married. The place is over ten thousand square feet of sprawling space.

The first few times I explored the palatial estate, I got lost in the maze of ornately decorated hallways and gigantic rooms. They all bear a striking resemblance to one another with my stepfather's highly coveted art collection displayed throughout most of it. Sculptures and busts are prominently showcased on pedestals. This place is more museum than home, and it's a far cry from the tiny shoebox we came from. There's an Olympic-sized pool in the backyard next to a perfectly pruned English garden complete with spectacular fountain. It's all a little surreal. Even with the massive workout room in the basement and spa-like amenities, I still prefer the house I spent most of my childhood in.

Once the Volkswagen is parked, I take a moment to steel myself for the handful of hours I'll have to spend socializing before escaping back to campus. My silent pep talk is interrupted when the driver's side door is yanked open, and a valet outfitted in tux-like garb impatiently waits for me to vacate the vehicle.

With a slight smile, I swipe my purse from the passenger seat and head up the wide stone stairs to the front porch. I can't help but hesitate under the arched portico before pushing open the massive mahogany door and peering cautiously inside. Even though this has been my home for six and a half years, most of the time, I feel like a guest.

Mom refused to bring any of our old furniture when we moved. Everything was packed up and dumped at the Salvation Army. When she attempted to donate my old bedroom set, I put my foot down, unwilling to part with the last piece of my childhood. Not that it was expensive or an antique like everything carefully curated to fill this house, but it's mine. It's the only thing that made me feel like it was sort of my home, too. Now the bedroom set is at the apartment and guest furniture fills my bedroom here.

"Good evening, Miss Brooke," an older woman greets, hustling into the grand double story foyer. Her voice echoes off the cavernous walls and gleaming marble floors. "Your mother was just wondering when you'd arrive."

I paste a smile on my face.

Mrs. Folly is the house manager slash housekeeper. Her ability lies in making sure everything on the vast estate runs like clockwork. It didn't take long for her to become my mother's right-hand woman. I don't know how she does it, but she manages to be a cross between cheery grandmother and five-star general. Luckily, she took an instant liking to me and made living in this mausoleum bearable, which I know sounds crazy.

Who wouldn't enjoy living in a mansion with every conceivable luxury at their fingertips?

I guess the answer would be me.

"Sorry, I'm running a little late." More like I was hoping to slip inside the house unnoticed right before the party began without having to deal with Elaine. She'll be fluttering around like a manic butterfly, making sure everything is carefully arranged to her meticulous specifications.

"Your gown has been pressed and is waiting upstairs in the bedroom."

"Thank you, Mrs. Folly. I appreciate it."

She nods before bustling off down the long stretch of marble corridor where the bar is located. A few guys decked out in black and white formalwear are busy checking the liquor and polishing stemware.

I hurry up the sweeping staircase to the second floor and swing a left on the landing before reaching my bedroom. Once inside, I find the gown Mrs. Folly was talking about hanging in a clear plastic bag on the closet door. I drop my purse on the bed before gravitating to the garment.

I'm almost afraid of what my mother picked out. If I know her—and I do—it'll be something tight and clinging, which is exactly what she enjoys wearing. The only problem is that we don't have the same body type. Elaine is petite, barely reaching five foot three. She's more china doll-like with big blue eyes and thick, ash-colored blonde hair. She's been a size six her entire life. Even though I'm only a couple inches taller, our bodies couldn't be more different. I'm curvier with big boobs and an ass.

I'm also someone who enjoys consuming food.

When I'm not in her presence, that is.

I pull off the plastic wrapper to inspect the gown. It's a beautiful V-neck A-line champagne colored dress that glitters under the lights. There's a long slit on the left side. Matching heels have been set out along with jewelry. It goes without saying that I will be all but poured into this garment. It's doubtful I'll be able to breathe for the next few hours.

With a huff, I strip off everything except my thong. There's no way the bra I wore will fit under the dress. Upon closer inspection, it appears the bodice has a built-in shelf. I suppose that's better than nothing.

Although not by much.

It takes several attempts to zip up the back. I have to suck everything in and hold my breath. Then I slip my feet into the heels, add the sparkling diamond necklace and matching earrings, and head into the en suite to touch up my makeup and give my hair a few more waves. With one final adjustment to my boobs, I leave the safety of my bedroom behind.

Reaching the open gallery on the second floor that overlooks the foyer, I pause and survey the already thick crowd. A babble of voices greets my ears as the front door opens and a handful of couples stroll inside. They're immediately greeted by a waiter holding a silver tray of crystal champagne flutes. The women help themselves as the men head for the bar where the stronger stuff is being served.

With my hand wrapped around the iron banister, I carefully descend to the first floor. Elaine and Garret stand sentinel in the entryway, greeting their guests with welcoming smiles. I hear mention of the silent auction taking place in one of the other rooms.

For a moment, I study her. It's obvious that Mom is in her element. Both the curve of her lips and the excitement dancing in her eyes are genuine. I don't doubt that she loves Garret, but would she be just as content with him if he didn't have a fat portfolio or a beautiful mansion she gets to call home?

I think we all know the answer to that one.

Her gaze flickers to mine as I arrive on the last tread. Rather gracefully, she lifts a slender arm to wave me over. Air gets clogged in my throat as I reluctantly close the distance between us. I can practically feel the heat of her gaze running over the length of me, assessing what she finds, mentally cataloguing the flaws on display. Not once does her expression falter. She's a pro at masking her inner thoughts behind a pleasant façade.

She makes introductions and I'm asked a handful of surface level questions regarding college and potential career paths. After about ten minutes, the couple I've been conversing with departs, wanting to check out the silent auction items. Garret kisses me on the cheek before taking off for a refill on his scotch. As soon as I wrap up this little convo with Mom, I also plan on dulling the pain with an alcoholic beverage. I'll Uber it home if it's necessary.

"Hello, darling." She air kisses both cheeks, careful not to make contact. God forbid she smudge her lipstick.

"Hi, Mom."

She steps back just enough to give me another once over. "I saw that gown while out shopping and knew it would be perfect with your coloring." Her gaze flickers to mine before dropping to my breasts, which are on full display. "Although, it does seem a tad snug."

It takes everything I have inside to resist the urge to tug at the bodice. "Oxygen is overrated, right?"

She pats my cheek. "You're so amusing. Perhaps I'll book us a week at that amazing spa in Arizona over Christmas break. I think we could both use a gentle cleanse to flush out all the poisonous toxins and impurities." She gives me a knowing look as if we're co-conspirators. "It'll also be beneficial in shedding some of this excess water weight."

"Ahhh..." The thought of spending a full week confined with my mother for company is a fate worse than death. I give my head a violent little shake. "I'm not sure that'll work, but thanks for the offer."

She waves a manicured hand in the air between us. "Nonsense. It'll do wonders for your complexion."

Actually, the only thing it will end up doing is bringing on a massive case of self-loathing.

Been there, done that. Bought the T-shirt for posterity.

"As amazing as that sounds, I might have a project to work on. I'm not sure."

One perfectly sculpted brow rises. I'm shocked those muscles even work with all the Botox and fillers that have been injected. "Over Christmas break?"

"Maybe," I mumble as inspiration strikes. "For extra credit."

"Hmmm. I suppose we can discuss it another time."

I really hope not.

Just as I'm about to make up an excuse to flee, the front door opens and another couple walks in. A smile magically appears on Mom's face as she waves them over.

I plaster fake happiness across my features as they stop to greet us.

"Hello, so good to see you again! Jeremy and Anne, correct?"

The older man nods before slipping his arm around the woman at his side. My guess is that she's at least twenty years younger. What I've discovered is that it's not an uncommon age gap in these circles. The men continue to get older, and the women get increasingly younger. And more plastic looking. Although, this one looks significantly less fake than my mother.

"And this is my son—"

My gaze collides with familiar dark eyes.

"Crosby." The name slips free on a surprised gasp.

Mom's attention bounces between us. "I take it you two know each other?"

It takes effort to look away from him. He's the last person I expected to see this evening. Other than a handful of guests I'd met at their wedding, I hadn't anticipated knowing anyone.

"Yes," I say. "We both attend Western."

Mom nods before extending a hand for Crosby to shake. "Delighted to meet you."

As he smiles, his lip ring glints beneath the crystal chandelier. It's a little mesmerizing. I'm instantly flooded with memories of what it felt like when he kissed me.

"Same. It's obvious where Brooke gets her beauty from."

I almost choke out a laugh when he lifts her hand to his lips and brushes a kiss against her knuckles. Even more surprising is the light blush that blooms in Mom's cheeks. Crosby dazzles her with one of his patented panty-dropper smiles before setting her free.

It's so tempting to roll my eyes.

Who knew Crosby Rhodes could turn on the charm to this degree?

Certainly not me.

Until very recently, I've only been treated to surly and moody with a side of asshole. This is an entirely different animal all together.

A far more dangerous animal.

His attention returns to me before sweeping down my length as our parents chat about their golf games and future trips to the Bahamas. I had no idea they were even acquainted.

Although, why would I?

It's not like I've ever mentioned Crosby before. For the most part, I've done my best to pretend he didn't exist.

That's no longer possible.

His fingers close around my elbow before he carefully leads me away from the group. Garret returns just as we disappear through the elegantly attired crowd toward a room where there are fewer people milling around.

"You look gorgeous. That dress," he whispers against my ear, "is fucking spectacular."

Heat fills my cheeks. It's on the tip of my tongue to admit that it's cutting off my circulation. Instead I say, "Thank you."

"You're welcome."

I give him a bit of side-eye. "You look pretty handsome yourself."

What is it about a good-looking man in a tux?

Add the lip ring, and he's ridiculously sexy. I'm certainly not the only one who's noticed. We've only been here for a handful of minutes, and already I can feel the hungry gazes tracking his progress throughout the room. It's like these women are tigers stalking prey.

My attention slips to the silver hoop. I wish I could stop thinking about what it felt like when we kissed. Or how much I'd like to feel it again. I force myself to look up, only to find a smirk lifting his lips and a dark intensity filling his eyes.

The combination is enough to have my belly hollowing out in response.

Before I can blink, he swallows up the distance until his warm breath can ghost across the outer shell of my ear. "I've given you a couple of days, but I couldn't stay away any longer. Have you given any more thought to our conversation?"

Unfortunately, I've been able to think about little else since we spoke in the school parking lot. And since I had a test to study for yesterday, that was a problem.

As I open my mouth to tell him that it's not a good idea for us to get involved, we're interrupted by two couples. The men slap Crosby on the back and ask about Western's prospects in the playoffs, while their wives boldly eat him up with their eyes.

After about ten minutes, I decide it's time to circulate and extricate myself from the group. With one last glance over my shoulder, I leave the handsome football player behind. After ninety minutes of talking, my cheeks hurt from the smile plastered across my face and I'm in desperate need of a break.

With a few waves in greeting, I navigate my way through the thick congestion of people before slipping into the kitchen where the caterers are working their magic, and I take the back staircase to the second floor. Once inside the peace and quiet of my room, I collapse against the door. It's a relief to finally be alone. If only for a few minutes to clear my head and regroup.

I've been here for less than two hours and I'm exhausted. I'd like nothing more than to change into my clothes and sneak away. Although, if I do that, Elaine will notice my absence and remark upon it. I'll give it another hour or so, and then I'm out of here.

Whether she approves or not.

As far as I'm concerned, I've done my due diligence.

A sigh escapes from my lips as I gravitate toward the French doors that lead out to a private balcony and rest my forehead against the cool glass. Now that it's almost winter, the trees in the expansive backyard have been tightly wrapped with burlap. The heated pool has been closed for the season, and the patio furniture has been moved into storage.

One more semester, I remind myself. And then I'll be free to make my own decisions. Mom won't be able to control me so easily if I can pay my own way. I have an idea of what my salary will be once I graduate and start working. It's not great, but it'll certainly be enough to live on.

Frugally.

In a tiny apartment.

I'm knocked from those thoughts when the bedroom door creaks open, and Crosby slips silently inside. He has the same look in his eyes that he had downstairs.

It's one that sends my belly into freefall.

25

CROSBY

*I*t might have taken me a while to untangle myself from the growing group of people before sweeping the first floor and poking around upstairs, but I finally found her.

Alone.

I've been dying to get my hands on Brooke since I walked in earlier and caught sight of her. I wasn't lying when I said she looked gorgeous. That dress is killer and does amazing things for her body. In the year and a half I've known her, this is the first time I've seen Brooke wear something so revealing. I almost hate that she's wearing it in front of all these lecherous old men.

When we were together earlier, I caught a number of them eyeing her up like she had the potential to be their next sugar baby. I gave them hard stares in return. If I could have bared my teeth and growled, I would have. Most quickly turned away. A few smiled smugly in challenge.

Over my dead fucking body.

Her eyes widen as she swings around. "How did you find me?"

I shrug before pushing away from the door and eating up the distance between us. "I figured you probably needed a break." I stick two fingers beneath the collar of my shirt and pull it away from my neck. It feels like I'm being strangled to death. "I wanted one as well."

The corners of her lips twitch as her expression softens. "There'd been quite a crowd gathered around you when I left."

I lift a brow. "You mean when you deserted me?""

The smile grows. "Oh, come on. I'm sure you're used to it by now. You seemed just fine amongst your adoring fans."

I almost snort.

Most of the men had wanted to discuss football along with my prospects for the NFL, while a few bolder women squeezed my bicep and cooed over my muscles before inquiring if I'd be interested in making some money on the side as a personal trainer.

I'm willing to bet they weren't interested in my lifting regimen.

"A couple of those *adoring fans* had the audacity to stuff their numbers in my pocket." I shake my head before shoving my hand inside my pants and pulling out three different slips of paper. Without looking at them, I crumple the tiny sheets in my fist before walking to the wastepaper basket near the desk and tossing them inside.

"Aww, poor baby," she mocks with a pout. "Being a celebrity is so tough."

"Yup," I say with a grin, because I'm well aware I have nothing to bitch about. Being swamped by fans comes with the territory.

Now that we're alone, I allow my gaze to linger and really soak her in the way I wasn't able to downstairs. "I did mention earlier that you look gorgeous, right?"

"Yes, you did."

The way her sharp teeth sink into her plump lower lip makes my dick stir. It's been difficult to control my lust all evening, but what other choice was there? Walking around with a raging boner certainly wasn't an option. There were a few times I had to mentally run through our playbook in an attempt to focus on something else.

Her fingers flutter to the bodice before giving it a slight tug. If she's not careful, her breasts will spill from their confines. Not that I would mind, but still...

"Elaine picked it out."

I should thank her for having such excellent taste. "She did a phenomenal job."

"It's a little tight," she says, pulling again at the top.

"No, it's perfect."

She's perfect. I only wished she realized it.

"I'm pretty sure my mother did it on purpose so I wouldn't be able to eat."

A mixture of sorrow and embarrassment flickers in her eyes before it's quickly shuttered away. If I hadn't been watching her so carefully, I would have missed the emotions. Brooke might not realize it, but I've always been standing by, watching. Even when she belonged to someone else.

Before I can overthink my decision, I close the remaining distance between us until I'm able to lay my hands on her cheeks and angle her head until she has no other choice but to meet my steady gaze.

"You're perfect just the way you are. There's nothing about you that needs to be altered. Whatever issues your mom has, they're hers alone, not yours. Do you understand me?"

She searches my eyes carefully, as if trying to discern if I'm being truthful or feeding her a line of bullshit. Hopefully, with enough time, I'll be able to prove my trustworthiness.

"You're built like a fucking goddess," I add when she remains silent, "and if you want me to drop to my knees and worship at your feet, I'll do it."

When her eyes widen, I release her cheeks before sinking to the floor.

"Crosby," she says in a choked-out whisper. "What are you doing? Get up!" Her face turns beet red as she tugs at my arm.

"Nope. I want you to understand just how serious I am. You have no idea how much I fucking love your curves. They're all I can think about." I place my hands on her hips before sweeping them upward until my thumbs are able to brush against the outer edges of her breasts. "You have no idea how damn sexy you are, do you?"

I allow them to trail down again over the sparkly fabric until my left hand arrives at the slit in the gown. When I slip beneath it to stroke her thigh, a needy whimper escapes from her.

Goddamn, but she feels like silk. My fingers drift to the elastic of her panties before trailing to her calf and gliding upward for a second time. Her underwear is hardly more than a scrap of material barring the most intimate part of her. It's so damn tempting to tear it away until she's bared to my sight. With my gaze locked on hers, I slip two fingers inside the thin band and caress the soft skin beneath.

Her breath hitches, getting clogged in her throat as she flattens against the French door she'd been staring out when I'd stepped inside the room. Her palms are pressed against the glass. I'd much rather they tunnel through my hair or draw me closer.

"You never answered my question." Not once do I stop exploring her flesh. Back and forth my fingers strum as her pupils dilate, the blackness all but swallowing up the forest green.

"Question?" She gulps.

A smile hovers around the corners of my lips. "Whether or not you'll forgive me so we can move forward."

"Oh." She drags a lungful of air into her body before forcing it out again. "Right."

When she lapses into silence, I grow impatient. "There's something here, Brooke. Don't you feel it when we're together?" My fingertips sink into the suppleness of her hips to add emphasis to the question.

"Yes."

Good.

I don't know what I would have done if she'd said she felt nothing. There would be no choice but to prove what a liar she is.

"Give me a chance to show you I'm not that guy. That I never was that guy."

Maybe it's unfair to touch her all the while demanding answers, but I don't give a damn. I'll play dirty and do what's necessary to make her mine.

She presses her lips together as I loosen my grip, continuing to stroke my hands over her. I graze her inner thigh, once again coming dangerously close to her pussy. Her eyelids grow heavy, and her breathing turns ragged as I torment her.

Or maybe I'm the one being tortured.

It's difficult to discern.

This girl has always driven me crazy. The more I touch her, the more desire is ignited within me. It no longer feels possible to push this desperation to a place where I can ignore its existence and pretend it isn't consuming every part of me.

Her tongue darts out to moisten her lips as fear flickers across her expression. "Crosby…"

"What, baby?"

"I couldn't bear it if you hurt me again."

Even though her words are little more than a forced whisper, it's enough to send a tidal wave of shame crashing over me. "I swear to you that I won't." I can only hope to God it's a promise I can keep.

Unable to resist the temptation any longer, I sweep my fingers beneath the material to graze her slit. A fine tremble wracks her body, and I have to stop myself from raising her leg and draping it over my shoulder.

Instead of delving in the way I want to, I slip my fingers free before wrapping my hands around her hips and pulling her forward until I can bury my face against her heat. For one blissful moment, I breathe in the sweet scent of her before pressing my lips against the silky material covering her pussy.

Unwilling to take it any further, I rise to my feet until she has to crane her neck in order to hold my gaze. What I love most is that I'm the one who put that dazed expression on her face.

"I want to spend time with you after this." I kiss one corner of her mouth before giving the other side the same treatment. "Are you up for that?"

When she only continues to stare, I nip at her lower lip, sucking the fullness into my mouth before releasing it with a soft pop. "Hmmm?"

"Yes."

Everything rioting inside me calms, knowing that tonight won't end with this fundraiser.

"Good. You should probably get back downstairs before Elaine realizes you've gone missing."

With a quick kiss against her lips, I give her a little nudge toward the bedroom door.

She stumbles forward on her heels before throwing a heavy-lidded look over her bare shoulder. It takes every ounce of self-control not to stop her from walking away.

It's only when she slips through the door that I release the pent-up breath in my lungs and begin the silent countdown until I can once again lay my hands on her.

26

BROOKE

Nerves tap dance up and down my spine as I glance in the rearview mirror and find Crosby's Mustang trailing a couple of car lengths behind my Volkswagen. My fingers tighten around the steering wheel in an odd concoction of anticipation and anxiety.

What is it about him that gets to me?

That burrows beneath my skin like an itch I can't quite scratch. The attraction I've felt for him has always been there, forever simmering beneath the surface. It was so much easier to keep him at bay when I thought he was just an arrogant player with a massive case of the assholes.

Crosby Rhodes is turning out to be different from what I assumed. And I can't decide if that's a good thing or not. What I do know is that I'm horny as hell. The kiss we shared the other night coupled with what happened in my bedroom has sent my hormones into a frenzy. Even thinking about what it felt like to stand pressed against the French doors while he'd been on his knees, slowly running his hands up and down my body has heat flooding my panties and my core tightening with need.

Has anyone ever taken their time to carefully stoke the flames of my desire?

Most of the guys I've been with were out for one thing, and it was like a race to the finish line to get there.

For them.

For me, it ended in inevitable disappointment.

I get the feeling that sex with Crosby would be like nothing I've ever experienced before.

By the time I pull up in front of the building, I'm a jittery mess. Once I cut the engine, I gather up my clothes and purse from the passenger seat. By the time I turn around, Crosby is there, yanking open the driver's side door and reaching for my hand.

Not once does he release me as we make our way to the entrance. When I slip the key into the lock, he pulls the handle and holds the door. A group of giggling girls trails in after us as we wait for the elevator.

From the corner of my eye, I watch them check out Crosby. I can't blame them for their interest. He's ridiculously handsome in his tux. Tall. Muscular. Broad in the shoulders with a tapered waist. There's a lot of whispering amongst them as the elevator doors trap us inside together.

The boldest one flashes him a smile. In response, he slips his arm around my waist before tugging me against him and leisurely trailing his other hand up and down my spine. That's all it takes for their quiet chatter to fade away. Once we reach my floor, the doors open, and he practically drags me into the hallway.

"Alone at last," he mutters under his breath.

I can't help the smile that springs to my lips. "Oh come on, I'm sure you must be used to all the attention."

When he gives me a mock glare, I add, "Older women slipping their numbers into your pocket, coeds trying desperately to snag your attention... Just another normal night in the life of Crosby Rhodes, right?"

Before I can unleash any more teasing comments, he swings

around and sweeps me off my feet. A squeak of protest escapes from me as my arms slip around his neck.

"Crosby! What are you doing?"

"What does it look like?" There's barely a pause before he answers his own question. "I'm carrying you to your apartment."

It only takes a handful of steps to reach my door. When he holds out his hand for the key, I give it to him without protest. After he shoves the thin metal into the lock and twists the handle, I'm brought inside. Darkness swallows us up as he closes the door. Silvery fingers of moonlight slant through the windows in the living room but don't touch the entryway.

Even though I'm enjoying the closeness, I force myself to say, "You can put me down now."

"What if I don't want to?" he shoots back. "What if I want to keep you tucked safely in my arms."

His softly spoken words break down the last of my resistance as I give into the urge to tunnel my fingers through his dark strands, pushing them away from his forehead and looking my fill.

It goes without saying that Crosby has a gorgeous face. Arresting, really, with eyes that are nearly black. If I'm not careful, I'll end up drowning in their inky depths. Thick brows and angular cheekbones that lead to a strong, prominent jawline complete the picture.

My gaze unconsciously drops to the lip ring.

This obsession I have with it is ridiculous, but that doesn't make it any less true. When his tongue peeks out to play with the thin slice of metal, liquid heat pools in my core.

"You like it, don't you?"

There's no need to ask what he's talking about.

"Yes."

Every time I'm around him, I find my attention getting snagged by the little silver hoop. The urge to run my fingers over the ring or kiss him so I can feel the smooth slide against my skin thrums through me. Just thinking about it has goosebumps breaking out across my flesh.

He must feel my reaction, because his arms tighten as he presses me closer until I can feel all of his steely strength. Arousal ricochets through my body, lighting up every nerve ending.

I don't think I've ever wanted another guy more. Even though I'm not entirely sure if I trust him, I understand what's going to happen tonight. It feels like there has been a combustible energy brewing between us for as long as we've known each other and only now has it turned explosive.

Instead of fighting against the inevitable, my fingers slip to the nape of his neck, drawing him closer until I can feel the heat of his breath drifting across my lips. That's all the coaxing it takes for his mouth to descend.

The moment we collide, I open, wanting to feel the velvety softness of his tongue as it mingles and dances with my own. Our mouths stay fused for an endless amount of time. No one has ever kissed me quite so thoroughly or deeply. The way he consumes me, drinking in every part, is like a revelation.

It only makes me realize how truly dissatisfied I've been all these years and how much I crave his long, drawn-out kisses and the soft caresses against my bare flesh. I'm all but starving for him.

He pulls away enough to ask, "Which room is yours?"

When I point to the one on the left, Crosby stalks toward the open door with me held securely in his arms. Once inside the dark space, another kiss unfolds. He devours me one sigh at a time until I'm squirming against him, needy for more.

Needy for everything he's willing to give.

He only breaks contact long enough to lower me to the floor until my heels are firmly planted on the carpet. My heart pounds a painful staccato against my ribcage as I take a shaky step in retreat.

"Where do you think you're going?"

Instead of answering, one hand slips behind me before finding the zipper that lies against the curve of my spine. His gaze stays pinned to mine as I gradually drag it down the length of my back. Other than our breathing, the grind of the little metal teeth is the only sound that fills the room. The sparkly fabric loosens from around my body.

Once I reach my lower back, the gown falls away, revealing my breasts as it pools around my waist before eventually puddling at my feet. Even though it's tempting to glance away and cover my bare breasts, I keep my arms firmly at my sides and allow Crosby to silently look his fill. I can almost feel the heat of his gaze as it licks over every dip and curve of my naked flesh. The only piece of clothing shielding me from his view is a thong that barely covers anything.

It takes effort to draw in a shaky breath. It's probably the first one I've taken since zipping up that gown.

"You're so fucking perfect I almost can't stand it," he growls.

Pleasure floods through me. There has never been a time in my life when I felt perfect. It's always been the opposite. My mother's voice has been a constant chirp in my ear since I was twelve years old and slammed headfirst into puberty. No matter how hard I try, eradicating a decade of her passive aggressive comments from my brain has been nearly impossible.

For some reason, I believe Crosby when he says I'm beautiful. There's a certain look a man gets in his eyes when he's admiring an attractive woman, and that's exactly the way he's staring at me.

"I've dreamed about this moment for years," he says, moving forward.

When he's close enough, his hands rise to cup my breasts. A little sigh of pleasure escapes from me as he palms my flesh, squeezing the soft weight as if attempting to learn the shape and feel of them. It doesn't take long for my nipples to stiffen into hard little points. Each pinch has an arrow of pure arousal shooting to my core before exploding like a firework.

Just when it feels like my knees will turn to jelly, he forces me toward the queen-sized bed in the middle of the room. The backs of my knees hit the mattress before I'm falling onto the softness.

Straightening to his full height, he takes a moment to stare down at me. One hand rises to scratch the stubble that covers both his chin and cheeks. "Do you have any idea how sexy you look with your hair spread out around you like a fucking halo? You're like an angel. One I can't wait to dirty up."

His words detonate another round of explosions deep inside me as I squirm beneath his penetrating stare. I've never wanted sex with anyone the way I do with him. It feels like years of buildup have culminated into this single, crystalline moment.

The longer he stares, the more restless I become for his touch.

A knowing look enters his eyes as he loosens the tie from around his neck. "You're all but crying for it, aren't you?"

Is there any point in denying the accusation?

"Yes." Unable to help myself, I shift against the comforter as need pumps through every fiber of my being. The way he watches me makes my skin feel feverish and tight. It's as if something is scratching beneath the surface, attempting to claw its way out. I'm almost frightened of the need he'll unleash within me.

"Good. I want you to fucking crave me the way I've always craved you. You need to understand that there was never a time I didn't feel this way."

His large hands settle on my thighs and squeeze the flesh beneath. The tips of his fingers sink into me before his grip loosens and he slides them upward, grazing my hip bones and dancing across my ribcage until he can once again cup my breasts. He palms the warm flesh, stroking and tweaking the nipples. It doesn't take long for them to turn achy.

We've barely begun, and this encounter already feels different. He takes his time to carefully stoke the flames of my desire and breathe life into what he alone has kindled inside me. With his hands cupping the outer sides of my breasts, he brings them together before leaning down and sucking one taut peak between his lips. He draws me deep into the warm confines of his mouth before allowing me to pop free so he can give the same ardent attention to the other side. My eyelids feather shut as I enjoy the feel of him tugging at the firm flesh. The metal of his lip ring grazes my skin, and a thousand shivers reverberate throughout my being. It's such a foreign sensation and I love it. I have no idea how I'll ever get enough.

He seems to realize the thoughts running rampant through my head.

His lips curve against my flesh as my fingers tunnel through his hair, raking across his scalp in an attempt to tug him closer. There's so much unrestrained desire coursing through me. As he licks and sucks at one bud, his fingers toy with the other. I writhe helplessly beneath him, lost in a sea of sensation, as my thong floods with arousal.

Just when I don't think I can stand another second of this sweet torture, he drifts along my body, kissing and nipping his way down the middle of my ribcage until he reaches my belly button. His progression is slow and steady, specifically designed to force me closer to the brink.

When his fingers hover over the elastic band of my panties, he glances up so that our gazes can collide. My body trembles with all the need I've spent years trying to tamp down. I don't think I've ever felt this kind of combustible energy rush through my veins, lighting me up from the inside out.

I've been turned on before, but it's never been to this degree. It feels like a living, breathing entity that will consume me in one tasty gulp if I allow it to.

"How much do you want this?" The deep scrape of his voice has my belly hollowing out.

"So much."

His gaze never falters as he presses a kiss against my lower abdomen. He's so close to the part of me that's crying for him...

"That's not good enough. I want to hear you say the words."

"Crosby," I whimper, shifting impatiently beneath him, anxious for his touch. Already, I know it will be masterful. Commanding. And that's exactly what I want.

What I need.

"Answer me."

I groan and reach for the comforter, twisting my fingers into the soft fabric. "I want this—*you*—more than I've ever wanted anything else. I feel like I'll die if you don't touch me."

Satisfaction flashes in his dark eyes. It's not smug, like he's just won a prize. More like relief that we're on the same page. "I'm glad to hear that, because I refuse to take you unless you're there with me all the way."

His words send a burning arrow of lust straight to my core, where it bursts into a million little sparks of fire.

"I want you, Crosby." My tongue darts out to moisten my lips as I force out the rest. "I want you to fuck me."

A powerful concoction of heat and desire ignites in his eyes, eclipsing all other emotion.

He tugs the material down a few inches until the top of my slit is exposed. Cool air rushes over my delicate flesh as he presses a kiss against me.

Oh god.

The gentle pressure of his mouth is like heaven. There's the barest press of metal against my pussy before it disappears.

"I'm going to take these off now."

I nod, eager for him to strip me bare. In the past, getting naked with a guy for the first time was always shrouded in uncertainty and embarrassment. Bearing yourself to someone new requires a certain amount of trust and vulnerability. No matter how much I attempted to shove the negative thoughts from my head, I was always left holding my breath, wondering what they thought.

Did they like what they saw?

I don't feel that way with Crosby. The questions and discomfort that usually clutter my mind are absent. I can tell by the flames crackling in his eyes that he's turned on.

His fingers slip beneath the fabric before lowering it one painstaking inch at a time. A scream builds in my lungs as I wait for him to finally rip them free. His attention stays locked on my center until I can feel the burn of his gaze on my bare skin.

It's as if he's leisurely unwrapping a Christmas present and wants to savor each second of the experience, prolonging the excitement until it becomes excruciating. He slides the material down my hips and over my thighs before tugging off the thong and tossing it over his shoulder, where it sails carelessly to the carpet.

Now that I'm completely bare, I tremble beneath the intensity of his stare as it drifts over every inch. There's something strangely erotic about being stripped naked while he looms over me, fully dressed in a crisp looking tux.

"I know I've said it before," he murmurs more to himself than to me, "but you're the most beautiful woman I've ever laid eyes on." His gaze flickers to mine before dropping to my core.

Reaching out, he caresses my inner thighs with strong hands. Back and forth, his calloused palms scrape against me.

Air clogs my throat as he lowers himself to the floor until his warm breath can ghost across my core. My teeth sink into my lower lip to keep the anticipation trapped inside. Seconds tick by before the velvety softness of his tongue makes contact, stroking over me, running from the bottom of my slit to the top where he circles my clit with the tip. A groan works its way loose as my eyelids feather closed. A series of fireworks explodes behind them in a colorful array. There's absolutely nothing rushed about what he's doing. It's as if he has all the time in the world for discovery. And that's exactly what it feels like. An exploration as his tongue dances over every delicate inch.

Unable to help myself, my body twists. His hands lock around my inner thighs, the fingertips sinking into the muscle, pinning me in place as he works my delicate flesh, forcing me closer to the edge.

A whimper escapes from me as I arch against him. His tongue dips inside before taking a long, leisurely lap of my pussy. My muscles tighten as arousal builds, ratcheting up in intensity. It only takes one more stroke of his tongue against my clit and I'm splintering apart beneath his firm hold. The cry tears from my lips as he continues to feast on my flesh, licking and sucking until I'm dizzy with the sensation. Until it feels like I'll burst right out of my skin. He doesn't stop until every drop has been wrung from my over sensitized body. Until all I can do is lie there, a limp mess, breathing hard as I stare sightlessly at the ceiling. Nothing I've experienced to this point has ever felt so cataclysmic. As if it were a spiritual awakening rather than a sexual one.

That thought is enough to leave me smirking. Of course I've heard the whispers around campus regarding Crosby's prowess.

Who hasn't?

He's legendary with the ladies at Western.

What I can now tell you from personal experience is that it's all true. Not only is the man talented on the football field but in this department as well.

And the lip ring...

Another shudder spirals through me.

I'm knocked from those hazy thoughts when he crawls up my body and hovers over me until our gazes can lock. Arousal lights his dark eyes as he presses his lips to mine. I open, and our tongues slide against each other.

"Do you taste your sweetness on me?"

My breath catches as I nod.

"Fucking delicious," he growls.

His tongue darts out again, moving in tandem with my own.

"I don't know how I'll ever get enough of you."

My belly hollows out as fresh desire explodes inside me.

"Are you ready for more?"

The thought of there being more is dizzying. Before I can respond, his heavy weight disappears, and he rises to his feet. A shiver courses through me as his fingers settle on the loosened tie around his neck before dragging it from the collar. After it's been dispatched, he works on the buttons, setting them free one at a time. Slowly, the crisp white fabric parts, revealing a snowy-colored T-shirt beneath. The starched dress shirt gets discarded before the undershirt is yanked over his head and he's left standing before me bare-chested with just the black trousers.

Every line of Crosby's body is hard and sculpted. I can only imagine the hours he spends in a gym to look like this.

He grabs something from the pocket before unfastening the black leather belt and unsnapping the button. My heartbeat kicks up a notch as the zipper is slowly lowered. There's a grind of metallic teeth before the pants are forced past his hips and down muscular thighs.

Shoes are toed off as socks get removed and then, finally, he's left in black boxer briefs.

Need crashes over me before settling in my core as I take in his masculine form. He makes an impressive figure, standing with his legs braced apart. Eyes locked on mine, he rips the square packet with his teeth before pulling out the condom and sheathing his rock-hard length in a thin layer of latex. One knee settles on the bed as he crawls up my body before aligning the head of his cock with my entrance.

I steel myself, prepared for him to drive inside me with one hard thrust. After all, he took his time and made sure that I came. Now, it's his turn to get off.

With the tip of his dick poised at my entrance, he stills. "Are you sure about this?"

Time grinds to a halt as he studies me. After a few seconds of intense scrutiny, I squirm beneath him as he continues to hold himself motionless.

With his obsidian-colored eyes fastened on mine, I realize how much I want this to happen. "Yes."

He nods once. "Okay."

When he finally moves, his strokes are shallow and measured. Even though I've just experienced the most intense orgasm of my life, desire is already stirring deep inside me as I lift my hips, attempting to meet his tempered thrusts. Instead of sliding further inside my body the way I crave, he holds back, making me ache for more. It feels as if I'm being carefully caressed from the inside out, and nothing has ever felt so good.

His face looms inches above me as his bulging biceps cage me in, surrounding me with his strength until it feels as if no one exists outside this bedroom. Every muscle strains. Each flex of his hips is purposeful. Powerful. He grits his teeth, the muscle in his jaw ticking as he deepens the thrusts. Pleasure ripples inside me, fanning outward. Even though we've just begun, I realize that it won't take much to force me over the edge.

"I want you to come with me," he growls.

I want that, too. It's not something I've experienced with another partner. By the time we have sex, they're usually so turned on, they go off like a shot. It's never mattered if I'm not quite there.

His warm breath mingles with my own until we're breathing one another in. I don't think I've ever felt this connected during sex. And it's never been this intimate. It feels like there's an invisible string linking us so that our bodies are in perfect harmony. In this moment, I am the yin to his yang and vice versa.

Balancing on one arm, he slips a hand between our bodies until the blunt pads of his fingers find my clit and are able to gently rub. My eyes widen and my mouth opens when he gives me a little pinch.

That little maneuver is all it takes for me to come unhinged, and my inner muscles contract around him.

"Fuck," he hisses, slipping his hand from between us and bracing himself on both elbows as his thrusts turn demanding.

My eyes stay locked on him as he throws back his head. Have I ever seen anything as beautiful as Crosby in the throes of orgasm?

He truly looks like the god people claim he is.

The thick muscles of his throat constrict as a low, guttural groan tears from his lips. His hips piston, rocking against me as his cock swells. The moment seems to last forever as his pelvis grinds against my clit, giving me sparks of pleasure. For the first time, I wish there were nothing between us and I could feel his cum painting my womb.

This will be a memory I tuck away in the back of my head and take out when I'm alone.

With a low growl, he collapses on top of me before burying his face in the hollow of my neck until his warm breath can feather across my flesh. My heart thumps a steady beat, filling my ears as the silence of the room settles around us. And still, I feel his cock pulsing inside me as it gradually softens.

After a long stretch of moments, he picks up his head until our gazes can fasten. Air gets clogged in my throat wondering what I'll find. It's entirely possible that this was a one and done kind of thing. Sure, he flattered me with a bunch of pretty words, but who knows?

Clearly, I'm not the best judge of character.

If that turns out to be the case, I'll be fine with it. The orgasm—both of them—were much too delicious to regret even for a second.

"You realize that you belong to me now, right?"

My belly hollows out as I open my mouth. Before I'm able to respond, he swoops in for a kiss.

That's all it takes for any protests to die a quick death on my tongue.

27

CROSBY

I glance at the girl sleeping soundly next to me. Something about her deep and even breathing calms everything that normally rages within. Her caramel-colored hair is spread out across the snowy white pillowcase. She really does look like an angel. Tearing my eyes away feels impossible.

After we had sex—for the second time—she fell asleep curled up in my arms almost immediately. Even though I want to be smug about exhausting her, it's the last thing on my mind. I can't stop thinking about what a fucking mess this has turned into. It's one I have no idea how to solve.

How ironic is it that I finally have the girl of my dreams, and now there's a huge secret sitting between us? One that doesn't allow me to be honest with her. I have to carefully consider everything that comes out of my mouth.

I've been lying awake for hours, going over all of it in my brain. Sure, I'm a football player, but I'm also a mechanical engineering student. I'm used to problem solving. It's part of the process.

But this particular problem?

Yeah, there's no easy solution. I've either got to reveal the truth or...

Ghost her as my alter ego. But I'm loath to do that. The last thing I want to do is inflict any more damage than I already have.

Let's just say a miracle occurs and I avoid getting booted to the curb…there's still the matter of Andrew. News that I'm with his ex will go over like a lead balloon. He'll freaking lose his mind, and it'll most likely destroy our friendship.

So…yeah.

It's a real clusterfuck.

I stare sightlessly up at the ceiling as all this swirls through my head. The only way to avoid this blowing up in my face is to walk away. But how can I do that?

The answer is that I can't. I've waited too damn long to have her, and now that I've had one small taste, there's no way I can go without. I wasn't kidding when I told her that she'd been claimed. Brooke McAdams belongs to me. I just need to figure out how to keep it that way.

She shifts and opens her eyes. Even though sleep still clouds her green depths, they stay fastened to mine.

"What time is it?" she asks, turning onto her side to face me before dragging the comforter over her shoulders and snuggling into it.

Could this girl be any more adorable?

I still as the silent question rolls around in my head before shoving it away.

"Really early."

"Is something wrong?" Some of her sleepiness falls away as her expression turns wary. "Why aren't you sleeping?"

As tempting as it is to admit the truth, I bite back the words, keeping them locked inside where they can't fuck anything up. The last thing I want to do is destroy the intimacy we just found in each other's arms.

"No reason."

As her caution recedes, she reaches out and strokes her fingertips over the hard ridges of my bare chest, skimming them across taut abdominals, before sinking south of the border.

"No reason at all?" she asks, voice dipping as one brow lifts.

Well...

I hiss out a breath when her hand settles on my dick. Up until now, it had been lying prone. Dwelling on all the lies I'm caught up in will do that to a man. As soon as she touches me, those thoughts vanish and I'm rising like a champ to the occasion.

"None I can think of," I groan.

"Hmmm. That's too bad."

Her fingers wrap around my length before slowly sliding down it. When she reaches the base, her grip intensifies before retracing her path in the opposite direction. Once she reaches the head of my cock, her fingers circle the tip. Round and round she swirls until it feels like I'll lose my damn mind.

When moisture beads the tiny slit, her fingers glide over the slickness, smoothing it into my skin. Her hold intensifies as she pumps my erection. I can't resist arching into her palm as my balls stir with the beginnings of an orgasm. I've had countless hand jobs, but none have ever affected me like this.

No one has ever affected me like this.

Just as I thrust into her hand, it loosens from around my girth before disappearing. My brows slam together as she rolls away, giving me her back.

"Sweet dreams."

What the—

I blink before realizing that she's messing with me and grab her from behind. "You little tease."

Her shoulders shake with silent laughter as I turn her toward me. A grin simmers around the corners of her mouth.

With wide eyes, she asks, "I'm sorry, is there a problem?"

A growl rumbles up from my chest as I pounce, rolling on top of her until she's pinned to the mattress. My cock nudges the entrance of her pussy, only to find it already slick with need. When she widens her legs, I sink inside her warmth. Not much. Just an inch or two.

Fuuuuck.

I've never been inside a girl without a condom, and even though it's only the tip, it feels like pure nirvana. It would be all too easy to drive deep inside, burying myself to the hilt. If only to feel her velvety softness surrounding me for one blissful moment. But if I do that, there's no way I'll be able to pull out without coming.

Knowing what needs to be done, I thrust my hips just once, sinking a little deeper inside her warmth, before slipping free. Even though we've only just begun, my breathing has turned labored as I bury my face against the crook of her neck and nip at the delicate flesh. She squeals, tilting her head as her nails dig into my back before scoring the skin.

"I need a condom," I say, as the mental fog begins to clear. "I can't be inside you without one. And I'm fresh out."

"Who said you needed to be inside me?"

I'm sorry?

I pull back enough to meet her eyes before searching them carefully in the shadowy darkness of the room. Her hands graze my back, drifting over my ass before the fingers sink into the taunt muscle.

"Slide upward."

Slide—

I pause as a fresh punch of arousal hits me full force.

She tightens her fingers around my backside, urging me into movement. I crawl up her length until I'm able to straddle her ribcage. Careful not to place my full weight on her, I balance on my knees as my cock settles in the valley between her breasts.

The sight of her stretched out beneath me with the tip of my dick a few inches from her lips is sexy as hell.

She looks so damn beautiful with her tousled hair spread out around her as she presses her breasts together until my erection is nestled between the soft flesh. I'm struck with the realization that this is exactly what I whispered to her over the phone when we both got off.

Does she realize she's intent on living out that fantasy?

Unable to hang onto the question for long, I flex my hips, sliding my hard length against her. With her gaze fastened to mine, she tucks her chin to her chest. Once the tip is within striking distance, her tongue flicks out to lick it.

Holy shit.

Unable to help myself, I repeat the maneuver. With each thrust, my body strains forward, attempting to close the distance between us until she's able to draw the crown between her lips. Tension coils tightly in every muscle as I flex my hips before pulling back.

Even though nothing can compare to the feel of her tight heat, this is pretty damn amazing. There's something erotic about this position. The way her tits are pressed against my dick as the backs of my thighs brush against her soft flesh. The heat of her mouth wrapping around my tip, drawing it inside before her tongue swirls around it.

It doesn't take long before we fall into a natural rhythm which only intensifies the arousal building within me. My balls draw up against my body as the orgasm stirs, making my cock swell and the muscles become whipcord tight.

Just when I'm about to come, I slip from between her breasts before jerking upright. My fingers tighten almost painfully around my shaft as I pump it with quick movements. The tip turns a mottled purplish hue as Brooke's arms fall to the mattress. Her breasts bounce a few times as her gaze stays locked on my throbbing erection.

Even though I want to close my eyes and allow my head to roll back so I can enjoy this, I can't stop staring at the gorgeous picture she makes sprawled beneath me. I can't stop watching as the first jets of cum erupt, painting her chest. My grip tightens until it feels like I'm on the verge of strangling my cock as the orgasm roars through me like a freight train.

I groan when she arches her back, thrusting out her tits. Pearly ropes decorate her nipples. The notion that I'm marking her skin in such a primal way only makes my dick swell more.

How is it possible she's this perfect?

It's only when I soften that my fingers loosen and a huff of breath escapes from me. Hovering over her, I close the distance between us before brushing my lips across hers. She immediately opens so that our tongues can tangle. Before I can get lost in the taste of her, I pull back and grab a couple of tissues from the nightstand to clean her off. Once her chest has been wiped, I pull her into my arms before rolling onto my back so she can sprawl out across me.

It doesn't take long before we're both drifting off to sleep.

And this time, there aren't any conflicting feelings to cloud my mind.

I'm strangely content.

Maybe for the first time in my life.

28

BROOKE

I wake with a stretch, unable to remember the last time I slept this deeply. It takes a couple of seconds for everything from last night to slam into me like a ton of bricks.

The fundraiser.

Crosby unexpectedly showing up with his parents.

Us leaving the event together.

My eyelids spring open as my head twists, only to find the bed empty and the sheets already cool to the touch. It's almost enough to make me wonder if it was all a dream. One shift against the cotton is all it takes for the dull ache between my thighs to flare to life.

Plus—

I peek cautiously under the covers, only to reconfirm my bare state. I usually sleep in panties and a tank top, not full-on naked.

So yeah…it happened.

I slept with Crosby Rhodes.

Out of all the guys on Western's campus I could have hooked up with, I never expected it to be him. Even though he apologized and explained the reasons for his behavior…

I'm still blown away.

Did I fantasize about it?

Guilty.

What red blooded female with a beating pulse at this university hasn't?

Even when I hated the guy, I couldn't stop thinking about him.

Everything happened so fast. I have no idea if us sleeping together meant anything. I know what he told me, but men will say a lot of things when they're trying to sweettalk a girl into sex.

I release a steady breath as memories of what his lip ring felt like against my clit tumble through my head. That's all it takes for a shiver of desire to dance down my spine and heat to rush to my core. If I were wearing panties, they'd already be soaked.

All right, enough of that. I need to get my head on straight where Crosby is concerned. It's probably for the best that he took off. His nearness clouds my better judgment.

Shaking away all thoughts of the sexy football player, I reach for my phone on the nightstand before scrolling through some messages and firing off a few quick responses. My gaze falls on the text convo from Chris, and I wince as a wave of guilt crashes over me, threatening to suck me under. My fingers fly over the miniature keyboard, tapping out a message.

Hey. Sorry I didn't get back to you last night.

I stare at the cell and will him to respond. There aren't even those three little dots to tell me he's typing out a reply. Last evening was the first time we've skipped talking or texting. It's only been a few weeks, but I look forward to our nightly conversations. Chris isn't like any of the other guys I've met at school, and we've become close fast. What I love most is that I can be myself and tell him anything.

Well...just about anything.

Even though I'm confused about the guy I just slept with, I don't want to lose my friendship with Chris. At the end of the day, I have no idea what to expect from Crosby.

He sleeps around and doesn't date.

Like a lot of the athletes on this campus, he seems to enjoy the perks of being a high-profile football player at Western. People treat him like a god.

Am I really willing to take a chance with another jock who's known for fucking around with groupies?

The question circles viciously in my head until my temples begin to throb.

Unable to sit still for another moment, I toss off the covers, ready to head to the bathroom for a long, hot shower. Last night was enjoyable and I refuse to regret it, but his scent is all around me, permeating the air. It clings to my skin and sheets, making it impossible to focus on anything else. As much as I hate to admit it—even privately to myself—it does strange things to my insides. What I need to do is wash it away and get a little perspective.

As I rise to my feet, a text pops up on my phone. I fall back to the mattress and drag the covers over my naked breasts before settling against the pillows.

No worries. Did you have a good time?

My teeth nibble at my lower lip as guilt and shame scald my cheeks.

How am I supposed to answer that?

It was a fundraising event at my parents' house. What do you think?

I tack on a laughing emoji and pray he doesn't dig deeper. The last thing I want to do is start off our relationship with deceit. Although technically, omissions of the truth are still considered lies. You don't have to watch reruns of *Law and Order* to understand that.

I'm knocked from those thoughts by his next question.

Sounds boring. Meet anyone interesting?

My fingers hesitate, hovering over the screen as another wave of remorse washes over me. If not for Crosby, the party would have been excruciating. And if that isn't one of the most bizarre thoughts that's ever popped into my brain, I don't know what is. If you'd asked a month ago if I'd be grateful for his presence, the answer would have been an unequivocal no.

Turns out that's no longer the case.

His growled-out words crash unwantedly through my head.

You realize that you belong to me now, right?

My belly does a little flip at the memory.

Did he mean it?

Do I even want him to?

I have no idea.

The thought makes me realize that no matter how uncomfortable the conversation, I can't hold back the truth from Chris.

I need to be honest with you.

Okay. Sounds serious.

It takes a moment to gather my courage as I carefully press each letter. Before I hit send, I suck in a breath and read over the text.

I slept with someone last night.

My nerves ratchet up to unprecedented levels as I clench the phone in my hand and wait for a reaction to the bomb I just dropped.

Oh.

That's it. That's his response. Another burst of apprehension explodes inside me.

I'm so sorry. It was after the fundraiser and just kind of...happened.

I wince. That sounds so lame.

When an immediate reply isn't forthcoming, I tap out another message.

Are you mad?

My teeth sink into my lower lip. He has every right to be upset. As stupid as it sounds, it feels like I cheated on him.

No.

I blink at the screen in surprise.

Really?

We're friends. We never made any promises to each other.

Relief rushes from my lungs in a burst of air.

It was never my intention to hurt you.

You didn't. It's all good.

My shoulders loosen. Before I can fire off anything more, another text pops up on the screen.

Do you like this guy?

For a long moment, I can only stare as the question circles through my head.

Do I?

Do I like Crosby?

It takes a few seconds to dredge my mind for an answer.

It's complicated.

Why?

Unsure how to respond, I stare across the room and force myself to be completely honest.

He's my ex's best friend. Even though the guy has always been a jerk to me, everything seems different now. I can't explain it.

Not even to myself.

You seem conflicted. Are you sure it's a good idea to get involved?

A mirthless laugh falls from my lips. Of course I'm not sure. Part of me feels like it's one of the stupidest decisions I could possibly make. But...

I don't know. He's not the person I'd assumed he was. Or maybe he's different now. The only thing I know for certain is that I can't get him out of my head. I have no idea if anything more will happen, but it doesn't feel right to lead you on after I slept with another guy. I need to figure out this situation before I do anything else. I'm sorry.

Again, there's a long stretch of silence.

No worries. We're good, okay?"

Tears sting the backs of my eyes. I hate that this feels like goodbye. I really like Chris and I've enjoyed our conversations. Maybe, if circumstances had been different, our relationship could have deepened and grown into something more. I guess we'll never know.

You're such a good guy.

I appreciate that. But I'm not the one you're thinking about, am I?

If I owe Chris anything, it's my honesty.

No.

I didn't think so. Your happiness is all that matters to me. If this guy makes you happy, then you should give it a chance.

His maturity and easy acceptance of the situation makes me feel like I'm making a terrible mistake. One that will haunt me for the rest of my life.

That's the problem. I have no idea if he's capable of giving me what I need.

The unvarnished truth is what makes me question everything.

You'll never know unless you give it a try.

My heart clenches as the finality of this conversation hits me.

Bye, Chris.

Bye, beautiful. Take care.

My fingers hover over the keyboard before deciding to leave it alone. It feels like we've said everything we needed to.

Confusion rolls over me as I set the phone on my nightstand and bury my face in my hands. Chris is such an amazing guy. If I were smart, I'd forget about Crosby and hold him at a firm distance.

But I can't do that.

Even if it means that I've just let the perfect guy slip through my fingers.

29

BROOKE

"What the hell is going on with you?"

I lift my gaze to my cousin, who is parked across from me on the other side of the table. I've got a bit of homework to finish up and Ryder is studying for a test. Since the hockey house is usually overflowing with rowdy teammates who like to party into the wee hours of the night, he dragged me to the library for a little peace and quiet. Ryder hasn't always taken his grades seriously, but that seems to have changed this year.

Which I find…interesting.

"What do you mean?"

His gaze narrows. "You keep staring at the book in front of you. We've been here for at least thirty minutes, and you haven't turned the page once. Is there something I need to know about?" He straightens on the chair. "Someone's ass I need to beat?"

Unfortunately, that's not an offhanded joke. The guy is dead serious.

There's no way in hell I'm going to tell him about Crosby. Ryder had a front row seat to my relationship with Andrew and its abrupt demise. It's only given him more ammunition to hate the football players. I would never point it out to him, but his teammates are just as bad when it comes to the groupies, and he shouldn't try to pretend otherwise.

"Is this about that guy you've been texting with? The one Sasha's worried about luring you into the sex trade?"

I roll my eyes.

Hard.

It takes effort to keep my voice light. "I'm sure you'll be thrilled to know that it fizzled out."

His expression softens. "That's probably for the best. What did you really know about him?"

Only that he was a really great guy. Probably the most decent one I've ever met. But there's no point in releasing those words into the atmosphere. That fledgling relationship is over.

What I'm loath to admit is that hours later, I can't stop wondering if I made the right decision. There have been too many times to count when I picked up the phone and scrolled through our messages as an ache grew in my heart.

Did I really choose Crosby over Chris?

Am I insane?

Unable to sit for another moment as all this churns through my head, I rise to my feet. Maybe stretching my legs will help refocus my attention.

"I'm going to get a drink of water."

He jerks his shoulders before grumbling, "I guess I'll get back to this boring-ass shit."

"If you want, I'll quiz you on it when I get back."

"Awesome." He holds his hand up before circling his finger in the air. "Yay. Can't wait."

My lips tremble around the corners as I take off. I love my cousin to death, but he's never been one to hit the books hard. It makes me curious as to what's changed. Especially since this is our last year before graduation.

As I weave my way through the stacks, both guys push their way back into my thoughts. No matter what I do, nothing banishes them for long.

Once I reach the water fountain, I grab a long drink before retracing my steps.

Just as the table I've been camped out with Ryder comes into view, strong fingers lock around my wrist. A gasp falls from my lips as I spin around before finding myself staring up into nearly black eyes framed by thick, sooty lashes.

My breath catches, getting clogged at the back of my throat.

Crosby.

I blink. It's almost as if my thoughts have conjured him up.

His grip on my wrist disappears before his fingers wrap around my upper arms, forcing me backward until my spine hits the bookshelves. Before I can say anything, his mouth crashes onto mine and metal drags across my lips as he nips at me. That's all it takes for my brain to click off as I give in, allowing myself to get swept away on a sea of sensation. His tongue delves inside to mingle with my own. There's something so dominant and commanding about the way he takes control of the situation.

Of me.

I would be lying through my teeth if I didn't admit how much I love it.

All the doubts that had been popping up in my head disappear with that one kiss. I have no idea what will happen between us, but in this moment, I realize that I need to see this through. Maybe it'll end disastrously, and I'll be chock-full of regrets, but walking away no longer feels like an option.

He pulls back just enough to growl, "I missed you today."

It takes effort to swallow down the pleasure that sparks to life within me. As much as I want to keep the words trapped deep inside and play it cool, they tumble free in a torrent.

"I missed you, too."

"I hope you realize that this morning wasn't a fuck and flee situation."

My lips quirk at the corners before I give a tiny shrug, not wanting to admit the truth. "I wasn't sure."

He angles his head, capturing my lips again before nipping at the lower one. "I assumed you wouldn't want Sasha to know I spent the night in your bed. I meant every word I said." His gaze searches mine. "You know that, right?"

A shiver of awareness scampers down my spine as I silently acknowledge that it wouldn't take much to fall into...*something* with him. And that's a scary prospect. Even though I'm mentally trying to pump the brakes and slow things down, it's not working. It feels as if I'm careening out of control. If there's one guy I should be wary of, it's Crosby Rhodes.

"Hey." His brows slant together, drawing me back to the moment. "What are you thinking about?"

I run my palms up his chest and stroke the hard muscles that lie beneath the T-shirt.

"That the situation is complicated."

He dips his head in agreement. "You're right, but that doesn't change how much I want you." There's a pause. "Or this."

I release an unsteady breath. How does he know exactly what I need to hear in order to stomp out all the questions mushrooming up inside me?

When I remain silent, he asks, "Do you feel the same way?"

I suck my lower lip into my mouth before blurting, "Yes."

As much as I wish I didn't, there's no denying the truth. I reach up onto the tips of my toes and align my mouth with his.

His rigidly held muscles loosen. "Thank fuck."

The delicate slide of metal against my lips sends an arrow of lust to my core. My tongue peeks out to lick it as my gaze remains fastened on his dark one.

"I love that the piercing turns you on."

Heat floods my cheeks. "Is it that obvious?"

He grins before pressing his body into mine until I can feel every hard line. "Yup."

A thick shudder that feels like warmed honey slides through me as I attempt to regain my bearings. I've never met anyone who has the power to knock me off balance so completely.

"Do you want to come over tonight?" I ask.

"Try to keep me away," he growls, pressing a quick kiss against my lips.

His deep voice strums something inside me and weakens my knees. The strange emotions he rouses are nothing short of addictive. All it takes is one heated look aimed in my direction and I'm going up in flames.

"What time?" he asks.

As I chew my lower lip, the minty taste of him explodes on my tongue. It has my belly hollowing out. All I can think about is delving in for more.

"Give me your number, and I'll text you after Sasha goes to bed."

One hand slips to his back pocket before stalling. "That won't work. There's something wrong with my phone." Breaking eye contact, he clears his throat. "I dropped it the other day and it's been jacked up ever since. I probably need to get it fixed. Or just get a new one."

"Oh."

"As soon as I get it figured out, I'll give it to you. Okay?"

I nod. It's a little strange, but whatever.

Before I can turn over the situation in my brain and really think about it, his head dips until he can feather his mouth against mine. "There's some homework I need to knock out. How about I stop over after eleven?"

"That should work."

"Perfect." With a grin, he jerks his head toward my cousin. "You should probably get moving."

Unable to resist, I steal one more kiss for the road before ducking out of his arms and backing away.

"I'll see you later," I say with a little wave.

His eyes darken with the same need that courses through me. "Yeah, you will."

30

CROSBY

As I push open the apartment door, a throaty groan hits my ears.

What the hell?

I make it two steps over the threshold before my gaze lands on my roommate sprawled out on the couch. His legs are spread, and his fingers are tunneled through long blonde strands as he holds the girl's head to his groin. The slurping action only solidifies what I've walked in on.

Again.

Andrew fucks around like it's his main job in life. My guess is that he's plowed his way through half the girls at this university. I don't give a shit how many chicks he screws, take it to your goddamn room. There's no reason to get it on in the middle of the living room.

I try hard not to think about the body fluids that are probably soaked into the couch.

With my lips pressed together, I keep my eyes averted and stalk to my bedroom before slamming the door shut. I'll give them five minutes to wrap this shit up and then I'm grabbing something to eat. It feels like my stomach is in the process of consuming itself.

I open my backpack and swap out a couple of books before

glancing at my phone. The plan had been to study here for a couple of hours, but for obvious reasons, those plans have changed.

Two minutes trickle by.

Fuck it.

If he doesn't care, why should I?

I grab the doorknob and yank it open, only to find the blonde now perched on Andrew's lap. Her arms are entwined around his neck as they go at it, all hot and heavy. At least this is an improvement from watching him get a BJ.

They break apart and he glances at me as I beeline for the kitchen.

"Hey, man. When did you get back?"

"Just a couple minutes ago."

"Huh." He rubs his jaw. "I didn't hear you come in."

"Yeah," I say, grabbing a Gatorade and twisting off the cap, "you seemed kind of preoccupied."

The girl grins as Andrew paws at her boob. "I couldn't help it. Cassy's the best there is, aren't you sweetheart?"

"Kelsey," she corrects with a high wattage smile that never falters.

He squeezes her again before nodding in my direction. "How's that jaw feeling? Think you can give him the same expert attention you just treated me to?"

She spears me a look from beneath a fringe of mascara-laden lashes before taking a leisurely tour down my body. Her tongue darts out to swipe at her lips as she flutters her fingers in my direction. "Hey, Crosby."

Andrew's other hand slides along her bare thigh, shoving the short skirt up until it's bunched around the juncture of her legs. "You've got such a pretty little pussy. Why don't you show him the goods, baby?"

It doesn't take any further encouragement for her to spread her legs wide. FYI—this is a girl who likes to go commando.

My gaze jerks away as Andrew uses his fingers to spread her lips.

"Mmm, don't you just want to pound that all night long?"

Not really.

"Hard pass. I've got to take off, but you have fun with that." I glance at my phone, needing to get out of here ASAP. I'll grab something to eat at the Union before chilling at the football house for a couple of hours.

I'm kicking myself for not bailing on this living situation earlier. In the beginning, the constant fucking around didn't bother me. You want to get laid—hey, go for it. Screw all you want. But I'm tired of coming home and wondering what BS I'm going to walk in on next.

At this point, all I want is to get through senior year and focus on football and my classes.

He wraps his hands around her waist and hoists her off his lap before giving her ass a little smack. The force of it has her stumbling forward on her heels. "Go wait in my room, babe. I'll be there in a few minutes."

Not questioning the directive, she heads toward the hallway.

"And take those damn clothes off. I want you naked, ready, and waiting."

She giggles, throwing a sultry look over her shoulder before closing the door to his bedroom.

Andrew relaxes into the couch before turning back to me. "Are you taking off already? For fuck's sake, you just got here. I thought we were gonna play a little COD later."

"Can't. I've got a test to cram for." And I sure as shit won't be doing it here.

Annoyance flickers across his face. "You're never around, dude. I'm starting to take it personally. This is our last year to fuck around before the real world comes calling. You're not taking advantage of it like you should be."

I shrug, antsy to get away from him. "It's been busy. These engineering classes are kicking my ass."

"You should have picked a blowoff major."

I almost snort. Yeah, my parents would never have allowed that to happen. Since Andrew's father will eventually be handing over the keys to the kingdom, it doesn't matter what kind of degree he gets. He just needs a diploma. Even if he does get drafted and play professional football for a couple of years, he'll end up working for his father at some point. It's a foregone conclusion.

Since there's been a pause in the sex-a-thon, I rummage around in the fridge, grabbing some leftover quinoa and chicken breast to nuke in the microwave. Sure, it's bland, but it's a good mix of complex carbs and protein. Throw some hot sauce on there, and you've got something that's fairly edible. It takes less than two minutes to wolf it down and throw the dirty dish in the sink before I grab my bag and hoist it over my shoulder, ready to flee the situation.

"You're seriously not interested in blowing your load on Candy?" He jerks his head toward his room. "Even if you just wanted to get sucked off, she would have happily gotten on her knees. She's cool like that."

"Her name is Kelsey."

He jerks his shoulders before sneering, "Does it really matter what her name is? She'll be whoever the fuck I want her to be. And you didn't answer the question."

"No, I'm not interested," I mutter, wishing I hadn't bothered to stick around. This isn't a convo I want to get ensnared in. The less I want to bone random chicks, the more he seems to jump down my throat for it.

"I heard you waltz through the door around six this morning. Where were you?" His gaze sharpens on me. "Who'd you shack up with?"

My throat turns bone dry as I shift my weight, unsure how to respond. "No one you know."

He sits up a little straighter. "Wait a minute, you're actually seeing someone?"

Fuck. I should have pleaded the fifth. "Sort of. It's kind of new. We're keeping it on the downlow for the time being."

He studies me as if I'm an exotic animal he's never seen before as he kicks his feet up onto the coffee table. "Does she party at the football house?"

"Not really."

A sly grin spreads across his face as he stabs a finger in my direction. "So she *does* hang out there." He rubs his meaty hands together. "Describe her. I bet I've seen her around."

I throw a glance at the door, wishing for escape before I let something slip. "Isn't Kelsey waiting for you?" I ask, trying to shift the conversation.

He rolls his eyes. "She's probably getting herself off." His brows rise. "Wanna go watch?"

Fuck no.

With a shake of my head, I inch my way toward the door. "Sorry, I need to get moving."

"Come on," he whines, "tell me who this chick is. I'm dying over here. It's a jersey chaser, isn't it? You're fucking a groupie." Before I can open my mouth to deny the claim, he goes on. "Hey, it's totally cool if you are. There's something to be said for boning a girl who knows the drill. And has probably been drilled in both holes." His head drops back onto the couch cushion. "Fuuuuck, I love a chick who can take a good ass pounding."

"She's not a cleat sniffer," I grunt. It takes effort to stop the muscle from ticking in my jaw as I grit my teeth.

He shrugs as if he doesn't really give a shit. "Just trying to figure out what's going on, since you're being all secretive. I've never known you to get serious. Not even in high school."

"Yeah, well, maybe things are different now."

He snorts out a laugh. "Yeah, right. You've always hit that pussy hard before moving on to the next. Are you really telling me that after all these years of nailing groupie ass, you're suddenly interested in being tied down?"

"Maybe I am," I mutter. A few more steps and I'll be at the door. I need to get out of here before he can fire off any more questions. "I've got to get moving, but I'll catch you later."

He waves me off before rising to his feet and stretching. "Whatever, dude."

Just as I grab the handle, he says, "Candy will be here for a few hours if you change your mind. Girlfriend or not, a man's got to nail as much ass as he can."

Not bothering to respond, I slam the door shut and head down the stairwell to the first floor before pushing into the lobby. Normally, I take the Mustang if I'm going anywhere. But the football house is only a couple blocks away, and I need the cold air to help clear my mind.

A few teammates acknowledge me with chin lifts as I step inside the house. There's a ton of people chilling in the living room, watching a show. Asher has his arms wrapped around the two blondes cozied up to him. He flashes a grin when he catches sight of me.

Typical Asher.

I search the room for Easton. My guess is that he's with Sasha at her apartment, which is exactly why I need to hang here for a couple of hours. I'd much rather be over there, too. Everything just feels better when I'm with Brooke.

"There's pizza in the dining room if you're hungry," Rowan Michaels says, walking down the staircase with his arm draped around his better half. Demi Richards is Coach's daughter. I wasn't shocked when they got together. It was always obvious that our QB had feelings for her. I'm just surprised it took him so long to make his move.

"Thanks, but I grabbed something at the apartment." I glance at the dark-haired girl. "Hey, Demi. Will you do me a favor? Tell your dad to stop running our asses into the ground."

She grins before lifting a brow. "You really want me to do that?"

On second thought…

I shake my head. "Nah, it'll only make him more sadistic."

"Sounds like you know him well."

"We're heading out to a movie. Any interest?" Rowan asks.

Brayden strolls out of the kitchen with his girlfriend, Sydney Daniels. She's teammates with Sasha and Demi for the Western Wildcats women's soccer program. Like me, they're all seniors.

I fist bump Brayden before nodding to his girlfriend. It's kind of unbelievable that these guys are now in relationships. There was a time when we'd all head out on a Saturday, looking to get drunk and laid. Instead of partying, they're double dating.

"Are you heading to the movies, too?" I ask her.

Sydney nods. "Yup, we're dragging them to that new romantic comedy that just hit the theater."

Brayden rolls his eyes and grumbles, "Did you really have to tell him that? It makes us look pussy whipped."

Sydney elbows him sharply in the ribs. "That's because you are."

"Maybe."

She smiles sweetly at me. That's one thing about Sydney. She'll give just as good as she gets, which makes her the perfect match for Bray.

Rowan glances at his sports watch. "We'd better take off. Time's ticking, Rhodes. What's it gonna be?"

I shake my head, not interested in being a fifth wheel. "Do you mind if I hang out in your room for a while and get some studying done?"

"Sure," he says, "have at it. What's going on at your place?"

My gaze flickers to the girls before I jerk my shoulders. "Andrew has company."

Brayden snorts. "That sounds about right."

"Feel free to crash here if you need to," Rowan offers before walking toward the front door. "Catch you later."

"Yeah, later." As I watch the four of them head out, a strange ache mushrooms up at the bottom of my gut.

It takes a moment to realize what it is.

Longing.

For the first time in my life, I want what they have.

31

CROSBY

By the time I make it to Brooke's, it's almost eleven o'clock on the dot. Even though it's late, people are still coming and going. Two girls smile and hold the door open for me as they step inside the lobby. Instead of heading toward the elevator with them, I push into the stairwell and take the steps two at a time. It's only been a couple of hours since I ran into her at the library, and already I'm impatient to get my hands on her. Once I reach the third floor, I pass by a couple of doors before stopping in front of her apartment.

Just as I lift my hand to knock, the thick wood swings open. Fingers reach out, locking around my wrist before I'm tugged inside the dark entryway. Brooke's lips find mine as I wrap my arms around her body and haul her close. All I want to do is devour this girl until I've consumed every piece of her.

By the time we finally pull apart, we're both breathing hard. With our hands clasped, she drags me through the apartment. There's just enough light slanting in through the windows at the far end of the living room to keep me from knocking into the furniture.

As we pass through the short hallway, she glances over her shoulder before holding one finger to her mouth and nodding toward

Sasha's room. Once we step over the threshold, she carefully closes the door and twists the lock.

"Easton's spending the night, so you should probably head out early again."

"No problem."

"Did you get a chance to fix your phone yet?" she asks, knocking me out of those thoughts.

Right.

My phone.

These lies will seriously be the death of me.

I suck my lip ring into my mouth and chew on it, trying to decide how to answer.

When I fail to respond, she pushes away from the door and swallows up the distance between us. Her palms settle on my chest before stroking them upward to my shoulders. She squeezes them before they flutter to my cheeks. Stretching onto the tips of her toes, her lips settle on mine. That's all it takes for the warring thoughts swirling through my head to empty.

My arms slip around her body before dragging her close. This girl is everything I've always wanted, and I'm so afraid of losing her. I don't know what the right thing to do here is.

Well...I do.

I'm just reluctant to tell her the truth.

After a few heated minutes, she breaks away. Her hands drift from my face as one trails down my chest to the waistband of my jeans before flipping open the button.

I still her movements, knowing what I've got to do. "Maybe we should talk for a minute."

A confused smile quirks her lips. "Really? Is that what you want to do right now?"

Hell, no.

"There's something I need to—"

As I try to force out the rest, she knocks my hand away and takes hold of the zipper before dragging it down. A hiss of breath escapes from me as her hand slips inside my boxers and wraps around my hard shaft. Even in the shadowy darkness of the room, a knowing glint enters her eyes as she works her fingers up and down my length.

"I'm sorry, were you about to say something?"

"Ahhhh." A mental fog descends. Whatever it was, it's long gone. All I can focus on is her tight grip.

"How about we talk after?"

"Yeah," I agree. "That sounds good."

"I'm more concerned about *this* feeling good."

"It feels fucking fantastic." I don't want her to ever stop. I've had dozens of girls give me hand jobs before, but this is different. What I'm discovering is that everything with Brooke is different.

I almost groan when her hand slips from my boxers. Before I can protest, she tugs at the thick denim until it's around my hips before shoving it down my thighs until my cock is able to spring free. She drops to her knees until she's eye level with my groin. Her tongue darts out to moisten her lips as she tilts her head until her gaze can fasten on mine.

"You've got a gorgeous cock. I've been fantasizing about giving you a blowjob for a while now."

Another groan rumbles up from deep in my chest. If I wasn't hard as steel before, that admittance does the trick. I've never wanted another girl to take me in her mouth the way I do this one.

With her gaze locked on mine, she closes the distance between us before her tongue darts out to lick the head of my cock like a lollipop. Slowly, she swirls it around my crown. Moisture leaks from the tiny slit as she laps at it. The appreciative sounds that escape from her only arouse me more.

She draws me even deeper into her mouth as I tunnel my fingers through her thick strands.

Holy fuck.

Even though it's tempting to close my eyes and enjoy the feel of all that warmth surrounding me, my gaze stays pinned to hers. Other than when I was buried deep in her body last night, I can't remember the last time something felt this amazing.

Never in a million years did I imagine that Brooke would be on her knees in front of me. Sure, I dreamed about it, even whacked off to thoughts of it, but I never expected it to become a reality.

My fingers tighten in her long hair as I angle her head just a fraction so she can take me further inside. Watching my hard length disappear between her pink lips is the most erotic thing I've ever witnessed.

She's so damn beautiful.

And mine.

Whether she realizes it or not, this girl is mine now. We'll hash out our issues and I'll make her understand.

Another tortured sound escapes as she takes me so deep that it feels like I'm nudging the back of her throat. Both of her hands are splayed wide against the backs of my thighs, urging me forward. After a few moments, one slides around to the front of my leg before drifting upward to cup my balls.

Aw, hell.

With each pass, she takes more of me into her mouth. The muscles of her throat constrict with each swallow, tightening around my length. Sharp shafts of pleasure explode inside me, and my eyes nearly cross. There's no damn way I'll last much longer.

"Brooke," I groan, wanting to push her away, "I'm going to come."

Instead of releasing me, her movements become more voracious. And it feels so fucking good. My balls tighten as my cock swells. Every muscle in my body stiffens before I lose control, my seed spurting in a torrent. At least, that's the way it feels. My fingers tighten around her scalp, drawing her closer. Even though tears sparkle in her eyes and slide down her cheeks, she doesn't attempt to fight her way free. Instead, she continues to massage my balls with one hand while the other presses the backs of my thighs. A fist grips my heart, squeezing it painfully, as I watch her deep throat my cock, swallowing down every drop of cum.

It's only when I soften in her mouth that she releases me, pressing a kiss against the tip of my length. Before she's able to rise to her feet, I scoop her up and haul her against me. No matter how many years slip by, that blowjob will live on in infamy. It'll be a moment of pure bliss I relive a million times.

"That was so fucking amazing." I smack a kiss against her lips. The saltiness of my release teases my senses and only turns me on more. There's something both primitive and erotic about it. As if she's been marked and now belongs to me. "You taste delicious."

"I taste like you," she says with a husky laugh.

"Damn right." It's definitely something I could get used to.

Now that I've been satisfied, all I can think about is returning the favor. I want to bury my face between her thighs and eat her up until she's screaming my name. I don't give a fuck if Sasha and Easton are in the room across the hall. And I sure as shit don't care if they hear us.

This feels like a runaway train barreling down the tracks, and there's not a damn thing I can do to stop it. Even more than that, I don't want to.

It's gently that I thumb the tears from her cheeks.

"I didn't hurt you, did I?"

"No, I enjoyed it. And I liked it even more when you came." Her voice drops, turning raspy. "I liked swallowing you down."

That's all it takes for my dick to stiffen up again. "You're sexy as hell, you know that?"

Her fingers slip between us to stroke my cock. "Hard already?"

I press my lips to hers. "I have the feeling I'm going to be like this all night long."

"Good. My first class doesn't start until nine, so I can sleep in."

"Challenge accepted."

With that, I swing around and carry her to the bed.

32

BROOKE

It's the incessant ringing of my phone that rouses me from a deep slumber. With a groan, I roll toward the nightstand and reach for the slim device. It takes a few fumbling attempts to locate it. My eyes are barely cracked open as I press the green button and force out a greeting.

"Brooke?" There's a pause. "Are you there?"

The sound of my mother's clipped tone has me jerking wide awake. Sunlight streams through the unadorned windows, bathing everything in brightness. My eyes water as I blink, trying to find my bearings.

I clear my throat, hoping I don't sound as groggy as I feel. "Um, yeah."

"You're not still in bed, are you?" Disapproval fills her voice. "It's almost nine. Aren't you supposed to be in class?"

Surprised that she knows my schedule, I glance at the clock next to the bed.

Well, shit. She's right. I overslept.

"Yeah. I had a late night..." My voice trails off before I tack on hastily, "Studying."

Don't ask what my attention was focused on, but the session lasted into the early hours of the morning.

And you know what?

I don't regret it one bit. Even if I am having to tap dance through an early morning conversation with Elaine before I've had any caffeine to assist the blood flow to my brain.

"I should probably get moving so I'm not late." Although, unless it's possible for me to teleport, there's no way I'll make it to class on time.

Just as I'm about to disconnect, Mom says, "I did call for a reason."

"Oh?"

I glance at Crosby as he shifts before throwing an arm across his face. The sinewy muscle that makes up his bicep and chest bunches and flexes with the movement. My mouth dries as my attention gets snagged by his gorgeous body.

"Brooke?" Mom's tone turns sharp. "Are you listening?"

I rip my gaze away from the gorgeous male sprawled out next to me. There's no way I can pay attention to her while eating him up with my eyes. No female with a beating pulse could pull off just such a feat.

Crosby Rhodes is hotness personified.

"Yeah, sorry," I mutter, only wanting to get this over with.

"So, you'll be able to make it tonight?"

"Make it to what?"

"Dinner," she snaps, losing her patience. "I called to invite you to dinner this evening."

"Oh..."

Crap. I wasn't expecting another invitation to be issued so soon. Barely have I recovered from the last two interactions.

"I don't know," I hedge. "I've got a lot of homework to do, not to mention an upcoming test."

"I'm sure you can shift a few things around and spare an hour or so for your family. Garret will be joining us. I really do hope you aren't too busy for him after everything he's done for you. I have to say, that's not the way you repay someone for taking care of all your expenses," she chides.

Ugh.

Guilt. Always with the guilt. The woman is a master manipulator.

"Fine," I grumble. "I'll be there."

"Excellent. Reservations have been made for six sharp at Les Nomades. And please dress appropriately. No jeans."

"All right."

My attention once again becomes snagged by Crosby as his eyelids flutter, and he angles his head toward me. If he's going for the sexy bedroom look, he's nailed it without even trying. I just want to kiss him.

Actually, I want to do way more than that.

"Goodbye, Brooke."

"Bye." Without taking my gaze off him, I stab the red button and drop the phone on the nightstand.

"Who was that?" he asks with a stretch. The languid motion has the sheet slipping further down his body, revealing rock-hard abs and an enviable V that disappears beneath the covers.

"Elaine."

"Oh, yeah? What'd she want this early in the morning?" he asks around a yawn.

This guy is beyond delicious. My core dampens as a fresh wave of arousal crashes over me. No matter how many times I have him, it's not nearly enough to satiate the deep well of need he's managed to tap into. I've never felt this turned on in my life. It's nothing short of a revelation. Now that I've experienced this kind of all-consuming lust, there's no way I can go back to lackluster, unfulfilling sexual encounters.

Distracted by the play of muscles across his body, I mutter, "I have to meet her and my stepfather for dinner tonight."

As he rolls toward me, his hand wraps around the nape of my neck before pulling me to him so his mouth can brush over mine.

"That sucks."

"That's an understatement."

His lip ring drifts across my flesh.

"Want me to come with?"

I blink, jerking away in surprise so I can search his eyes. I can't tell if he's fucking with me or not. Whatever this is between us is still in its baby stages. Why would he want to have dinner with my parents?

"Is that a serious offer?"

The sleep falls away from his expression. "Yeah. If you want me to come with for moral support, I will. It's not a big deal. Are you forgetting that I've already met them?"

That's true.

But still...

After giving it a moment of consideration, I shake my head. "No, I don't want to put you in that kind of position."

He reaches out and slowly strokes his fingers along the curve of my jaw. "I wouldn't have offered if I didn't want to go."

I raise a brow and he smirks, amending the statement. "What I meant is that I want to be there for you."

When his hand slides upward, I squeeze my eyes tightly shut and press my cheek against the warmth of his palm. Whatever this is between us feels like it's moving at the speed of light.

"Okay."

He nods. "Good. Then it's settled."

Before I can say anything else, he slips his arms around my body and flips me over so that my back is pressed flat against the mattress as he looms over me. My heart picks up its tempo, pounding into overdrive as I stare at him with wide eyes.

"And we can move on to more pressing matters."

I swallow thickly as my mouth turns cottony. "More pressing matters?"

A slow smile spreads across his face. "Yup."

There's a brush of metal as he presses a kiss against my lips. Just as I open my mouth so that our tongues can tangle, he dips lower, trailing hot kisses along my jaw before sweeping over the hollow of my neck. The pulse flutters as he sucks the delicate flesh into his mouth. Pleasure ricochets through my body as I groan, baring more for him.

Instead of taking advantage of the offering, he continues to slip lower, grazing over my collarbone before nipping and licking his way to my breasts. He draws one stiff little peak into his mouth before giving the same treatment to the other side. I shiver with need each time the piercing drags across my flesh.

"I fucking love your tits," he mutters, almost as if he's talking more to himself than me.

He nips at the undersides before drifting further along my body and past my ribcage, arriving at the indent of my belly button. Just when I don't think I can stand another moment of this sweet torture, he shoulders his way between my legs, pushing them apart before flicking his gaze upward.

"Eating your pussy just so happens to be one of those pressing matters."

Even though he kept me up most of the night, forcing several orgasms from me, my body is already trembling with need.

His gaze drops to my core.

An appreciative gleam enters his eyes as a smirk curves his lips. "Mmm, so creamy. I love how greedy you are."

Under normal circumstances, having something like that pointed out would embarrass the hell out of me, but at the moment, I don't give a damn if he sees all the wetness glistening on my lips. The more he talks, the more arousal floods my pussy.

And just like last night, it's a revelation of sorts.

When I writhe beneath him, eager for his touch, both hands settle on my inner thighs to pin me in place. His thumbs massage the delicate flesh, pulling my lips apart until he can see every pink inch. I'm much too aroused to be embarrassed by his intense scrutiny. All I want is for him to touch me with his tongue and lips. I want to feel the cool metal of his ring scraping across my skin.

"Hmmm. I should check to make sure you're ready."

He swirls one thick finger around the plush opening. Instead of dipping inside, he continues his lazy strokes until my body is a tightly wound ball of pent-up agitation. I spread my legs further, arching off the mattress, silently begging for more.

"So impatient." He taps my clit with the tips of his fingers.

It's just enough to get my attention and my eyes widen. I gasp as a strange mixture of pleasure-infused pain explodes inside me. That's all it takes for my pussy to flood with more arousal. By the low chuckle that slides from his lips, he understands the effect the little slap had.

"You like that, don't you?"

When he strikes me for a second time, I nearly come off the bed. I press a hand over my mouth to keep the scream buried deep inside. I have no idea if Sasha is here at the apartment, but I don't want to find out by having her bang on my door to see if I'm all right.

"He never understood what he had, did he?" Crosby growls.

There's no need to ask who he's talking about.

"But I do, and I'm not going to let you get away." He glances up at me. "Understand?"

My lower lip catches on my teeth. I'm too far gone to dwell on what he's saying. The best I can do is tuck the words away to pull out at a later time.

Slowly he presses his finger inside me until it's buried to the third knuckle. Unconsciously, my inner muscles clench around him. As good as it feels, it's nowhere near the girthy size of his cock. I need more.

"You're so turned on, you're practically dripping." He pumps his finger a few times before dragging it from my body. The moment he pulls out, I feel bereft. Empty.

"How much do you want it, baby? How much does this sweet little pussy need to be filled?"

Whatever escapes from me is an incoherent babble of consonants and vowels all mashed together.

The smirk grows. "That much, huh?"

Before I can say anything more, his mouth descends, closing over me. My eyelids feather shut as a throaty moan escapes. The ring drags across my skin before circling my clit.

That's all it takes before I'm exploding like a firework.

33

CROSBY

Since I've pushed off giving Brooke my digits with the whole my-phone-is-busted excuse, I rap my knuckles against her apartment door. Sooner or later, I'm going to have to tell her that she already has my number and explain the situation. The only alternative I've been able to come up with is to change it, and I don't really want to do that. Although, honestly, that might be for the best.

How many people do I actually care to hear from?

Probably a quarter of the ones who bother my ass.

Before I can knock for a second time, the door swings open, and Brooke stands across from me in a soft looking black sweater that hugs her curves, a brown suede skirt that hits mid-thigh, and tall black boots that end above her knees. There's only about four inches of tantalizing skin visible.

Have I mentioned how much I love those boots?

If I'm lucky, she'll let me fuck her in them later and nothing else. The thought has me popping a boner. Since that probably won't go over well with the 'rents, I force it down. With her looking damn near edible, it's not easy.

"Hey, gorgeous."

"Hi." She beams before closing the distance and feathering her lips over mine. It's not nearly enough.

When she attempts to retreat, I grab hold of her and reel her to me. "Where do you think you're going?"

She squeals when I bury my face against the side of her neck and nip at her throat. "Stop it or we'll be late."

"Is it really a big deal if we keep Elaine and Garret waiting ten or fifteen minutes?" I ask, warming to the idea of a quickie to hold me over.

She pulls back just enough for me to see one brow rise. "Is that all it'll take?"

When I bare my teeth and bite her neck again, she dissolves into giggles. "Crosby!"

Before she can fight her way free, I drop a kiss against her forehead and allow her to escape unscathed. As she swipes her purse from the small table in the entryway, her expression sobers. I know exactly what's going to tumble from her lips before it has a chance to burst free.

"Are you sure about this?" She steps closer before placing a hand on my chest and dropping her voice. "I won't be mad if you've changed your mind and want to bail. Promise."

I nab her fingers before bringing them to my lips and pressing a kiss against her knuckles. "I've already told you that I don't mind tagging along, and I meant it. There's no need to try to talk me out of it."

Her shoulders loosen as a smile of relief curves her lips. "Okay."

Even though she was fighting my hold only moments ago, I tug her to me and wrap my arms around her. The way she fits perfectly against my chest makes it feel as if she were made especially for me.

If any other chick inspired these kinds of emotions, I'd probably freak out and ghost her ass. With Brooke, it only solidifies that I've already spent too much time fighting my feelings, and I'm done with that.

After a few silent moments, she tips her head until she can meet my eyes. "I don't want you to think I'm forcing you into this dinner, that's all."

"You didn't ask, I offered," I remind lightly. "End of story."

"Okay."

"You ready to get your sexy ass moving?"

Brooke huffs out an exaggerated breath before a chuckle slips free. "Not really. I'd much rather stay here with you." Heat fills her eyes. "Preferably naked."

I give her a wink. "If you play your cards right, that's exactly what will happen after." My gaze drops to her long, lean legs. "And if I play mine right, you'll leave the boots on."

Her eyes widen, sparking with interest. "Ohhh…kinky. I like it."

"Trust me, I'll make sure you do."

With that, I capture her fingers and pull her from the apartment. It's apparent from the way she drags her feet that she doesn't want to go. Hopefully, she'll feel a little better with me by her side. Speaking of which…

"You did mention you're bringing a friend, right?"

Guilt flashes across her face as she closes and locks the apartment door. "Umm, I meant to…"

"So that's a no," I finish for her.

"Don't worry. It won't be a problem." She brightens before adding, "And if it is, we'll just leave. Easy peasy lemon squeezy."

I snort and shake my head as we walk to the elevator and ride it down to the lobby before pushing out into the cold. With my arm wrapped around her, I steer us toward my Mustang parked in the lot near the entrance. Once we're both inside, I twist the key and the engine roars to life. I encircle her fingers, giving them a gentle squeeze and pull out of the lot. The restaurant we're meeting at is about a twenty-minute drive from her building.

Brooke tells me about her day and the classes she's taking. Although she was a no-show for her nine o'clock. You'd better believe I made damn sure of that. Hell, I would have kept her ass in bed the entire day if I could. But I had classes and practice that couldn't be missed.

It doesn't escape me that there was a time in the not-so-distant past when she'd be hanging out at my apartment and doing the exact same thing with Andrew. Because I was a glutton for punishment and couldn't help myself, I'd sit sprawled in a chair, pretending not to pay her the slightest bit of attention, all the while hanging on every word. Sometimes, I'd throw out a barbed comment and watch the hurt bloom across her face before being shuttered away behind a mask of stoic indifference.

The only way to keep her at a distance was to be an asshole, and I hated it. Relief pumps through me that the façade is no longer necessary. Now I'm the one she's sitting beside and talking about her day with. The sound of her voice is sweet music to my ears. My fingers tighten around her more delicate ones. If I have my way, I won't ever let go.

Maybe some guys would be pumping the brakes and wanting to slow their roll, but I'm not interested in that. I've spent way too much time fantasizing about this girl and craving every part of her. Now that she's mine, I want to hang on with both hands and enjoy the ride.

Even though there are a few things that need to get straightened out, I'm confident we'll work through it. I just need to find the right moment to tell her.

I hit the turn signal and swing into the crowded parking lot before pulling into a spot and killing the engine. I turn to her as she swipes both palms down the front of her short skirt before straightening it with tense fingers. I know Brooke well enough to realize that a burst of nerves has flared to life inside her.

"Everything'll be fine, I promise."

I slip my hand around the nape of her neck and pull her toward me, nipping at her lower lip before my mouth settles more firmly over hers. She opens almost immediately. One brush of my tongue and her muscles turn slack as she sinks into the caress.

I just want to kiss her all night long.

Fuck her parents. They can eat by themselves.

It's only when her hands settle on my chest that I break away. A hazy quality fills her eyes.

"Mmm, do we have to go?"

A pained chuckle slips free from me. "I really wish we didn't, but yeah, we do."

Her teeth sink into her lower lip before she tears her gaze away and stares at the restaurant that looms in front of us. It takes a moment for the sexual fog to clear before she jerks her head into a reluctant nod. "Okay. We should probably go before I change my mind."

"You might not believe this, but I'm actually good with parents."

She releases a steady breath on something that sounds suspiciously like a laugh. "Is that so? Well, I look forward to seeing just how smooth you can be."

"Oh, baby." I grin. "You've already seen it and you had no complaints."

She snorts before flashing me a full-on grin. My comments do exactly what they're meant to and lighten her mood.

We exit the vehicle before meeting around the front of the sleek hood. With clasped hands, we stroll toward the entrance. I hold open the door before following her inside. My gaze unconsciously drops to her backside as it sways from side to side. Damn, but she's got the best ass. I love palming the rounded cheeks when I'm eating her out.

Once we arrive at the hostess stand, Brooke gives the older woman her parents' names and we're immediately ushered to a table in the main dining room.

"Here's your party," the woman says, waving to a table set for four. "Please let me know if you need anything."

Elaine glances up from the compact she'd been staring at before blinking as her gaze lands first on her daughter and then on me. There's the slightest furrow to her brow as she snaps the gold case shut and slips it into her purse.

Unfazed by the response, Brooke leans over and air kisses her mother's cheeks. The older woman's attention never deviates from me. Her stepfather rises and presses an actual kiss on Brooke's cheek before drawing her in for a quick hug. He's a bigger, burlier guy. Tall and broad in the shoulders. He looks like a man who would be comfortable wearing an expensive cowboy hat and five-thousand-dollar shitkickers. With an easy smile, he thrusts out his hand for me to shake.

"Garret Bollinger, and this is my wife, Elaine."

His wife's lips rise marginally. She looks none too pleased by my presence. But that's tough shit for her. Little does she realize I'm here to stay.

"Crosby Rhodes. We met at the fundraiser over the weekend."

He shakes his finger at me as recognition sets in. "Right. I remember." He waggles the same thick digit between us. "You both attend Western, right?"

Brooke clears her throat and jumps in to answer the question. "Yes, we do." She glances at me for a moment. "We've just started seeing each other."

He grins as if that's good news. "Well, isn't that—"

"Inconvenient," Elaine cuts in with a frown. Sort of. She spears her daughter with a glare. "I really wish you would have mentioned that you planned to bring a," her gaze flickers to me, *"friend."*

Brooke's spine goes ramrod straight. "Does it matter?"

"Actually, it does. We've invited a guest to join us this evening. This will make it awkward."

"Who?" Brooke's eyes turn frosty.

Elaine doesn't get a chance to respond before the hostess shows up with another person in tow. When my gaze crashes into Andrew's, the smile falls clear off his face.

His brows slam together as he grinds to a halt five feet from the table. "Crosby? What are you doing here?"

When I slip an arm around Brooke and tug her to my side, his eyes flare before narrowing. Even though this isn't how I intended for him to find out, it's happening, and there's nothing I can do about it.

"Wait a minute," his hard gaze bounces between us, "you two are together?"

An uncomfortable silence falls over the table as I clear my throat. "Yeah. I'm sorry. I should have said something sooner."

Another wave of shock crashes over his features as his mouth falls open. He drags a hand through his short blond hair before shaking his head. "So, when I asked you the other day if you were hooking up with someone, you were actually talking about my ex-girlfriend?"

A dull heat creeps up my cheeks. Not because I'm embarrassed or ashamed, but more because I don't want her parents to know the intimate details of our relationship. It's none of their damn business, just like it's none of his.

"Yeah."

He grits his teeth as his hands bunch at his sides. "How the fuck could you go after my girl?"

Brooke straightens her shoulders. "I'm not your girl and haven't been since I broke up with you."

A muscle tics in his jaw as Elaine shoots to her feet and slips around the table before sliding an arm around Andrew's waist.

"I am so sorry about this." She pats his chest. "Apparently, my daughter has yet to learn that we all make mistakes and are in need of forgiveness."

"We've been through this before, Mom. He didn't cheat just once. It was the entire time we were together."

A wounded look flickers across Andrew's face as he focuses on Elaine. "I didn't realize what I had until it was gone. All I want is for her to give me another chance to prove how much I love her."

"I know, sweetie," she coos before glaring at Brooke. "I invited Andrew here tonight to help you two work through your issues and get back on the right track. I had no idea you were going to invite someone else." She shakes her head. "You really should have informed me of this."

"And you should have given me the same courtesy instead of ambushing me. I've told you repeatedly that I have no intention of getting back together with Andrew." Her cool gaze flickers to her ex. "The trust between us has been broken, and you're the one who did that. Whether you want to take responsibility for it or not. There's no way for us to go back and rewrite the past. The only option we have is to move forward. And I will not be moving forward with you."

Her mother's lips flatten into a barely perceptible thin line. "Perhaps it's time to say goodbye to your friend so the four of us can sit down and have a nice meal. I'm sure Andrew can see you back to school afterward. A little time alone would do you two some good."

Garret clears his throat. "Darling, I don't think that's a—"

She shoots him a cool look. "It's an excellent idea."

"No," Brooke growls, "it's not."

This woman is off her damn rocker if she thinks I'll walk away and leave her daughter alone with them. Garret seems like a decent enough guy, but it doesn't escape me that until now, he's sat by silently and allowed Elaine to dictate the conversation.

Before the discussion has a chance to escalate, Brooke swings toward me. "I'm ready to leave."

We haven't even sat down and this dinner has already imploded. With my arm wrapped protectively around her, we walk past Andrew. Our gazes lock as he knocks his shoulder into mine.

"This isn't over," he growls so only I can hear.

No, it's not.

34

BROOKE

I'm so fucking angry. I can't believe my mother had the audacity to invite my ex without telling me.

What am I saying?

Of course I can. She's been hounding me since the breakup to give Andrew another chance. Honestly, I should have expected her to try shoving us together at some point.

"Hey." Crosby squeezes my fingers as he shoots a concerned look in my direction. "Are you okay?"

My other hand drifts to my lips as I shake my head. "I don't think so."

"That was…" His voice trails off before he clears his throat. "Something."

Laughter bubbles up from deep within my chest. "Yes, it was."

"If you're looking for any silver linings, it's doubtful your mother will try that again."

Hopefully.

"There is that." A heavy silence falls over us before I add softly, "But now you have to work everything out with Andrew. I'm sure that wasn't the way you wanted him to find out."

A muscle in his cheek twitches as his jaw tightens. "No, it wasn't, but I'll deal with it."

When he doesn't say anything more, I continue. "I know you've been friends for a long time. It was never my intention to get between you two." Even though it's painful, I force out the rest. "If this has become too complicated, we—"

"Don't you dare say it." His gaze narrows, flicking to mine and holding it for a quick second before returning to the dark road stretched out beyond the windshield.

I swallow down the lump of sawdust that has settled in the middle of my throat. It takes effort to keep my voice light. "I just want you to know I wouldn't have hard feelings."

"Really? Because I'd be fucking furious if you ended this over Andrew."

The deep scrape of his voice and bite of his words leaves me faltering. "I don't want to be the one who destroys your friendship."

Silently, he swings into my building parking lot before pulling into a space and cutting the engine. Only then does he swivel around, trapping me in place with his furious gaze.

"Don't you get it?" His dark eyes scrutinize me, pushing past the surface to the emotion simmering below. "Andrew had his chance and blew it. That's a truth he needs to reconcile and live with. But I'll be damned if it ruins what we've found."

His words leave me reeling. I don't understand how Crosby can choose me over someone he's so tight with.

My tongue darts out to moisten my lips. "But you two have been friends for so long. You're teammates," I add stupidly.

"You're right, we are. And we've played ball together for years. I'm also sure I don't have to tell you that Andrew can be a selfish prick. As much as I love the guy, I'm unwilling to walk away from something I've wanted for so long. If he can't understand that, then fuck him. Not once did I involve myself in your relationship. In fact, I did everything I could to keep my distance. Even after you broke up, I had to fight myself to stay away." He looms closer until the world shrinks around us and he's all I can see. "But you're mine now, and I refuse to let you go. Do you understand that?"

Everything he's just declared swims viciously around in my brain. My teeth scrape against my lower lip as I nod. "I don't want you to resent me if Andrew can't accept that we're together."

And my guess is that he won't. My ex is unable to see past his own wants and needs. I wish it hadn't taken me so long to see the character flaw. Especially when it was staring me right in the face the entire time.

"Trust me, that won't happen."

"How can you be so sure?" I persist, unable to believe that I could mean that much to him.

He tugs me closer until his mouth can settle over mine. The slide of his lip ring makes my knees weaken. Somewhere in the far recesses of my brain, I realize it's the last thing I should be focused on.

"Because I've waited too damn long for this to happen," he murmurs. "And maybe you're forgetting that I'm the one who came after you. Now let's go inside."

A smile tilts my lips as another thought occurs to me. "I guess we don't have to hide this anymore. It's all out in the open. No more secrets."

Guilt flickers in his dark eyes before disappearing.

It's there and gone before I can interpret what it means.

"You're right," he says quietly, "no more secrets."

Relief floods through me. I was never a fan of all the sneaking around and hiding. Hopefully, Crosby is right, and at some point, Andrew will get over our breakup and move on. No matter how much he continues to insist that he loves me, I know he doesn't.

We exit the Mustang and meet up on the sidewalk. Hands clasped, we stroll to the entrance before stepping inside the lobby and waiting for the elevator. He draws me close until his mouth can settle on mine. It's only when the doors slide open that we break apart and step inside. A few girls jump in at the last minute.

If I needed a reminder that he's nothing like my ex, everything he's done and said this evening has reinforced that. He's put me first. It's like he doesn't notice the females who are so obviously clamoring for his attention. Even with me standing by his side, Andrew would be flirting back and egging them on.

Crosby couldn't be more different.

Once the doors separate, we step onto the floor. Before we can start down the narrow hallway, I twine my arms around his neck and pull him close before pressing my mouth to his. The babble of female voices rises, meeting my ears as the doors close again, trapping them inside.

I lose all sense of time and place as the kiss deepens, continuing to unfold.

Heated moments pass as my body vibrates with need.

He breaks away to growl, "Unless you want to get fucked right here, you need to stop that."

I stare at the wall before flicking my gaze to him. "That might be interesting."

A low rumble emanates from his chest as he swings me into his arms and stalks toward the apartment. I slip the key from my purse before handing it over. He shoves the thin metal into the lock and throws open the door with such force that it ricochets off the doorstop. With me still held securely in his arms, he kicks it shut and beelines for my room. It's only when the sound of the television hits my ears that I realize Sasha is home. I glance toward the living room, only to find her and Easton staring at us with wide eyes.

Neither of them says a word.

Crosby stops, pressing me closer to his chest as if they might try to wrestle me free. "We're together now. Get used to it."

A knowing smile spreads across Easton's face. "It's about time, man."

The guy holding me jerks his head in acknowledgment before stalking into my room, where he slams the door behind us.

"By tomorrow morning, everyone will know," I say lightly.

"Yup, that's the plan."

His arms loosen until I can slide down his muscular length and my feet are able to touch the floor. Impatience vibrates off him as his fingers rise to the hem of my sweater. He drags it up my body and over my head before tossing it to the carpet.

"You're wearing way too much clothing." There's a pause as he unfastens the suede skirt. "But the boots can stay."

35

CROSBY

I grind to a halt outside my apartment door before pushing it open. Even though I stayed the night with Brooke, hoping it would give Andrew time for the shock to wear off, I know he'll be pissed. We've been friends too long for me not to anticipate his reaction. If I had to guess, I'd say he probably ended up at someone's house and got fucked up, all the while running his mouth about how I stole his girlfriend from beneath his nose.

My muscles tense as I step over the threshold and glance around the quiet apartment. The only sign that he's been here recently is half a dozen empty beer bottles strewn across the coffee table.

Relief rushes from my lungs as my muscles loosen. It might be a small reprieve, but I'll take it. With any luck, he'll cool off by the time we sit down and talk. The guy needs to get it through his head that Brooke was never getting back together with him. That ship sailed months ago.

I dump my bag on the couch and head into the bathroom for a quick shower. I have class in an hour and can't afford to miss it. I wasn't kidding when I said these engineering courses were kicking my ass. There are times when it feels like my head will explode.

Ten minutes later, I wrap a plush navy towel around my waist and saunter into the hallway. My footsteps falter as the apartment door swings open, and Andrew stalks in before slamming it shut again. He stutters to a halt as our gazes catch.

One look is all it takes to reconfirm that he got shitfaced last night. His hair is a mess, sticking up from all angles, and his eyes are bloodshot. A scowl overtakes his features as he stalks toward the small dining room table and leans against the back of a chair before crossing his arms over his chest. If he thinks the aggressive stance does anything to intimidate me, he's sadly mistaken.

With my feet braced slightly apart, I tighten the towel around my waist. I wish to hell he'd come in five minutes later when I was dressed.

I give him a chin lift. "Hey."

He snorts, eyes sparking with anger. "Seriously, asshole? That's all you've got to say to me? *Hey?*"

It does seem a little inadequate, even to my own ears.

"What would you like me to say?"

"Oh, I don't know…" He cocks his head. "How about that the situation isn't what it looks like and you're not actually fucking my ex." There's a pause. "The very same one I've spent months trying to get back together with. That would be an excellent place to start."

Unable to tell him what he wants to hear, I drag a hand through my hair. "I'm sorry."

A muscle throbs in his cheek as he clenches his jaw. His voice drops to more of a growl. "I thought you hated her guts, huh? What the fuck happened to *that?*"

"I never felt that way," I mutter. Only then does it occur to me that I've been lying to him for far longer than I realized.

"Yeah," he says with a bark of disbelief, "I'm beginning to piece that together."

I shift my weight, uncomfortable with the intense scrutiny. We both realize nothing I say will make this better, but that doesn't stop me from throwing out a platitude. "I never meant for any of this to happen. It just did."

He jerks a brow and continues to glare. "Yeah, I seriously hate it when accidents like that occur. You're just walking down the street, minding your own damn business and your dick falls into some chick's pussy."

A dull heat creeps into my cheeks. "It wasn't like that."

He throws his hands up in the air. "Then explain it, bro. Explain how you started boning my ex behind my back. And you didn't even have the balls to give me a heads up. I had to find out in front of her family. Do you have any idea how messed up that is?"

It's so damn tempting to fight back and lay the blame at his feet. If he hadn't grabbed my phone that night and called her, none of this would be playing out. I'd still be tormenting her every chance I got, pretending to hate her.

But then I wouldn't have Brooke.

She wouldn't belong to me.

And there's no way I can regret that.

"Sorry," I say again.

He arches a brow. "That's it? All I get is a fucking lame-ass apology?"

I jerk my shoulders. "What do you want me to say? That I've always had feelings for Brooke? Fine, I'll admit it. Even before you started going out with her, I thought she was a cool chick. But she wasn't a groupie and didn't hang all over the football players. There was no mistaking that she had 'relationship' stamped all over her, so I didn't bother pursuing anything. And then you brought her around and started dating her. Being an asshole seemed like the best way to make sure she kept her distance. It was easier to deal with the situation when she hated me."

A mixture of shock and anger ignites in his eyes as he pushes away from the chair and stalks closer. He grinds to a halt when we're no more than a few feet apart. Unsure of his next move, I tighten the towel around my waist.

When he stabs a finger in my direction, I brace for contact. The last thing I want is to get into a physical altercation with him, but I'm also not going to stand here and let him beat my ass.

Even if I deserve it.

"You're un-fucking-believable. We've been friends since elementary school, and you go and steal my girl?"

"She hasn't been your girl for six months."

A growl rumbles up from deep inside him as he barrels toward me, shoving his hands against my chest. The force of it has me stumbling back a step before I'm able to steady myself.

"Fuck you! You knew how much I loved her."

"I get that you're pissed, but don't blow smoke up my ass. How much could you have loved her if you cheated every damn chance you got?" Maybe that's not what he wants to hear, but it's the goddamn truth, and I'm tired of tiptoeing around it.

His lips flatten as he sneers. "Who the hell do you think you are, acting holier than thou? You're no better than me. Like you haven't been out there, fucking any girl who spread her legs for you?"

"I don't think I'm better at all. My point is if you'd actually cared for Brooke, then you wouldn't have put your relationship at risk."

"You want to pick some bitch over me, go for it. We're done here."

Before I can attempt to walk him back from the ledge, he spins away, stomping toward his bedroom and slamming the door. It rattles on its hinges before an uncomfortable silence settles around me.

I don't necessarily want to leave our relationship fractured this way, but I don't think there's any point in trying to reason with him. At least not now. Andrew needs to calm his ass down. Although, after that conversation, I'm not sure if he'll ever come around to my point of view.

I knew that was a possibility when I decided to move forward with Brooke. As much as I hate that my friendship with Andrew has been blown apart, I don't regret my relationship with her.

Not for one damn second.

36

BROOKE

My eyelids flutter open and I find myself draped across Crosby's chest. Ever since the blow-up with Andrew, he's been sleeping at my apartment. I can't say that I don't love it. If this is what my new normal looks like, I could easily get used to it.

Last night, we had sex twice before falling asleep in each other's arms.

The first time had a frantic quality to it. We tore at each other's clothing with desperate fingers before tumbling onto the mattress. There's nothing like the feel of his hard body stretched out across mine, pinning me in place. One quick thrust and he was buried deep inside me, driving us both toward an orgasm that sated the need pumping wildly through both of our veins. Even though it took all of five minutes, we were both breathing hard and laughing by the time he rolled onto his back.

The second time couldn't have been more different. There was a deliberateness to the act. Gentle thrusts, all the while holding each other's gazes before leaping off the precipice. I could feel the bond between us already strengthening. Coalescing into something more.

In this moment, I can't imagine being anywhere else. Or with anyone else. I realize it's early, but I'm happy. Happier than I've ever been with any other guy.

I lift my head from his chest and allow my gaze to roam over his face. His eyes are closed, and there's a sweep of dark lashes kissing his cheeks. He has a strong profile with a straight nose and full lips. Kissable lips. A shadow of stubble covers both his chin and cheeks.

And don't even get me started on that lip ring...

Desire slides through me like warmed honey before settling in my core as his chest rises and falls with each steady inhalation. It would be all too easy to lay here, snuggled up, staring in fascination for hours.

Careful not to wake him, I reach over and swipe my phone from the nightstand. Even though I didn't get much sleep last night, I'm wide awake. I scroll through my email, Snapchat, and Insta until he finally stirs.

It takes a few seconds for his lashes to lift as he stretches his powerful body beside me. The sheet slides down his abdomen as his muscles ripple with movement. It's enough to make my mouth turn bone dry and forget all the thoughts filling my head.

"Morning," he murmurs.

His voice is all low and raspy. It strums something deep inside, and my belly hollows out in response. It seems crazy that I just had him last night and could want him again so quickly. All he has to do is glance in my direction and I turn into a puddle of need.

Unable to resist the lure of his lips, I lean over and kiss him. My tongue darts out to gently suck the silver hoop into my mouth before whispering, "Morning, sunshine."

He smiles as an easy chuckle escapes from him. "What time is it?"

"Seven. There's no rush, you don't have to get up for a while."

How sad is it that I already know his schedule?

Don't answer that.

"Good. I'm tired." When he rolls onto his side to face me, I set down the phone and sift my fingers through the soft strands of his hair.

With barely cracked open eyes, he reaches out and strokes his thumb over the curve of my cheek. "I was thinking we could go out to eat tonight."

Another burst of happiness explodes inside me. It's strange to think that we no longer have to hide our relationship. We can go out and grab dinner, go to the movies, or walk around campus holding hands. It no longer matters who sees us. Maybe there'll be some fallout when Andrew's friends and a few of his closer teammates discover what's going on, but we'll deal with it just like we've handled all the other obstacles in our path.

"That sounds good."

"Do you like Taco Loco?"

"Love it. It's one of my favorites."

"Me, too." He smirks. "See how perfect we are for each other? We're a match made in taco heaven."

He could be right about that. I do love my tacos.

As we stare at each other, a sense of rightness fills me. After a long stretch of moments, his eyelids close.

"You wore me out last night, babe," he whispers.

Hmmm. I kind of like the sound of that. Maybe I'll get it printed on a T-shirt.

As I reach for my phone, it occurs to me that I still don't have Crosby's number. That needs to change. I can't be in a relationship and not be able to call or text him. With my cell in hand, I tap the screen and open the message app. He rolls onto his back before throwing one brawny arm over his eyes.

"What's your number?"

With a yawn, he rattles off a string of digits and I quickly punch them in. As I do, my conversation with Chris pops up.

My brows slide together as my forehead furrows. I haven't talked or texted with him since I ended our relationship the morning after the fundraiser.

"What the hell?" I mutter, more to myself than him.

Instead of asking Crosby to repeat the number, I type one word.

Hey

My finger hovers over the send button and the muscles in my belly tighten as I force myself to hit it. I have no idea why my heartbeat picks up its tempo, slamming painfully against my ribcage. One second ticks by and then another in the stillness of the room.

Just as my muscles loosen and relief rushes in to fill the void, a faint ding comes from somewhere in the vicinity of Crosby's joggers on the floor.

My lips part in shock as gooseflesh prickles along my arms and legs.

No.

This has to be some kind of weird coincidence, right?

It's not possible to have his number, because that would mean…

My brain shies away from the implications of that thought.

I glance at Crosby. His breathing has turned deep and even again. My teeth scrape against my lower lip as I type out another message with shaking fingers. The faint whisps of nausea curling through my belly have become more pronounced. The acidic taste of bile rises in my throat, threatening to explode.

Who is this?

Again, I hit send and silently send up a prayer that these two boys are not one and the same.

There's another corresponding ding, announcing a new message.

This can't be happening.

I throw off the blankets and shoot from the bed before stumbling toward his haphazard pile of clothing. We'd been in such a hurry last night to get naked. All I'd wanted was to feel him sinking inside my body.

That thought makes my insides churn.

I can't focus on that right now. I can't think about how we'd stared into each other's eyes the entire time he was inside me, carefully stroking us both to orgasm. The realization that I've been lied to cuts me to the very bone. Once I have his joggers, I make quick work of searching his pockets. Delving inside, I wrap my fingers around the slim device before pulling it out and staring at it.

A glance at the exterior shows that there aren't any scratches, dings, or dents. Nothing to confirm that it was dropped or broken. As soon as I tap the screen, it lights up. Clearly, it's in perfect working order.

Just another lie he fed me.

More damning than that are the messages I just sent.

It's almost comical the way Crosby jerks upright on the bed. Except there's nothing humorous about this situation. How could there be when it feels like my beating heart is being ripped out of my chest and I can barely breathe?

My jaw turns slack as I stare at him with wide, disbelieving eyes.

"Brooke, it's not what you—"

"Think?" I supply, dropping my gaze to the phone once more. If I weren't looking at the evidence in my hand, I'd be tempted to dismiss it.

Even though I've made a concerted effort to keep Chris and Crosby separate, I allow all my interactions with them to crash through my head. As a timeline develops, horror fills me, rising in my throat, until it's almost enough to choke on.

"Is that what you were going to say?" My voice escalates with each word that sprays from my mouth like bullets as I hold up his phone. "Are you really going to sit there, look me in the eyes, and tell me you're not Chris?"

He smashes his lips into a tight line before shaking his head. "No, I can't tell you that."

I suck in an unsteady breath. Even though I'd quickly pieced together the truth, it still feels like a slap in the face to hear him confirm it.

My brain slows as I mentally rake over every interaction with more care. All the secrets I'd confided without much prodding. Masturbating on the phone. Crosby pulling me aside and apologizing out of the blue. Asking Chris to meet up for coffee and Crosby showing up instead. Him loitering outside my apartment after the dinner with Mom. And like an idiot, I'd invited him up. It was the first time we'd kissed. Then the convo in the car the next morning. Him showing up at the fundraiser and us having sex.

It all swirls through my head like a tempest. I feel like such an idiot for the way he played me.

"It was never a random call, was it?" I blink back the tears that threaten to spill down my cheeks.

He throws off the covers and jumps naked from the bed, cutting a path directly to me. When he hunkers down, I scramble backward, popping to my feet to keep a safe distance between us. It's only when my hand shoots out that he grinds to a halt.

Color drains from his face. "Just give me a chance to explain." His voice drops as he pleads, "I promise it's not as bad as it looks."

Laughter bubbles up in my throat as I give my head a few violent shakes. "There's nothing you could say to make this right." My fingers tighten around his phone before I throw it at him. *"Nothing."*

It hits him square in the chest before he lifts his hands and fumbles with the device. Not once does his gaze deviate from mine as he tosses it to the bed.

"Was this all some kind of sick joke?" Another thought slams into me, knocking the air from my lungs. Barely can I force out the question. "Was it a game you and Andrew concocted to fuck with me?" The idea of them plotting to hurt me has nausea exploding in the pit of my belly. I want to wrap my arms around my waist and double over with the pain of it before curling into a tight ball.

"What?" His eyes widen. "No, of course not."

"Of course not?" I repeat, voice rising until it sounds more like a screech. *"Of course not?"*

He winces.

My voice reaches such a high octave that I'm almost surprised when the window doesn't shatter into a million pieces.

"Brooke." His tongue darts out to moisten his lips as a thick waver threads its way through his voice. It's as if he's trying to calm someone standing on a ledge, threatening to jump. "Please, let's sit down and talk this out."

"What rational explanation is there for what you did?"

When he remains silent, I continue, "You called and pretended to be someone else to gain my trust." My eyes narrow.

"Do you think I would have told you anything about my life if I'd known I was actually texting and talking with Crosby Rhodes?"

"No." He drags a hand through his already disheveled hair.

"Nope," I agree. "I wouldn't have. So, as you can surmise, we have nothing further to discuss." I stab a finger toward the door and try to keep my voice from wobbling with all the emotion rushing through me. "You need to leave."

When he remains frozen in place, gaze locked on me, I scream, "Now! Get out now! I don't want to see you again!"

When he swallows, the muscles in his throat constrict, and his expression turns pained. "I never set out to trick you."

"And yet, that's exactly what happened," I whisper harshly through stiff lips.

His broad shoulders slump under the weight of my accusation.

When he remains silent, I say, "You could have come clean at any time, and you didn't." I point to the phone on my bed. "When I asked for your number the first time, you could have told me what was going on at that point, and you chose not to."

"I tried."

With a glare, I carefully inch my way toward the dresser. I can't stand here naked in front of him for another moment.

"Not hard enough." There's a pause before I bite out, "You didn't try hard enough."

"I was afraid—"

"That it would all seem like a terrible game meant to humiliate me?" I bark out a hoarse laugh.

"It was never a game. I swear it wasn't."

"I don't believe you."

With my attention fastened on him, I slide open the drawer and grab the first thing my fingers come in contact with before whipping the T-shirt over my head. Now that my body is shielded from his view, I don't feel quite so vulnerable.

When he takes a tentative step in my direction, I bare my teeth and he grinds to a halt.

"Please, just give me ten minutes, and if you still want me to leave, I will. You'll never hear from me again."

"You used everything I told you against me." Another punch of queasiness hits my belly. "You knew *exactly* how to play me. For fuck's sake, I practically gave you a step-by-step guide to seduce me."

"It wasn't like that."

"You keep telling me that, and yet, there's all this evidence that claims otherwise. I told you exactly how I liked to be touched and what I needed from a guy." Hurt flares to life inside me. "And that's exactly what you gave me."

"Brooke," he whispers.

I shake my head, unable to listen to any more lies as memories flood my brain, making me feel like even more of a dumbass for thinking he could be trusted.

"Just tell me one thing..." It's a constant battle to swallow down the rising nausea.

"Anything." His eyes widen, pleading with mine as he inches closer. "Whatever you want to know, I'll tell you."

"Was Andrew involved in this? Did he know what you were up to?"

"No." He shakes his head before shifting his stance. "Do you really believe I'm capable of something so malicious?"

Hot tears sting my eyes. "After everything I've just learned? Yeah, I do."

"If you would just—"

"No," I snap. The rage burning brightly inside me is the only thing that keeps the pain at bay. "I don't want to hear any more lies. And you know what? I wouldn't believe them anyway."

A mixture of guilt and grief settles over his expression. "Fine, I'll leave." His gaze flickers to mine. "Just know that it was never my intention to hurt you."

As much as I want to believe him, there's no way to do that.

"Get out."

Instead of continuing to argue, he jerks his head into a nod. I keep my eyes averted as he scoops up his clothing and makes quick work of yanking on his boxers, joggers, and T-shirt, along with a sweatshirt before shoving his feet into his shoes. After he's dressed, his movements stall, and even though my attention is carefully averted, I feel the heat of his gaze resettle on me.

The floorboards creak beneath his weight, and I stiffen when his fingers wrap around my shoulders before I'm dragged to him and crushed against the hard ridges of his chest.

The warmth of his breath ghosts over the outer shell of my ear. "Even when I was pretending to be Chris, everything we shared was real. They were my thoughts and feelings. I wanted you to know me. The person buried deep down inside. The one I don't share with many people."

I screw my eyelids tightly closed in an attempt to battle back all the rioting emotions fighting to break free. "I wish I could believe that."

"So do I."

He presses a kiss against the side of my face before squeezing me one last time.

And then he's gone.

Walking out of my room and life forever.

37

CROSBY

With my backpack hoisted over one shoulder, I stalk across campus. There must be a look on my face, because the people walking toward me scramble out of my way. Even though it's been a few days, the fallout with Brooke still feels painfully fresh.

No matter how hard I suspected she'd take the truth, it was a thousand times worse.

After I tried texting and calling a few times, she blocked my number. I should have expected it. That's exactly what she did to Andrew. Once she'd decided she was done with him, she was done. There's something about her determination to move on from a crap situation I can't help but respect.

At the same time, I wish she'd give me a chance to explain. Not that it would necessarily change anything, but still…

Maybe I didn't set out with the intention to mislead or trick her, but in the end, that's exactly what happened. I should have been upfront from the beginning and not allowed the situation to spiral so far out of control.

Except, I knew how she'd react, and that the friendship we'd been building would come crashing down around our heads.

And that's exactly what happened.

I'm so lost in the tangle of my thoughts that I don't immediately hear my name being shouted above the babble of voices. It takes a moment for me to shift mental gears before swinging around and searching the crowd. That's when I see Ryder McAdams barreling straight through a sea of students. A few innocent bystanders get shoved to the side. By the grim set of his lips, I can already tell this won't be a pleasant conversation.

Perfect.

This is exactly what I need.

"Hey, asswipe," he bellows when our gazes lock. "Stop running away."

I lift my hands and glare. "Do I look like I'm going anywhere?"

If he's looking for a fight, he came to the right place.

Just like Brooke blocking my number, I should have expected Ryder to seek me out. He might not be her brother, but they're family, and he's always been protective. Shit got a little physical with Andrew after their breakup.

Rage vibrates off him in thick, suffocating waves as he eats up the distance between us with long-legged strides. I straighten and brace for the oncoming attack. As soon as he's within striking distance, he plows his hands into my chest, knocking me back a few steps.

Before I can find my footing and right myself, he steps further into my personal space, knocking me harder this time. When I keep my arms at my sides, not bothering to defend myself, anger sparks in his eyes as a low growl emanates from deep in his chest.

He takes a swing, and a second later, his fist connects with my eye. A starburst of color and pain explodes around my socket as my vision goes blurry. I hiss out a breath and straighten, ready for more.

"You just gonna stand there and let me pound your ass, Rhodes?"

"Yup." That's the plan. How can I defend myself when my actions were indefensible?

He yanks back his arm before slamming it into the side of my jaw. It feels like slow motion as my head whips to the side and another burst of agony explodes in my face. I stumble back, knocked off balance as my hand slides over my jawbone. I'm almost afraid that one knocked a few teeth loose.

"Put up a fucking fight. I can't beat the shit out of you if you refuse to defend yourself."

Even though the right side of my face feels like it's on fire, pulsating with a life all its own, I jerk my shoulders before lifting my arms and making a come-on gesture with my hands. "Do your worst, McAdams. I won't fight you."

My words only seem to piss him off more. With a growl, he slams his fist into my gut. No matter how prepared you are for that kind of blow, it still robs all the breath from your lungs. I grunt and double over before wheezing. Just as I straighten, he catches me in the lip.

Goddammit.

The metallic taste of blood floods my mouth. When it becomes too much, I spit it on the sidewalk.

Some people would say that football is a brutal sport filled with Neanderthals. Clearly, they don't watch hockey. These guys are a bunch of bruisers who live for the fights that break out on the ice and in the locker rooms. Ryder just so happens to be one of those guys who enjoys a good brawl.

Be it on or off the ice.

He grabs me by the shirtfront and hauls me close. Only now do I become aware of the growing crowd gathered around us to watch the show. A few have whipped out their phones to capture the moment for posterity.

"You better start defending yourself, because I can keep this up all day long. You fucked with my cousin, and now I'm gonna mess you up. Be prepared to kiss your football playing days goodbye."

The threat must give him pleasure, because a sadistic grin curves his lips.

"I deserve the ass kicking, so just finish it," I grunt. I've spent the last couple of days mentally beating myself up. The physical pain blooming throughout my face and body feels good. Like penance. "I've got a class that starts in twenty minutes, and I can't afford to miss it."

Confusion flickers across his face, mixing with the rage. He tightens his hold before swearing under his breath and shoving me away. I stumble back a few paces and bring my hand up to swipe my mouth. Already, my lip feels swollen. It comes away with an ugly smear of blood.

He cracks his knuckles and shakes out his hand. "You gonna tell me why the hell you would do that to her?"

Now that we're no longer fighting—or maybe I should say, now that Ryder is no longer pummeling the shit out of me—the disappointed crowd disperses.

"Did she tell you what happened?"

His eyes narrow as he shifts his weight. It wouldn't surprise me if he decided to get in a few more licks. I've known Ryder since freshman year. I've seen him throw down half a dozen times. He's always had a quick temper. He's more of a hit first and ask questions later kind of guy.

"She told me enough."

I drag a hand through my hair. "I know the situation looks bad, but I really do care about her. I just…" My voice trails off, unsure how to arrange my thoughts into words that make sense.

When I fall silent, he raises a brow, waiting for me to do the impossible and explain myself.

Shoulders collapsing, I shake my head. "I never meant to hurt her. It started off as a couple of texts back and forth before morphing into something more. By the time I realized what was happening, it seemed too late to tell her the truth without losing her."

"Yeah, well that's exactly what you should have done, asshole."

I snort and throw up my hands in irritation. "Don't you think I know that? If I could go back and make different decisions, I'd do it in a heartbeat. But that's not possible."

His gaze turns glacial. "You fucking hurt her, man. Brooke's a sweet girl. She doesn't deserve what you did."

I wince. Hearing him say that is more painful than the beatdown I was just treated to.

"I know, and it fucking kills me." I stare at him through my good eye, since the other is now swollen shut. "I can't stop thinking about it."

Or her.

No matter what, Brooke is never very far from my thoughts.

"Hey, what's going on here?" Easton pushes his way between us before forcing the hockey player back a couple of steps and glaring at him. "Is there a problem here?"

Ryder shifts his gaze from me to my teammate. "Nothing that concerns you, Clark. Do yourself a favor and stay the fuck out of it, or I'll give you a taste of what he just got."

It's not an idle threat, and we both know it.

Easton's brows wing up as he gives me a sidelong glance, taking in my face, which feels like a pulpy mess. "Rhodes? Is there an issue?"

"No. It's all good." A mirthless chuckle slips free as I keep my good eye on Ryder.

Easton nods but looks unconvinced.

An uncomfortable silence falls over the three of us before Brooke's cousin forces out a grunt. "Whatever. I need to take off." He points to me as he walks backward. "You better hope I don't catch sight of your ass again or you'll get more of the same. Got it?"

When I jerk my head into a nod, he gives me one last glare before swinging around and pushing his way through the throng of students.

Easton watches him go with narrowed eyes before glancing at me. "I really hate that guy."

I snort as the tension filling my muscles gradually dissipates. "Yeah, but you don't hate him because he just beat the shit out of me. You can't stand him because he took Sasha out before you two got together."

"That motherfucker is lucky I didn't give him a little taste of his own medicine..." His voice trails off, and I almost see the realization as it flashes across his face before he points to mine. "This is because of Brooke?"

I release a steady breath and nod. "Yup."

His brow furrows as he stares at the last place Ryder was seen before disappearing. "He didn't even have a scratch on him. You just stood there and let him hit you?" There's a pause. "Why would you do that?"

"Because I deserve it."

And I'd been prepared to take much more.

As far as I'm concerned, Ryder McAdams let me off easy.

38

BROOKE

"Are you sure you don't want to talk about it?"

I glance up from the chicken, black bean, and quinoa bowl to meet Sasha's concerned gaze from across the table before shaking my head.

Nope. I feel like a complete idiot for being catfished. Do you have any idea how humiliating that is?

Apparently, I can't pick a good guy to save my life. That's the only conclusion I've been able to arrive at after much soul searching on the subject.

A couple of days have slid by, and thankfully, I haven't run into him. It's like we've fallen into our old habit of avoiding one another. We just have to keep it up until the end of spring semester.

Shouldn't be a problem, right?

Exactly.

"Come on, girl. You need to eat. All you've been doing is picking at that poor bowl."

With a sigh, I set down the fork. "I probably shouldn't have bothered to buy it. I'm not really hungry." I suppose that's one tiny silver lining in all this. No appetite. Maybe I'll shed a few pounds and my mother will stop threatening to take me to the spa over break.

A rush of sympathy floods her eyes. "I'm sorry he hurt you." There's a pause. "I still can't believe he was the guy you were texting with. That's so messed up."

"Tell me about it," I force myself to say lightly.

"I always thought Crosby was a dick, but this stunt only solidifies it."

"Yup." Except...after we started talking and I got to know him on a deeper level, he didn't seem like such a jerk. Truth be told, I'd actually come to like him.

A lot.

The hardest part is not knowing where the truth lies.

Did he ever have feelings for me?

Or was it all just a big charade to screw me over?

It's tempting to scrub a hand down my face. I'm tired of lying awake at night, unable to stop the questions from circling around in my brain. It's mentally and emotionally exhausting. I don't want to think about Crosby anymore. Unfortunately, it's not that easy. He refuses to be banished.

Here's what I do know—it'll take a long time before I'm able to trust another guy with my heart again, if ever. The last two I've allowed into my life have inflicted permanent damage.

Sasha clears her throat, and I blink out of my inner turmoil before shoving it to the back of my brain where it belongs.

"Just know that I'm here to listen when you're ready to talk, okay?"

I nod in relief that she won't force the issue. Sasha is a good friend. Probably the best I've ever had. There's never been a time when she didn't have my back. As much as I want to graduate and move on with my life, I'll miss seeing her smiling face on a daily basis. The thought is enough to bring tears to my eyes.

Ugh.

This breakup has made me super emotional, and I hate it.

"It's okay to be sad," she says quietly as if reading my thoughts. Or maybe it's my facial expressions that give me away.

I force the edges of my lips to lift into a slight smile. "I don't understand why I'm so upset. We weren't together that long. It shouldn't be such a big deal."

Reaching across the table, her hand settles over mine. "Aw, babe... it always hurts when someone breaks our hearts."

I guess she's right about that. I just wish my heart hadn't been involved in the first place.

"All I need is a few more days to wallow, and then I'll be over it." Even as I force out the words, they don't ring true. And the way Sasha's dark brows wing upward confirms that she doesn't believe me either.

"Want me to beat him up? Would that make you feel better?" She retracts her hand so she can crack her knuckles.

Even though the popping sound is like fingernails on a chalkboard, the offer brings the first genuine smile to my lips since the incident. "Trust me, he's not worth breaking a nail over."

She stretches out her arm before admiring her unpolished ones. They're short and perfectly filed. Acrylics and soccer don't mix, but Sasha doesn't mind. She's always been more of a jock than a girlie girl.

"I'm willing to break a nail or two for you."

A chuckle slips free. "That's because you're a good friend."

She puckers her lips and sends an air kiss in my direction. "Right back at you, chickie poo poo."

From the corner of my eye, my attention gets snagged by my cousin as he walks by with a few teammates. They're a loud, boisterous group with a gaggle of puck bunnies trailing in their wake. Every men's sports team seems to have their fair share of groupies.

As we make eye contact, he says something to the closest one before breaking away from his friends and beelining for my table. A number of girls nearby perk up as he saunters past. Once he arrives, he gives Sasha a quick chin lift in greeting before focusing his attention on me.

"Hi, Ryder." She gathers up her belongings before scooting from the booth and popping to her feet. "Bye, Ryder."

"Catch you later, Sasha," he says.

She turns to me. "We'll talk more after practice."

I raise my hand in a wave as she takes off. With any hope, that won't happen. I refuse to give Crosby another moment of my precious time or headspace.

My cousin drops down onto the bench across from me before carefully scouring my face. After a few silent moments, I shift beneath his intense scrutiny.

"Are you doing all right?"

I paste a fake smile on my face. "Of course. Never better." He caught me right after I found out about the whole Crosby-Chris thing, and in a moment of weakness I now regret, I blurted out the entire sordid story. He'd been furious. I wish he'd just forget about it. The fewer people who know, the better off I'll be. I can't go through another chlamydia-gate again.

Fool me once, shame on you.

Fool me twice, and I'm an idiot who deserves what I get.

His lips flatten. "You're a terrible liar, you know that? I'm being serious. I want to make sure you're okay."

I jerk my shoulders. "I promise that I'm as fine as I can be. That's the best I can do." I clench my hand under the table until the rounded nails bite into the soft skin of my palm before adding, "I just need you and Sasha to stop making a big deal out of this so I can forget about it and move on."

An uncomfortable silence settles over us as he continues to assess me until I'm practically squirming beneath his relentless gaze.

"Well, that's weird. It sure seemed like a big deal to Rhodes."

I jerk upright as my chest constricts until it feels like there's a thousand-pound elephant sitting in the middle of it, making it impossible to suck in full breaths. "What?" I can barely force out the next question. "You talked to him?" My voice elevates with each word that tumbles out. "Why would you do that?"

Oh my god. Why would he do that?

The situation is humiliating enough without my cousin sticking his nose where it doesn't belong and making everything worse.

A tortured groan escapes from me.

Oblivious to my inner turmoil, he points to the untouched quinoa bowl in front of me. "You gonna finish that or what?"

"No." I shove it toward him. Maybe I'm jumping to conclusions and it's not as bad as I think. "Please tell me you didn't talk to Crosby."

Why am I even asking?

I can already tell by the hard glint in his eyes that he did.

Instead of answering, he stabs a piece of blackened chicken with the fork and pops it into his mouth before chewing it methodically. Only when he's swallowed it down does he say nonchalantly, "We might have had a few words in passing."

"Ryder..." I groan before burying my face in my hands. "The situation doesn't include you. It wasn't that big a deal. You shouldn't have gotten involved."

He scoops up another spoonful of quinoa and beans before shoving it into his mouth. Once it's down the hatch, he points his fork at me. "Listen, you're my cousin. I'm not going to sit back and watch one of those football playing douchebags get away with hurting you." He gives me a steely look. "Again."

Some of the tension filling my shoulders drains away. Even though I don't need him to do it, how can I be mad at him for wanting to come to my defense? That's what family does, right?

They stand up for each other when no one else will.

Everything in me softens. "Thanks, Ry."

He shrugs as a smile plays across his lips.

"Do I even want to know what you talked about?"

"Probably not."

Movement catches the corner of my eye, and my head swivels in that direction. My gaze lands on Crosby as he walks with Asher, Rowan, and Carson through the main part of the Union.

My eyes widen as my mouth falls open. Not only is his eye blackened, but his lip is split, and there's an angry bruise that has bloomed on his right cheek. It looks like someone beat the shit out of him.

Someone like...

When I continue to stare, my cousin swings around to look before turning back with a smirk. Almost as if he's proud of his handiwork.

"You did that?" I whisper, a mixture of horror and sorrow filling me. Even though Sasha had jokingly threatened to hurt Crosby, I didn't actually want to see it happen.

"Yup." He returns his attention to the bowl as if it's not a big deal. And to Ryder, it probably isn't. "Like I said before, no one hurts you and gets away with it."

Everything from the past few weeks churns in my head as we lapse into silence. He finishes off my lunch before lounging against the bench.

"Do you want my opinion on the matter?"

My gaze is reluctantly drawn across the large, open space until it lands on Crosby for a second time. A shiver of awareness slides through me when I find his broody stare pinned to mine. It takes effort to rip my gaze away and refocus on my cousin. After all the lies and subterfuge, it shouldn't be difficult.

Even though Ryder's thoughts won't change anything, I shrug. "I guess."

"The guy refused to defend himself."

My brows pinch together. Out of everything he could have said, that's not what I was expecting. "I don't understand."

He nods toward Crosby and his friends. "Just look at him. He's a fucking mess. I beat the crap out of him in front of a crowd of people, and he just stood there and took it. Didn't even try to hit me back. Trust me, I could have done far more damage, but after a while, I felt kind of bad." His forehead furrows as if he doesn't quite understand why that would matter to him.

The muscles in my belly contract until they're pinched and painful. There are so many questions swirling through my head.

Before I can wrap my lips around any of them, he continues, "Do you have any idea how annoying it is to beat the shit out of someone, and they won't even fight you back? They just stand there like a punching bag and let you do your worst." His face contorts before he shakes his head and folds his arms across his broad chest. "Takes the fun right out of it."

My tongue darts out to moisten my lips. "Why would he do that?"

Instead of answering the question, he turns it back on me. "I have my theory, but I'm more interested in what you think."

My teeth scrape over my lower lip as my gaze reluctantly slides back to Crosby. His attention is still fastened on me. "I don't know." More like I'm afraid to acknowledge the kernel of hope that has taken root inside me.

He cocks his head. "You can try to fool me, but don't lie to yourself. I guarantee it won't help anything."

I force out a shaky breath as confusion crashes through me, destroying all the lies I've been reassuring myself with. "Why are you doing this? You've always hated the guys I've dated." I wrack my brain for an exception but come up empty. "Every single one of them."

He jerks his shoulders. "Is it my fault you pick assholes?"

Ironically enough, that's exactly what I pegged Crosby to be for most of the time I've known him. A moody jerk who enjoyed screwing as many girls as he could. But the guy I'd gotten to know over the phone was different.

He's someone I could have easily fallen for.

It sucks to realize that maybe I already had.

I've spent the past couple of days trying to convince myself that he was exactly the asshole I'd always assumed. Now, my cousin is stirring up trouble and making me question everything I'd thought was true.

I don't like it.

More than that, I don't appreciate it.

"I don't understand why you're doing this," I whisper for a second time.

"Maybe I don't want to see you make a mistake." He reaches across the table and places his hand over mine before quickly withdrawing it. The touch is fleeting. There and gone before I can process the tenderness of the gesture. "Although, I think we can both admit that I'm the last person who should be giving you advice on your love life."

I snort out a laugh.

Even though I love my cousin dearly, he's no better than a lot of the football players on campus. Hell, he might even be worse.

Although, I would fight anyone who repeated the sentiment. That's just how we roll.

Since high school, he's left a trail of broken hearts in his wake. Sometimes, I have my doubts that he'll ever settle down.

Why would he bother?

Girls come out of the woodwork just for the chance to throw themselves at him, and I don't see that changing anytime soon. This is his last year playing college hockey before he enters the draft. And there's no doubt in my mind he'll end up playing professionally. He could have gone straight to the NHL from high school, but he chose to attend Western and play for one of the best coaches in Division I college hockey.

"Whatever you decide," he says, "I'll stand by you."

My lips lift into a smile.

No matter what happens, I have my family. That's not always a comforting thought, but right now, staring at Ryder, it means the world to me.

39

CROSBY

I unsnap the chin strap and yank off my helmet before shaking out my damp hair. Even though the air is cold, I'm sweating from a grueling two-hour practice. Now that it's over and I'm not focused on the physical pain ricocheting through my body, thoughts of Brooke rush in, inundating every cell in my brain. If there were a way to switch it off, I'd do it in a heartbeat.

Andrew laughs with a couple of guys from the O line as they shuffle toward the locker room. A few seconds later, Coach barks out a handful of names. My guess is that it's for an ass chewing. Relief floods through me that I'm not on the list.

Was today one of my best practices?

Nope. Not even close.

My head isn't in the game. I'm a second too slow and not where I should be on the field. I need to get my shit together before it becomes more of a problem.

As a couple of players beeline toward Coach, Andrew meets my gaze before giving me a slight chin lift in acknowledgement. It's the most I've gotten from him in days. The apartment has turned into one hell of a frosty place to be. It's enough to freeze my nuts off. I've been spending a lot of time hanging out at the football house, crashing on their couch.

This is the first time in more than a decade of solid friendship that we've had a problem. All right, so maybe that isn't one hundred percent true. Even though I've had my fair share of issues with the guy, I've always shrugged them off. I've pushed his irritating tendencies aside, refusing to let them crawl under my skin. When he's riled me up or pissed me off, I've let it go, not wanting to make waves. This is the first time I haven't been able to do that.

No one other than Brooke could have come between us.

Instead of turning his back the way I expect, he closes the distance before falling into line with me and staring at my face. "What the fuck happened to you?"

"Ryder's fist happened."

His lips quirk as a few chuckles escape. "Yeah, that sounds about right." There's a pause before he adds, "All I gotta say is better you than me, dude."

I snort. Leave it to Andrew to find the humor in this situation. There's no love lost between him and Brooke's hot-headed cousin. Although, my teammate didn't stand there and take it like I did. You better believe he gave as good as he got. They both walked away with blackened eyes and split lips.

An uncomfortable silence settles over us as we walk toward the tunnel that leads to the locker rooms beneath the bleachers. There's a part of me that feels like I should apologize so we can smooth this over and move on. Football ends in January, but the lease on our apartment won't be up until May. It's an awfully long time to go without talking or interacting.

Except...I don't regret getting together with his ex. Sure, I'm sorry about how it went down and the lies I told, but that's it.

Before I can figure it out, he plows a hand through his blond hair, making the short strands stand on end. "Look man, I don't want to have a problem with you."

My feet stutter to a halt as he does the same. A couple of guys slap us on the shoulders before sauntering past. It takes a moment for the field to completely empty.

"I feel the same." I clear my throat. "I didn't mean for everything to go down the way it did. I've always tried to keep my distance from her so it wouldn't happen."

He releases a steady puff of air before glancing away. "Yeah, I know. I guess..." His voice trails off as he jerks his shoulders. "I guess part of the reason I couldn't let it go is because she's the one who dumped my ass. Maybe I wanted to prove that I could get her back. It had more to do with my ego than anything else."

I shift my weight, unsure how to respond to the admittance.

Is it what I suspected all along?

Yeah, it is.

When it comes down to it, Andrew doesn't actually want a girlfriend. He never did. He wants to screw around with all the groupies who spread their legs for him. And you know what?

As long as everyone understands the score and is cool with it, have at it. Enjoy yourself. Maybe there'll come a day when he meets a girl who changes the way he views relationships and makes him rethink his priorities. I don't know. So far, that hasn't happened. Maybe it never will.

"So, what now?" I ask.

His gaze resettles on me. "I let it go and we move on. We've been friends for too fucking long to let some chick come between us."

For him, that's the truth.

For me, it's not.

As far as I'm concerned, Brooke is worth it. If I wanted her before all this happened, it's nothing compared to the way I ache for her now that we've drilled beneath the surface and got to know each other on a deeper level.

When he starts walking again, I do the same.

"Maybe it's better this way," he continues.

Confused, I glance at him. "What do you mean?"

"That neither of us is with her."

I force out a long, slow breath. For a flicker of a second, I consider holding back the truth. But how can I do that after all the lies that have rocked the foundation of our friendship?

I'm tired of keeping my real feelings buried deep inside where they can't see the light of day.

"I like her," I blurt, surprising even myself.

"What?" He shoots a frown in my direction as if he didn't hear me correctly.

I clear my throat and strengthen my voice so there's no confusion about my feelings. "I don't know if it's possible for her to forgive me, but I need to try to work things out. There's no way I can just let her go."

40

BROOKE

"I can't believe that I let you drag me here," I grumble as we head up the concrete stadium steps with our drinks and popcorn in hand.

"Oh, come on," Sasha says, "it'll be fun. You needed to get out of the apartment. You've been moping for way too long."

Fun?

Ha! The last thing this will be is fun.

The moping part?

Yeah, unfortunately, that's true. I've been brooding. And no, it's not a good look on me. If it were possible to snap out of it, I'd do it in a heartbeat. I want to forget about Crosby and enjoy the last six months of college. I'd assumed it would take a few days to shake off this funk, but it's continued to linger like a bad stench. If anything, it's worse now than it was before, which doesn't make a damn bit of sense. Our relationship was fleeting. Here and gone before I could blink my eyes. And yet, it feels like I've lost something special.

How's that for a kick in the ass?

So, no...sitting in the stadium bleachers at a football game for three plus hours and staring at Crosby on the bright green turf isn't going to help hasten that along. If anything, it'll make matters worse, and I can't afford to slide backward.

There have only been a handful of times when I've spotted him at the Union or on one of the paths that cut across campus. Normally, I'll swing around and head in the opposite direction. Even if that means arriving late to class. A couple of times, he's caught sight of me, too. He'll hold my gaze, refusing to look away. Thankfully, he doesn't take it a step further and approach. It's doubtful my heart could withstand that kind of onslaught. I'm barely holding it together as it is.

I frown as Sasha points to empty seats about ten rows up from the fifty-yard line instead of heading to the student section where we normally sit. If there's anything that will distract my attention from the field, it's all the noise and antics that take place there.

"You want to sit here?"

This is primo seating for season ticket holders.

Sasha shrugs, nonchalantly saying over her shoulder as she moves steadily up the staircase, "Professor Donaldson had a pair of tickets and asked if I wanted to use them since he couldn't attend the game this weekend. I thought it'd be a nice change of pace to get away from all the chaos."

Chaos is right. The student section can get pretty rowdy with all the jostling and yelling. Sometimes, I walk out of the stadium after a game with my ears ringing, barely able to hear myself think. Although, at the moment, that would be preferable. Reluctantly, I trail after Sasha as she scoots past a few people who look old enough to be our parents.

Once we're settled in our seats, I wind my scarf more tightly around my neck. Even with the sun shining brightly overhead, there's a distinct chill to the early December air. Nerves flare to life in the pit of my gut as my gaze combs over the players warming up on the field. Rowan Michaels is easy to spot as he windmills his arms before doing a few light passing drills. Brayden Kendricks is standing next to a guy on the sidelines who is decked out from head to toe in Wildcats paraphernalia. He looks too young to be an assistant coach. More like a superfan.

Sasha rises to her feet and waves to Easton before flashing him a big smile. She's decked out in a jersey with his name and number stamped across the back. There are black smudges under her eyes, and her thick hair is pulled up into a ponytail. There's no question as to who this girl belongs to, and she wouldn't have it any other way. Easton grins, waving back before giving her a wink.

These two...

They're way too cute for words.

My gaze slides to Carson Roberts and Asher Stevens. Both are moving through a series of stretches. The only time Asher looks serious is on the football field. Otherwise, he's kind of a goofball and always horsing around. He plays a ton of video games, smokes weed, and drinks like he's triple majoring in all three.

He's blond and blue eyed with muscles galore. The girls go crazy for him. And he, in turn, enjoys them with an equal amount of fervor. There's a revolving door of females in his bed. And if the rumors that circulate around campus are to be believed, sometimes more than one.

I force my attention away from him to scour the field. It takes a few moments to realize what I'm doing. Or rather, who I'm searching for. Irritated with myself, I release a slow breath and reluctantly accept that the next three and a half hours will be brutal. I'll be hyper focused on him all the while reliving our relationship one painful frame at a time.

I'm almost grateful when Sasha knocks her shoulder into mine, recapturing my distracted attention. Glancing at her with raised brows, I find a smile dancing around the edges of her lips as she points to the turf.

"Check it out."

Ugh.

I'm trying my damnedest *not* to do that. The last thing I need is more reminders of Crosby. He's the one person I haven't been able to find. Maybe if I'm lucky, he'll be out for the game, and I won't have to torment myself with his presence.

I force myself to glance at the field, only to find Crosby standing on the sidelines directly in front of me. Electricity jolts through me as our gazes lock. He holds a thick sheet of white posterboard in his hands.

I'm sorry I hurt you.

My breath catches, becoming wedged at the back of my throat as he drops the first sign. I'm almost shocked to discover another one ready to take its place.

The weeks we spent getting to know each other were the best of my life.

It would be a lie if I didn't admit—at least privately to myself—that I felt the same. I enjoyed all of it.

The posterboard falls to the turf and is replaced by a third one.

I don't want to lose you.

Another sign drops as my heartbeat picks up tempo, crashing painfully against my ribcage as I wait to see if there's more.

Please forgive me for not being honest.

My teeth sink into my lower lip.

I…can't believe he's doing this.

Players gather around him as the crowd quiets in the stands. People turn, searching the sea of spectators before pointing me out. My attention stays locked on Crosby. Looking away feels impossible.

When he drops the fourth poster, there's yet another.

Can we talk after the game?

There's a tap on my shoulder. It's almost difficult to pry my gaze away from him as I turn and find a smiling girl holding an oversized bouquet.

"These are for you," she says, shoving them into my hands.

They're a beautiful mix of brightly colored wildflowers.

When I glance back at Crosby, he's holding one last sign.

Please, baby? Don't leave me hanging.

Even though I told myself there wasn't anything he could say or do to change my mind, I find myself caving with a quick nod. A slight smile tips the corners of his lips before he jogs off the field. It's only when he disappears inside the tunnel that I become aware of the crowd cheering around me.

Heat fills my face as I bury my nose in the fresh blooms. As I do, a thought occurs to me, and I turn to Sasha. "You knew about this, didn't you?"

The happiness radiating from her face is a clear giveaway. "Maybe."

Even though I shake my head, I'm finding it impossible to be angry with her.

She wraps an arm around my shoulders and tugs me close. "Just consider it payback for setting me up with your cousin."

A chuckle escapes from me. I'd almost forgotten about that.

"Bitch," I mutter.

"Right back at you, babe."

And this, my friends, is why Sasha will always be my bestie.

41

CROSBY

I huff out a breath as I slam the locker door closed and grab my athletic bag. Even though I should be riding high from our win this afternoon, a thick knot of tension has taken up residence in the pit of my belly. Brooke might have agreed in front of a packed stadium full of fans to meet up, but I have no idea if she'll actually wait around. Maybe she only agreed because I put her on the spot.

At the time, standing on the sidelines with the posterboards and declaring my feelings had seemed like a grand romantic gesture.

Chicks like that kind of thing, right?

Now, after a couple of hours, I'm not so sure. It's entirely possible that all I've done is push her further away when all I want to do is keep her close.

A heavy hand lands on my shoulder, knocking me from the tangle of my own thoughts. I glance up and find Andrew. Unsure how he'll react, my muscles stiffen. The last thing I want to do is stir up more shit when the dust has barely had a chance to settle from the last time.

"I saw what you did out there, man. It was pretty cool. Good luck."

That's all it takes to have everything loosening inside me. "Thanks."

I think we can all agree that I'm going to need it.

He jerks his head into a nod before walking away. Even though we've been good since hashing everything out after practice, I'd be lying if I didn't admit the easy camaraderie we've always had is no longer there. Sometimes I wonder if we've stayed close for this long because we both played football and attended the same school. We seemed to have more in common when we were younger.

That's no longer the case.

Normally, when those thoughts pop into my brain, I shove them away, not wanting to inspect them too closely.

But now...

I've come to accept that maybe we've grown apart over the years. Some of the teammates I've met at Western have become better friends. Guys like Easton, Carson, Asher, Brayden, and Rowan. These are the ones I turn to if something happens, or I need their bullshit advice. They're the ones I'll remain in contact with long after we graduate and move on with our lives. Not because we've been friends for a long time but because I actually like who these guys are, and I respect them.

Even Asher.

Trust me, that's a painful admittance.

But he's a good dude.

Deep down.

Beneath all the pot, pussy, and beer.

It's only after the locker room clears that I realize there's no point in dragging my feet and delaying the inevitable. Brooke will either be out there waiting for me or not. Even if she does take pity on me and decide to hear me out, there's no guarantee she'll forgive me for deceiving and hurting her.

When it comes down to it, that's exactly what I did. Nothing I say or do will change that truth. It's a regret I'll have to live with for the rest of my life.

With my duffel thrown over my shoulder, I push through the locker room door and into the brightly lit corridor. Air clogs my lungs as I glance around. My heartbeat stutters a painful beat when I don't immediately find her. There are a few pockets of people shooting the shit and rehashing the game. Under normal circumstances, that's exactly what I'd be doing.

Deep down, I should have realized she wouldn't stick around. Obviously, she'd felt pressured into agreeing to meet up with me. I can't blame her for being a no-show.

I fucked up.

A couple of players slap me on the shoulder before taking off. There's some chatter about a party to celebrate our win.

Want to guess whose ass won't be in attendance tonight?

Yup. That's right…me. I plan on drowning my sorrows in a couple bottles of beer.

Once they disappear, I fight my way free of the disappointment before taking a step toward the exit. As I do, the crowd shifts and I catch sight of the beautiful girl leaning against the white cinderblock wall with the flowers I'd picked out earlier this morning clutched in her hand. My steps falter as our gazes collide.

Unsure what to do, I lift my hand into a tentative wave.

I've been with my fair share of females over the years, and no one has ever stirred up these kinds of emotions in me. It's kind of like I want to throw up and kiss her all at the same time.

It's unnerving.

When she returns the gesture, I force my feet into movement. It's only when I'm a few feet away that I stop and shove my hands into the pockets of my joggers in order to resist the urge to reach out and yank her into my arms.

"Hi." I force the word through stiff lips as my heart slams against my ribcage. If I'm not careful, it'll break free of its confines before falling to the floor and flopping around pathetically.

Straightening, she tucks an errant lock of caramel-colored hair behind her ear. "Thanks for the flowers. They're beautiful."

"No problem."

An awkward silence descends as I shift my weight. The distance between us feels palpable. Everything swirling through my head since she discovered the truth and forced me from her life sits perched on the tip of my tongue.

"I'm sorry about the lies." Before she can respond, I hurry on, knowing this might be the only chance I get to clear the air. "There were so many times I could have come clean and told you the truth, and I didn't. It was never my intention to hurt or deceive you. That night, when you got the first call, it was from Andrew. He'd been drunk and grabbed my phone when I wasn't looking because you'd blocked his number. When I realized what he was doing, I took it back and hung up."

The memory flickers in her eyes.

"When you texted, asking who it was, I told you it was a wrong number. I assumed it would end there, but then we started messaging back and forth. I thought by the next morning, it would be forgotten, but I couldn't let it go. The more we texted and then talked, the more ensnared in the lie I became, and the harder it was to find a way out. And then at the coffee shop—"

"You showed up." Her brow furrows.

"I was planning to tell you then, but..." My voice trails off.

"I'd thought it was someone else," she says.

Everything inside me deflates. "Yeah."

When she opens her mouth, I cut her off, "But that's not an excuse. I should have told you the truth."

She releases a steady breath. When she doesn't immediately tell me to go to hell, I inch closer, craving her nearness. It's been more than a week since she forced me from her life, and I've missed her more than I thought possible. We might not have been together long, but it feels like we opened up, got close.

What I don't know is if she feels the same way.

Or anything, where I'm concerned.

"I understand that what I did can't be swept under the rug, but is there any chance you can forgive me? Can we go back to the beginning and have a fresh start? Only this time, it wouldn't be Chris you'd be getting to know. It would be Crosby." I move closer. "Just Crosby."

She nibbles her lower lip before breaking eye contact and staring down at the bouquet.

"I don't know." She peeks up at me from beneath a thick fringe of lashes. "How can I trust you after what you did?"

Even though her response cuts me to the bone, I nod, accepting responsibility for my mistakes. If I was looking for an answer, I'm pretty sure I have it. I can't blame her for feeling that way. She's right, I did all those things.

"If I could go back and do everything differently, I would. I hope you realize that."

"I appreciate the sentiment."

When she says nothing further, the flicker of hope inside me is snuffed out and I awkwardly hitch a thumb over my shoulder. "I should probably get moving."

"Okay."

It blows to walk away, but there's nothing else for me to say.

When I take a quick step in retreat, her voice halts me. "Crosby?"

"Yeah?" My gaze stays fastened on hers.

"If we were to…get back together, it would take time to earn my trust. There's no way I can just hand it over again."

My heart stutters.

"I'll do whatever it takes to prove that I'm worthy of it. That I'm deserving of you." I close the distance between us until she has to crane her neck to hold eye contact. "I won't let you down again. I promise."

"I'm scared," she admits so softly that it almost breaks my heart. I'm the one who did that to her. I gave her a reason to withhold her love and affection by not being truthful.

"I know." Unable to stop myself, I cradle her cheek in my palm. "There's no reason for you to believe I'm telling the truth, but I swear I am. I want you, Brooke. I always have. Even when I was too busy denying it to myself, I wanted you. Even when you were dating my best friend, I wanted you. I never stopped, and when I found a way to get close, I took it. That doesn't make it right," I tack on quickly. "All I can do is promise to give you total honesty moving forward."

Her eyelids flutter shut as she presses the side of her face against me. "Okay."

My brows lift as I tug her into my arms and hold her close. I don't give a shit about the flowers now crushed between our bodies. I'll buy her new ones. Hundreds of them. "Really? You mean it?"

"Yeah, I do. I'll give this a shot." There's a pause. "I'll give *you* a shot."

"I promise, babe, you won't be sorry."

With that, my mouth crashes onto hers. All it takes is one sweep of my tongue against the seam of her lips for her to open, and then I'm delving inside where I belong.

42

BROOKE

The party rages around us as Crosby holds me close, his arm thrown over my shoulders. We've been together for more than a month now. Never in my wildest dreams did I expect to give him a second chance to redeem himself, but how could I let him walk away after everything he stirred within me?

The answer is that I couldn't.

I'd had every intention of telling him that there was no way I could trust him again, but something deep inside prodded me to give him a chance to prove that he's the man I need him to be. It's possible that I'll regret that decision in the not-so-distant future. But so far, I'm glad I opened my heart and let him in.

As soon as I glance up, our gazes collide. He lowers his face until his lips can brush across mine. The slow slide of metal against my flesh still makes me shiver with awareness. No matter how many times he kisses me, it never gets old. I'm fascinated by the piercing.

Actually, I'm just fascinated by him.

That hasn't changed, and I hope it never does.

"Love you, babe," he whispers against my mouth.

"Love you, too."

We haven't been together long, but it seems like our relationship has shifted into hyper speed. As soon as the air was cleared, everything else fell into place. It's crazy to admit, but I've never been happier. The one guy I was desperate to avoid is the very same one I can't get enough of.

"Aww. It's adorable the way you two play kissy face."

My lips twitch as Asher makes a few gagging noises. He can be such an ass sometimes. The caveat being that he's a lovable ass. There are two blondes cozied up against him who look suspiciously similar.

Unbothered by the comment, Crosby smirks. "Maybe you should give monogamy a try, man. You might just enjoy it."

The girls perk up at the notion of Asher getting exclusive.

"No, thanks," he snorts. "I'm not interested in getting wifed up like everyone else around here. You jokers must be forgetting that variety is the spice of life." He winks at both girls. "Right, ladies?"

They giggle, all the while running their hands over his chest.

"I think we could all use some liquid refreshments," he says.

With that, Asher moves his entourage toward the back of the house where the kitchen is located. His posse grows as they move through the dining room.

I shake my head as he disappears through the crowd. "He's kind of a pig."

"Yeah," he agrees easily, "but he's *our* pig."

My lips twitch. "True."

My bestie and her boyfriend make an appearance on the second-floor landing before walking down the staircase hand in hand. They're both wearing goofy smiles, making it obvious what they've been up to. They've been together for a couple of months and still can't keep their hands off each other. It's like they're trying to make up for all the time they lost when they were platonic.

For a while, I was envious of their relationship.

I mean, how could I not be?

But that's no longer the case. I don't want to jinx it, but what I've found with Crosby feels like the real deal. I'm excited to see how life unfolds and where it takes us.

Sasha gives me a quick hug before waving to a couple of teammates, Demi Richards and Sydney Daniels. There's another girl with them that I don't immediately recognize.

Demi makes introductions before throwing an arm around her shoulders. "This is Lola. We went to high school together. I had to bribe her into coming out with us tonight."

The dark-haired girl smirks. "Don't think I'm forgetting about the extra-large pizza I was promised. It's the only reason I'm here."

Demi snorts. "I know you won't. Margarita. Extra buffalo mozzarella and basil."

"You know me well," Lola says with a grin before glancing around and taking in the drunken people making complete asses out of themselves. "This looks like it's going to be painful. I probably should have insisted on two pizzas and a side order of garlic knots."

Western is a well-known party school with an extensive Greek system, and most of the students who attend enjoy taking full advantage of that.

"Oh, come on. It'll be fun."

She gives Demi a mock glare. "We both know this isn't my idea of a good time."

As I continue to stare, recognition niggles at the back of my mind. There's something familiar about her. Even though it's a huge university, you tend to see the same people walking around campus, at the library, or at parties.

When her gaze lands on me, I give her a friendly smile. "Hi, I don't think we've met. I'm Brooke."

"Lola."

I pat my newly minted boyfriend's chest, unable to deny that I'll shamelessly use any excuse to touch his rock-hard body. "And this is Crosby."

The tension on her face eases as her shoulders loosen.

"Any chance you work at Taco Loco?" Crosby asks.

Just as the question leaves his lips, another lightbulb clicks on, and I realize that's exactly where I've seen her.

"Yup. My uncle owns the place, so I fill in from time to time when they're short staffed."

"I thought you looked familiar." A huge grin spreads across his face as his shoulders shake with silent laughter.

When Demi launches into a story about the two of them in high school, I whisper to Crosby, "What's so funny? You love Taco Loco."

"It's nothing. Really."

I narrow my eyes, and his expression morphs into one of innocence. He might have stopped chuckling, but the corners of his lips are still twitching. When he says nothing more, I shake my head.

Craning his neck, he glances around the packed space. "I wonder where Asher is. He really needs to get his ass back in here. He's gonna love this."

"What's he going to love?"

A better question would be why Crosby is talking in riddles.

"You'll see. It shouldn't be long now."

Just as I'm about to pump him for more information, Asher saunters back into the living room. I blink, realizing the blondes he took off with fifteen minutes ago aren't the same ones now clinging to his brawny biceps. Although, in the world of Asher, that's nothing new. He goes through girls like most people go through underwear. Whatever he's packing in his pants must be pure magic, because there has never been a shortage of females throwing themselves at him.

With an arm slung around each girl, Asher rejoins us.

Crosby is all smiles as he clears his throat. "Hey, Ash, did you get a chance to meet Demi's friend Lola?"

Asher glances around the group until his gaze lands on the one girl he doesn't know. His lips lift into a lazy smile before it wavers, gradually dissolving into a frown. His eyebrows snap together as he stares at her with narrowed eyes.

I shift my gaze to Lola, only to find that she's wearing a similar expression.

"Yeah, unfortunately we've met," she says with a frown.

Asher's blue eyes flare before he spits, "Who let you in, taco girl?"

Even with the dim party lighting, it would be impossible not to see the color that flares to life in her cheeks. "That's not my name."

He jerks his broad shoulders. "I don't give a shit who you are. If you're standing in my house, you better have brought tacos."

She bares her teeth like a rabid dog before swinging toward Demi. "Sorry, I can't do this. I'm out." Before her friend can respond, she turns on her heel and stomps out the door.

"What the hell?" Demi stares at Asher with wide, disbelieving eyes before leaping into action and hurrying after her friend.

Sydney scrunches her face before eyeing up the blond football player. "What was that about? Why are you calling her taco girl?"

When Crosby's shoulders continue to shake with silent laughter, I elbow him in the stomach. Not that it does much good.

"Right," Brayden says slowly, "I remember that night. I thought for sure we were gonna get thrown out of Taco Loco. That girl was our waitress. Her and dipshit here," he points to his friend, "exchanged a few words."

My gaze settles on Asher, only to find that the scowl marring his expression has disappeared.

"I'm gonna need a little help getting back into the party spirit." He squeezes the girls against him. "You ladies think you can assist with that?"

They perk up like they just won the lottery before nodding eagerly. He flashes a lazy smile before steering them into the dining room and then hallway where his room is located.

I glance at Crosby and shake my head. It all makes sense now. "You must have been there too, because you couldn't wait for Asher to see her."

Guilt flickers across his expression. "There aren't many girls who take an instant dislike to the guy. Can I help it if I take pleasure in finding the one that does?"

I rise onto my tiptoes and nip his lower lip between my teeth before giving it a tug.

Heat sparks in his dark eyes as I release him. "You know how much I like it when you get aggressive."

I can't help but snort.

He doesn't just like it, the guy loves it.

"Now that the show's over, are you ready to get out of here?"

Actually, I am.

With a nod, we wave to our friends and take off. Our hands are clasped as we head out the front door and down the sidewalk.

"You know that I'd much rather spend my time alone with you, right?"

I glance up at him as everything inside me softens. "And you know I feel the same."

"I do." He gives me a wink. "Play your cards right tonight, and I might just buy you a pizza afterward."

Hmmm. The promise of sexy times with my handsome, football playing boyfriend and then pizza?

It sounds like the perfect evening to me.

EPILOGUE

CROSBY

wo years later...

I GRAB a glass of champagne and maneuver my way through the thick crowd, searching for Brooke. There has to be at least two hundred people at the fundraising event her mother and stepfather are throwing. We flew in this morning from California especially for it. Just as I catch sight of her on the other side of the room, delicate fingers wrap around my bicep, halting my progress.

"Crosby, darling, I've been searching everywhere for you."

I glance at the petite blonde who has sidled up beside me and paste a smile in place.

"Looks like you've found me," I say easily.

Her lips lift at the corners ever so slightly. What I've come to learn throughout the years is that this is what a full-blown smile looks like on Elaine. She's been injected with so much Botox that her face barely moves.

She loops her arm through mine as if afraid I might try to make a run for it. "There are a few friends I'd like to introduce you to."

"Sure, no problem."

For a tiny woman, she's awfully strong. Not to mention bossy. She drags me easily through the sea of formally attired guests until we reach a group of people where introductions are made. It might have taken Elaine six months to let go of the idea that her daughter and ex would be getting back together, but she finally came around to it. Even if she didn't, it wouldn't have mattered. Once I'd made Brooke mine, there was no letting go.

Not ever.

A couple of the men bombard me with questions. As I talk about the team and season prospects, my gaze coasts over the crowd for the only woman I have eyes for. After a few minutes, I find her watching me from across the open space. A smile trembles around the corners of her red-slicked lips.

She understands how much I hate this shit.

She also realizes I'd do anything for her, and that includes being paraded around by her mother like a circus animal. Plus, I know how turned on the sight of me in a tux makes her. So, I'm anticipating a good night ahead for yours truly.

After roughly ten minutes, I make my excuses and break away from the group before Elaine can coerce me into meeting more of her friends. I've played this game before. She'll monopolize hours of my time if I let her.

I keep my focus pinned to Brooke as I wind my way through the sea of glittering people. She looks gorgeous in a pale pink, low-cut gown with spaghetti straps. The sight is enough to have my cock stirring. I'm looking forward to getting her alone. As much as I enjoyed assisting her into that dress, I'll enjoy stripping it off before laying her out on the bed like a fucking feast even more—because that's exactly what her body is.

Uncaring of the people who surround us, I lean down and cover her mouth with my own. No matter how many times I kiss her, it never gets old. The need that rushes through my veins only continues to intensify.

Even though we'd only been together for six months when we

graduated from Western, I didn't want us parting ways. Luckily for me, she felt the same and was able to find a job in sunny California as a fashion merchandising buyer for a major high-end retailer. We found an apartment in San Francisco near the bay and couldn't be happier.

It's kind of unbelievable just how good life is at the moment. And if I have my way, it'll only get better.

"I see Elaine has already sunk her hooks into you," she whispers when I pull away. "Now that you're a famous professional football player, you're her new favorite person."

Unable to resist her lure, I smack another kiss against her mouth. "The only thing that matters is that I'm *your* favorite person. Other than that, I don't give a damn."

Her lips curve into a soft smile. It's one that punches me in the gut every time.

"You are definitely that."

"Good."

"Have I thanked you for agreeing to this?"

"Yeah, but you can always thank me again later if you want." I waggle my brows. "In your special way."

She slaps at my chest, but the knowing glint that ignites in her eyes tells me that I can count on it happening.

Hell, yeah.

"Plus," I say, wanting to sound a little more altruistic, "they're raising money for a good cause, and that makes you happy. So, it's a win-win in my book."

Over the last couple of years, Brooke and her mother have been working on repairing their fractured relationship. When I have time off, we fly home for a long weekend. Is it anywhere near perfect?

Nope. Not by a long shot.

But every day it gets a little better. During the last two years, Brooke has become more open with her mom about things that hurt her feelings. Maybe Elaine isn't the mother she would have picked for herself if given a choice, but she's the only one she has. They're both trying to make the best of that situation.

I glance around the crowded room before locking my fingers around her wrist and hustling her sweet ass down a long stretch of hallway. Our shoes click against the ocean of marble floor, and the crowd thins as we reach one of the darkened galleries near the back of the house.

"Crosby," she gasps as I force her spine to the wall and pin my body against her softer one, "what are you doing?"

I nip at her lips and then chin before sliding down the delicate column of her neck. "What does it look like?"

A whimper escapes from her as I press my mouth against her overflowing cleavage. I really fucking love her tits and the way this dress showcases them.

"Someone could walk in any moment," she whispers.

"Yup."

Her fingers tunnel through my hair. Instead of pushing me away, she pulls me closer. I bite the hardened tips of her nipples through the silky material covering them as I drop to my knees and stare up at her. She looks like a fucking goddess with the glittery gown molding to every curve and her hair piled on top of her head with a few stray tendrils left to frame her face.

Her teeth scrape against her lower lip as she throws a cautious glance toward the entrance of the room. Darkness swirls around us as moonlight pours in through the unadorned windows that stretch from floor to ceiling.

My hands delve under her gown, settling on her bare thighs before slowly sliding upward until they reach her panties. I push the fabric out of my way before shoving against the lacy scrap covering her center. A hiss of breath escapes from her as I close over her pussy. Unable to wait, my tongue dips into her sweetness, taking a long lap as the taste of her explodes in my mouth.

This right here is what I live for. And there was no damn way I'd make it through the party without getting a taste.

Even though she's right, and someone could stumble upon us at any moment, I'm not concerned. We're in a distant part of the house, away from the festivities taking place, and it won't take long for her to cry out my name.

After running my tongue over her plump lips, I nibble at her clit, knowing that it's her Kryptonite. The way she arches her pelvis tells me that she's close.

"Come for me, baby girl," I whisper against her soaked flesh.

That's all it takes for her to splinter apart. I continue to lap at her shuddering softness until her muscles turn lax and her knees weaken. Only then do I place a tender kiss against her damp flesh before tugging the panties back into place. I straighten her gown and rise to my feet. When I press my lips to hers, she opens until our tongues can tangle. I love the taste of her on my lips.

"Feel good, baby?"

"Mmmm, you know it did. I came in record time."

I can't help but grin, because she's right about that. The girl goes off like a firework lighting up the sky every time.

Her fingers drift across my erection. "Should I return the favor?"

As tempting as the offer is, I shake my head. "Tonight, after this is all over, I'll let you have your wicked way with me." I steal one last kiss before snagging her fingers with my own. "Ready to return to the party?"

A soft sigh falls from her lips as she leans her head against my chest. "I'll go anywhere as long as you're with me."

My heart softens. She has a way of doing that to me.

This is the one girl who makes me want to be a better man. And for her, I will be. I'll do whatever I need to make her happy.

"Ditto."

There's a moment of silence before she whispers as we walk through the cavernous hallway, "I love you, Crosby."

I pull her into the warm circle of my arms and hold her tight. "I love you, too. More than I ever thought possible."

More than I ever dared to dream.

Brooke McAdams owns me heart and soul. And I don't see that ever changing.

"Let's make the rounds and then get the hell out of here so you can fulfill your promises."

She bats her lashes as a grin curves her lips. "Oh, did I promise something?"

"You bet your sweet ass you did. And I plan to hold you to it."

All night long.

The End

Want more of Crosby & Brooke? Subscribe to my newsletter and get a free bonus epilogue!
https://dl.bookfunnel.com/93vkcqnii2

Turn the page for a sneak peak at Campus Legend!
https://books2read.com/campuslegend

CAMPUS LEGEND

LOLA

"Hey," Carmen calls out as she rushes past with a tray loaded down with food, "you've got a new table in the back."

I give her a nod and continue preparing a bill for a customer. "Thanks for the heads up."

"No problem." She throws a sassy smile over her shoulder. "He's hot with a capital H." To emphasize the comment, she uses one hand to hold up the large circular tray while fanning herself with the other.

I lift a brow.

Here's the thing you need to know about my cousin—while I love her to death, she isn't overly picky when it comes to men as proven by a long string of ex-boyfriends that goes way back to high school. There are so many, they could start their own club if they wanted.

So…do I think her assessment of the situation will turn out to be accurate?

Nope. Not even a little.

As soon as I'm finished, I tear off the piece of paper from my notepad and beeline toward the couple before laying the check face down on the table.

"Thanks for coming in," I tell them. "Have a great night."

They smile in return, telling me to do the same. They're regulars at Taco Loco. Even though I only work part time, I see them here at least once a week. The guy is usually a good tipper. The girl...not so much. I'm lucky if she leaves ten percent.

Here's hoping that he'll be the one taking care of the check today.

I glance at my watch and huff out a breath. Only three more hours until my shift ends for the night. As much as I'd love to fall face first into bed and sleep for a solid seven hours, that's not going to happen. I have a ton of homework to plow through and a marketing test to study for.

Whoever said there's no rest for the weary was spot on. I'm only twenty-two years old and already mentally and physically exhausted.

The grind, unfortunately, is all too real.

And from what I've discovered, it never ends.

Just as I swing around, ready to head to the table in my section that was seated a few minutes ago, my gaze lands on the trio occupying the booth and my feet grind to a halt.

Oh, fuck no.

For a second or two, I remain frozen in place before slowly retreating, not wanting them to catch sight of me. I almost roll my eyes at such an absurd thought. Like they would glance up long enough to notice their waitress?

Unlikely.

The guy and two girls are much too wrapped up in one another to pay attention to the people around them. I quickly scan the crowded area before beelining to the kitchen where I find Carmen loading entrees from the long stretch of silver counter onto her serving tray.

"How would you like to do a favor for your favorite cousin?"

"I have a favorite cousin?" she asks, grabbing plates and strategically placing them on the massive platter. "Wait a minute—is Valeria here? I must have missed her."

"Ha-ha, very funny." When she grins, I say, "I need you to take the table that was just seated. I'll love you forever if you do."

"Don't you already love me?"

"We're talking forever," I say, impatient to secure her agreement. "Promise."

"Which table? The one with the hot guy?" She glances at me with a furrowed brow. "Why? What's the problem?"

I jerk my shoulders and try to keep my response casual. "Who said anything about a problem?"

With her attention focused on me, she searches my face with more care. "Do you know them or something?"

"Ummm…" I wave a hand. "Not really. I've met the guy a couple times." There's a pause before I reluctantly admit, "We don't exactly get along."

"What? I can't imagine that happening." She feigns shock by widening her eyes. "You've got such a sunny disposition and are so easy to get along with. Who wouldn't like you?"

With a scowl, I give her the finger. José, one of the line chefs, smirks before setting another plate under the lamps.

"As much as I wouldn't mind waiting on that hottie, I can't. I've got three tables left and then I'm out of here." She gives her booty a little shake. "We're heading to a couple of the clubs downtown. You should join us."

"Can't. I'm here until close and then I have a ton of homework to finish up."

"Sucks to be you, girl."

Sometimes, it really does.

My teeth scrape across my lower lip. If there's one thing I loathe, it's asking for help. I'd much rather suck it up and do what needs to be done, no matter how painful, challenging, or time consuming. That being said, when it comes to dealing with Asher Stevens, I'm willing to make an exception.

I steeple my hands together. "Please? Just take this table. I'm sure they'll be quick."

Hopefully.

If they can stop making googly eyes at each other long enough to order their food and eat.

Her expression softens as she shakes her head. "Sorry, I really need to get home and shower before I head out tonight. If I didn't already have plans, I'd stay. I could use the extra money."

Damn.

Once she loads up the rest of the food, she swings away without another word.

It's just my luck to get stuck dealing with that guy after an already long day. I don't have much in the way of patience left. Although, that doesn't seem to matter when it comes to Asher. All I have to do is look sideways at him and my irritation skyrockets through the roof.

With no other options available, I straighten my shoulders.

Maybe I'm worrying over nothing.

So what if we've had two explosive run-ins?

That doesn't necessarily mean he'll recognize me. Asher is a major player on campus. Every time I catch sight of the guy, there are different girls hanging all over him. Western is a large Division I college and there are a ton of athletes who go on to play professional sports, but only a select few are treated with his celebrity status.

It's a little sickening.

All right, maybe more than a little.

I spend the next thirty seconds giving myself a silent pep talk before forcing my feet into movement. The smile pasted across my face feels brittle as I stalk through the dining room before grinding to a halt in front of their table.

Just like when I caught sight of them a few minutes ago, they're all wrapped up in each other. It takes effort to swallow down the acidic taste of bile rising in my throat. If I'm not careful, I'll spew chunks everywhere.

It's doubtful that would be appreciated.

Which makes it tempting.

"Hello," I mutter. "My name is Lola and I'll be waiting on you today. Can I start you off with something to drink?"

The girls barely glance at me. They're way too busy pawing the six-foot, golden-haired man sprawled out in the semi-circle booth between them.

Like a sandwich.

Gross.

He stares straight at me as a slow smile spreads across his handsome face. It's obvious that he remembers our encounters.

He only reinforces that suspicion by saying, "If it isn't taco girl, my favorite waitress. What a surprise to find you here."

My jaw locks as I grit my teeth. Keeping the faux smile firmly in place is no easy feat, especially when all I want to do is bear my teeth and growl.

"How about we skip the pleasantries, and you tell me what you want to order?"

The last time he showed up here with a group of friends, I might have called him a dick in front of my uncle and ended up getting my ass chewed out. I have zero interest in being treated to another lecture. Plus, my *tía* and *tío* have been good to me. I don't want my behavior to be a reflection on their restaurant. Trust me, I was obsessively checking Yelp reviews after the incident occurred.

So...if that means I need to be cordial to this knuckle dragging jerk, then that's what I'll do.

But that doesn't mean I have to like it.

Or that it'll be easy.

It doesn't go unnoticed that he has a brawny arm wrapped around each girl. With his bright blue gaze pinned to mine, he hauls them even closer. The smile turns into more of a smirk as a strange sizzle of electricity zips through my veins before settling like a heavy stone in my core.

As soon as the unwanted desire bursts to life, I ruthlessly stomp it out like it's a kitchen fire that has the potential to burn down the joint. Asher Stevens is the very last guy on the face of the earth I want to find myself attracted to.

Other women might be taken in by his handsome face, chiseled body, and athletic prowess, but not me. I see him for what he is—a muscle bound, steroid-infused meathead who drinks like a fish, smokes weed, and screws like he's being sent to prison for a life sentence without the possibility of conjugal visits.

When you live paycheck-to-paycheck and have to continually

worry about having enough money to pay for groceries, utilities, along with all the little necessities, you don't have the luxury of getting caught up in frivolous things that don't matter. At that point, life becomes very black and white. There aren't many shades of gray.

"Now where's the fun in that?"

Fun?

There's nothing about this situation that even resembles a good time.

I narrow my eyes before shifting my weight. Is it really too much to ask that they give me their order so I can get the hell away from this table?

The less interaction I have with him, the better off we'll all be.

What's funny is that I've waited on my fair share of conceited jerks while working here and I've always been able to smile and take their order without incident. Even the ones who hit obnoxiously on me.

For whatever reason, this guy is the exception to the rule. It defies logic how he's managed to burrow under my skin like a nasty infection that's in need of a steroid treatment.

Possibly two rounds.

When he remains irritatingly silent, I rip my gaze from him and glance at the girls. "Would either of you like to order?"

Neither of the blondes pay attention to me. One is nibbling her way along the thick column of Asher's neck while the other strokes lethal looking acrylics down his chest. It's almost a surprise when the T-shirt doesn't shred beneath her sharp claws.

"They'll both have your hard taco platter with sides of rice and beans. And a couple glasses of water." He squeezes them again. "Right, ladies?"

When they coo and laugh, it takes every ounce of self-restraint not to roll my eyes.

I stare at my note pad while jotting down the order. "And for you?"

A few more seconds and I can escape his insufferable presence.

"You know what I'd like? A little eye contact."

I pause, lifting my gaze to stare even though it's the last thing I want to do. "Excuse me?"

"I said I like a little eye contact when I'm being serviced. Is that too much to ask?"

My mouth falls open. He really is an insufferable asshole.

When I snap my teeth, barely able to suppress the growl rumbling up from deep in my chest, he actually has the audacity to chuckle. I quickly glance around for my uncle. That's the last thing I need.

When my attention returns to him, he's tapping his forefinger against his lips as his gaze roves over the menu. "I'll have four hard tacos, one beef burrito—you know what—make that two beef burritos. Three chicken enchiladas, and—"

I stop scribbling and glance up from the notepad. "Seriously? Aren't you afraid you'll ruin your girlish figure?"

He pops a brow as humor sparks in his eyes. "It kind of sounds like you've been checking me out. If you're interested, I'd be more than happy to show you that there's not an ounce of fat on me."

My cheeks heat as I scowl. "Hard pass. Anything else?"

"Yeah, throw a couple chicken taquitos on there."

I write down the last of the order before swinging away in relief. I hate how the air gets clogged in my throat, making it impossible to breathe whenever I have the sad misfortune to be around him. Sure, I'll admit that Asher is good looking, but I don't have time for guys who are under the misguided assumption they're god's gift to the female species.

Actually, I don't have time for guys.

Period.

I don't get more than two steps before I hear, "Lola?"

I stiffen and grind to a halt before reluctantly glancing over my shoulder.

"I'd like a glass of water as well."

It's so tempting to give him the middle finger. Except I've done that before, and it didn't end well for me.

I jerk my head into a tight nod and stomp away.

Since Taco Loco is close to campus and the food is delicious, not to mention reasonably priced, we get a ton of student traffic. Most of the college kids I wait on are decent. Sometimes we'll get a group of guys who are asshats, but I've never had a problem handling them. A few well-placed snarky comments usually cuts them down to size. They're like wild animals, as long as you don't show fear, they'll grudgingly respect you.

For whatever reason, waiting on this one annoys the crap out of me. Instead of dwelling on the reason for that, I shove Asher from my brain and focus on the tasks at hand. The faster I get their order to them, the quicker they can eat and get the hell out of here.

I fill three glasses of water and drop them off at their table. Even though Asher's penetrating gaze feels more like a physical caress, I refuse to give him the time of day before taking off to wait on other customers. As I bustle around the dining area, I can't shake the feeling that I'm being watched.

Or maybe it's just my imagination.

It's a relief when I circle back to the kitchen and find their entrees waiting on the counter under the lamps. I shake my head, slightly awed yet sickened by the sheer amount of food Asher plans on consuming. If he actually eats all of it, we'll have to call Guinness World Records. And if I'm really lucky, he'll explode, and I'll never have to tangle with him again.

Wouldn't that be nice?

It takes two trips to bring out all the food. The blondes are barely able to stop pawing at him long enough to eat their meals.

I just can't with these girls.

"Is there anything else I can get for you?" I ask, ready to sprint away.

Asher's gaze stays locked on mine. "Nope, I think we're all good."

"Great." My pulse picks up its tempo as I force my attention from him, swinging away to check my other tables.

Fifteen minutes later, the girls have eaten half their meals and Asher has amazingly managed to plow through most of his entrees. It's a relief when he catches my eye and makes the universal sign with his hand for the bill.

Yay! As soon as he walks out the door, I'll finally be able to relax.

I give him a nod before grabbing his check. Usually, I write a little note of thanks, but I can't bring myself to do that this time. I glance at their table again and watch as one of the girls nips at his lower lip while the other snuggles against the broad expanse of his chest.

Ugh.

What a male chauvin—

An idea takes root as my pen flies over the paper before adding a few finishing touches. My shoulders shake with silent mirth as I lay the paper face down on the table before saying sweetly, "Thanks so much for coming in. I really hope you enjoy the rest of your evening."

Before he can reply, I take off, laughter bubbling up inside me. There's no way I'll be able to contain it for much longer.

And here I thought waiting on Asher would piss me off.

Turns out, he managed to put a smile on my face.

Want to read more of Lola & Asher's story? You can do it here -)
https://books2read.com/campuslegend

HATE TO LOVE YOU

BRODY

"Dude, I thought you'd be back earlier." Cooper, one of my roommates, grins as I walk through the front door. There's a half-naked chick straddling his lap. "We had to get this party started without you." He shrugs as if he's just taken one for the team. "It couldn't be helped."

I snort as my gaze travels around the living room of the house we rent a few blocks off campus. Even though there are only four of us on the lease, our place seems to be a crash pad for half the team. By the looks of the beer bottles strewn around, they've been at it for a while. I'm seriously thinking about charging some of these assholes rent.

Although, I guess if I were stuck in a shoebox of a dorm, I'd be desperate for a way out, too. I played juniors straight out of high school for two years before coming in as a freshman at twenty. I skipped dorm living and went straight to renting a place nearby. There was no way I was bunking down with a bunch of random eighteen-year-olds who'd never lived away from home. Not to mention, having an RA up my ass telling me what I could and couldn't do.

That sounds about as much fun as ripping duct tape off my balls.

Which is, I might add, the complete opposite of fun. Hazing sucks.

And for future reference, you don't rip duct tape off your balls, you carefully cut it away with a steady hand while mother-fucking the entire team.

My other two roommates, Luke Anderson and Sawyer Stevens, are hunched at the edge of the couch, battling it out in an intense game of NHL. Their thumbs are jerking the controllers in lightning-quick movements, and their eyeballs are fastened to the seventy-inch HD screen hanging across the room.

I can only shake my head. Every time they play, it's like a freaking National Championship is at stake.

I arch a brow as the girl on Cooper's lap reaches around and unhooks her bra, dropping it to the floor. Apparently, she doesn't mind if there's an audience. Cooper's lazy grin stretches as his fingers zero in on her nips.

I'd love to say this scene isn't typical for a Sunday night, but I'd be lying through my teeth. Usually, it's much worse.

Deking out Luke with some impressive video game puck handling skills, Sawyer says, "Grab a beer, bro. You can take over for Luke after I make him cry again like a little bitch."

"Fuck you," Luke grumbles.

I glance at the score. Luke is getting his ass handed to him on a silver platter, and he knows it.

"Sure." Sawyer smirks. "Maybe later. But I should warn you, you're not really my type. I like a dude who's packing a little more meat than you."

My lips twitch as I drop my duffle to the floor.

"Hey, you see that bullshit text from Coach?" Cooper asks from between the girl's tits.

I groan, hoping I didn't miss anything important while I was out of town for the weekend. I'm already under contract with the Milwaukee Mavericks. My dad and I flew there to meet with the coaching staff. I also got to hang with a few of the defensive players. Saturday night was freaking crazy. Next season is going to rock.

"Nah, didn't see it," I say. "What's going on?"

"Practice times have changed," Cooper continues, all the while playing with the girl's body. "We're now at six o'clock in the morning and seven in the evening."

Fuck me. He's starting two-a-days already?

"You think he's just screwing around with us?" I wouldn't put it past Coach Lang. I don't think he has anything better to do than lie awake at night, dreaming up new ways to torture us. The guy is a real hard-ass.

Then again, that's why we're here.

But six in the morning...that sucks. Between school and hockey practice, I already feel like I don't get enough sleep. And it's only September. That means I'll need to be up and out the door by five to make it to the rink, get dressed, and be on the ice by six. By the time eleven o'clock at night rolls around, I'll fall into bed an exhausted heap.

Sawyer shrugs, not looking particularly put out by the time change.

Cooper pops the nipple out of his mouth and fixes his glassy-eyed gaze on me. "Can't you have your dad talk some freaking sense into the guy?"

Luke grumbles under his breath, "I can barely make it to the seven o'clock practice on time."

"Nope." I shake my head. I'd do just about anything for these guys, except run to my father with anything related to hockey. Coach and my dad go way back. They both played for the Detroit Redwings. I've known the man my entire life. He helped me lace up my first pair of Bauers. So, you'd think he'd have a soft spot for me. Maybe take it easy on me.

Yeah...fat chance of that happening.

If anything, he comes down on me like a ton of bricks *because* of our personal relationship. I think Lang doesn't want any of the guys to feel like he's playing favorites.

Mission accomplished, dude.

No one would ever accuse him of that.

"Then prepare to haul ass at the butt crack of dawn, my friend."

With that, Cooper turns his attention elsewhere, attacking the girl's mouth.

Luke eyes them for a moment before yelling, "Hey, you gonna take that shit to the bedroom or are we all being treated to a free show?"

Not bothering to come up for air, Cooper ignores the question.

Luke shakes his head and focuses his attention on making a comeback. Or at least knocking Sawyer's avatar on its ass. "Guess that means we should make some popcorn."

I pick up my duffel and hoist it over my shoulder, deciding to head upstairs for a while. I love hanging with these guys, but I'm not feeling it at the moment.

"Hi, Brody." A lush blonde slips her arms around me and presses her ample cleavage against my chest. "I was hoping you'd show up."

Given the fact that this is my house, the chances of that happening were extremely high.

I stare down into her big green eyes.

"Hey." She looks familiar. I do a quick mental search, trying to produce a name, but only come up with blanks.

Which probably means I haven't slept with her recently.

When it comes to the ladies, I've come up with an algorithm that I've perfected over the last three years. It's simple, yet foolproof. I never screw the same girl more than three times in a six-month period. If you do, you run the risk of entering into the murky territory of a quasi-relationship or a friends-with-benefits situation. I'm not looking for any attachments at this point.

Even casual ones.

I'm at Whitmore to earn a degree and prepare for the pros. I'm focused on getting bigger, faster, and stronger. The NHL is no place for pussies. If you can't hack it, the league will chew you up and spit you out before you can blink your eyes. I have no intention of allowing that to happen. I've worked too hard to crash and burn at this point.

Or get distracted.

In a surprisingly bold move, Blondie slides her hand from my chest to my package and gives it a firm squeeze to let me know she means business.

I have no doubts that if I asked her to drop to her knees and suck me off in front of all these people, she would do it in a heartbeat. Other than a thong, the girl grinding away on Cooper's lap is naked.

My first year playing juniors, when a girl offered to have no-strings-attached-sex, I'd thought I'd hit the flipping jackpot. Less than five minutes later, I'd blown my load and was ready for round two. Fast forward five years, and I don't even blink at a chick who's willing to drop her panties within minutes of me walking through the door. It happens far too often for it to be considered a novelty.

Which is just plain sad.

When I was in high school, I jumped at the chance to dip my wick.

Now?

Not so much.

It's like being fed a steady diet of steak and lobster. Sure, it's delicious the first couple of days. Maybe even a full week. You can't help but greedily devour every single bite and then lick your fingertips afterward. But, believe it or not, even steak and lobster become mundane.

Most guys, no matter what their age, would give their left nut to be in my skates.

To have their pick of any girl. Or, more often than not, *girls*.

And here I am...limp dick in hand.

Actually, limp dick in *her* hand.

Sex has become something I do to take the edge off when I'm feeling stressed. It's my version of a relaxation technique. For fuck's sake, I'm twenty-three years old. I'm in the sexual prime of my life. I should be ecstatic when any girl wants to spread her legs for me. What I shouldn't be is bored. And I sure as hell shouldn't be mentally running through the drills we'll be doing when I lead a captain's practice.

I pry her fingers from my junk and shake my head. "Sorry, I've got some shit to take care of."

And that shit would be school. I have forty pages of reading that needs to be finished up by tomorrow morning.

Blondie pouts and bats her mascara-laden lashes.

"Maybe later?" she coos in a baby voice.

Fuck. That is such a turnoff.

Why do chicks do that?

No, seriously. It's a legitimate question. Why do they do that? It's like nails on a chalkboard. I'm tempted to answer back in a ridiculous, lispy-sounding voice.

But I don't.

I'm not that big of an asshole.

Plus, she might be into it.

Then I'd be screwed. I envision us cooing at each other in baby voices for the rest of the night and almost shudder.

"Maybe," I say noncommittally. Although I'm not going to lie, that toddler voice has killed any chance for a later hookup. But I'm smart enough not to tell her that. Chances are high that she'll end up finding another hockey player to latch on to and forget all about me. Because let's face it, that's what she's here for.

A little dick from a guy who skates with a stick.

Just to be sure, I run my eyes over the length of her again.

Toddler voice aside, she's got it going on.

And yet, that banging body is doing absolutely nothing for me.

Which is troublesome. I almost want to take her upstairs just to prove to myself that everything is in proper working order. But I won't.

As I hit the first step, Cooper breaks away from his girl. "WTF, McKinnon? Where you going?" He waves a hand around the room. "Can't you see we're in the middle of entertaining?"

"I'll leave you to take care of our guests," I say, trudging up the staircase.

"Well, if you insist," he slurs happily.

My bedroom is at the end of the hall, away from the noise of the first floor. As a general rule, no one is allowed on the second floor except for the guys who live here. I pull out my key and unlock the door before stepping inside.

My duffel gets tossed in the corner before I open my Managerial Finance book. I thought I'd have a chance to plow through some of the reading over the weekend, but my dad and I were on the go the entire time. Meeting people from the Milwaukee organization, hitting a team party, checking out a few condos near the lakefront. Just getting the general lay of the land. On the plane ride home, I had every intention of being productive, but ended up sacking out once we hit cruising altitude.

Three hours later, there's a knock on the door. Normally an interruption would piss me off, but after slogging through thirty pages, my eyes have glazed over, and I'm fighting to stay awake. This material is mind-numbingly boring, and that's not helping matters.

"It's open," I call out, expecting Cooper to try cajoling me back downstairs.

When that guy's shitfaced, he wants everyone else to be just as hammered as he is. I've never seen anyone put away alcohol the way he does. It's almost as impressive as it is scary. And yet, he's somehow able to wake up for morning practice bright-eyed and bushy-tailed like he wasn't just wasted six hours ago. Someone from the biology department really needs to do a case study on him, 'cause that shit just ain't normal.

When I suck down alcohol like that, the next morning I'm like a newborn colt on the ice who can't keep his legs under him.

It's not a pretty sight. Which is why I don't do it. Been there, done that. Moving on.

The door swings open to reveal Blondie-With-The-Toddler-Voice. And she's not alone. She's brought a friend.

I raise my brows in interest as they step inside the room.

In the three hours since I've seen her, Blondie has managed to lose most of her clothing. The brunette she's with appears to be in the same predicament. They stand in lacy bras and barely-there thongs with their hands entwined.

My gaze roves over them appreciatively.

How could it not?

Their tummies are flat and toned. Hips are nicely rounded. Tits jiggle enticingly as they saunter toward the bed where I'm currently sprawled.

I should be a man of steel over here. I haven't gotten laid in three weeks. Which is almost unheard of. I haven't gone that long without sex since I first started having it.

But there's nothing.

Not even a twitch.

Which begs the question—What the hell is wrong with me?

It must be the stress of school and the skating regimen I'm on. Even though I'm already under contract with Milwaukee and don't have to worry about the NHL draft later this year, I'm still under a lot of pressure to perform this season.

National Championships don't bring themselves home.

I'd be concerned that I have some serious erectile dysfunction issues happening except there's one chick who gets me hard every time I lay eyes on her. Rather ironically, she wants nothing to do with me. I think she'd claw my eyes out if I laid one solitary finger on her.

Actually, all I have to do is stare in her direction, and she bares her teeth at me.

Maybe these girls are exactly what I need to relieve some of my pent-up stress. It certainly can't hurt.

Decision made, I slam my finance book closed and toss it to the floor where it lands with a loud thud. I fold my arms behind my head and smile at the girls in silent invitation.

And the rest, shall we say, is history.

WANT to read more of Natalie & Brody's story? You can buy the book here -) https://books2read.com/u/bPXN6x

ABOUT THE AUTHOR

Jennifer Sucevic is a USA Today bestselling author who has published twenty New Adult novels. Her work has been translated into German, Dutch, and Italian. Jen has a bachelor's degree in History and a master's degree in Educational Psychology. Both are from the University of Wisconsin-Milwaukee. She started out her career as a high school counselor, which she loved. She lives in the Midwest with her husband, four kids, and a menagerie of animals. If you would like to receive regular updates regarding new releases, please subscribe to her newsletter here- Jennifer Sucevic Newsletter (subscribepage.com) Or contact Jen through email, at her website, or on Facebook.
sucevicjennifer@gmail.com
Want to join her reader group? Do it here -)
J Sucevic's Book Boyfriends | Facebook

Social media links-
https://www.tiktok.com/@jennifersucevicauthor
www.jennifersucevic.com
https://www.instagram.com/jennifersucevicauthor
https://www.facebook.com/jennifer.sucevic

Amazon.com: Jennifer Sucevic: Books, Biography, Blog, Audiobooks, Kindle

Jennifer Sucevic Books - BookBub

CPSIA information can be obtained
at www.ICGtesting.com
Printed in the USA
BVHW062333060123
655722BV00003B/509